Decade: The 1960s

Brian W. Aldiss and Harry Harrison are known to everyone who reads science fiction. Individually, each enjoys an outstanding reputation founded on innumerable successes. Jointly, they have achieved international renown as editors.

Decade
The 1960s

edited by Brian W. Aldiss and Harry Harrison

Pan Books in association with Macmillan London

First published 1977 by Macmillan London Ltd
This edition published 1979 by Pan Books Ltd,
Cavaye Place, London SW10 9PG
in association with Macmillan London Ltd
Introduction and selection © SF Horizons Ltd 1977
ISBN 0 330 25767 6
Made and printed in Great Britain by
C. Nicholls & Company Ltd, Philips Park Press, Manchester

Contents

1960's Commercels & Ads

Acknowledgements

'The Assassination of John Fitzgerald Kennedy Considered as a Downhill Motor Race', by J. G. Ballard, Copyright © 1967 by *Ambit*; reprinted by permission of the author.

'Gravity', by H. Jacobs, Copyright © 1969 by *New Worlds in Science Fiction*; reprinted by permission of the author.

'Harrison Bergeron', by Kurt Vonnegut, Jr, Copyright © 1961 by Mercury Press, Inc.; reprinted by permission of the author.

'Computers Don't Argue', by Gordon R. Dickson, Copyright © 1965 by The Condé Nast Publications, Inc.; reprinted by permission of the author.

'The Food Goes in the Top', by Will Worthington, Copyright © 1961 by *Science Fantasy*; reprinted by permission of the author.

'Subversive', by Mack Reynolds, Copyright © 1962 by The Condé Nast Publications, Inc.; reprinted by permission of the author and his agent, Scott Meredith Literary Agency.

'Descending', by Thomas M. Disch, Copyright © 1964 by Ziff-Davis Publications, Inc.; reprinted by permission of the author.

'The Village Swindler', by Brian W. Aldiss, Copyright © 1968 by International Publications; reprinted by permission of the author.

'Manscarer', by Keith Roberts, Copyright © 1966 by *New Worlds in Science Fiction*; reprinted by permission of the author.

'Hybrid', by Keith Laumer, Copyright © 1961 by Mercury Press, Inc.; reprinted by permission of the author.

'Heat Death of the Universe', by Pamela Zoline, Copyright © 1967 by *New Worlds in Science Fiction*; reprinted by permission of the author.

'Devil Car', by Roger Zelazny, Copyright © 1965 by Galaxy Publishing Corp.; reprinted by permission of the author.

Introduction

Suppose you want to boil yourself a perfect egg, the kind in which the white is hard and the golden centre still fluid like a medium-consistency honey. You are alone in the kitchen, there is no clock, you have lost the egg-timer, and your watch has stopped. How can you time the egg exactly?

One answer is that you could put a record of Mozart's overture to *The Marriage of Figaro* on the record-player. The overture lasts four minutes. At its conclusion, remove your egg from the pan and it will be done to perfection.

We recognise that this useful culinary tip has nothing to do with music. It is a misapplication. It is using Mozart as a utility; we are amused by the inappropriateness of the idea, or perhaps we think it is vaguely immoral.

Literature is a bit different from music, and maybe science fiction is a bit different from literature. For science fiction authors, among them some of the best known, like to claim practical applications for their fiction. Not that their fiction boils eggs – although of course there is a fortune awaiting a man who writes the story which will boil the first four-minute egg – but, less modestly, that it changes opinions, that it turns them into scientists, or even that it helps Man on his Way to the Stars.

Other authors would claim the opposite, that their fiction can have no justification unless it succeeds as fiction. This would seem to them glory enough. In imaginative literature and in poetry, the human spirit has risen to some of its greatest heights. To turn fiction into propaganda is to demean it.

The two opposed views can best be exemplified by a juxtaposition Mark Adlard made (in an article entitled 'The Other Tradition of Science Fiction') of statements by Isaac Asimov and C. S.

Lewis. In a film he made about the history of magazine SF, Asimov says in essence that the SF of the 1940s (when Asimov's SF was in full spate) became the fact of the 1960s. He went on to imply that when Neil Armstrong stepped on the Moon it justified the work done by Campbell's stable of writers in *Astounding* (see *Decade 1940s*).

In *Of Other Worlds* (1966), Lewis by contrast has this to say: 'If some fatal process of applied science enables us in fact to reach the moon, that real journey will not at all satisfy the impulse which we now seek to gratify by writing such stories.'

This argument about the role of SF is highly germane to the sixties. It was a period of tremendous popular intellectual ferment, when everything was called into question. The great issues of the day found SF writers divided, whether on Vietnam, on the Space Race, on Marxism, on drugs, or on race. The question of one's life-style became crucially important; beards were political.

It was a highly political decade, starting promisingly with a glamorous president in the White House and the dandyish Macmillan in 10 Downing Street, and continuing with ominous vibrati from all over the world. The two great communist countries, China and the Soviet Union (with its luckless satellites), turned their arts from aesthetic purposes to expressions of political intention, and many people in the West were prepared to do the same thing. But there is a gulf of difference between personal belief and state-imposed belief; certainly SF authors, whose very material has of necessity economic and political implications, often forsook aesthetic goals for the causes in which they believed. The Third World lay uneasy on their consciences. In the United States, despite its racial upheavals, some found time to wonder at the justice which permitted a small number of people to consume something like ninety per cent of the world's resources. There was reason to think of SF as ammunition in a global battle.

As change was inevitable in the world at large, so it was inevitable in the realm of SF. Each decade shows a changing pattern, although the basic arts of story-telling are perennial and less susceptible to alteration than readers may imagine. The forties was Campbell's and *Astounding*'s decade. The fifties saw the great change in taste which brought in *Galaxy* and *The Magazine of Fantasy & Science Fiction,* with emphasis on sociology and human values. The sixties re-emphasized this swing; in addition, it was the decade in which space travel and the future became less of an overriding concern.

The point needs some examination. Before the first Sputnik sailed up into the skies of the fifties, magazine SF seemed at times to have turned itself into a propaganda machine for space travel. Werner von Braun was one of the heroes of this machine, as he laid before Congress and the general public grandiose plans for a fleet of ships to annex Mars. Yet, according to the mythology, sales of SF magazines declined with the launching of the first satellites. If this is what really happened, it justifies C. S. Lewis's dictum and provides an argument for SF as an imaginative literature, SF as reverie rather than prophecy; its proper subject is the things that may be, not the things that are.

Many of the older SF writers held as an article of faith the belief that space travel was possible. When the possibility became actuality, a sense of *déjà vu* set in. And more than that. In the context of the times, aspirations foundered. The multi-million-dollar and -rouble programmes aimed at getting men into space contrasted gratingly with the mess they left behind on Earth. Arguments were sometimes short-sighted on either side. The 'space race' eased an emergence from the Cold War which had dominated the fifties, as well as proving a tremendous and undeniable success in its own right, a technological miracle on a scale we may not witness again for many years.

And yet . . . Had the natural aggressiveness of mankind merely stumbled on a new arena for its working-out? Commenting on man's arrival on Luna, J. G. Ballard said, 'If I were a Martian, I'd start running now.'

The tremendous process of which journeys to the Moon are part has by no means unfolded fully. And yet . . . Propaganda apart, the brilliance of the success served to emphasize to one half of the world how grandiosely the other half lived.

Disenchantment or curiosity made many writers look away from space and the future to the world about them. There was plenty to explore, from computers to over-population, from injustice to the Pill, from heart-transplants to emergent nations. The sixties was the decade in which SF discovered the Present. It is no coincidence that it was also the decade in which the general reading public discovered SF.

A few milestones are in order.

In 1961, Kingsley Amis's survey of SF, *New Maps of Hell*, was published in England. It had been condemned in some quarters; Amis wrote lightly and amusingly about a subject on which he felt deeply, and some people understand only the ponderous. But *New Maps* remains a shrewd, reliable guide to what it's all about, and certainly paved the way to more general acceptance of the genre. Amis emphasizes the satiric aspects of SF at the expense of the fantastic side; there he was merely being prophetic. As this anthology shows, the decade following his book relied heavily on forms of satire – including satires on prose styles.

Within forty-eight hours of the death of President Kennedy in 1963, two writers died whose names, for all their other achievements, are still closely associated with the upper pastures of the science fiction field: Aldous Huxley and C. S. Lewis. Huxley's *Brave New World* (1932) has long ranked as SF; so does the neglected but equally penetrating *Ape and Essence* (1948); while his last novel, *Island* (1962), is a remarkable utopian novel which repays careful attention. Lewis, a connoisseur of romances and science fiction, wrote the beautiful trilogy which begins with *Out of the Silent Planet* (1938).

In 1965, Professor J. R. R. Tolkien's great trilogy *The Lord of the Rings* was published in paperback; it went on to become the cult book of the sixties. While not in itself SF,* its enormous success has directed attention towards the enchantments of alternate worlds to ours. During a period when SF was expanding and becoming increasingly departmentalised, the Tolkien syndrome encouraged alternate-worldery, so that alternate worlds have increasingly become a part of SF. Other cult books included Frank

*Although the jacket of the first hardcover edition in 1954 quoted the perceptive Naomi Mitchison as saying, 'It's really super science fiction'.

Herbert's *Dune*, which began life as a serial in *Analog* and won the first Nebula Award for the best novel of 1965, and Robert Heinlein's *Stranger in a Strange Land* (Hugo award-winner 1962), a campus favourite for some years. Other award-winners of the decade included Daniel Keyes' *Flowers for Algernon* (Nebula, 1966), Samuel Delany's *The Einstein Intersection* (Nebula, 1967), Ursula Le Guin's *The Left Hand of Darkness* (Nebula, 1969), Walter Miller's *A Canticle for Leibowitz* (Hugo, 1961), Philip K. Dick's *The Man in the High Castle* (Hugo, 1963), Fritz Leiber's *The Wanderer* (Hugo, 1965), Roger Zelazny's *Lord of Light* (Hugo, 1968) and John Brunner's *Stand on Zanzibar* (Hugo, 1969).

One interesting thing about this list is that few of the award-winners can be classified as adventure or action novels. Their equivalents only a decade earlier would have been so classifiable. After all, magazine SF largely grew out of men's adventure fiction. In the sixties, a more meditative mood set in.

Another milestone of the decade was the Stanley Kubrick–Arthur C. Clarke film, *2001: a space odyssey*, which had its European première in May 1968. Significantly, it is cast as an adventure, but it concludes with a psychedelic trip followed by meditation.

Another comparatively new feature of SF was that it began to stand outside itself and look at itself. 'Heat Death of the Universe' (included here) is not so much traditional SF as a story which takes SF for granted and uses its vocabulary. Among the great successes of the decade are two novels by my collaborator on this series, Harry Harrison. Both his *Bill, the Galactic Hero* and *The Technicolor Time Machine* make ingenious fun of all the clichés of the genre – the former with particular reference to the novels of Heinlein and Asimov.

It was hardly to be expected that changes which infiltrated every facet of life should not have their effect on the way the writers wrote as well as what they wrote about. The mood became dis-passionate, hard-hearted at least on the surface. To be 'cool' was the height of fashion.

In the mid-sixties, London was the height of fashion. For a few years – which now seem as remote as the Ming Dynasty – London was the place where culture lived and thrived as it had done in Paris in the twenties. An electricity was generated. We all felt it. The time and the place acquired a label which was instantly mocked: Swinging London. But the phenomenon needed a label, however absurd.

Behind the ballyhoo, the hippies, the Flower Power, and the youth cult, many dark things lurked. Writers have always been abnormally aware of dark things. They did not forget them as they made hay with the rest while the sun shone.

This go-where-you-please, do-your-own-thing, turn-on-freak-out mood found particular embodiment in the pages of a British SF magazine, *New Worlds*.

New Worlds was the oldest-established British magazine. Under its editor E. J. Carnell it had achieved regular publication and modest success but, as the sixties dawned, its sales were dwindling and illness afflicted the dedicated Ted Carnell. Also, it must be said, its formula was growing somewhat threadbare. Although most of its fiction was by British writers, many of them copied American models of some vintage and assumed a Transatlantic tone of voice. Not infrequently, the stories were rejects from the more profitable American market.

It seemed as if only a miracle could save *New Worlds* and its companion *Science Fantasy*, also edited by Carnell. He handed over editorships to Michael Moorcock and Kyril Bonfiglioli respectively. Moorcock had already made a name for himself as a writer of fantasy and his hero Elric was well established, although not taken too seriously (least of all by the genial Moorcock himself). Kyril Bonfiglioli was a hitherto semi-respectable antiquarian-book- and art-dealer and *bon viveur* residing in Oxford.

Bonfiglioli was an important influence in the life of several new authors, among them Johnny Byrne, who went on to write *Groupie* with Jenny Fabian (a real sixties-flavour book) and to work on the TV series *Space 1999*; Thom Keyes, who went on to write *One Night Stand*, which was filmed; and Keith Roberts, who became editor of *Science Fantasy* when Bonfiglioli changed the name to *SF Impulse*, and did much of the excellent artwork as well as contributing stories. The best known of these stories were those which formed the novel *Pavanne*; in that book and others since, Roberts has shown himself master of the alternate-world story, pitching his tone deliberately in a minor key. He is represented here by 'Manscarer', a story of artists in an over-populated world, which was first published in *New Writings in Science Fiction*, the paperback magazine started by Carnell when he left *New Worlds*; *NW in SF* still continues, with even greater success, edited by Kenneth Bulmer who, like Carnell before him, has shown himself generous, reliable and discerning.

SF Impulse faded out, but *New Worlds* went from strength to strength. Aided by a dedicated editorial team, including such lively men as Charles Platt, Mike Moorcock kicked out the old gang and installed the new. Galactic wars went out; drugs came in; there were fewer encounters with aliens, more in the bedroom. Experimentation in prose styles became one of the orders of the day, and the baleful influence of William Burroughs often threatened to gain the upper hand.

The revolution was inevitable. The bathwater had become so stale that is was scarcely to be avoided if the baby sometimes went out with it. When an Arts Council grant was secured for *New Worlds* and it became glossy and filled with illustrations, it was the only SF magazine in the mid-sixties which looked as if it belonged to the mid-sixties. All the others seemed like fossils. Life was where *New Worlds* was.

Of course, individual issues were often disappointing. But the ritual of a magazine, its layout, its expectations, its continuity, its hazardous pact with readers and authors, elevates it to a sort of protolanguage which speaks as strongly as its actual fiction content. The ritual suggested that the future had arrived with a flutter of colour supplements and mini-skirts and was securely nailed to *New Worlds'* editorial desk. The rather twitchy hedonism of *New Worlds* had no need to look ahead, and the galaxy began in Ladbroke Grove.

In the decidedly more sombre mood of the seventies, all this may sound silly. Naturally, it was easy to hate *New Worlds*, which often opted for trendiness rather than depth – though trendiness in those days was almost a philosophy in itself. But the feeling that the future has happened is not as perverse as it seems. Our Western culture has in many ways fulfilled the targets established in the early Renaissance: to take control of our world through observation and understanding and application. Enormous benefits have accrued to us. The life of the average man in the West, as regards both his physical and his mental horizons, has been much enhanced by the impetus of that aspiration. Now the bills for our astonishing performance, centuries long, are coming in. We see that progress and pollution, medical discoveries and over-population, technical development and nuclear escalation, improved communications and terrorism, social care and public apathy are sides of the same coin. Further advances are increasingly hard-won; moreover, the Oil Crisis in the early seventies rang like a tocsin through the West, reminding its citizens that the hour grew late and Toynbee's Civilisation Number Twenty-Two was losing autonomy. Our alternatives grow less. *New Worlds* was the first SF magazine in the world to abandon the idea that technological progress could be extrapolated for ever; as such, it may be honoured for having been truly prodromic.

Hardly surprising, then, that it often radiated a hard shiny surface of scepticism, the cool of slight desperation. Boiling eggs to Mozart – the whole comedy of misapplication – was *New Worlds'* thing. The dominant figure here was J. G. Ballard, with his postlapsarian guilts and a genuine power to embody the landscapes of subtopia in skeletal fiction. It is possible that *New Worlds* ultimately damaged Ballard's development by overlauding the sadistic side of his work; but he is and remains a genuine original and an acute observer. Ballard threw away the old pack of cards. His new ones may not be to everyone's taste, but they are his own. He has the courage of his convictions, and his best stories remain the best. If he often seems to use other authors as models – Jarry, as in the piece we anthologise here, Kafka, Greene, Conrad, Burroughs – the benefit of a post-Renaissance period is that we are heirs to all styles, and Ballard moulds each to his own purpose.

Moorcock rightly seized upon Ballard, but also forged his own fictional hero, Jerry Cornelius. Cornelius is in fact neither hero nor anti-hero, but a sort of myth of the times. He can be male or female, white or black. Moorcock encouraged this ambiguous aspect by persuading other writers to chronicle the adventures of Cornelius; included here is Norman Spinrad's Jerry, in the typically cool and comic account of 'The Last Hurrah of the Golden Horde'.

Spinrad was one of a number of American writers who found the English cultural climate more congenial than the American one. His chief contribution to *New Worlds* was *Bug Jack Barron*, serialised at inordinate length; its use of four-letter words, together with a modicum of sexual intercourse, oral sex and other pleasures, led to a banning of *New Worlds* by W. H. Smith and the denunciation of Spinrad in Parliament as a degenerate – the sort of accolade most writers long for. *Barron* is a powerful novel about the role of television and government, powerfully overwritten.

Among other expatriates who drifted through was Thomas M. Disch, a distinguished writer whose stories move easily between being flesh, fowl, and good red herring. Disch's greatest contribution to *New Worlds* was the novel *Camp Concentration*. A friend of his, John Sladek, settled in London, and has become one of SF's leading comedians and parodists. Pamela Zoline, primarily an artist, also came over and settled here; we reprint her fine story 'Heat Death of the Universe'.

Among the English authors encouraged by Moorcock were Langdon Jones, Hilary Bailey, David Masson, Robert Holdstock and Ian Watson. Moorcock has gone on to greater things and is a legend in his own time. With the maverick *New Worlds*, he brought British SF kicking and screaming into the twentieth century.

News of the English revolution percolated back to the United States, where it had imitators who seem mainly to have thought the issue rested on writing as wildly and fuzzily as possible. But the times they were a-changing rapidly in the States as elsewhere, and many authors emerged with genuine fresh approaches to experience. One of them was Harvey Jacobs. Comic writers are always welcome in a field which frequently inclines to the ponderous; but Jacobs found he was most welcome by Mike Moorcock. Among the other new names were Will Worthington, who showed, like Disch, some kinship with the Theatre of the Absurd; he came and went all too fast, but shall be remembered here by his excellent story, first published by Ted Carnell, 'The Food Goes in the Top'.

Roger Zelazny came and stayed. A genuine baroque talent, often too much in love with the esoteric, but shining forth clearly here with 'Devil Car'. His story is a persuasive embodiment of the sixties' passion for the automobile.

Keith Laumer rose to great popularity in the sixties, when his name was associated with Retief, his hero whose military adventures had a satiric edge. He is represented here by 'Hybrid', a good safe space story of the kind *New Worlds* ceased to print.

The other authors include Kurt Vonnegut, Jr, Gordon R. Dickson, Philip K. Dick, Frederik Pohl, Robert Silverberg and Mack Reynolds – distinguished names all, and old hands at SF. All manifest the spirit of the sixties in one form or another – Reynolds in his enquiry into capitalist economics, Vonnegut in his satire on equality, Pohl in his sparky creation of Day Million, Dickson in his preoccupation with the blindness of computers. Silverberg re-creates the past, the far past. Dick does his own thing on the Dickian subject of reality. Reality trembled in the sixties. As many of us discovered, when things settled back into place again and the music died, life ceased to be quite so much fun.

B.W.A.

J. G. Ballard
The assassination of John Fitzgerald Kennedy considered as a downhill motor race

Author's note: The assassination of President Kennedy on 22 November 1963 raised many questions, not all of which were answered by the Report of the Warren Commission. It is suggested that a less conventional view of the events of that grim day may provide a more satisfactory explanation. In particular, Alfred Jarry's The Crucifixion Considered as an Uphill Bicycle Race *gives us a useful lead.*

Oswald was the starter.

From his window above the track he opened the race by firing the starting-gun. It is believed that the first shot was not properly heard by all the drivers. In the following confusion Oswald fired the gun two more times, but the race was already under way.

Kennedy got off to a bad start.

There was a governor in his car, and its speed remained constant at about fifteen miles an hour. However, shortly afterwards, when the governor had been put out of action, the car accelerated rapidly, and continued at high speed along the remainder of the course.

The visiting teams. As befitting the inauguration of the first production-car race through the streets of Dallas, both the President and the Vice-President participated. The Vice-President, Johnson, took up his position behind Kennedy on the starting-line. The concealed rivalry between the two men was of keen interest to the crowd. Most of them supported the home driver, Johnson.

The starting-point was the Texas Book Depository, where all bets were placed on the presidential race. Kennedy was an unpopular contestant with the Dallas crowd, many of whom showed outright hostility. The deplorable incident familiar to us all is one example.

The course ran downhill from the Book Depository, below an overpass, then on to the Parkland Hospital and from there to Love Air Field. It is one of the most hazardous courses in downhill motor-racing, second only to the Sarajevo track discontinued in 1914.

Kennedy went downhill rapidly. After the damage to the governor the car shot forward at high speed. An alarmed track official attempted to mount the car, which continued on its way, cornering on two wheels.

Turns. Kennedy was disqualified at the Hospital, after taking a turn for the worse. Johnson now continued the race in the lead, which he maintained to the finish.

The flag. To signify the participation of the President in the race Old Glory was used in place of the usual checkered square. Photographs of Johnson receiving his prize after winning the race reveal that he had decided to make the flag a memento of his victory.

Previously, Johnson had been forced to take a back seat, as his position on the starting-line behind the President indicates. Indeed, his attempts to gain a quick lead on Kennedy during the false start were forestalled by a track steward, who pushed Johnson to the floor of his car.

In view of the confusion at the start of the race, which resulted in Kennedy, clearly expected to be the winner on past form, being forced to drop out at the Hospital turn, it has been suggested that the hostile local crowd, eager to see a win by the home driver Johnson, deliberately set out to stop him completing the race. Another theory maintains that the police guarding the track were in collusion with the starter, Oswald. After he finally managed to give the send-off Oswald immediately left the race, and was subsequently apprehended by track officials.

Johnson had certainly not expected to win the race in this way. There were no pit stops.

Several puzzling aspects of the race remain. One is the presence of the President's wife in the car, an unusual practice for racing drivers. Kennedy, however, may have maintained that as he was in control of the ship of state he was therefore entitled to captain's privileges.

The Warren Commission. The rake-off on the book of the race. In their report, prompted by widespread complaints of foul play and other irregularities, the syndicate lay full blame on the starter, Oswald.

Without doubt Oswald badly misfired. But one question still remains unanswered: who loaded the starting-gun?

Harvey Jacobs
Gravity

I am Bogardus Blik. But I use the name *Morris Nucleus* in my writings.

Nucleus, naturally, for direct association with the Atomic Age, of which I am the proudest citizen. *Morris* because that name has always been exotic to me – musky, tumescent, hairy, benevolent, and the wise kind of shy.

My actual name will be new to you. My *nom de plume* will mean nothing. Don't sweat.

I have been innocuous as a pebble. I work as a computer-programmer in a bank just outside Houston, Texas. I hardly socialize. I live alone in a rented room. And I have published nothing. Not yet. With reason. I am saving.

When my work is done to satisfaction I will release it – ah, it will fall off by itself. Then you will know me. I will be a household word in palaces of power and workers' flats. Such fame will follow that a sun will blaze always in my mottled eyes. Notoriety is pain. I despise it. But it is inevitable since the work I am coping with is epic. And I am more *humous* than *posthumous* by nature.

For now I relish privacy and the dank-dark of obscurity. Later I will suffer plenty from flashbulbs burning the skin off my bones. So let these be tranquil years, years of sweet study and discipline, years of peace.

Dammit, why do they pick at me? Am I a dessert? Yes, in a way.

I am watching television. A cub of a poetess in a literary magazine described the light of television as 'blue cellophane'. Lovely and accurate. I wrote her a letter. The blue cellophane crackles through my room. There on the launch-pad at Cape Kennedy (Cape Canaveral to my soul – I have never accepted the change) is the latest of our Moonships poised and smouldering like a young phallus. Look at it and sing.

Morris Nucleus sits eating a mallomar straining for flight. I feel the selfish power of that steaming rocket. I have all to do to keep from yanking myself around the room by my organ. Not in the spirit of a *Portnoy* who masturbates to pull things from within. In the spirit of *Icarus*, in an age beyond wings. It is marvellous to be alive at this hour. We are spreading the legs of the Universe. We will be remembered, if there are memories at work.

Only yesterday I read that 53.2 per cent of our population would divert funds from the Space Programme. The poor idiots fail to comprehend. I am last to blame them. The New Technology has not communicated its mystique or its message. The sheep see Science as a diplomat of death. Why not? Who has shown them a neutron smiling? They have seen smoking Japs. When my book is published things will be different. They will clamour. There will be demonstrations. Flowers will cover our laboratories. Cut the Space budget? Castrate God?

Give me time. I need time and leisure. Cancer, go home.

They are counting down. Emotion puffs my blue cellophane bag. Ten. Nine. Eight. Seven. Six. Aieeee. There is trouble. The countdown is holding. My insides are ignited. Let me off the ground!

The smooth voice of Mission Control. The trouble is minor. Nothing. It is repaired. Now. Five. Four. Three. Two. One. Zero. Blast-off. What a word! Oops. I am lifting. I am pushing. I am a rising vibration. I am gone.

Minutes into my flight I detach my first stage. I wait, count seconds, burn. My second stage is gone. My useless leaden arse falls backwards into water. I have attained orbital velocity. Glory to this glorious nation and the glories known and unknown and boons and gifts she has bequeathed. Oh, beautiful for spacious skies. Oh, beautiful. I would not like to be a Bulgarian sulking at home today. Of course we fly for Bulgarians too, but it is better to be part of the heart. And this is an American story.

An animation is on the screen. Jules Bergman tells me that my Spaceship is streaking around the globe. We have made another star. Inside there are men and they are giants. I am proud for every race.

Why am I listed? Soon the telephone will ring.

* * *

The telephone rings. Little bitch. Our Ship is barely in range of the Canary Islands tracking-station much less Jodrell Bank. Flesh-monger. She must begin her dialling, area code and all, at the moment of lift-off. She must wait for the last digit. She knows how I feel about actual staging and confirmation of apogee and peri-gee. She knows by now. When it is determined that the mission is safely away she tugs at the dial. And my passive turd of a Princess phone does its *dingle*. This cretin answers.

'Huh? What is it?' (My voice is rage and rejection.)

'Morris?' (Honey flows out of my Princess' tunnel.)

'Don't ever call me that.' (A spasm, not a voice.)

'Bogardus, then.' (She is really frightened.)

'Yes.' (Mellowing. Why?)

'You know who this is, don't you?' (Bath-water on soapy thighs.)

'I know.' (A shortness of breath. My plague.)

'Did you watch? He got off all right.' (Would she call through tragedy?)

'Of course I watched. What would I do – not watch?' (I am too soft.)

'Then come to me.' (Leaves from last summer blowing in new spring wind.)

'You can't be serious. We pledged . . .' (Liquid oxygen turning to mist.)

'Bogardus, I need you. I can't help the way I feel. And it's the only time we can be absolutely sure.' (Petulant appetite. I feel her wet.)

'It is not right. It is wrong.'

'How can anything so . . . holy . . . be wrong? You'll come. I know you won't leave me like this.'

'You trade on my worst instincts. You interrupt my work. You make stalactites grow from my soul. You give me such astounding guilt that I'll end up like a parsnip. Oh, I'll come. I'll lumber over. But you won't get one hot drop out of me, not this time.'

'Let me try.'

'Then try, bitch. You risk a noisy divorce. I risk damnation. A hell of a lot you care.'

'I care so I'm careful. Hurry, dear fool.'

'If I leave now I will arrive before first pictures are sent live. Is your television working?'

'Yes. The colour is fabulous. You won't miss anything. And, if you do, you can see it all on the Late News.'

'I am not interested in the Late News.'

'Then stop talking and move yourself.'

'What about the press?'

'Been and gone. The kids are with Mother. They won't be back until splashdown. It's a five-day mission, Bogardus.'

'I was just getting into Chapter Nine.'

'Hurry.'

'Yes. I'm already out the door.'

Forgive me, Chapter Nine. Forgive me, neighbours in my century. I know your needs. But I have mine.

On the bus going toward the Space Centre I have a lovely fantasy, the kind that eats like acid at your own intestines. I am dead and being judged by my peers. The charge is procrastination and fornication. They sit listening as my life is read from a lucite roll – Goddard, Meliès, Tsiolkovski, Verne, Avicenne, Von Guericke, Von Humboldt, Gauss, da Vinci, Euler, Kepler, Mercator, Stefanic, Caldas, Boskovic, Roemer, Kuang Chi, Nervander, Le Sage, Poincaré, Laplace, Flammarion, Newton, Verrier, Pope Sylvestre II, Galileo, Eddin, Maimonides, Einstein, Huyghens, Kimura, Lomonsov, Koulibine, Arrhenius, Swedenborg, Struve, Gokman, Kucera, Planck, Curie, Mrs Curie, Röntgen, Perrin, Lavoisier, Becquerel, Bohr, Democritus, Mendeliev, Bjerknes and assorted Chinese. Every one has had a postage stamp for a tombstone. Oh, it is old home week.

I stand naked at an aluminium podium struck silent. My jury mutters back and forth in the poetry of equations. As witnesses for the prosecution empty pages fly like unformed foeti through that chamber of dreams. The faces of husbands I have wronged, wearing the helmets and goggles of their occupation, flash wildly on a cinemascope screen.

Then the jury of genius, men I know and love more than my

family, begin a slow tapping at their privates. Tap tap. Thump thump. The din grows. Should I plead? It would be out of order. *Responsibility* is the subject, really, and I have no case. Guilty, I am sentenced to eternal wakefulness. I will hang in ether as a footnote suspended from a page as blank as the endless light. The bus reaches my stop. I am trembling as I navigate the aisle.

But I am trembling as much from anticipation of her starved, stunning body as I am from the anger of those educated eyes.

Clams on the half-shell and navel oranges. Her fridge is filled with them. And Bonbell cheese, which I also like. Phosphorus, proteins, vitamins and minerals that go straight to the genitals is the name of her game.

'You should live in trees that give fruit every day. Ripe, gushy fruit like fresh figs. You are an animal.'

'I would rather be a bird than an animal, Bogardus, if it's all the same to you.'

'So. A bird. Eat, tweet, flutter, evacuate and lay eggs. I ask myself a thousand times, "Why did *he* marry *you*?" '

'You know we met at college. He was so specialized. I was drifting in Liberal Arts. We had plenty for each other in those long-ago days.'

'Do you have Jules Bergman's station turned on? He is the only one who knows anything about it up there.'

'The T.V. is on in the bedroom.'

'Naturally. Hey, how do you live with yourself?'

'I don't want to live with myself. That's why you're here, Bogardus. Lord, where did you get that outfit? Green slacks, a blue jacket, a plaid shirt and brown tie. Your hair is standing like Dr Zorba's. And it's receding. You've lost whole tufts since I saw you right over your forehead. Look at your shoes. And that beard looks like an abandoned nest. You don't take care of yourself.'

'Now tell me my belly is hanging over my belt.'

'I noticed.'

'You look lovely. Not a blemish.'

'Thank you, Bogardus. I know how hard it is for you to spare me any candy.'

'It's the truth.'

It is. She looks as lovely as a sunshower. I was in a growl when I came sneaking like a mole to her back door. A mole at the bung of the split-level built and furnished by a great national magazine in exchange for the exclusive rights to *his* memoirs. What would they give for hers? An igloo in Zambia. When she opened her door to me she wore only a Turkish towel, a pink affair with flowers. She dropped it and came into my arms.

'Are you advertising your thing to the street? Cover yourself.'

'Cover me.'

'This is ridiculous. Impossible. You're getting worse. You carry on like a yippie. Act your age, dammit. Keep some grace and style. We don't live in the zoo.'

'I'm penitent, Bogardus. How do I feel to your touch?'

'Delicious.'

'Come have a surprise. Look in the refrigerator.'

And there they are, clams, oranges and cheese. She knows my taste for bivalves, citrus and Bonbell. They are aphrodisiac. And I am no teenager. My fountain needs priming. I am ugly and slowing down, but I always have women. I am some kind of toy to them.

On hard nights I go over the names of the girls I have penetrated. I list them. I divide them into the beautiful, the near-beautiful and the unbeautiful. The married, the unmarried. The young and old. The mothers, the childless. The Christians, Jews, Quakers, Adventists, Buddhists, Mohammedans and B'hais. The fat and thin. The white, black, yellow, red and in-between shades. I break them into luscious categories. One time. Twice. Thrice. Good. Bad. Winners, losers. I arrange them by alphabet. I count them. I lump them. Then I sleep.

'Are you hungry, darling?'

'As a whale.'

'Let's nibble, then. I'll take plates into the bedroom. Go, be comfortable and watch the tube.'

'Why do you call the miracle of television "the tube"? I dislike that expression. Do you do it to detract from the marvel? To drag down? Does that give you pleasure, saying "the tube"?'

'It's an expression the children use.'

'And you let them use it?'

'Please, go inside. There's a robe if you want one. And slippers. I'll get the goodies.'

'Goodies. There's another lovely crappy word.'

'The nutrients. The food. Is that better?'

'To my ear, yes. If you're getting food, say it that way.'

'I'll get food.'

'Bravo.'

'You are in a mood. You need a long massage, Bogardus, and you're going to get one – toes to nose.'

'Your hands are cool authority. I am grateful for those hands.'

'That's good of you to say, Bogardus, considering how disturbed your feelings are. God, I'm thankful that I'm not a deep person.'

'You are deep. Deeper than deep. Deep.'

'I'll rush.'

'Yes. Rush. Deep as deep. Making love with you is like drilling for offshore gold. Really.'

'You turn me on.'

'I turn you on! That's three gorgeous phrases in three minutes.'

'I'll shut up, Bogardus. I promise to please you soon and make restitution for my lackings.'

'A lick for a lack.'

'What a mind you have, Bogardus. What a sense of humour.'

Later I draw slow circles on her belly with one finger. My perfume is on her breath. I splash into her and my gravy runs through her terrain like vapour. She feeds me a Cherrystone while I peel an orange with one hand.

'You love to take squishy creatures out of the security of their shells. Creatures like me. You pry us open and suck our juices, pearls, everything.'

'It's you who are eating the clams, Bogardus.'

'I saw you eat at least three. Besides, I am speaking in simple symbols.'

'Symbols or thimbles, clams don't make pearls. On top of that, this month has no *r* in it.'

'Well, you've destroyed this conversation. You make rubble and garbage out of ideas.'

'You're an idea factory, Bogardus. Don't begrudge me a few measly ideas. Be generous.'

Another report from the Spaceship is due in half an hour. But the television is left on in case of emergency. In the space race one never knows, and the hazards – the terrible hazards – lurk everywhere. We are just babies in the cosmos and an alien form.

'How is your work coming?'

'The words come like snails.'

'Are you pleased with it?'

'Yes and no. I don't know if it's worth it. Yes, I know it's worth it.'

'I'm sure.'

'You are sure of nothing except that you must get yours. The only thing you're sure of is that you want Bogardus Blik's pole in your throbbing hole.'

'Be crass if you want to. But don't sit up to yell at me. Just rest, Bogardus. I have a gift for you.'

'Oh, wow, ah, Jesus Christ, oh darling, how that feels.'

'Thank you, Bogardus. But you don't have to say a single word.'

A sea is torn from me. I let it go. As it flows I think that I have lost enough little sperms to fill a cathedral with bright faces. Where are my unborns? Also, there is more waste. I am sublimating my writing. I do not share those thoughts with her. She is busy anyhow. I stroke her silk hair and rub her shoulders. She moans.

After rest I ask her if she can say that her children are also his.

'Do you want me to answer?'

'Yes.'

'I'm pretty sure of two. The third might be yours.'

'Werner?'

I roll her over and slap her behind. My hand leaves its map. You can see my life-line.

'You are getting a varicose vein on your left thigh.'

'Bogardus, love me a little.'

'I love you a lot. I also hate every cell. With red hate. Pus hate. Hate.'

'I know all that.'

'You have no patriotism. You have no sense of what your husband is doing. You have no comprehension of the religious nature of his vocation, much less of the blind courage and dedication. Married to him you should feel like the priestess of a gleaming tomorrow. You shouldn't involve yourself in adultery.'

'It's partly that they train them so hard, Bogardus. Everything is hardwear, hardwear. Have some mercy for me. The only part of the whole ball of wax that I like is when they talk about the umbilical cords. The rest is cold glass and beryllium.'

'Do you know how much I envy your husband?'

'Yes, I do.'

'He is perfectly Apollonian, pure, strong, clear as a lamp. He is an action man. In me dregs of seminal wine pollute my blood. I moved across the land to Houston to be near the great computers that direct the Space Programme and I meet you.'

'At a supermarket no less. You were arguing about the plumpness of a barbecued chicken. And you turned to me to act as impartial arbitrator. Impartial. You didn't even suspect that I had watched you push your cart in that bent-over way you have for days and weeks before we ever spoke. I dreamed of knowing you.'

'And I of knowing you. Which does not alter the fact that your husband walks in space. I walk on ladies.'

'Don't pluralize. That's insulting. You walk on me.'

'Imagine stepping out into a weightless world.'

'Bogardus, if a person ejaculates in space, are they propelled backward?'

'Ask your husband.'

'He would give me a programmed answer. Don't you see?'

'Imagine making love in a weightless world.'

'Attached to the mother ship by an umbilical.'

'Look, frankly that word *umbilical* bothers me. It downgrades the entire vocabulary of the Programme. Do you notice how Jules Bergman winces when he uses that word? He must feel in his heart as I do. *Tether* is enough.'

'You put me down every chance you get, Bogardus. Well, go ahead. Put me down. So long as you jump on top of me. I don't care for your words. I don't care if you roast a billion years with recrimination. I am only selfish when it comes to you. I adore the way you glump around like a teddy bear. I go to butter when you touch me with your chubby hands. When I feel you swelling up despite yourself I die. When I kiss you I let myself go into you and I get me back down below. As for the marriage, I do my part. I give interviews about how I wasn't nervous while he was up there and how glad I am that he came down intact. And I do worry about him. Don't you think I don't remember how it was back in college? He's the father of most of my children. I love him, Bogardus, in my fashion. If that's what bothers you, know I love him. But you are simply another story. And that's the way of it.'

'Give me a clam.'

'Give me a section of orange.'

Why do I come here? Discovery would mean instant dismissal from the bank and international mortification. Chapter Nine was moving like water. It's a crucial chapter. It relates my theory to the emotions. Why don't I have my scrotum filled with plaster?

'Take me.'

'But there is a report due in seconds from the capsule.'

'Do me and watch at the same time.'

'Your own husband is reporting live on the first attempt at docking, and you want me to do you and watch at the same time?'

'They dock. We dock.'

'Now it's you with the humour. Did He who made the lamb make thee?'

'Yes. I swear it. Now take me, Bogardus, Morris, whoever you are.'

There is Jules Bergman with urgency in his voice.

*　　*　　*

'Gently. Please. Gently. Nice.'

I suspected complication. There is a slow water-leak into a battery that connects with a generator.

'Oh, good. Good. There, yes. Like that.'

The generator is vital. It helps cool a motor involved with re-circulation of coolants involved with the heating system. If the heating system should be impaired in the sub-frigid void of hostile space, all is lost.

'Quicker. You're breaking me. Quicker. You're touching my centre. I'm coming. I'm coming.'

Jules Bergman is definitely worried.

'Ow. Yow. Oooo. Yes. More. Now. Now.'

If he is worried, there is worry. Here comes the announcement. They will scrap the mission. The mission is failed. Down they come.

'Now. Now. Now. Now. Oh, dear, wonderful, splendid man.'

Down. Millions of dollars gone. Hours of preparation gone. So what? We will try again, and next time we will prevail.

'I am exhausted. I feel like a beach. Oh, thank you.'

Failure is the price of success. Now, I suppose 55.4 per cent will vote to cut funds.

'The mission is over. They are bringing them down.'

'Oh, no.'

'Say at least thank heaven the men are spared.'

'Thank heaven the men are spared. Give me a towel or build us an ark. I'm making a lake.'

'Won't reporters ask for your reaction?'

'Any minute. I've got to get to the shower.'

'You see? You see the price of our shame?'

'It was worth any price, Bogardus.'

'Shower. And change your facial expression. You are smiling slightly with that enigmatic, it's-still-inside grin. Your face is flushed. Compose yourself, please.'

'Don't worry.'

'The door-bell. I hear the door-bell.'

'Just take your clothes and go into the broom closet. I'll say I'm too upset to talk. I'll use statement A-15, which covers this. I'll say I'm upset but confident.'

'You want me to stand in the broom closet?'

'Take an orange, darling. I'll be back in a jiff. Then we'll take one of our famous bubble-baths.'

'Oh, sure. We'll splish-splash for the Associated Press. Maybe the President will call. They do that.'

'The broom closet, Bogardus.'

I go into the broom closet. I close the door. There is me. And some brooms. A mop. A folded ironing-board. And detergent. We make a quaint grouping.

I eat my orange in the dark. I hear her running on bare feet. Even the sound of her arches excites my outrageous balls.

While I wait I will use the time to think. About repression, elimination, definition, construction, conquest and liberation. The repression of war. The elimination of disease and hunger. A clear definition of life and death. The construction of alabaster cities. Conquest of the galaxy. The liberation of love through vigorously applied Technology. I will think about Chapter Ten.

Kurt Vonnegut, Jr
Harrison Bergeron

The year was 2081, and everybody was finally equal. They weren't only equal before God and the law, they were equal every which way. Nobody was smarter than anybody else; nobody was better looking than anybody else; nobody was stronger or quicker than anybody else. All this equality was due to the 211th, 212th and 213th Amendments to the Constitution, and to the unceasing vigilance of agents of the United States Handicapper-General.

Some things about living still weren't quite right, though. April, for instance, still drove people crazy by not being springtime. And it was in that clammy month that the H-G men took George and Hazel Bergeron's fourteen-year-old son Harrison away.

It was tragic, all right, but George and Hazel couldn't think about it very hard. Hazel had a perfectly average intelligence, which meant she couldn't think about anything except in short bursts. And George, while his intelligence was way above normal, had a little mental-handicap radio in his ear – he was required by law to wear it at all times. It was tuned to a government transmitter and, every twenty seconds or so, the transmitter would send out some sharp noise to keep people like George from taking unfair advantage of their brains.

George and Hazel were watching television. There were tears on Hazel's cheeks, but she'd forgotten for the moment what they were about, as the ballerinas came to the end of a dance.

A buzzer sounded in George's head. His thoughts fled in panic, like bandits from a burglar alarm.

'That was a real pretty dance, that dance they just did,' said Hazel.

'Huh?' said George.

'That dance – it was nice,' said Hazel.

'Yup,' said George. He tried to think a little about the baller-inas. They weren't really very good – no better than anybody else would have been, anyway. They were burdened with sashweights and bags of birdshot, and their faces were masked, so that no one, seeing a free and graceful gesture or a pretty face, would feel like something the cat dragged in. George was toying with the vague notion that maybe dancers shouldn't be handicapped. But he didn't get very far with it before another noise in his ear radio scattered his thoughts.

George winced. So did two out of the eight ballerinas.

Hazel saw him wince. Having no mental handicap herself, she had to ask George what the latest sound had been.

'Sounded like somebody hitting a milk bottle with a ballpeen hammer,' said George.

'I'd think it would be real interesting, hearing all the different sounds,' said Hazel, a little envious. 'The things they think up.'

'Um,' said George.

'Only, if I was Handicapper-General, you know what I would do?' said Hazel. Hazel, as a matter of fact, bore a strong resembl-ance to the Handicapper-General, a woman named Diana Moon Glampers. 'If I was Diana Moon Glampers,' said Hazel, 'I'd have chimes on Sunday – just chimes. Kind of in honour of religion.'

'I could think, if it was just chimes,' said George.

'Well – maybe make 'em real loud,' said Hazel. 'I think I'd make a good Handicapper-General.'

'Good as anybody else,' said George.

'Who knows better'n I do what normal is?' said Hazel.

'Right,' said George. He began to think glimmeringly about his abnormal son who was now in jail, about Harrison, but a twenty-one-gun salute in his head stopped that.

'Boy!' said Hazel, 'that was a doozy, wasn't it?'

It was such a doozy that George was white and trembling, and tears stood on the rims of his red eyes. Two of the eight ballerinas had collapsed to the studio floor, and were holding their temples.

'All of a sudden you look so tired,' said Hazel. 'Why don't you stretch out on the sofa, so's you can rest your handicap bag on the pillows, honeybunch.' She was referring to the forty-seven pounds of birdshot in a canvas bag, which was padlocked around George's neck. 'Go on and rest the bag for a little while,' she said. 'I don't care if you're not equal to me for a while.'

George weighed the bag with his hands. 'I don't mind it,' he said. 'I don't notice it anymore. It's just a part of me.'

'You been so tired lately – kind of wore out,' said Hazel. 'If there was just some way we could make a little hole in the bottom of the bag, and just take out a few of them lead balls. Just a few.'

'Two years in prison and two thousand dollars fine for every ball I took out,' said George. 'I don't call that a bargain.'

'If you could just take a few out when you came home from work,' said Hazel. 'I mean – you don't compete with anybody around here. You just set around.'

'If I tried to get away with it,' said George, 'then other people'd get away with it – and pretty soon we'd be right back to the dark ages again, with everybody competing against everybody else. You wouldn't like that, would you?'

'I'd hate it,' said Hazel.

'There you are,' said George. 'The minute people start cheating on laws, what do you think happens to society?'

If Hazel hadn't been able to come up with an answer to this question, George couldn't have supplied one. A siren was going off in his head.

'Reckon it'd fall all apart,' said Hazel.

'What would?' said George blankly.

'Society,' said Hazel uncertainly. 'Wasn't that what you just said?'

'Who knows?' said George.

The television programme was suddenly interrupted for a news bulletin. It wasn't clear at first as to what the bulletin was about, since the announcer, like all announcers, had a serious speech impediment. For about half a minute, and in a state of high excitement, the announcer tried to say, 'Ladies and gentlemen—'

He finally gave up, handed the bulletin to a ballerina to read.

'That's all right,' Hazel said of the announcer, 'he tried. That's the big thing. He tried to do the best he could with what God gave him. He should get a nice raise for trying so hard.'

'Ladies and gentlemen—' said the ballerina, reading the bulletin. She must have been extraordinarily beautiful, because the mask she wore was hideous. And it was easy to see that she was the strongest and most graceful of all the dancers, for her handicap bags were as big as those worn by 200-pound men.

And she had to apologize at once for her voice, which was a very unfair voice for a woman to use. Her voice was a warm, luminous, timeless melody. 'Excuse me—' she said, and she began again, making her voice absolutely uncompetitive.

'Harrison Bergeron, age fourteen,' she said in a grackle squawk, 'has just escaped from jail, where he was held on suspicion of plotting to overthrow the government. He is a genius and an athlete, is under-handicapped, and is extremely dangerous.'

A police photograph of Harrison Bergeron was flashed on the screen – upside down, then sideways, upside down again, then right-side up. The picture showed the full length of Harrison against a background calibrated in feet and inches. He was exactly seven feet tall.

The rest of Harrison's appearance was Hallowe'en and hardware. Nobody had ever borne heavier handicaps. He had outgrown hindrances faster than the H-G men could think them up. Instead of a little ear-radio for a mental handicap, he wore a tremendous pair of earphones, and spectacles with thick, wavy lenses besides. The spectacles were intended not only to make him half-blind, but to give him whanging headaches besides.

Scrap metal was hung all over him. Ordinarily, there was a certain symmetry, a military neatness to the handicaps issued to strong people, but Harrison looked like a walking junkyard. In the race of life, Harrison carried 300 pounds.

And, to offset his good looks, the H-G men required that he wear at all times a red rubber ball for a nose, keep his eyebrows shaved off, and cover his even white teeth with black caps at snaggle-tooth random.

'If you see this boy,' said the ballerina, 'do not – I repeat, do not – try to reason with him.'

There was the shriek of a door being torn from its hinges.

Screams and barking cries of consternation came from the television set. The photograph of Harrison Bergeron on the screen jumped again and again, as though dancing to the tune of an earthquake.

George Bergeron correctly identified the earthquake, and well he might have – for many was the time his own home had danced to the same crashing tune. 'My God!' said George. 'That must be Harrison!'

The realization was blasted from his mind instantly by the sound of an automobile collision in his head.

When George could open his eyes again, the photograph of Harrison was gone. A living, breathing Harrison filled the screen.

Clanking, clownish and huge, Harrison stood in the centre of the studio. The knob of the uprooted studio-door was still in his hand. Ballerinas, technicians, musicians and announcers cowered on their knees before him, expecting to die.

'I am the Emperor!' cried Harrison. 'Do you hear? I am the Emperor! Everybody must do what I say at once!' He stamped his foot and the studio shook.

'Even as I stand here,' he bellowed, 'crippled, hobbled, sickened, I am a greater ruler than any man who ever lived! Now watch me become what I *can* become!'

Harrison tore the straps of his handicap harness like wet tissue-paper, tore straps guaranteed to support 5000 pounds.

Harrison's scrap-iron handicaps crashed to the floor.

Harrison thrust his thumbs under the bar of the padlock that secured his head harness. The bar snapped like celery. Harrison smashed his headphones and spectacles against the wall.

He flung away his rubber-ball nose, revealed a man that would have awed Thor, the god of thunder.

'I shall now select my Empress!' he said, looking down on the cowering people. 'Let the first woman who dares rise to her feet claim her mate and her throne!'

A moment passed, and then a ballerina arose, swaying like a willow.

Harrison plucked the mental handicap from her ear, snapped off her physical handicaps with marvellous delicacy. Last of all, he removed her mask.

She was blindingly beautiful.

'Now—' said Harrison, taking her hand. 'Shall we show the people the meaning of the word "dance"? Music!' he commanded.

The musicians scrambled back into their chairs, and Harrison stripped them of their handicaps, too. 'Play your best,' he told them, 'and I'll make you barons and dukes and earls.'

The music began. It was normal at first – cheap, silly, false. But Harrison snatched two musicians from their chairs, waved them like batons as he sang the music as he wanted it played. He slammed them back into their chairs.

The music began again, and was much improved.

Harrison and his Empress merely listened to the music for a while – listened gravely, as though synchronizing their heartbeats with it.

They shifted their weight to their toes.

Harrison placed his big hands on the girl's tiny waist, letting her sense the weightlessness that would soon be hers.

And then, in an explosion of joy and grace, into the air they sprang!

Not only were the laws of the land abandoned, but the law of gravity and the laws of motion as well.

They reeled, whirled, swivelled, flounced, capered, gambolled and spun.

They leaped like deer on the moon.

The studio ceiling was thirty feet high, but each leap brought the dancers nearer to it.

It became their obvious intention to kiss the ceiling.

They kissed it.

And then, neutralizing gravity with love and pure will, they remained suspended in air inches below the ceiling, and they kissed each other for a long, long time.

It was then that Diana Moon Glampers, the Handicapper-General, came into the studio with a double-barrelled ten-gauge shotgun. She fired twice, and the Emperor and the Empress were dead before they hit the floor.

Diana Moon Glampers loaded the gun again. She aimed it at the musicians and told them they had ten seconds to get their handicaps back on.

It was then that the Bergerons' television tube burned out.

Hazel turned to comment about the blackout to George. But George had gone out into the kitchen for a can of beer.

George came back in with the beer, paused while a handicap signal shook him up. And then he sat down again. 'You been crying?' he said to Hazel, watching her wipe her tears.

'Yup,' she said.

'What about?' he said.

'I forget,' she said. 'Something real sad on television.'

'What was it?' he said.

'It's all kind of mixed up in my mind,' said Hazel.

'Forget sad things,' said George.

'I always do,' said Hazel.

'That's my girl,' said George. He winced. There was the sound of a riveting-gun in his head.

'Gee – I could tell that one was a doozy,' said Hazel.

'You can say that again,' said George.

'Gee—' said Hazel. 'I could tell that one was a doozy.'

Gordon R. Dickson
Computers don't argue

Treasure Book Club

PLEASE DO NOT FOLD, SPINDLE OR MUTILATE THIS CARD

Mr: Walter A. Child Balance: $4.98

Dear Customer: Enclosed is your latest book selection. *Kidnapped*, by Robert Louis Stevenson.

Treasure Book Club
1823 Mandy Street
Chicago, Illinois

Woodlawn Drive
Panduk, Michigan
16 Nov 1965

Dear Sirs:

I wrote you recently about the computer punch card you sent, billing me for *Kim*, by Rudyard Kipling. I did not open the package containing it until I had already mailed you my cheque for the amount on the card. On opening the package, I found the book missing half its pages. I sent it back to you, requesting either another copy or my money back. Instead, you have sent me a copy of *Kidnapped*, by Robert Louis Stevenson. Will you please straighten this out?

I hereby return the copy of *Kidnapped*.

Sincerely yours,
Walter R. Child

Treasure Book Club

SECOND NOTICE PLEASE DO NOT FOLD, SPINDLE OR MUTILATE THIS CARD

Mr: Walter A. Child Balance: $4.98

For *Kidnapped*, by Robert Louis Stevenson.

(If remittance has been made for the above, please disregard this notice)

Treasure Book Club
1823 Mandy Street
Chicago, Illinois

437 Woodlawn Drive
Panduk, Michigan
21 Jan 1966

Dear Sirs:

May I direct your attention to my letter of 16 November 1965?
You are still continuing to dun me with computer punch cards for
a book I did not order. Whereas, actually, it is your company that
owes *me* money.
Sincerely yours,
Walter A. Child

Treasure Book Club
1823 Mandy Street
Chicago, Illinois
1 Feb 1966

Mr Walter A. Child
437 Woodlawn Drive
Panduk, Michigan

Dear Mr Child:

We have sent you a number of reminders concerning an amount
owing to us as a result of book purchases you have made from us.
This amount, which is $4.98, is now long overdue.

This situation is disappointing to us, particularly since there
was no hesitation on our part in extending you credit at the time
original arrangements for these purchases were made by you. If
we do not receive payment in full by return mail, we will be forced
to turn the matter over to a collection agency.
Very truly yours,
Samuel P. Grimes
Collection Mgr

437 Woodlawn Drive
Panduk, Michigan
5 Feb 1966

Dear Mr Grimes:

Will you stop sending me punch cards and form letters and make
me some kind of a direct answer from a human being?

I don't owe you money. *You* owe me money. Maybe I should
turn your company over to a collection agency.
Walter A. Child

FEDERAL COLLECTION OUTFIT

Mr Walter A.Child   88 Prince Street
437 Woodlawn Drive   Chicago, Illinois
Panduk, Michigan   28 Feb 1966

Dear Mr Child:

Your account with the Treasure Book Club, of $4.98 plus interest and charges, has been turned over to our agency for collection. The amount due is now $6.83. Please send your cheque for this amount or we shall be forced to take immediate action.

Jacob N. Harshe
Vice-President

FEDERAL COLLECTION OUTFIT

Mr Walter A. Child   88 Prince Street
437 Woodlawn Drive   Chicago, Illinois
Panduk, Michigan   8 April 1966

Dear Mr Child:

You have seen fit to ignore our courteous requests to settle your long-overdue account with Treasure Book Club, which is now, with accumulated interest and charges, in the amount of $7.51.

If payment in full is not forthcoming by 11 April 1966 we will be forced to turn the matter over to our attorneys for immediate court action.

Ezekiel B. Harshe
President

MALONEY, MAHONEY, MACNAMARA & PRUITT Attorneys

Mr Walter A. Child   89 Prince Street
437 Woodlawn Drive   Chicago, Illinois
Panduk, Michigan   29 April 1966

Dear Mr Child:

Your indebtedness to the Treasure Book Club has been referred to us for legal action to collect.

This indebtedness is now in the amount of $10.01. If you will send us this amount so that we may receive it before 5 May 1966, the matter may be satisfied. However, if we do not receive satisfaction in full by that date, we will take steps to collect through the courts.

I am sure you will see the advantage of avoiding a judgment against you, which as a matter of record would do lasting harm to your credit rating.

Very truly yours,
Hagthorpe M. Pruitt, Jr
Attorney at law

Mr Hagthorpe M. Pruitt, Jr   437 Woodlawn Drive
Maloney, Mahoney,   Panduk, Michigan
MacNamara & Pruitt   4 May 1966
89 Prince Street,
Chicago, Illinois

Dear Mr Pruitt:
You don't know what a pleasure it is to me in this matter to get a letter from a live human being to whom I can explain the situation.

This whole matter is silly. I explained it fully in my letters to the Treasure Book Company. But I might as well have been trying to explain to the computer that puts out their punch cards, for all the good it seemed to do. Briefly, what happened was I ordered a copy of *Kim*, by Rudyard Kipling, for $4.98. When I opened the package they sent me, I found the book had only half its pages, but I'd previously mailed a cheque to pay them for the book.

I sent the book back to them, asking either for a whole copy or my money back. Instead, they sent me a copy of *Kidnapped*, by Robert Louis Stevenson – which I had not ordered; and for which they have been trying to collect from me.

Meanwhile, I am still waiting for the money back they owe me for the copy of *Kim* that I didn't get. That's the whole story. Maybe you can help me straighten them out.

Relievedly yours,
Walter A. Child

P.S: I also sent them back their copy of *Kidnapped*, as soon as I got it, but it hasn't seemed to help. They have never even acknowledged getting it back.

MALONEY, MAHONEY, MACNAMARA & PRUITT Attorneys

Mr Walter A. Child   89 Prince Street
437 Woodlawn Drive   Chicago, Illinois
Panduk, Michigan   9 May 1966

Dear Mr Child:

I am in possession of no information indicating that any item purchased by you from the Treasure Book Club has been returned.

I would hardly think that, if the case had been as you stated, the Treasure Book Club would have retained us to collect the amount owing from you.

If I do not receive your payment in full within three days, by 12 May 1966, we will be forced to take legal action.

Very truly yours,

Hagthorpe M. Pruitt, Jr

COURT OF MINOR CLAIMS Chicago, Illinois

Mr Walter A.Child
437 Woodlawn Drive
Panduk, Michigan

Be informed that a judgment was taken and entered against you in this court this day of 26 May 1966 in the amount of $15.66 including court costs.

Payment in satisfaction of this judgment may be made to this court or to the adjudged creditor. In the case of payment being made to the creditor, a release should be obtained from the creditor and filed with this court in order to free you of legal obligation in connection with this judgment.

Under the recent Reciprocal Claims Act, if you are a citizen of a different state, a duplicate claim may be automatically entered and judged against you in your own state so that collection may be made there as well as in the State of Illinois.

COURT OF MINOR CLAIMS Chicago, Illinois

PLEASE DO NOT FOLD, SPINDLE OR MUTILATE THIS CARD

Judgment was passed this day of 27 May 1966, under Statute $15.66

Against: Child, Walter A. of 347 Woodlawn Drive, Panduk, Michigan. Pray to enter a duplicate claim for judgment.

In: Picayune Court – Panduk, Michigan.

For Amount: Statute 941

Samuel P. Grimes
Vice-President, Treasure Book Club
1823 Mandy Street
Chicago, Illinois

437 Woodlawn Drive
Panduk, Michigan
31 May 1966

Grimes:

This business has gone far enough. I've got to come down to Chicago on business of my own tomorrow. I'll see you then and we'll get this straightened out once and for all, about who owes what to whom, and how much!

Yours,
Walter A. Child

From the desk of the Clerk Picayune Court

1 June 1966

Harry:

The attached computer card from Chicago's Minor Claims Court against A. Walter has a 1500-series Statute number on it. That puts it over in Criminal with you, rather than Civil with me. So I herewith submit it for your computer instead of mine. How's business?

Joe

CRIMINAL RECORDS Panduk, Michigan

PLEASE DO NOT FOLD, SPINDLE OR MUTILATE THIS CARD

Convicted: (Child) A. Walter
On: 26 May 1966
Address: 437 Woodlawn Drive, Panduk, Mich.

Crim: Statute: 1566 (Corrected) 1567
Crime: Kidnap
Date: 16 Nov 1965
Notes: At large. To be picked up at once.

POLICE DEPARTMENT, PANDUK, MICHIGAN. TO POLICE DEPARTMENT
CHICAGO ILLINOIS. CONVICTED SUBJECT A. (COMPLETE FIRST
NAME UNKNOWN) WALTER, SOUGHT HERE IN CONNECTION REF.
YOUR NOTIFICATION OF JUDGMENT FOR KIDNAP OF CHILD NAMED
ROBERT LOUIS STEVENSON, ON 16 NOV 1965. INFORMATION HERE
INDICATES SUBJECT FLED HIS RESIDENCE, AT 437 WOODLAWN
DRIVE, PANDUK, AND MAY BE AGAIN IN YOUR AREA.

POSSIBLE CONTACT IN YOUR AREA: THE TREASURE BOOK CLUB,
1823 MANDY STREET, CHICAGO, ILLINOIS. SUBJECT NOT KNOWN TO
BE ARMED, BUT PRESUMED DANGEROUS. PICK UP AND HOLD,
ADVISING US OF CAPTURE . . .

TO POLICE DEPARTMENT, PANDUK, MICHIGAN. REFERENCE YOUR
REQUEST TO PICK UP AND HOLD A. (COMPLETE FIRST NAME
UNKNOWN) WALTER, WANTED IN PANDUK ON STATUTE 1567,
CRIME OF KIDNAPPING.
SUBJECT ARRESTED AT OFFICES OF TREASURE BOOK CLUB,
OPERATING THERE UNDER ALIAS WALTER ANTHONY CHILD AND
ATTEMPTING TO COLLECT $4.98 FROM ONE SAMUEL P. GRIMES,
EMPLOYEE OF THAT COMPANY.
DISPOSAL: HOLDING FOR YOUR ADVICE.

POLICE DEPARTMENT PANDUK, MICHIGAN TO POLICE DEPARTMENT
CHICAGO, ILLINOIS.

REF: A. WALTER (ALIAS WALTER ANTHONY CHILD) SUBJECT
WANTED FOR CRIME OF KIDNAP, YOUR AREA, REF: YOUR
COMPUTER PUNCH CARD NOTIFICATION OF JUDGMENT, DATED 27
MAY 1966. COPY OUR CRIMINAL RECORDS PUNCH CARD HEREWITH
FORWARDED TO YOUR COMPUTER SECTION.

CRIMINAL RECORDS Chicago, Illinois
PLEASE DO NOT FOLD, SPINDLE OR MUTILATE THIS CARD
SUBJECT (CORRECTION – OMITTED RECORD SUPPLIED)
APPLICABLE STATUTE NO. 1567
JUDGMENT NO. 456789
TRIAL RECORD: APPARENTLY MISFILED AND UNAVAILABLE
DIRECTION: TO APPEAR FOR SENTENCING BEFORE JUDGE JOHN
ALEXANDER MCDIVOT, COURTROOM A, 9 JUNE 1966

From the Desk of Judge Alexander J. McDivot

June 2 1966

Dear Tony:

I've got an adjudged criminal coming up before me for sentencing
Thursday morning – but the trial transcript is apparently misfiled.

I need some kind of information (Ref: A. Walter – Judgment
No. 456789, Criminal). For example what about the victim of the
kidnapping. Was victim harmed?

Jack McDivot

3 June 1966

Records Search Unit
Re: Ref: Judgment No. 456789 – was victim harmed?
Tonio Malagasi
Records Division

3 June 1966

To: United States Statistics Office Attn: Information Section
Subject: Robert Louis Stevenson
Query: Information concerning

Records Search Unit
Criminal Records Division
Police Department
Chicago, Ill.

5 June 1966

To: Records Search Unit
Criminal Records Division
Police Department
Chicago, Illinois

Subject: Your query re Robert Louis Stevenson (File no. 189623)
Action: Subject deceased. Age at death 44yrs. Further informa-
tion requested?
A.K.
Information Section
U.S. Statistics Office

6 June 1966

To: United States Statistics Office
Attn: Information Division
Subject: Re: File no. 189623
No further information required.
Thank you.
Records Search Unit

Criminal Records Division
Police Department
Chicago, Illinois

7 June 1966

To: Tonio Malagasi
Records Division
Re: Ref: Judgment No. 456789 – victim is dead.
Records Search Unit

7 June 1966

To: Judge Alexander J. McDivot's Chambers
Dear Jack:
Ref: Judgment No. 456789. The victim in this kidnap case was
apparently slain.

From the strange lack of background information on the killer
and his victim, as well as the victim's age, this smells to me like a

gangland killing. This for your information. Don't quote me. It seems to me, though, that Stevenson – the victim – has a name that rings a faint bell with me. Possibly one of the East Coast Mob, since the association comes back to me as something about pirates – possibly New York dockage hijackers – and something about buried loot.

As I say, above is only speculation for your private guidance. Any time I can help . . .

Best,
Tony Malagasi
Records Division

MICHAEL R. REYNOLDS Attorney-at-law

49 Water Street
Chicago, Illinois
8 June 1966

Dear Tim:

Regrets: I can't make the fishing trip. I've been court-appointed here to represent a man about to be sentenced tomorrow on a kidnapping charge.

Ordinarily, I might have tried to beg off, and McDivot, who is doing the sentencing, would probably have turned me loose. But this is the damnedest thing you ever heard of.

The man being sentenced has apparently been not only charged, but adjudged guilty as a result of a comedy of errors too long to go into here. He not only isn't guilty – he's got the best case I ever heard of for damages against one of the larger book clubs headquartered here in Chicago. And that's a case I wouldn't mind taking on.

It's inconceivable – but damnably possible, once you stop to think of it in this day and age of machine-made records – that a completely innocent man could be put in this position.

There shouldn't be much to it. I've asked to see McDivot tomorrow before the time for sentencing, and it'll just be a matter of explaining to him. Then I can discuss the damage suit with my freed client at his leisure.

Fishing next weekend?

Yours,
Mike

MICHAEL R. REYNOLDS Attorney-at-law
49 Water Street
Chicago, Illinois
10 June

Dear Tim:

In haste –

No fishing this coming week either. Sorry.

You won't believe it. My innocent-as-a-lamb-and-I'm-not-kidding client has just been sentenced to death for first-degree murder in connection with the death of his kidnap victim.

Yes, I explained the whole thing to McDivot. And, when he explained his situation to me, I nearly fell out of my chair.

It wasn't a matter of my not convincing him. It took less than three minutes to show him that my client should never have been within the walls of the County Jail for a second. But – get this – McDivot couldn't do a thing about it.

The point is, my man had already been judged guilty according to the computerized records. In the absence of a trial record – of course there never was one (but that's something I'm not free to explain to you now) – the judge has to go by what records are available. And, in the case of an adjudged prisoner, McDivot's only legal choice was whether to sentence to life imprisonment or execution.

The death of the kidnap victim, according to the statute, made the death penalty mandatory, Under the new laws governing length of time for appeal, which has been shortened because of the new system of computerizing records, to force an elimination of unfair delay and mental anguish to those condemned, I have five days in which to file an appeal, and ten to have it acted on.

Needless to say, I am not going to monkey with an appeal. I'm going directly to the Governor for a pardon – after which we will get this farce reversed. McDivot has already written the Governor, also, explaining that his sentence was ridiculous, but that he had no choice. Between the two of us, we ought to have a pardon in short order.

Then, I'll make the fur fly . . . And we'll get in some fishing.

Best,

Mike

OFFICE OF THE GOVERNOR OF ILLINOIS

17 June 1966

Mr Michael R. Reynolds
49 Water Street
Chicago, Illinois

Dear Mr Reynolds:
In reply to your query about the request for pardon for Walter A.
Child (A. Walter), may I inform you that the Governor is still on
his trip with the Midwest Governors Committee, examining the
Wall in Berlin. He should be back next Friday.

I will bring your request and letters to his attention the minute
he returns.
Very truly yours,
Clara B. Jilks
Secretary to the Governor

27 June 1966

Michael R. Reynolds
49 Water Street
Chicago, Illinois

Dear Mike:
Where is that pardon?
My execution date is only five days from now!
Walt

29 June 1966

Walter A. Child (A. Walter)
Cell Block E
Illinois State Penitentiary
Joilet, Illinois

Dear Walt:
The Governor returned, but was called away immediately to the
White House in Washington to give his views on interstate sewage.

I am camping on his doorstep and will be on him the moment
he arrives here.

Meanwhile, I agree with you about the seriousness of the situation. The warden at the prison there, Mr Allen Magruder, will bring this letter to you and have a private talk with you. I urge you to listen to what he has to say; and I enclose letters from your family also urging you to listen to Warden Magruder.
Yours,
Mike

30 June 1966

Michael R. Reynolds
49 Water Street
Chicago, Illinois

Dear Mike:
(This letter being smuggled out by Warden Magruder)
As I was talking to Warden Magruder in my cell, here, news was brought to him that the Governor has at last returned for a while to Illinois, and will be in his office early tomorrow morning, Friday. So you will have time to get the pardon signed by him and delivered to the prison in time to stop my execution on Saturday.

Accordingly, I have turned down the Warden's kind offer of a chance to escape; since he told me he could by no means guarantee to have all the guards out of my way when I tried it; and there was a chance of my being killed escaping.

But now everything will straighten itself out. Actually, an experience as fantastic as this had to break down sometime under its own weight.
Best,
Walt

FOR THE SOVEREIGN STATE OF ILLINOIS

I, Hubert Daniel Willikens, Governor of the State of Illinois, and invested with the authority and powers appertaining thereto, including the power to pardon those in my judgment wrongfully convicted or otherwise deserving of executive mercy, do this day of 1 July 1966 announce and proclaim that Walter A. Child (A. Walter), now in custody as a consequence of erroneous conviction upon a crime of which he is entirely innocent, is fully and freely pardoned of said crime. And I do direct the necessary authorities having custody of the said Walter A. Child (A. Walter), in whatever place or places he may be held, to immediately free, release, and allow unhindered departure to him . . .

Interdepartmental Routing Service
PLEASE DO NOT FOLD, MUTILATE, OR SPINDLE THIS CARD
Failure to route Document properly.
To: Governor Hubert Daniel Willikens.
Re: Pardon issued to Walter A. Child, 1 July 1966

Dear State Employee:
You have failed to attach your Routing Number.
PLEASE: Resubmit document with this card and form 876, explaining your authority for placing a TOP RUSH category on this document. Form 876 must be signed by your Departmental Superior.

RESUBMIT ON: Earliest possible date ROUTING SERVICE office is open. In this case, Tuesday, 5 July 1966.

WARNING: Failure to submit form 876 WITH THE SIGNATURE OF YOUR SUPERIOR may make you liable to prosecution for misusing a Service of the State Government. A warrant may be issued for your arrest.

There are NO exceptions. YOU have been WARNED.

Will Worthington
The food goes in the top

Mr Beavers was in a rancid mood when he came up out of the subway on Saturday evening. It had been a disturbing week. Two incidents conspired to make it so – two, that is, which could be clearly defined, described and blamed for his darkening mood, but these events were only superficially discrete; on some unlighted level of mind where common logic had no authority, where any question commencing with 'why' was a disembodied hand groping in emptiness, these incidents were somehow connected. More than that, some unknown catalytic agent united them to produce a series of images which were likewise disturbing because they were familiar images jarred out of their usual context and so rendered new and strange. All the way uptown – nineteen blocks – he had struggled to marshal these thoughts, whip them into some meaningful sequence and so exercise their demonic powers, but his efforts had only raised more dust.

On Monday morning a hysterical female clerk had run screaming through the offices of Albumin Ltd. Old Mr Byles of the Shipping Department had died at his desk and she had found him there. Beavers had helped put him on a stretcher when the ambulance came, but they had encountered grotesque difficulties. The old man's body was curved – just as though he were shaped that way for the purpose of bending over bills of lading – and kept tumbling from the stretcher.

It had been necessary for Beavers to hold the old man's hairless ankle while the body was borne through the clots of curious employees to the waiting ambulance. The expressions, or perhaps the absence thereof, on the faces of the others had shocked him then. They were all faces which should have been familiar to him, but he might have been walking through an aquarium of weird tropical fish. Some even smirked – or so it seemed. No one knew Byles well, though he had been with the firm of Albumin Ltd for twenty-three years.

Mr Beavers had reflected later that he really knew nothing of Mr Byles, though he had certainly spoken to him often enough. If Byles had ever mentioned a family, a home town, a life beyond Albumin Ltd, the intelligence had gone the way of such facts as old high-jumping records and the dates of obscure acts of Congress. To all intents he had come from nowhere, unannounced, and silently like the ambulance, which as swiftly and silently took him away again.

There had been a notice on the main bulletin board to the effect that employees could have time off to attend funeral rites on Wednesday. This was pointedly addressed to people in the Shipping Department. Mr Beavers had not attended. He was in the Accounting Department.

The second incident that served to make the week distinct from all other weeks Beavers could remember happened on Thursday. A notice on the bulletin board announced that placement examinations were to be given to certain qualified younger employees, presumably to select trainees for future junior executive positions. Clearly it did not apply to men like Beavers, who had never seriously considered advancing themselves beyond the comfortable sphere of their known capabilities, and it had not occurred to Beavers to feel 'out of it' in any way. Or it wouldn't have occurred to him if it hadn't been for the inane comment passed by one of the more offensive office boys who happened to be standing there while Beavers was reading the bulletin board. Rizzio, the kid's name was . . . one of those papuliferous young louts who always has something snide to contribute to any situation.

'Happy is the clot
        who has found his proper slot . . . ,' said the kid, and a girl next to him had giggled in a wax-loosening voice.

'*What* did you say?' Beavers had demanded, although he had heard the impertinent jingle quite clearly.

'Don't let it bug ya, dad,' the kid had replied. There had been nothing to do but stalk away from the scene. To himself he had said, 'Not even a week after poor old Byles . . . ,' and then it had occurred to him that his complaint and sense of outrage was based on an irrelevancy. What had Byles to do with it? Why, for that matter, should Rizzio's wry comment touch Melvin P. Beavers of the Accounting Department? Why, indeed? Nevertheless, it did.

After that Mr Beavers had begun to notice things, but his observations exploded upon his awareness one at a time. Taken singly, they were as senseless as the random forms of puzzle-pieces, but by their very randomness they suggested – and persistently – that they were part of a picture not yet seen. The dirtiness of the subway was a case in point, as was the great amount of litter on the platforms and the stairs. On that Saturday evening the stairway to the street was so silted in with newspapers and other rubble that Beavers had been unsure of finding the steps and had clung to the railing in case his feet should miss one of them. He did not remember having done this before.

They were leaving more litter around than ever before.

But also:

They were not cleaning up the subways and streets.

(*They* had wasted no time in coming for the body of old Byles, though, and *They* had taken him away without a word. Then *They* had posted a bulletin . . .

The calendar indicated that it was mid-October, and the evening air should have been cool, clear and bracing when he came up out of the subway at 23rd and Market, but it wasn't. There was carbon monoxide in it and carbon dioxide and just plain carbon. There was something else. It was *used* air – even *re-used*.

They were getting careless about the air. Even the sky . . .

Mr Beavers lived at Mrs Geppert's boarding-house on Market Street. The air inside of that old-fashioned dwelling was much like the vitiated air of the streets, only more so: stiller, staler and polluted not only with Mr Geppert's cigars but with Geppert himself, who silently scorned the fastidious and who was past caring. Mr Beavers had once dreaded coming back to the boarding-house on Saturday evenings because Geppert had chided him about working on Saturdays. 'Why do you *do* it, Beavers? What are you saving it all up *for*?' Beavers had cut him short one particularly tense evening, but he could not remember with what comment. This much he knew: it was not with any cogent answer to the offensive question. Surely some kind of merit accrued. Was it time? Money? Something else?

In time he had thrust the question from the spotlight of his mind, at least, though it would not be expelled altogether. Some echo of it was evoked each evening when he saw Geppert, whom he despised. Mr Geppert had no function. He did no work of any kind and he slept alone. Having abdicated function he had also relinquished all prerogatives of voice, except for an occasional word to Mr Beàvers.

This also was resented by Beavers – that he alone should be thought lowly enough to be spoken to by Geppert, and even addressed by his last name, but in fact Geppert had very little to say. Along with the ignominious privilege of sitting inert in *his* Morris chair in the parlour went that of selecting all television programmes and watching these all day long and much of the night.

There was no conflict with Mrs Geppert concerning the TV, for that lady was totally preoccupied with gaining entrance to TV studios as a member of the 'live' audience, especially for quiz programmes. Beavers had seen her face among the bland, bovine masks of the 'live'-audience ladies, but it was always hard to distinguish her from the rest, with their pastry-fed look, child-like eyes swimming euphorically behind rimless glasses, anachronistic bobby-soxer enthusiasm. (*They* turned it on and off as the script required. Perhaps *They* had installed shockers in the seats. More likely *They* merely selected highly suggestible types – unintelligence tests, possibly. One thing was certain: *They used the same ladies over and over and over again*. Nothing changed. They didn't actually come *from* anywhere.

Geppert was in *his* Morris chair when Mr Beavers entered the house. The TV was giving forth the painful falsetto banalities which were directed downward at the kiddies of the Nation by *Geeko and His Friends*, sponsored by Vita-Shards, the fortified lemon-flavoured dry cereal. Geppert would watch it with the same unchanging attention with which he would subsequently favour *Frontier Bondsman* sponsored by . . . who was it now? Last year it had been Vita-Nuggs, the dietary supplement for growing children. Same programme. Same stories. All reruns. *They had no new material*. No one was writing, acting, producing, composing, arranging . . . anything. All tape or wire or something let out of bottles. Only quizzes were 'live'.

Geppert was eating something out of a tinfoil tray. He did not take his eyes from the grey screen when Mr Beavers came in, but indicated the kitchen with his thumb

'The wife's out. Dinner inna oven.'

Why did the man always have to be the *same*, thought Mr Beavers as he washed up for 'dinner'. One could ignore the man, perhaps, but how escape his ambiance? It was not the one, grubby, inconsiderate individual that sometimes made you want to light fires and claw down walls; it was drifts of rumpled newspapers, grey undershirts, mustiness in clothes, upholstery, carpets – cigar-ends in the toilet. (And even that homely convenience seemed now to lack the vitality to flush completely. *They* were skimping on the water-pressure. *Cut off . . .*

'Dinner', which had cooled enough so that Mr Beavers could remove it from the oven without burning himself, was Mother Darb's All-Meat Hackettes with Gr. Peas and Fr. Fr. Pot. One was forewarned of this by the lettering on the placental covering which had to be removed somehow without spilling the contents.

Mr Beavers could hear the gunplay of *Frontier Bondsman* in the parlour and so decided to eat his 'dinner' right there in the kitchen. He had no intention of lingering over it, not that it was what could be called a revolting experience exactly. Such food merited no such strong language. But there was no joy in it either.

He was not so obviously hungry as he was simply aware that it was after five o'clock. He would eat it and he would not then be hungry. It would be as though *They* had somehow taken the measure of one's stomach at mean post-prandial distension and adjusted the amount of food, allowing for expansion, to fit the space as precisely as a piston fits into a cylinder. Beavers had once tried to imagine brown hands picking such Gr. Peas from a vine, or field-hands in bright shirts bending to pluck the Fr. Fr. Pot. from freshly turned earth – all under an open, sun-cleansed sky – but the image would not connect with the plastic-encysted reality, and it kept fading until it would have been just as easy to accept that the food came from another planet or another time.

To what extent had the entire outer world where things and creatures lived, grew and 'came from' dissolved and sloughed away? If one were tempted to speculate about such as the All-Meat Hack-ettes, perhaps it was not such a bad thing at that. Meanwhile the present contained nonce-realities which you accepted in the same spirit and by means of the same inner mechanism that enabled you to agree that movie characters on the screen in the other room were doing heroic things in the here and now, notwithstanding that the heroes wore vests and hard straws, made pursuits, and getaways in towering cars with running-boards, and with slouch-hatted heroines conversed in a language out of the ice-cream par-lours of the early nineteen thirties.

The food had no origin more than a block away. It was from nowhere. It conveyed nothing to your body or spirit beyond its own tasteless self – no fecund earth, no field-hand laughter, no bustling kitchens – and it sent you nowhere except, in due course, to the bathroom with its reluctant facility. It would not change you; you would neither wax nor wane from having partaken of it, neither would it warm you. Nothing would change.

The pause after dinner, never a cheerful epoch in the best of times Beavers could remember, now revealed itself too obviously as a window on nothingness. Prospects for the hours ahead – never mind how many – were not merely depressing now, but almost menacing. It was part of this queasy business of starting to *notice things*. Beavers sat with his elbows propped on the kitchen table, and over the nasal aggressions of the *Frontier Bondsman* and the sporadic phlegm-rattlings of Geppert in the other room he man-aged to think. It was a terrible mistake.

Suppose you wanted to talk to somebody – really talk?

Geppert was out. He didn't. He had nothing worth saying and a lifetime accumulation of wax in his ears. Mrs Geppert was pleasant enough, but she didn't hear you. She just rolled her big, vague, swimmy eyes at the ceiling and said something like 'Oh my yaaaa-aa-aaasss!' – her mind removed to some Western Paradise of gleaming new refrigerators and suave MC's.

The men in the office were out, except of course for the communication demands of Business – tightly limited by its very nature. They were all your superiors, hence forbidding and unapproachable, or they were in every imaginable sense your inferiors, like that young pustule Rizzio with his cracks about *slots* and things. You did not talk to the women in the office for fear that they would answer you. Where did these women come from?

They must have selected them with a view to ensuring stasis. These women would never leave or be borne away from Albumin Ltd by anybody – except in the sense that poor old Byles was borne away. They had the heads and voices of big, dusty carnivorous birds. Everything they did or said – and they did everything with an angry clatter – advertised their misanthropy, but when one did venture some coyness – it happened sometimes that they would roll their codfish eyes and say things like 'I'll saaay!' or 'You said it, kid!' – you were doing well not to vomit. The population would not increase because of these women. If in a fit of morbid whimsy, you tried to think of them as females, a sharp antisexual pang would stab at and suffuse your loins. It was a real physical sensation, much like a fever settling in the vitals. So you were celibate.

They must have sent scouts out to recruit these women, *but when*? *From what place?* Never and nowhere, obviously. They had always been there, like Albumin Ltd, the grey building in which its offices were, the subway, Market Street, Mrs Geppert's boarding-house, Geppert, *Frontier Bondsman*, All-Meat Hackettes w. gr. peas & fr. fr. pot., drifts of grey newsprint, cigar-ends in a constipated john . . . and a *clerk named Beavers*.

You never went out. The movies, like the television, showed only 'film classics' – three on the bill sometimes, and rarely one of any merit when it was new. Westerns starring heroes who had long since died or gone into 'semi-retirement', which is to say they were wistful old elevator-operators somewhere. Or *I Was a Teenage Clothing Fetishist*. That sort of thing. The movie-house two blocks down on Market was also a gathering-place for young punks. Beavers made no effort to conceal his fear and dislike of these superfluous creatures. It was tolerable to think that there were truly desperate men and even professional criminals pursuing their unpleasant work in the dark places of the city, but the young punks were without motive or purpose. They did not go there to see films but merely to stand there dredging their pants pockets and menacing passers-by. As Beavers thought about them, one observation emerged from all the others and burned behind his eyes like the after-image of a garish neon-sign.

They had no place to go.

Now he knew what his thoughts would look like if he could stand aside and watch them move. They were glass marbles hurled against a polished stone floor. Compact and discrete as they were, the thing they had in common was a single unyielding surface – something that would not be known. There were others – questions in search of answers; answers seeking questions – popping up from some inaccessible level of mind like the steel marbles in a pinball game, all waiting to be hurled against the Unyielding, each containing the mysterious possibility of ringing the unheard bell, turning on all the lights, earning the unknown and unimaginable Score.

The kitchen was unendurably small.

At one point, Mr Beavers had to snatch his billfold from his back pocket and rummage through it in search of something by which to establish *his age*. It was not quite believable, nor was his tenure at Albumin Ltd quite believable. He'd worked there every day except Sundays, which he hated because they were mere prolongations of his hollow, echoing time after 'dinner', and the idea of vacations was – had been – insupportable.

He never went anywhere.

The Office was nineteen blocks away on Market Street, but he knew only the extreme ends of the streets because he went by subway. Didn't everybody?

Was Market Street more than nineteen blocks long? Of course it was. Why would you suggest that it wasn't? Why?

Did any other streets cross Market Street? Of course they did! Didn't they?

And what do you mean 'The *same* cars and taxis, the *same* people walking, staring straight ahead past you or looking at the pavement as they hurried along to . . .' What do you mean *where*?

The living-room was much too small too. The ceiling was too low, the walls were too opaque and, besides, Geppert was in it, and *Frontier Bondsman* and the general staleness. You could almost see it now. It was like something coagulating on the surface of the eyeballs.

For what did you account? Now *that* was a stupid question. The vouchers came down from Miss Cloggett's office and you checked them against the records from the Dispersing Department, then entered the totals in the . . .

Totals of what? What do you mean, 'just sending arithmetic problems back and forth'? *Totals*, that's all . . .

Frontier Bondsman was waving to 'all his friends out there' now as he rode away on his horse. Marcus. The man and the animal silhouetted against the sky.

Sky. Have you ever actually *seen* a sky – an open sky? A horizon? On Market Street? Nonsense. Everybody knows what a sky is. A sky is light. There is a stream of electrons from a cathode, and these impinge against a fluorescent surface. It's all inside a thing like a bottle.

Of course there was such a thing as sky! They had sky between the Second National Trust Building and the Albumin Building. They used to change it with the seasons. Lately *They*'d been letting it get sort of crummy. It must still be there, though. Must!

Mr Beavers paused in the hallway long enough to put on his suit coat. It was not cool outside. It was supposed to be, but *They* hadn't changed it yet.

'You never go out!' whined Mr Geppert. He didn't stir from his chair – he wasn't *that* surprised – but he did register surprise. It had never happened before.

The streets were not as dark as Beavers had expected them to be. They should be dark by now, but everything was lighted up. Too much, actually. The air, as he had expected, had not changed. For the first time he noticed the continuous rustling sound in the streets and identified it for what it was. It was the sound of people walking through tons and tons of waste paper. That figured.

The glass-marble thoughts had not penetrated their target yet, but their flight was not random now; they became as a stream of machine-gun bullets – concerted.

He walked past the theatre (*The Sheepman's Revenge – I Was a Teenage Indigent – Selected Short Subjects*) almost hoping that one of the young bums under the marquee would start something. None did, as it happened, but a couple of them stared as he went by. He knew that he was walking at a pace they would think strange – too fast and too purposeful in contrast to other people on the street, who just bumbled along with their eyes focused on nowhere. When he turned the corner into a darker side-street he heard one of them shout, 'You'll be sorrr-ree!'

The paper got worse after he'd gone half a block, and up ahead he saw what appeared to be obstructions. But beyond these there was light. *Light* – great and diffuse, filling the sky! (See – there *is* a sky. You can almost see it.)

Under a street-lamp on a corner stood a policeman. He had seen the officer before, even nodded to him in passing, but they had never exchanged words. People didn't.

'Are you really sure you want to go over there, Mr Beavers?'

'Is there a law?' asked Beavers, not stopping. The policeman shook his head sadly but made no move to stop him. Strange. How could one cop know the names of everyone living in an area like this? Certainly he, Mr Beavers of Albumin Ltd, was of no extraordinary interest to the Law.

Within two blocks the paper was springy underfoot; so deep had it drifted. It was darker too and so impossible to tell how deep.

Sometimes his feet would encounter terrifying depths in the trash, and once he floundered completely. While struggling to get up-right again his hand grazed something furry. It was a dead dog. And now he heard other rustlings – not of people walking, but of rats. He saw a couple of them, and up ahead he could see the eyes of dozens of them peering from window-ledges and from under drifted paper, red points of reflected light.

He seemed to be struggling uphill over the trash, but the reality of it didn't reach him until he blundered into a large object which was shaped like one of those Mongolian *chortens* he remembered seeing in a movie. It was a moment before he realised that it was only a street-lamp. It was odd how such a familiar object sug-gested something so outlandish when seen at this range and angle. It was not lighted, of course, or the fantastic notion would never have come to his mind. The familiar-unfamiliar object, the rust-ling of rats, the faint, steamy warmth coming up from the tons of litter underfoot all conspired to throw him into panic, but he kept floundering straight ahead without looking to either side. There was light up there – a vast, open horizon. Never mind that no map of the city he'd ever seen admitted of such a possibility. What had maps to do with this? What real meaning had any map, geography book, old issue of the *National Geographic* or corny filmed travel-ogue *ever had*? Where was the connection?

Now he saw a man staggering towards him over the dunes of discarded stuff – the leaves and husks of other days (or weeks? Months? Longer? Oh, surely not!). Common drunk, most likely. His arms were outstretched and he had a foolish grin on his face. Oh, hell! He was going to pretend that he knew him . . . an old friend. To make a touch. But the man went right past Beavers, arms still spread, and he wasn't smiling at all. He was weeping like a child. What was he whimpering? To hell with him!

Now he could see other people standing silhouetted against that wonderful light. Were those clouds? Luminous coloured clouds? And why were those people holding their arms up like that and shaking their fists at the sky? Lunatics perhaps, or members of some far-out cult.

Funny thing about those clouds. They were unlike any old

memory of clouds that he was able to summon. They moved, but they seemed undecided about their direction of drift. Did clouds move one way and then the other? And the wind. *Where was the wind?*

There wasn't any. Hadn't been as long as anyone could remember.

Then Mr Beavers ran right into the transparent wall.

'All right now, Mr Beavers. All right! No use pounding on it like that. No use screaming at 'em either. Come home now, Mr Beavers. You know me. Hanrahan from the neighbourhood.'

The big cop held on to Beavers' wrists, but it wasn't easy. Beavers was beyond talking sense to, but if you talked at 'em gently they quieted down most of the time. This was the lousy part of the night's duties – fetching the Wanderers off the Wall. Other policemen wrestled with other hysterical citizens and one by one dragged them down over the drifted trash to a patrol parked in the street below.

Beavers collapsed, sobbing, out of breath, and Hanrahan picked him up bodily. He wasn't very heavy, and Hanrahan was one of the strong ones. The big cop talked angrily to the darkness.

'And such a nice, peaceable little gent, too. Dammit to hell! Why do they have to wander? Why do they get curious? They could go on about their lives for years and never have to know about the faces . . . never know about *Them* and their lousy Wall.'

Mack Reynolds
Subversive

The young man with the brown paper bag said, 'Is Mrs Coty in?'

'I'm afraid she isn't. Is there anything I can do?'

'You're Mr Coty? I came about the soap.' He held up the paper bag.

'Soap?' Mr Coty said blankly. He was the epitome of mid-aged husband complete to pipe, carpet slippers and office-slump posture.

'That's right. I'm sure she told you about it. My name's Dickens. Warren Dickens. I sold her—'

'Look here, you mean to tell me in this day and age you go around from door to door peddling soap? Great guns, boy, you'd do better on unemployment insurance. It's permanent now.'

Warren Dickens registered distress, 'Mr Coty, could I come in and tell you about it? If I can make the first delivery to you instead of Mrs Coty, shucks, it'll save me coming back.'

Coty led him back into the living-room, motioned him to a chair and settled into what was obviously his own favourite, handily placed before the telly. Coty said tolerantly, 'Now, then, what's this about selling soap? What kind of soap? What brand?'

'Oh, it has no name, sir. That's the point.'

The other looked at him.

'That's why we can sell it for three cents a cake, instead of twenty-five.' Dickens opened the paper bag and fished out an ordinary-enough-looking cake of soap and handed it to the older man.

Mr Coty took it, stared down at it, turned it over in his hands. He was still blank. 'Well, what's different about it?'

'There's nothing different about it. It's the same as any other soap.'

'I mean, how come you sell it for three cents a cake, and what's the fact it has no name got to do with it?'

Warren Dickens leaned forward and went into what was obviously a strictly routine pitch. 'Mr Coty, have you ever considered what you're buying when they nick you twenty-five cents on your credit card for a bar of soap in an ultra-market?'

There was an edge of impatience in the older man's voice. 'I buy soap!'

'No, sir. That's your mistake. What you buy is a telly show, in fact several of them, with all their expensive comedians, singers, musicians, dancers, news commentators, network vice-presidents, and all the rest. Then you buy fancy packaging. You'll note, by the way, that our product hasn't even a piece of tissue paper wrapped around it. Fancy packaging designed by some of the most competent commercial artists and motivational research men in the country. Then you buy distribution. From the factory all the way to the retail ultra-market where your wife shops. And every time that bar of soap goes from one wholesaler or distributor to another the price roughly doubles. You also buy a brain trust whose full-time project is to keep you using their soap and not letting their competitors talk you into switching brands. The brain trust, of course, also works on luring away the competitors' customers to their product. Shucks, Mr Coty, practically none of that twenty-five cents you spend to buy a cake of soap goes for soap. So small a percentage that you might as well forget about it.

Mr Coty was obviously taken aback. 'Well, how do I know this nameless soap you're peddling is, well, any good?'

Warren Dickens sighed deeply, and in such wise that it was obvious that he had so sighed before. 'Sir, there is no difference between soaps. Oh, they might use a slightly different perfume-colour, but for all practical purposes common hand-soap, common bath-soap, is soap, period. All the stuff the copy-writers dream up about secret ingredients and health for your skin, and cosmetic qualities, and all the rest, is Madison Avenue gobbledygook and applies as well to one brand as another. As a matter of fact, often two different soap companies, supposedly keen competitors, and using widely different advertising, have their products manufactured in the same plant.'

Mr Coty blinked at him. Shifted in his chair. Rubbed his chin as though checking his morning shave. 'Well . . . well, then, where do you get *your* soap?'

'The same place. We buy in fantastically large lots from one of the gigantic automated soap-plants.'

Mr Coty had him now. 'Ah, ha! Then how come you sell it for three cents a cake, instead of twenty-five?'

'I've been telling you. Our soap doesn't even have a name, not to mention an advertising budget. Far from spending fortunes redesigning our packaging every few months in attempts to lure new customers, we don't package the stuff at all. It comes to you, in the simplest possible wrappings, through the mails. A new supply every month. Three cents a cake. No middlemen, no wholesalers, distributors. No nothing except soap at three cents a cake.'

Mr Coty leaned back in his chair. 'I'll be darned.' He thought it over. 'Listen, do you sell anything besides soap?'

'Not right now, sir. But soap flakes are coming up next week and I think we'll be going into bread in a month or two.'

'Bread?'

'Yes, sir, bread. Although we'll have to distribute that by truck, and have to have almost hundred-per-cent coverage in a given section before it's practical. A nickel a loaf.'

'Five cents a loaf! You can't *make* bread for that much.'

'Oh, yes, we can. We can't advertise it, package it, and pay a host of in-betweens, is all. From the bakery to you, period.'

Mr Coty seemed fascinated. He said, 'See here, what's the address of your office?'

Warren Dickens shook his head. 'Sorry, sir. That's all part of it. We have no swanky offices with big, expensive staffs. We operate on the smallest of shoestrings. No brain trust. No complaint department. No public relations. No literature on how to beautify yourself. No nothing, except good soap at three cents a cake, plus postage. Now, if you'll sign this contract, we'll put you on our mailing list. Ten bars of soap a month, Mrs Coty said. I brought this first supply so you could test it and see that the whole thing is bona fide.'

Mr Coty had to test it, but then he had to admit he couldn't tell any difference between the nameless soap and the product to which he was used. Eventually, he signed, made the first payment, shook hands with young Dickens and saw him to the door. He said, in parting, 'I still wonder why you do this, rather than dragging down unemployment insurance like most young men fresh out of school.'

Warren Dickens screwed up his face. This was a question that wasn't routine. 'Well, I make approximately the same, if I stick to it and get enough contracts. And, shucks, they're not hard to get. And, well, I'm working, not just bumming on the rest of the country. I'm doing something, something useful.'

Coty pursed his lips and shrugged. 'It's been a long time since anybody cared about that.' He looked after the young man as he walked down the walk.

Then he turned and headed for the phone, and ten years seemed to drop away from him. He lit the screen with a flick, dialled and said crisply, 'That's him, Jerry. Going down the walk now. Don't let him out your sight.'

Jerry's face was in the screen but he was obviously peering down, from the helio-jet, locating the subject. 'O.K., Tracy, I make him. See you later.' His face faded.

The man who had called himself Mr Coty dialled again, not bothering to light the screen. 'All right,' he said. 'Thank Mrs Coty and let her come home now.'

Frank Tracy worked his way down an aisle of automated phonotypers and other office equipment. The handful of operators, their faces bored, periodically strolled up and down, checking that which seldom needed checking.

He entered the receptionist's office, flicked a hand at LaVerne Sandell, one of the few employees it seemed impossible to automate out of her position, and said. 'The Chief is probably expecting me.'

'That he is. Go right in, Mr Tracy.'

'I'm expecting a call from one of the operatives. Put it through, eh, LaVerne?'

'Righto.'

Even as he walked toward the door to the sanctum sanctorum, he grimaced sourly at her. '*Righto*, yet. Isn't that a bit on the maize side? Doesn't sound very authentic to me.'

'I can see you don't put in your telly time, Mr Tracy. Slang goes in cycles these days. They simply don't dream up a whole new set of expressions every generation anymore because everybody gets tired of them so soon. Instead, older periods of idiom are revived. For instance, scram is coming back in.'

He stopped long enough to look at her, frowning. 'Scram?'

She took him in quizzically, estimating. 'Possibly *dust*, or *get lost*, was the term when you were a boy.'

Tracy chuckled wryly, 'Thanks for the compliment, but I go back to the days of *beat it*.'

In the inner office the Chief looked up at him. 'Sit down, Frank. What's the word? Another exponent of free enterprise, prehistoric style?'

Frank Tracy found a chair and began talking even while fumbling for briar and tobacco pouch. 'No,' he grumbled, 'I don't think so, not this time. I'm afraid there might be something more to it.'

His boss leaned back in the massive old-fashioned chair he affected and patted his belly, as though appreciative of a good meal just finished. 'Oh? Give it all to me.'

Tracy finished lighting his pipe, flicked the match out and put it back in his pocket, noting that he'd have to get a new one one of these days. He cleared his throat and said, 'Reports began coming in of house-to-house canvassers selling soap for three cents a bar.'

'*Three cents a bar?* They can't manufacture it for that. Will the stuff pass the Health Department?'

'Evidently,' Tracy said wryly. 'The salesman claimed it's the same soap as reputable firms peddle.'

'Go on.'

'We had to go to a bit of trouble to get a line on them without raising their suspicion. One of the boys lived in a neighbourhood that was being canvassed for new customers and his wife had signed up. So I took her place when the salesman arrived with her first delivery – they deliver the first batch. I let him think I was Bob Coty and questioned him, but not enough to raise his suspicions.'

'And?'

'An outfit selling soap and planning on branching into bread and heavens knows what else. No advertising. No middlemen. No nothing, as the salesman said, except standard soap at three cents a bar.'

'They can't package it for that!'

'They don't package it at all.'

The Chief raised his chubby right hand and wiped it over his face in a stereotype gesture of resignation. 'Did you get his home office address? Maybe there's some way of buying them out – indirectly, of course.'

'No, sir. It seemed to be somewhat of a secret.'

The other's eyes widened. 'Ridiculous. You can't hide anything like that. There's a hundred ways of tracking them down before the day is out.'

'Of course. I've got Jerome Wiseman following him in a heliojet. No use getting rough, as yet. We'll keep it quiet . . . assuming that meets with your approval.'

'You're in the field, Frank. You make the decisions.'

The phone screen had lighted up and LaVerne's piquant face faded in. 'The call Mr Tracy was expecting from Operative Wiseman.'

'Put him on,' the Chief said, lacing his plump fingers over his stomach.

Jerry's face appeared in the screen. He was obviously parked on the street now. He said, 'Subject has disappeared into this office building, Tracy. For the past fifteen minutes he's kinda looked as though the day's work was through and, since this dump could hardly be anybody's home, he must be reporting to his higher-up.'

'Let's see the building,' Tracy said.

The portable screen was directed in such manner that a disreputable-appearing building, obviously devoted to fourth-rate business, was centred.

'O.K.,' Tracy said. 'I'll be over. You can knock off, Jerry. Oh, except for one thing. Subject's name is Warren Dickens. Just for luck, get a complete dossier on him. I doubt if he's got a criminal or subversive record, but you never know.'

Jerry said, 'Right,' and faded.

Frank Tracy came to his feet and knocked the rest of his pipe out into the gigantic ashtray on his boss's desk. 'Well, I suppose the next step's mine.'

'Check back with me as soon as you know anything more,' the Chief said. He wheezed a sigh as though sorry the interview was over and that he'd have to go back to his desk chores, but shifted his bulk and took up a sheaf of papers.

Just as Tracy got to the door, the Chief said. 'Oh, yes. Easy on the rough stuff, Tracy. I've been hearing some disquieting reports about some of the over-enthusiastic bully-boys on your team. We wouldn't want such material to get in the telly-casts.'

Lard bottom, Tracy growled inwardly as he left. Did the Chief think he liked violence? Did anyone in his right mind like violence?

Frank Tracy looked up at the mid-century-type office building. He was somewhat surprised that the edifice still remained. Where did the owners ever find profitable tenants? What business could be so small these days that it would be based in such quarters? However, here it was.

The lobby was shabby. There was no indication on the list of tenants of the firm he was seeking, nor was there a porter. The elevator was out of repair.

He did it the hard way, going from door to door, entering, hat in hand apologetically, and saying, 'Pardon me. You're the people who sell the soap?' They kept telling him no until he reached the third floor and a door to an office even smaller than usual. It was lettered *Freer Enterprises* and, even as he knocked and entered, the wording rang a bell.

There was only one desk but it was efficiently equipped with the latest in office gadgetry. The room was quite choked with files and even a Mini-IBM tri-unit. The man behind the desk was old-fashioned enough to wear glasses, but otherwise seemed the average aggressive executive type you expected to meet in these United States of the Americas. He was possibly in his mid-thirties and one of those alert, over-eager characters irritating to those who believe in taking matters less than urgently.

He looked up and said snappily. 'What can I do for you?'

Tracy dropped into an easy-going characterization. 'You're the people who sell the soap?'

'That is correct. What can I do for you?'

Tracy said easily, 'Why, I'd like to ask you a few questions about the enterprise.'

'To what end, sir? You'd be surprised how busy a man I am.'

Tracy said, 'Suppose I'm from the Greater New York *News-Times* looking for a story?'

The other tapped a finger on his desk impatiently. 'Pardon me, but in that case I would be inclined to think you a liar. The *News-Times* knows upon which side its bread is spread. Its advertisers include all the soap companies. It does not dispense free advertising through its news columns.'

Tracy chuckled wryly. 'All right. Let's start again.' He brought forth his wallet, flicked through various identification cards until he found the one he wanted and presented it. 'Frank Tracy is the name,' he said. 'Department of Internal Revenue. There seems to be some question as to your corporation taxes.'

'Oh,' the other said, obviously taken aback. 'Please have a chair.' He read the authentic-looking, but spurious credentials. Tracy took the proffered chair and then sat and looked at the other as though it was his turn.

'My name is Flowers,' the Freer Enterprises man told him, nervously. 'Frederic Flowers. Frankly, this is my first month at the job and I'm not too well acquainted with all the ramifications of the business.' He moistened his lips. 'I hope there is nothing illegal—' He let the sentence fade away.

Tracy reclaimed his false identity-papers and put them back

into his wallet before saying easily, 'I really couldn't say, as yet. Let's have a bit of question and answers and I'll go further into the matter.'

Flowers regained his confidence. 'No reason why not,' he said quickly. 'So far as I know, all is above board.'

Frank Tracy let his eyes go about the room. 'Why are you established, almost secretly, you might say, in this business back-woods of the city?'

'No secret about it,' Flowers demurred. 'Merely the cheapest rent we could find. We cut costs to the bone, and then shave the bone.'

'Um-m-m. I've spoken to one of your salesmen, a Warren Dickens, and I suppose he gave me the standard sales-talk. I wonder if you could elaborate on your company's policies, its goals, that sort of thing.'

'Goals?'

'You obviously expect to make money, somehow or other, though I don't see that peddling soap at three cents a bar has much of a future. There must be some further angle.'

Flowers said, 'Admittedly, soap is just a beginning. Among other things, it gives us a mailing-list of satisfied customers. Consumers who can then be approached for future purchases.'

Frank Tracy relaxed in his chair, reached for pipe and tobacco and let the other go on. But his eyes had narrowed, coldly.

Flowers wrapped himself up in his subject. 'Mr Tracy, you probably have no idea of the extent to which the citizens of Greater America are being victimized. Let me use but one example.' He came quickly to his feet, crossed to a small toilet which opened off the office and returned with a power-pack electric shaver which he handed to Tracy.

Tracy looked at it, put it back on the desk and nodded. 'It's the brand I have,' he said agreeably.

'Yes, and millions of others. What did you pay for it?'

Frank Tracy allowed himself a slight smirk. 'As a matter of fact, I got mine through a discount outfit, only twenty-five dollars.'

'*Only* twenty-five dollars, eh, when the retail price is supposedly thirty-five?' Flowers was triumphant. 'A great bargain, eh? Well, let me give you a rundown, Mr Tracy.'

He took a quick breath. 'True, they're advertised to retail at thirty-five dollars. And stores that sell them at that rate make a profit of fifty per cent. The regional supply-house, before them, knocks down from forty to sixty per cent, on the wholesale price. Then the trade-name distributor makes at least fifty per cent on the sales to the regional supply-houses.'

'Trade-name distributor?' Tracy said, as though ignorant of what the other was talking about. 'You mean the manufacturer?'

'No, sir. That razor you just looked at bears a trade name of a company that owns no factory of its own. It buys the razors from a large electrical appliances manufacturing complex which turns out several other name-brand electric razors as well. The trade-name company does nothing except market the product. Its budget, by the way, calls for an expenditure of six dollars on every razor for national advertising.'

'Well, what are you getting at?' Tracy said impatiently.

Frederic Flowers had reached his punch-line. 'All right, we've traced the razor all the way back to the manufacturing complex which made it. Mr Tracy, that razor you bought at a discount bargain for twenty-five dollars cost thirty-eight cents to produce.'

Tracy pretended to be dumbfounded. 'I don't believe it.'

'It can be proven.'

Frank Tracy thought about it for a while. 'Well, even if true, so what?'

'It's a crime, that's so-what,' Flowers blurted indignantly. 'And that's where Freer Enterprises comes in. Very shortly, we're going to enter the market with an electric razor retailing for exactly one dollar. No name brand, no advertising, no nothing except a razor just as good as though selling for from twenty-five to fifty dollars.'

Tracy scoffed his disbelief. 'That's where you're wrong. No electric-razor manufacturer would sell to you. They'd be cutting their own throats.'

The Freer Enterprises official shook his head, in scorn. 'That's where *you're* wrong. The same electric-appliance manufacturer who produced that razor there will make a similar one, slightly different in appearance, for the same price for us. They don't care what happens to their product once they make their profit from it. Business is business. We'll be at least as good a customer as any of the others have ever been. Eventually, better, since we'll be getting electric razors into the hands of people who never felt they could afford one before.'

He shook a finger at Tracy. 'Manufacturers have been doing this for a long time. I imagine it was the old mail-order houses that started it. They'd get in touch with a manufacturer of, say, typewriters, or outboard motors, or whatever, and order tens of thousands of these, not an iota different from the manufacturer's standard product except for the nameplate. They'd then sell these for as little as half the ordinary retail price.'

Tracy seemed to think it over for a long moment. Eventually he said, 'Even then you're not going to break any records making money. Your distribution costs might be pared to the bone, but you still have some. There'll be darn little profit left on each razor you sell.'

Flowers was triumphant again. 'We're not going to stop at razors, once under way. How about automobiles? Have you any idea of the disparity between the cost of production of a car and what they retail for?'

'Well, no.'

'Here's an example. As far back as about 1930 a barge company transporting some brand-new cars across Lake Erie from Detroit had an accident and lost a couple of hundred. The auto manufacturers sued, trying to get the retail price of each car. Instead, the court awarded them the cost of manufacture. You know what it came to, labour, materials, depreciation on machinery – everything? Seventy-five dollars per car. And that was around 1930. Since then, automation has swept the industry and manufacturing costs per unit have dropped drastically.'

The Freer Enterprises executive was now in full voice. 'But even that's not the ultimate. After all, cars were selling for as cheaply as $425 then. Let's take some items such as aspirin. You can, of course, buy small neatly packaged tins of twelve for twenty-five cents but supposedly more intelligent buyers will buy bottles for forty or fifty cents. If the druggist puts out a special for fifteen cents a bottle it will largely be refused since the advertising-conditioned customer doesn't want an inferior product. Actually, of course, aspirin is aspirin and you can buy it, in one-hundred-pound lots in polyethylene-film bags, at about fourteen cents a pound, or in carload lots under the chemical name of acetylsalicilic acid, for eleven cents a pound. And any big chemical corporation will sell you USP grade Milk of Magnesia at about six dollars a ton. Its chemical name, of course, is magnesium hydroxide, or $Mg(OH)$, and you'd have one thousand quarts in that ton. Buying it beautifully packaged and fully advertised, you'd pay up to a dollar twenty-five a pint in the druggist section of a modern ultra-market.'

Tracy had heard enough. He said crisply, 'All right, Mr Flowers, of Freer Enterprises, now let me ask you something: Do you consider this country prosperous?'

Flowers blinked. Of a sudden, the man across from him seemed to have changed character, added considerable dynamic to his make-up. He flustered, 'Yes. I suppose so. But it could be considerably more prosperous if—'

Tracy was sneering. 'If consumer prices were brought down drastically, eh? Mr Flowers, you're incredibly naïve when it comes to modern economics. Do you realize that one of the most significant developments, economically speaking, took place in the 1950s; something perhaps more significant than the development of atomic power?'

Flowers blinked again, mesmerized by the other's new domineering personality. 'I . . . I don't know what you're talking about.'

'The majority of employees in the United States turned from blue collar to white.'

Flowers looked pained. 'I don't—'

'No, of course you don't or you wouldn't be participating in a subversive attack upon our economy, which, if successful, would lead to the collapse of Western prosperity and eventually to the success of the Soviet Complex.'

Mr Flowers gobbled a bit, then gulped.

'I'll spell it out for you,' Tracy pursued. 'In the early days of capitalism back when Marx and Engels were writing such works as *Capital*, the overwhelming majority of the working class were employed directly in production. For a long time it was quite accurate when the political cartoonists depicted a working man as wearing overalls and carrying a hammer or wrench. In short, employees who got their hands dirty outnumbered those who didn't.

'But, with the coming of increased mechanization and eventually automation and the second industrial revolution, more and more employees went into sales, the so-called service industries, advertising and entertainment which has become largely a branch of advertising, distribution and, above all, government which in this bureaucratic age is largely a matter of regulation of business and property relationships. As automation continued, fewer and fewer of our people were needed to produce all the commodities that the country could assimilate under our present socio-economic system. And I need only point out that the average American *still* enjoys more material things than any other nation, though admittedly the European countries, and I don't exclude the Soviet Complex, are coming up fast.'

Flowers said indignantly, 'But what's this charge that I'm participating in a subversive—'

'Mr Flowers,' Tracy overrode him, 'let's not descend to pure maize in our denials of the obvious. If this outfit of yours, Freer Enterprises, was successful in its fondest dreams, what would happen?'

'Why, the consumers would be able to buy commodities at a fraction of the present cost!'

Tracy half came to his feet and pounded the table with fierce emphasis. '*What would they buy them with? They'd all be out of jobs!*'

Frederic Flowers bug-eyed him.

Tracy sat down again and seemingly regained control of himself. His voice was softer now. 'Our social system may have its strains and tensions, Mr Flowers, but it works and we don't want anybody throwing wrenches in its admittedly delicate machinery.

Advertising is currently one of the biggest industries of the country. The entertainment industry, admittedly now based on advertising, is gigantic. Our magazines and newspapers, employing hundreds of thousands of employees from editors right on down to news-stand operators, are able to exist only through advertising revenue. Above all, millions of our population are employed in the service industries, and in distribution, in the stock market, in the com-modity markets, in all the other branches of distribution which you Freer Enterprises people want to pull down. A third of our working force is now unemployed but, given your way, it would be at least two-thirds.'

Flowers, suddenly suspicious, said, 'What has all this to do with the Department of Internal Revenue, Mr Tracy?'

Tracy came to his feet and smiled ruefully, albeit a bit grimly. 'Nothing,' he admitted. 'I have nothing at all to do with that de-partment. Here is my real card, Mr Flowers.'

The Freer Enterprises man must have felt a twinge of premoni-tion even as he took it up, but the effect was still enough to startle him. 'Bureau of Economic Subversion!' he said.

'Now, then,' Tracy snapped. 'I want the names of your higher-ups, and the address of your central office, Flowers. Frankly, you're in the soup. As you possibly know, our hush-hush depart-ment has unlimited emergency powers, being answerable only to the President.'

'I . . . I've never even heard of it,' Flowers stuttered. 'But—'

Tracy held up a contemptuous hand. 'Many people haven't,' he said curtly.

Frank Tracy hurried through the outer office into LaVerne San-dell's domain, and bit out to her, 'Tell the Chief I'm here. Crisis. And immediately get my team together, all eight of them. Heavy equipment. Have a jet readied. Chicago. The team will rendezvous at the airport.'

LaVerne was just as crisp. 'Yes, sir.' She began doing things with buttons and switches.

Tracy hurried into the Chief's office and didn't bother with the usual amenities. He snapped, 'Worse than I thought, sir. This outfit is possibly openly subversive. Deliberately undermining the economy.'

His superior put down the report he was perusing and shifted his bulk backward. 'You're sure? We seldom run into such extremes.'

'I know, I know, but this could be it. Possibly a deliberate programme. I've taken the initiative to have Miss Sandell summon my team.'

'Now, see here, Frank—' The bureau head looked at him anxiously.

Tracy said, impatience there, 'Chief, you're going to have to let your field-men use their discretion. I tell you, this thing is a potential snowball. I'll play it cool. Arrange things so that there'll be no scandal for the telly-reporters. But we've got to chill this one quickly, or it'll be on a coast-to-coast basis before the year is out. They're even talking about going into automobiles.'

The Chief winced, then said unhappily, 'All right, Tracy. However, mind what I said. Curb those roughnecks of yours.'

It proved considerably easier than Frank Tracy had hoped for. Adam Moncure's national headquarters turned out to be in a sparsely settled area not far from Woodstock, Illinois. The house, in the passé ranch style, must have once been a millionaire's baby, what with an artificial fishing-lake in the back, kidney-shaped swimming-pool, extensive gardens and an imposing approach up a corridor of trees.

'Right up to the front door,' Tracy growled to the operative driving the first hover-car of their two-vehicle expedition. 'The quicker we move, the better.' He turned his head to the men in the rear seat. 'We five will go in together. I don't expect trouble; they'll have had no advance warning. I made sure of that. Jerry has equipment in his car to blanket any radio sending. 'We'll take care of phones in the house. No rough stuff, we want to talk to these people.'

One of the men growled, 'Suppose they start shooting?'

Tracy snorted. 'Then shoot back, of course. But just don't you start it. I shouldn't have to tell you these things.'

'Got it,' one of the others said. He shifted his shoulders to loosen the .38 Recoilless in its holster.

At the ornate doorway, the cars, which had been moving fast, a foot or so off the ground, came to a quick halt, settled, and the men disgorged, guns in hand.

Tracy called to the occupants of the other vehicle, 'On the double. Surround the house. Don't let anybody leave. Come on, boys.'

They scurried down the flagstone walk, banged on the door. It was opened by a houseman who stared at them uncomprehendingly.

'The occupants of this establishment are under arrest,' Tracy snapped. He flashed a gold badge. 'Take me to Adam Moncure.' He turned to his men and gestured with his head. 'Take over, boys. Jerry, you come with me.'

The houseman was terrified, but not to the point of being unable to lead them to a gigantic former living-room, now converted to offices.

There was an older man, and four assistants. All in shirt-sleeves in concession to the mid-western summer, none armed from all Tracy could see. They looked up in surprise, rather than dismay. The older man snapped, 'What is the meaning of this intrusion?'

Jerry chuckled sourly.

Frank Tracy said, 'You're all under arrest. Jerry, herd these clerks, or whatever they are, into some other room. Get any other occupants of the house together, too. And watch them carefully, confound it. Don't under-estimate these people. And make a search for secret rooms, cellars, that sort of thing.'

'Right,' Jerry growled.

The older of the five Freer Enterprises men was on his feet now. He was a thin, angry-faced type, grey of hair and somewhere in his sixties. 'I want to know the meaning of this!' he roared.

'Adam Moncure?' Tracy said crisply.

'That is correct. And to what do I owe this cavalier intrusion into my home and place of business?'

Jerry, at pistol point, was herding the four assistants from the room, taking the houseman along with them.

Tracy looked at Moncure, speculatively, then dipped into his pockets for pipe and tobacco. He gestured to a chair with his head. 'Sit down, Mr Moncure. The jig is up.'

'The *jig*?' the other blurted in a fine rage. 'I insist—'

'O.K., O.K., you'll get your explanation.' Tracy sat down on a couch himself and sized up the older man, even as he lit his pipe.

Moncure, still breathing heavily in his indignation, took control of himself well enough to be seated. 'Well, sir?' he bit out.

Tracy said curtly, 'Frank Tracy, Bureau of Economic Subversion.'

'Bureau of Economic Subversion!' Moncure said indignantly. 'What in the name of all that's holy is the Bureau of Economic Subversion?'

Tracy pointed at him with the pipe stem. 'I'll ask a few questions first, please. How many branches of your nefarious outfit are presently under operation?'

The other glared at him, but Tracy merely returned the pipe to his mouth and glowered back

Finally Moncure snapped, 'There is no purpose in hiding any of our affairs. We have opened preliminary offices only in Chicago and New York. Freer Enterprises is but in its infancy.'

'Praise Allah for that,' Tracy muttered sarcastically.

'And thus far we have dealt only in soap. However, as our organization gets under way we plan to branch out into a score, and ultimately hundreds of products.'

Tracy said, 'You can forget about that, Moncure. Freer Enterprises comes to a halt as of today. Do you realize that your business tactics would lead to a complete collapse of gainful employment and eventually to a depression such as this nation has never seen before?'

'Exactly!' Moncure snapped in return.

It was Tracy's turn to react. His eyes widened, then narrowed. 'Do you mean that you are deliberately attempting to undermine the economy of the United States of the Americas? Remember, Mr Moncure, you are under arrest and anything you say may be held against you.'

'Undermine it!' Moncure said heatedly. 'Bring it crashing to the ground is the better term. There has never been such an abortion developed in the history of political economy.'

He came to his feet again and began storming up and down the room. 'A full three-quarters of our employed working at nothing jobs, gobbledygook jobs, non-producing jobs, make-work jobs, red-tape bureacracy jobs. At a time when the nation is supposedly in a breakneck economic competition with the Soviet Complex, we put our best brains into advertising, entertainment and sales, while they put theirs into science and industry.'

He stopped long enough to shake an indignant finger at the surprised Tracy. 'But that isn't the worst of it. Have you ever heard of planned obsolescence?'

Tracy acted as though on the defensive. 'Well . . . sure . . .'

'In the Soviet Complex and, for that matter, in Common Europe and other economic competitors of ours, they simply don't believe in planned obsolescence and all its related nonsense. Razor blades, everywhere except in this country, don't go dull after two or three shaves. Cars don't fall apart after two or three years, or even become so out of style that the owner feels that he's losing status by being seen in it; the owners expect to keep them half a life time. Automobile batteries don't go to pieces after eighteen months; they last for a decade. And on and on!'

The old boy was really unwinding now. 'Nor is even that the nadir of this socio-economic hodgepodge we've allowed to develop, this economy of production for sale, rather than production for use.' He stabbed with his finger. 'I think one of the best examples of what was to come was to be witnessed way back at the end of the Second War. The idea of the ballbearing pen was in the air. The first one to hurry into production gave his pen a tremendous build-up. It had ink enough to last three years, it would make many carbon copies, you could use it under water. And so on and so forth. It cost fifteen dollars, and there was only one difficulty with it. It wouldn't write. Not that that made any difference because it sold like hotcakes what with all the promotion. He wasn't interested in whether or not it would write, but only whether or not it would sell.' Moncure threw up his hands dramatically. 'I ask you, can such an economic system be taken seriously?'

'What's your point?' Tracy growled dangerously. He'd never met one this far out before.

'Isn't it obvious? Continue this ridiculous economy and we'll lose the battle for men's minds. You can't have an economic system that allows such nonsense as large-scale unemployment of trained employees, planned obsolescence, union featherbedding, and an overwhelming majority of those who are employed wasting their labour on unproductive employment.'

Tracy said, 'Then, if I understand you correctly, Freer Enterprises was deliberately organized for the purpose of undermining the economy so that it will collapse and have to be reorganized on a different basis.'

'That is *exactly* correct,' Moncure said defiantly. 'I am devoting my whole fortune to this cause. And there is nothing in American law that prevents me from following through with my plans.'

'You're right there,' Tracy said wryly. 'There's nothing in American law that prevents you. However, you see, I have no connection whatsoever with the American government.' He slipped the gun from its holster.

Frank Tracy made his way wearily into LaVerne's domain. She looked up from the desk. 'Everything go all right, Mr Tracy?'

'I suppose so. Tell Comrade Zotov that I'm back from Chicago, please.'

She clicked switches, said something into an inter-office communicator, then looked up again. 'He'll see you immediately, Mr Tracy.'

Pavel Zotov looked up from his endless paperwork and wheezed the sigh of a fat man. He correctly interpreted the expression of his field-operative. 'Pour us a couple of drinks, Frank, or would you rather have it *Frol*, today?'

His best field-man grunted as he walked over to the bar. 'Vodka, eh? *Chort vesmiot* how tired one can become of this everlasting bourbon.' He reached into the refrigerator compartment and brought forth a bottle of iced Stolichnaya. He poured two three-ounce charges and brought them back to his bureau chief's desk.

They toasted silently, knocked back the colourless spirit. Pavel Zotov said, 'Well, Frol?'

The man usually called Frank Tracy said, 'The worst case yet. This one had quite a clear picture of the true situation. He saw the necessity – given *their* viewpoint, of course – of getting out of the fantastic rut their economy has fallen into.' He ran his hand over his mouth in a gesture of weariness. 'Chief, do you have any idea of how long it would take us to catch up to them, if we ever did, if they really turned this economy on full blast, as an alternative to their present foul-up?'

'That's why we're here,' the Chief said heavily. 'What did you do?'

The man sometimes called Tracy told him.

Zotov winced. 'I thought I ordered you—'

'You did,' Tracy told him curtly, 'but what alternative was there? The fire will completely destroy the records. I have the names and addresses of all the others connected with Freer Enterprises. We'll have to arrange car accidents, that sort of thing.'

The fat man's lips worked. 'We can't get by with this indefinitely, Frol. With such blatant tactics, sooner or later their CIA or FBI is going to get wind of us.'

Tracy came to his feet angrily. 'What alternative have we? We've been sent over here to do a job. We're doing it. If we're caught, who knows better than we that we're expendable? If you don't mind, I'm going on home.'

As he left the office, through the secret door that led through the innocuous-looking garage, the man called Frank Tracy was inwardly thinking, 'Frolov might be my superior, and a top man in the party, but he's too soft at this job. Perhaps I'd better send a report back to Moscow on him.'

Thomas M. Disch
Descending

Catsup, mustard, pickle relish, mayonnaise, two kinds of salad dressing, bacon grease, and a lemon. Oh, yes, two trays of ice cubes. In the cupboard it wasn't much better: jars and boxes of spice, flour, sugar, salt – and a box of raisins!

An empty box of raisins.

Not even any coffee. Not even tea, which he hated. Nothing in the mailbox but a bill from Underwood's: *Unless we receive the arrears on your account . . .*

$4.75 in change jingled in his coat pocket – the plunder of the Chianti bottle he had promised himself never to break open. He was spared the unpleasantness of having to sell his books. They had all been sold. The letter to Graham had gone out a week ago. If his brother intended to send something this time, it would have come by now.

– I should be desperate, he thought. Perhaps I am.

He might have looked in the *Times*. But, no, that was too depressing – applying for jobs at $50 a week and being turned down. Not that he blamed them; he wouldn't have hired himself, himself. He had been a grasshopper for years. The ants were on to his tricks.

He shaved without soap and brushed his shoes to a high polish. He whitened the sepulchre of his unwashed torso with a fresh, starched shirt and chose his sombrest tie from the rack. He began to feel excited and expressed it, characteristically, by appearing statuesquely, icily calm.

Descending the stairway to the first floor, he encountered Mrs Beale, who was pretending to sweep the well-swept floor of the entrance.

'Good afternoon – or I s'pose it's good morning for you, eh?'

'Good afternoon, Mrs Beale.'

'Your letter come?'

'Not yet.'

'The first of the month isn't far off.'

'Yes, indeed, Mrs Beale.'

At the subway station he considered a moment before answering the attendant: One token or two? Two, he decided. After all, he had no choice but to return to his apartment. The first of the month was still a long way off.

– If Jean Valjean had had a charge account, he would have never gone to prison.

Having thus cheered himself, he settled down to enjoy the ads in the subway car. *Smoke. Try. Eat. Give. See. Drink. Use. Buy.* He thought of Alice with her mushrooms: Eat me.

At 34th Street he got off and entered Underwood's Department Store directly from the train platform. On the main floor he stopped at the cigar stand and bought a carton of cigarettes.

'Cash or charge?'

'Charge.' He handed the clerk the laminated plastic card. The charge was rung up.

Fancy Groceries was on 5. He made his selection judiciously. A jar of instant and a two-pound can of drip-ground coffee, a large tin of corned beef, packaged soups and boxes of pancake mix and condensed milk. Jam, peanut butter, and honey. Six cans of tuna fish. Then he indulged himself in perishables: English cookies, an Edam cheese, a small frozen pheasant – even fruitcake. He never ate so well as when he was broke. He couldn't afford to.

'$14.87.'

This time after ringing up his charge, the clerk checked the number on his card against her list of closed or doubtful accounts. She smiled apologetically and handed the card back.

'Sorry, but we have to check.'

'I understand.'

The bag of groceries weighed a good twenty pounds. Carrying

it with the exquisite casualness of a burglar passing before a policeman with his loot, he took the escalator to the bookshop on 8.
His choice of books was determined by the same principle as his
choice of groceries. First, the staples: two Victorian novels he
had never read, *Vanity Fair* and *Middlemarch*; the Sayers' trans-
lation of Dante, and a two-volume anthology of German plays
none of which he had read and few he had even heard of. Then
the perishables: a sensational novel that had reached the best-
seller list via the Supreme Court, and two mysteries.

He had begun to feel giddy with self-indulgence. He reached
into his jacket pocket for a coin.

– Heads a new suit; tails the Sky Room.

Tails.

The Sky Room on 15 was empty of all but a few women chat-
ting over coffee and cakes. He was able to get a seat by a window.
He ordered from the *à la carte* side of the menu and finished his
meal with espresso and baklava. He handed the waitress his credit
card and tipped her fifty cents.

Dawdling over his second cup of coffee, he began *Vanity Fair*.
Rather to his surprise, he found himself enjoying it. The waitress
returned with his card and a receipt for the meal.

Since the Sky Room was on the top floor of Underwood's, there
was only one escalator to take now – Descending. Riding down,
he continued to read *Vanity Fair*. He could read anywhere – in
restaurants, on subways, even walking down the street. At each
landing he made his way from the foot of one escalator to the
head of the next without lifting his eyes from the book. When he
came to the Bargain Basement, he would be only a few steps from
the subway turnstile.

He was halfway through chapter VI (on page 55, to be exact)
when he began to feel something amiss.

– How long does this damn thing take to reach the basement?

He stopped at the next landing, but there was no sign to indicate
on what floor he was nor any door by which he might re-enter
the store. Deducing from this that he was between floors, he took
the escalator down one more flight only to find the same perplex-
ing absence of landmarks.

There was, however, a water fountain, and he stooped to take a drink.

– I must have gone to a sub-basement. But this was not too likely after all. Escalators were seldom provided for janitors and stockboys.

He waited on the landing watching the steps of the excalator slowly descend toward him and, at the end of their journey, telescope in upon themselves and disappear. He waited a long while, and no one else came down the moving steps.

– Perhaps the store has closed.

Having no wristwatch and having rather lost track of the time, he had no way of knowing. At last, he reasoned that he had become so engrossed in the Thackeray novel that he had simply stopped on one of the upper landings – say, on 8 – to finish a chapter and had read on to page 55 without realizing that he was making no progress on the escalators.

When he read, he could forget everything else.

He must, therefore, still be somewhere above the main floor. The absence of exits, though disconcerting, could be explained by some quirk in the floor plan. The absence of signs was merely a carelessness on the part of the management.

He tucked *Vanity Fair* into his shopping-bag and stepped on to the grilled lip of the down-going escalator – not, it must be admitted, without a certain degree of reluctance. At each landing, he marked his progress by a number spoken aloud. By *eight* he was uneasy; by *fifteen* he was desperate.

It was, of course, possible that he had to descend two flights of stairs for every floor of the department store. With this possibility in mind, he counted off fifteen more landings.

– No.

Dazedly, and as though to deny the reality of this seemingly interminable stairwell, he continued his descent. When he stopped again at the forty-fifth landing, he was trembling. He was afraid.

He rested the shopping-bag on the bare concrete floor of the landing, realizing that his arm had gone quite sore from supporting the twenty pounds and more of groceries and books. He discounted the enticing possibility that 'it was all a dream', for the dream-world is the reality of the dreamer, to which he could not weakly surrender, no more that he could surrender to the realities of life. Besides, he was not dreaming; of that he was quite sure.

He checked his pulse. It was fast – say, eighty a minute. He rode down two more flights, counting his pulse. Eighty almost exactly. Two flights took only one minute.

He could read approximately one page a minute, a little less on an escalator. Suppose he had spent one hour on the escalators while he had read: sixty minutes – one hundred and twenty floors. Plus forty-seven that he had counted. One hundred and sixty seven. The Sky Room was on 15.

$167 - 15 = 152$.

He was in the one-hundred-and-fifty-second sub-basement. That was impossible.

The appropriate response to an impossible situation was to deal with it as though it were commonplace – like Alice in Wonderland. Ergo, he would return to Underwood's the same way he had (apparently) left it. He would walk up one hundred and fifty-two flights of down-going escalators. Taking the steps three at a time and running, it was almost like going up a regular staircase. But after ascending the second escalator in this manner he found himself already out of breath.

There was no hurry. He would not allow himself to be overtaken by panic.

No.

He picked up the bag of groceries and books he had left on that landing, waiting for his breath to return, and darted up a third and fourth flight. While he rested on the landing, he tried to count the steps between floors, but his count differed depending on whether he counted with the current or against it, down or up. The average was roughly eighteen steps, and the steps appeared to be eight or nine inches deep. Each flight was, therefore, about twelve feet.

It was one-third of a mile, as the plumb drops, to Underwood's main floor.

Dashing up the ninth escalator, the bag of groceries broke open at the bottom, where the thawing pheasant had dampened the paper. Groceries and books tumbled on to the steps, some rolling of their own accord to the landing below, others being transported there by the moving stairs and forming a neat little pile. Only the jam jar had been broken.

He stacked the groceries in the corner of the landing, except for the half-thawed pheasant, which he stuffed into his coat pocket, anticipating that his ascent would take him well past his dinner hour.

Physical exertion had dulled his finer feelings – to be precise, his capacity for fear. Like a cross-country runner in his last laps, he thought single-mindedly of the task at hand and made no effort to understand what he had in any case already decided was not to be understood. He mounted one flight, rested, mounted and rested again. Each mount was wearier; each rest longer. He stopped counting the landings after the twenty-eighth, and some time after that – how long he had no idea – his legs gave out and he collapsed to the concrete floor of the landing. His calves were hard aching knots of muscle; his thighs quivered erratically. He tried to do knee-bends and fell backwards.

Despite his recent dinner (assuming that it had been recent), he was hungry, and he devoured the entire pheasant, completely thawed now, without being able to tell if it were raw or had been pre-cooked.

– This is what it's like to be a cannibal, he thought as he fell asleep.

Sleeping, he dreamt he was falling down a bottomless pit. Waking, he discovered nothing had changed, except the dull ache in his legs, which had become a sharp pain.

Overhead, a single strip of fluorescent lighting snaked down the stairwell. The mechanical purr of the escalators seemed to have heightened to the roar of a Niagara, and their rate of descent seemed to have increased proportionately.

Fever, he decided. He stood up stiffly and flexed some of the soreness from his muscles.

Halfway up the third escalator, his legs gave way under him.

He attempted the climb again and succeeded. He collapsed again on the next flight. Lying on the landing where the escalator had deposited him, he realized that his hunger had returned. He also needed to have water – and to let it.

The latter necessity he could easily – and without false modesty – satisfy. Also he remembered the water fountain he had drunk from yesterday, and he found another three floors below.

– It's so much easier going down.

His groceries were down there. To go after them now, he would erase whatever progress he had made in his ascent. Perhaps Underwood's main floor was only a few more flights up. Or a hundred. There was no way to know.

Because he was hungry and because he was tired and because the futility of mounting endless flights of descending escalators was, as he now considered it, a labour of Sisyphus, he returned, descended, gave in.

At first, he allowed the escalator to take him along at its own mild pace, but he soon grew impatient of this. He found that the exercise of running down the steps three at a time was not so exhausting as running *up*. It was refreshing, almost. And, by swimming with the current instead of against it, his progress, if such it can be called, was appreciable. In only minutes he was back at his cache of groceries.

After eating half the fruitcake and a little cheese, he fashioned his coat into a sort of sling for the groceries, knotting the sleeves together and buttoning it closed. With one hand at the collar and the other about the hem, he could carry all his food with him.

He looked up the descending staircase with a scornful smile, for he had decided with the wisdom of failure to abandon *that* venture. If the stairs wished to take him down, then down, giddily, he would go.

Then down he did go, down dizzily, down, down and always, it seemed, faster, spinning about lightly on his heels at each landing so that there was hardly any break in the wild speed of his descent. He whooped and haloo'd and laughed to hear his whoopings echo in the narrow, low-vaulted corridors, following him as though they could not keep up his pace.

Down, ever deeper down.

Twice he slipped at the landings and once he missed his footing in mid-leap on the escalator, hurtled forward, letting go of the sling of groceries and falling, hands stretched out to cushion him, on to the steps, which, imperturbably, continued their descent.

He must have been unconscious then, for he woke up in a pile of groceries with a split cheek and a splitting headache. The telescoping steps of the escalator gently grazed his heels.

He knew then his first moment of terror – a premonition that there was no *end* to his descent, but this feeling gave way quickly to a laughing fit.

'I'm going to hell!' he shouted, though he could not drown with his voice the steady purr of the escalators. 'This is the way to hell. Abandon hope all ye who enter here.'

– If only I were, he reflected.

– If that were the case, it would make sense. Not quite orthodox sense, but some sense, a little.

Sanity, however, was so integral to his character that neither hysteria nor horror could long have their way with him. He gathered up his groceries again, relieved to find that only the jar of instant coffee had been broken this time. After reflection he also discarded the can of drip-ground coffee, for which he could conceive no use – under the present circumstances. And he would allow himself, for the sake of sanity, to conceive of no other circumstances than those.

He began a more deliberate descent. He returned to *Vanity Fair*, reading it as he paced down the down-going steps. He did not let himself consider the extent of the abyss into which he was plunging, and the vicarious excitements of the novel helped him keep his thoughts from his own situation. At page 235, he lunched (that is, he took his second meal of the day) on the remainder of the cheese and fruitcake; at 523 he rested and dined on the English cookies dipped in peanut butter.

– Perhaps I had better ration my food.

If he could regard his absurd dilemma merely as a struggle for survival, another chapter in his own Robinson Crusoe story, he might get to the bottom of this mechanized vortex alive and sane. He thought proudly that many people in his position could not have adjusted, would have gone mad.

Of course, he *was* descending . . .

But he was still sane. He had chosen his course and now he was following it.

There was no night in the stairwell, and scarcely any shadows. He slept when his legs could no longer bear his weight and his eyes were tearful from reading. Sleeping, he dreamt that he was continuing his descent on the escalators. Waking, his hand resting on the rubber railing that moved along at the same rate as the steps, he discovered this to be the case.

Somnambulistically, he had ridden the escalators further down into this mild, interminable hell, leaving behind his bundle of food and even the still-unread Thackeray novel.

Stumbling up the escalators, he began, for the first time, to cry. Without the novel, there was nothing to *think* of but this, this . . .

– How far? How long did I sleep?

His legs, which had only been slightly wearied by his descent, gave out twenty flights up. His spirit gave out soon after. Again he turned around, allowed himself to be swept up by the current – or, more exactly, swept down.

The escalator seemed to be travelling more rapidly, the pitch of the steps to be more pronounced. But he no longer trusted the evidence of his senses.

– I am, perhaps, insane – or sick from hunger. Yet I would have run out of food eventually. This will bring the crisis to a head. Optimism, that's the spirit!

Continuing his descent, he occupied himself with closer analysis of his environment, not undertaken with any hope of bettering his condition but only for lack of other diversions. The walls and ceilings were hard, smooth, and off-white. The escalator steps were a dull nickel colour, the treads being somewhat shinier, the crevices darker. Did that mean that the treads were polished from use? Or were they designed in that fashion? The treads were half an inch wide and spaced apart from each other by the same width. They projected slightly over the edge of each step, resembling some-what the head of a barber's shears. Whenever he stopped at a land-ing, his attention would become fixed on the illusory 'disappear-ance' of the steps, as they sank flush to the floor and slid, tread in groove, into the grilled baseplate.

Less and less would he run, or even walk, down the stairs, con-tent merely to ride his chosen step from top to bottom of each flight and, at the landing, step (left foot, right, and left again) on to the escalator that would transport him to the floor below. The stairwell now had tunnelled, by his calculations, miles beneath the department store – so many miles that he began to congratu-late himself upon his unsought adventure, wondering if he had established some sort of record. Just so, a criminal will stand in awe of his own baseness and be most proud of his vilest crime, which he believes unparalleled.

In the days that followed, when his only nourishment was the water from the fountains provided at every tenth landing, he thought frequently of food, preparing imaginary meals from the store of groceries he had left behind, savouring the ideal sweetness of the honey, the richness of the soup which he would prepare by soaking the powder in the emptied cookie-tin, licking the film of gelatine lining the opened can of corned beef. When he thought of the six cans of tuna fish, his anxiety became intolerable, for he had (would have had) no way to open them. Merely to stamp on them would not be enough. What, then? He turned the question over and over in his head, like a squirrel spinning the wheel in its cage, to no avail.

Then a curious thing happened. He quickened again the speed of his descent, faster now than when first he had done this, eagerly, headlong, absolutely heedless. The several landings seemed to flash by like a montage of Flight, each scarcely perceived before the next was before him. A demonic, pointless race – and why? He was running, so he thought, toward his store of groceries, either believing that they had been left *below* or thinking that he was running *up*. Clearly, he was delirious.

It did not last. His weakened body could not maintain the fran-tic pace, and he woke from his delirium confused and utterly spent.

Now began another, more rational delirium, a madness fired by logic. Lying on the landing, rubbing a torn muscle in his ankle, he speculated on the nature, origin and purpose of the escalators. Reasoned thought was of no more use to him, however, than un-reasoning action. Ingenuity was helpless to solve a riddle that had no answer, which was its own reason, self-contained and whole. He – not the escalators – needed an answer.

Perhaps his most interesting theory was the notion that these es-calators were a kind of exercise wheel, like those found in a squirrel cage, from which, because it was a closed system, there could be no escape. This theory required some minor alterations in his con-ception of the physical universe, which had always appeared highly Euclidean to him before, a universe in which his descent seemingly along a plumb-line was, in fact, describing a loop. This theory cheered him, for he might hope, coming full circle, to return to his store of groceries again, if not to Underwood's. Perhaps in his abstracted state he had passed one or the other already several times without observing.

There was another, and related, theory concerning the meas-ures taken by Underwood's Credit Department against delinquent accounts. This was mere paranoia.

– Theories! I don't need theories. I must get on with it.

So, favouring his good leg, he continued his descent, although his speculations did not immediately cease. They became, if any-thing, more metaphysical. They became vague. Eventually, he could regard the escalators as being entirely matter of fact, re-quiring no more explanation than, by their sheer existence, they offered him.

He discovered that he was losing weight. Being so long without food (by the evidence of his beard, he estimated that more than a week had gone by), this was only to be expected. Yet, there was another possibility that he could not exclude: that he was ap-proaching the centre of the earth where, as he understood, all things were weightless.

– Now *that*, he thought, is something worth striving for.

He had discovered a goal. On the other hand, he was dying, a process he did not give all the attention it deserved. Unwilling to admit this eventuality, and yet not so foolish as to admit any other, he side-stepped the issue by pretending to hope.

– Maybe someone will rescue me, he hoped.

But his hope was as mechanical as the escalators he rode – and tended, in much the same way, to sink.

Waking and sleeping were no longer distinct states of which he could say: 'Now I am sleeping,' or 'Now I am awake.' Sometimes he would discover himself descending and be unable to tell whether he had been woken from sleep or roused from inattention.

He hallucinated.

A woman, loaded with packages from Underwood's and wearing a trim, pillbox-style hat, came down the escalator toward him, turned around on the landing, high heels clicking smartly, and rode away without even nodding to him.

More and more, when he awoke or was roused from his stupor, he found himself, instead of hurrying to his goal, lying on a landing, weak, dazed, and beyond hunger. Then, he would crawl to the down-going escalator and pull himself on to one of the steps, which he would ride to the bottom, sprawled head foremost, hands and shoulders braced against the treads to keep from skittering bumpily down.

– At the bottom, he thought, at the bottom . . . I will . . . when I get there . . .

From the bottom, which he conceived of as the centre of the earth, there would be literally nowhere to go but up. Probably by another chain of escalators, ascending escalators, but preferably by an elevator. It was important to believe in a bottom.

Thought was becoming as difficult, as demanding and painful, as once his struggle to ascend had been. His perceptions were fuzzy. He did not know what was real and what imaginary. He thought he was eating and discovered he was gnawing at his hands.

He thought he had come to the bottom. It was a large, high-ceilinged room. Signs pointed to another escalator: *Ascending*. But there was a chain across it and a small typed announcement.

'Out of order. Please bear with us while the escalators are being repaired. Thank-you. The Management.'

He laughed weakly.

He devised a way to open the tuna-fish cans. He would slip the can sideways beneath the projecting treads of the escalator, just at the point where the steps were sinking flush to the floor. Either the escalator would split the can open or the can would jam the escalator. Perhaps if one escalator were jammed the whole chain of them would stop. He should have thought of that before, but he was, nevertheless, quite pleased to have thought of it at all.

– I might have escaped.

His body seemed to weigh so little now. He must have come hundreds of miles. Thousands.

Again, he descended.

Then he was lying at the foot of the escalator. His head rested on the cold metal of the baseplate and he was looking at his hand, the fingers of which were pressed into the creviced grille. One after another, in perfect order, the steps of the escalator slipped into these crevices, tread in groove, rasping at his fingertips, occasionally tearing away a sliver of his flesh.

That was the last thing he remembered.

Brian W. Aldiss
The village swindler

The great diesel train hauled out of Naipur Road, heading grandly
south. Jane Pentecouth caught a last glimpse of it over bobbing
heads as she followed the stretcher into the station waiting-room.

She pushed her way through the excited crowd, managing to get
to her father's side and rejoin the formidable Dr Chandhari, who
had taken charge of the operation.

'My car will come in only a few moments, Miss Pentecouth,' he
said, waving away the people who were leaning over the stretcher
and curiously touching the sick man. 'It will whisk us to my home
immediately, not a mile distant. It was extremely fortunate that I
happened to be travelling on the very same express with you.'

'But my father would have been—'

'Do not thank me, dear lady, do not thank me! The pleasure is
mine, and your father is saved. I shall do my level best for him.'

She had not been about to thank this beaming and terrifying
Hindu. She trembled on the verge of hysterical protest. It was
many years since she had felt so helpless. Her father's frightening
attack on the train had been bad enough. All those terrible people
had flocked round, all offering advice. Then Dr Chandhari had
appeared, taken command, and made the conductor stop the train
at Naipur Road, this small station apparently situated in the
middle of nowhere, claiming that his home was near by. Irresis-
tibly, Jane had been carried along on the steamy tide of solicitude
and eloquence.

But she did believe that her father's life had been saved by Dr
Chandhari. Robert Pentecouth was breathing almost normally.
She hardly recognized him as she took his hand; he was in a coma.
But at least he was still alive, and, in the express, as he bellowed

and fought with the coronary attack, she had imagined him about to die.

The crowd surged into the waiting-room, all fighting to lend a hand with the stretcher. It was oppressively hot in the small room; the fan on the ceiling merely caused the heat to circulate. As more and more men surged into the room, Jane stood up and said loudly, 'Will you all please get out, except for Dr Chandhari and his secretary!'

The doctor was very pleased by this, seeing that it implied her acceptance of him. He set his secretary to clearing the room, or at least arguing with the crowd that still flocked in. Bending a yet more perfect smile upon her, he said, 'My young intelligent daughter Amma is fortunately at home at this present moment, dear Miss Pentecouth, so you will have some pleasant company just while your father is recovering his health with us.'

She smiled back, thinking to herself that the very next day, when her father had rested, they would return to Calcutta and proper medical care. On that she was determined.

She was impressed by the Chandhari household despite herself.

It was an ugly modernistic building, all cracked concrete outside – bought off a film star who had committed suicide, Amma cheerfully told her. All rooms, including the garage under the house, were air-conditioned. There was a heart-shaped swimming-pool at the back, although it was empty of water and the sides were cracked. High white walls guarded the property. From her bedroom, Jane looked over the top of the wall at a dusty road sheltered by palm trees and the picturesque squalor of a dozen hovels, where the small children stood naked in doorways and dogs rooted and snarled in piles of rubbish.

'There is such contrast between rich and poor here,' Jane said, surveying the scene. It was the morning after her arrival here.

'What a very European remark!' said Amma. 'The poor people expect that the doctor should live to a proper standard, or he has no reputation.'

Amma was only twenty, perhaps half Jane's age. An attractive girl, with delicate gestures that made Jane feel clumsy. As she herself explained, she was modern and enlightened, and did not intend to marry until she was older.

'What do you do all day, Amma?' Jane asked.

'I am in the government, of course, but now I am taking a holiday. It is rather boring here, but still I don't mind it for a change. Next week, I will go away from here. What do you do all day, Jane?'

'My father is one of the directors of the new EGNP Trust. I just look after him. He is making a brief tour of India, Pakistan and Ceylon, to see how the Trust will be administered. I'm afraid the heat and travel have over-taxed him. His breathing has been bad for several days.'

'He is old. They should have sent a younger man.' Seeing the look on Jane's face, she said, 'Please do not take offence! I am meaning only that it is unfair to send a man of his age to our hot climate. What is this trust you are speaking of?'

'The European Gross National Product Trust. Eleven leading European nations contribute one per cent of their gross national product to assist development in this part of the world.'

'I see. More help for the poor over-populated Indians, is that so?' The two women looked at each other. Finally, Amma said, 'I will take you out with me this afternoon, and you shall see the sort of people to whom this money of yours will be going, if they live sufficiently long enough.'

'I shall be taking my father back to Calcutta this afternoon.'

'You know my father will not allow that, and he is the doctor. Your father will die if you are foolish enough to move him. You must remain and enjoy our simple hospitality and try not to be too bored.'

'Thank you, I am not bored!' Her life was such that she had had ample training in not being bored. More even than not being in command of the situation, she hated failing to understand the attitude of these people. With what grace she could muster, she told the younger woman, 'If Dr Chandhari advises that my father should not be moved, then I will be pleased to accompany you this afternoon.'

* * *

After the light midday meal, Jane was ready for the outing at two o'clock. But Amma and the car were not ready until almost five o'clock, when the sun was moving towards the west.

Robert Pentecouth lay breathing heavily, large in a small white bed. He was recognizable again, looked younger. Jane did not love him; but she would do anything to preserve his life. That was her considered verdict as she looked down on him. He had gulped down a lot of life in his time.

Something in the room smelt unpleasant. Perhaps it was her father. By his bedside squatted an old woman in a dull red-and-maroon sari, wrinkled of face, with a jewel like a dried scab screwed in one nostril. She spoke no English. Jane was uneasy with her, not certain whether she was not Chandhari's wife. You heard funny things about Indian wives.

The ceiling was a maze of cracks. It would be the first thing he would see when he opened his eyes. She touched his head and left the room.

Amma drove. A big new car that took the rutted tracks uneasily. There was little to Naipur Road. The ornate and crumbling houses of the main street turned slightly uphill, became mere shacks. The sunlight buzzed. Over the brow of the slope, the village lost heart entirely and died by a huge banyan tree, beneath which an old man sat on a bicycle.

Beyond, cauterized land, a coastal plain lying rumpled, scarred by man's long and weary occupation.

'Only ten miles,' Amma said. 'It gets more pretty later. It's not so far from the ocean, you know. We are going to see an old nurse of mine who is sick.'

'Is there plague in these parts?'

'Orissa has escaped so far. A few cases down in Cuttack. And of course in Calcutta. Calcutta is the home town of the plague. But we are quite safe – my nurse is dying only of a malnutritional disease.'

Jane said nothing.

They had to drive slowly as the track deteriorated. Everything had slowed. People by the tattered roadside stood silently, silently were encompassed by the car's cloud of dust. A battered truck slowly approached, slowly passed. Under the annealing sun, even time had a wound.

Among low hills, little more than undulations of the ground, they crossed a bridge over a dying river and Amma stopped the car in the shade of some deodars. As the women climbed out, a beggar sitting at the base of a tree called out to them for baksheesh, but Amma ignored him. Gesturing courteously to Jane, she said, 'Let us walk under the trees to where the old nurse's family lives. It perhaps would be better if you did not enter the house with me, but I shall not be long. You can look round the village. There is a pleasant temple to see.'

Only a few yards farther on, nodding and smiling, she turned aside and, ducking her head, entered a small house with mud walls.

It was a long, blank village, ruled by the sun. Jane felt her isolation as soon as Amma disappeared.

A group of small children with big eyes was following Jane. They whispered to each other but did not approach too closely. A peasant farmer, passing with a thin-ribbed cow, called out to the children. Jane walked slowly, fanning the flies from her face.

She knew this was one of the more favoured regions of India. For all that, the poverty – the Stone Age poverty – afflicted her. She was glad her father was not with her, in case he felt as she did, that this land could soak up EGNP money as easily, as tracelessly, as it did the monsoon.

Walking under the trees, she saw a band of monkeys sitting or pacing by some more-distant huts, and moved nearer to look at them. The huts stood alone, surrounded by attempts at agriculture. A dog nosed by the rubbish heaps, keeping an eye on the monkeys.

Stones were set beneath the big tree where the monkeys paced. Some were painted or stained, and branches of the tree had been painted white. Offerings of flowers lay in a tiny shrine attached to the main trunk; a garland withered on a low branch above a monkey's head. The monkey, Jane saw, suckled a baby at its narrow dugs.

A man stepped from behind the tree and approached Jane.

He made a sign of greeting and said, 'Lady, you want buy somet'ing?'

She looked at him. Something unpleasant was happening to one of his eyes, and flies surrounded it. But he was a well-built man, thin, of course, but not as old as she had at first thought. His head was shaven; he wore only a white dhoti. He appeared to have nothing to sell.

'No, thank you,' she said.

He came closer.

'Lady, you are English lady? You buy small souvenir, some one very nice thing of value for to take with you back to England! Look, I show – you are please to wait here one minute.'

He turned and ducked into the most dilapidated of the huts. She looked about, wondering whether to stay. In a moment, the man emerged again into the sun, carrying a vase. The children gathered and stared silently; only the monkeys were restless.

'This is very lovely Indian vase, lady, bought in Jamshedpur, very fine hand manufacture. Perceive beautiful artistry work, lady!'

She hesitated before taking the poor brass vase in her hands. He turned and called sharply into the hut, and then redoubled his sales talk. He had been a worker in a shoe factory in Jamshedpur, he told her, but the factory had burned down and he could find no other work. He had brought his wife and children here, to live with his brother.

'I'm afraid I'm not interested in buying the vase,' she said.

'Lady, please, you give only ten rupees! Ten rupees only!' He broke off.

His wife had emerged from the hut, to stand without motion by his side. In her arms, she carried a child.

The child looked solemnly at Jane from its giant dark eyes. It was naked except for a piece of rag, over which a great belly sagged. Its body, and especially the face and skull, were covered in pustules, from some of which a liquid seeped. Its head had been smeared with ash. The baby did not move or cry; what its age was, Jane could not estimate.

Its father had fallen silent for a moment. Now he said, 'My child is having to die, lady, look see! You give me ten rupees.'

Now she shrank from the proffered vase. Inside the hut, there were other children stirring in the shadows. The sick child looked outwards with an expression of great wisdom and beauty – or so Jane interpreted it – as if it understood and forgave all things. Its very silence frightened her, and the stillness of the mother. She backed away, feeling chilled.

'No, no, I don't want the vase! I must go—'

Muttering her excuses, she turned away and hurried, almost ran, back towards the car. She could hear the man calling to her.

She climbed into the car. The man came and stood outside, not touching the car, apologetic, explaining, offering the vase for only eight rupees, talking, talking. Seven and a half rupees. Jane hid her face.

When Amma emerged, the man backed away, said something meekly; Amma replied sharply. He turned, clutching the vase, and the children watched. She climbed into the driving-seat and started the car.

'He tried to sell me something. A vase. It was the only thing he had to sell, I suppose,' Jane said. 'He wasn't rude.' She felt the silent gears of their relationship change; she could no longer pretend to superiority, since she had been virtually rescued. After a moment, she asked. 'What was the matter with his child? Did he tell you?'

'He is a man of the scheduled classes. His child is dying of the smallpox. There is always smallpox in the villages.'

'I imagined it was the plague . . .'

'I told you, we do not have the plague in Orissa yet.'

The drive home was a silent one, voiceless in the corroded land. The people moving slowly home had long shadows now. When they arrived at the gates of the Chandhari house, a porter was ready to open the gate, and a distracted servant stood there; she ran fluttering beside the car, calling to Amma.

Amma turned and said, 'Jane, I am sorry to tell you that your father has had another heart attack just now.'

The attack was already over. Robert Pentecouth lay unconscious on the bed, breathing raspingly. Dr Chandhari stood looking down at him and sipping an iced lime-juice. He nodded tenderly at Jane as she moved to the bedside.

'I have of course administered an anti-coagulant, but your father is very ill, Miss Pentecouth,' he said. 'There is severe cardiac infarction, together with weakness in the mitral valve, which is situated at the entrance of the left ventricle. This has caused congestion of the lungs, which means the trouble of breathlessness, very much accentuated by the hot atmosphere of the Indian sub-continent. I have done my level best for him.'

'I must get him home, Doctor.'

Chandhari shook his head. 'The air journey will be severely taxing on him. I tell you frankly I do not imagine for a single moment that he will survive it.'

'What should I do, Doctor? I'm so frightened!'

'Your father's heart is badly scarred and damaged, dear lady. He needs a new heart, or he will give up the ghost.'

Jane sat down on the chair by the bedside and said, 'We are in your hands.'

He was delighted to hear it. 'There are no safer hands, dear Miss Pentecouth.' He gazed at them with some awe as he said, 'Let me outline a little plan of campaign for you. Tomorrow we put your father on the express to Calcutta. I can phone to Naipur Road station to have it stop. Do not be alarmed! I will accompany you on the express. At the Radakhrishna General Hospital in Howrah in Calcutta is that excellent man, K. V. Menon, who comes from Trivandrum, as does my own family – a very civilized and clever man of the Nair caste. K. V. Menon. His name is widely renowned and he will perform the operation.'

'Operation, Doctor?'

'Certainly, certainly! He will give a new heart. K. V. Menon has performed many many successful heart-transplants. The operation is as commonplace in Calcutta as in California. Do not worry! And I will personally stand by you all the while. Perhaps Amma shall come too because I see you are firm friends already. Good, good, don't worry!'

In his excitement, he took her by the arm and made her rise to her feet. She stood there, solid but undecided, staring at him.

'Come!' he said. 'Let us go and telephone all the arrangements! We will make some commotion around these parts, eh? Your father is OK here with the old nurse-woman to watch. In a few days, he will wake up with a new heart and be well again.'

Jane sent a cable explaining the situation to the Indian headquarters of EGNP in Delhi (the city which ancient colonialist promptings had perhaps encouraged the authorities to choose). Then she stood back while the commotion spread.

It spread first to the household. More people were living in the Chandhari house than Jane had imagined. She met the doctor's wife, an elegant sari-clad woman who spoke good English and who apparently lived in her own set of rooms, together with her servants. The latter came and went, enlivened by the excitement. Messengers were despatched to the bazaar for various little extra requirements.

The commotion rapidly spread farther afield. People came to inquire the health of the white sahib, to learn the worst for themselves. The representative of the local newspaper called. Another doctor arrived, and was taken by Dr Chandhari, a little proudly, to inspect the patient.

If anything, the commotion grew after darkness fell.

Jane went to sit by her father. He was still unconscious. Once, he spoke coherently, evidently imagining himself back in England; although she answered him, he gave no sign that he heard. Amma came in to say good-night on her way to bed.

'We shall be leaving early in the morning,' Jane said. 'My father and I have brought you only trouble. Please don't come to Calcutta with us. It isn't necessary.'

'Of course not. I will come only to Naipur Road station. I'm glad if we could help at all. And, with a new heart, your father will be really hale and hearty again. Menon is a great expert in heart-transplantation.'

'Yes. I have heard his name, I think. You never told me, Amma – how did you find your old nurse this afternoon?'

'You did not ask me. Unhappily, she died during last night.'

'Oh! I'm so sorry!'

'Yes, it is hard for her family. Already they are much in debt to the moneylender.'

She left the room; shortly after, Jane also retired. But she could not sleep. After an hour or two of fitful sleep, she got dressed again and went downstairs, obsessed with a mental picture of the glass of fresh lime-juice she had seen the doctor drinking. She could hear unseen people moving about in rooms she had never entered. In the garden, too, flickering tongues of light moved. A heart-transplant was still a strange event in Naipur Road, as it had once been in Europe and America; perhaps it would have even more superstition attached to it here than it had there.

When a servant appeared, she made her request. After long delay, he brought the glass on a tray, gripping it so that it would not slip, and lured her out on to the verandah with it. She sat in a wicker chair and sipped it. A face appeared in the garden, a hand reached in supplication up to her.

'Please! Miss Lady!'

Startled, she recognized the man with the dying child to whom she had spoken the previous afternoon.

The next morning. Jane was roused by one of the doctor's servants. Dazed after too little sleep, she dressed and went down to drink tea. She could find nothing to say; her brain had not woken yet. Amma and her father talked continuously in English to each other.

The big family-car was waiting outside. Pentecouth was gently loaded in, and the luggage piled round him. It was still little more than dawn; as Jane, Amma and Chandhari climbed in and the car rolled forward, wraith-like figures were moving already. A cheerful little fire burned here and there inside a house. A tractor rumbled towards the fields. People stood at the sides of the road, numb, to let the car pass. The air was chilly; but, in the eastern sky, the banners of the day's warmth were already violently flying.

They were almost at the railway station when Jane turned to Amma. 'That man with the child dying of smallpox walked all the way to the house to speak to me. He said he came as soon as he heard of my father's illness.'

'The servants had no business to let him through the gate. That is how diseases spread,' Amma said.

'He had something else to sell me last night. Not a vase. He wanted to sell his heart!'

Amma laughed. 'The vase would be a better bargain, Jane!'

'How can you laugh? He was so desperate to help his wife and family. He wanted fifty rupees. He would take the money back to his wife and then he would come with us to the Calcutta Hospital to have his heart cut out!'

Putting her hand politely to her mouth, Amma laughed again.

'Why is it funny?' Jane asked desperately. 'He meant what he said. Everything was so black for him that his life was worth only fifty rupees!'

'But his life is not worth so much, by far!' Amma said. 'He is just a village swindler. And the money would not cure the child, in any case. The type of smallpox going about here is generally fatal, isn't it, Pappa?'

Dr Chandhari, who sat with a hand on his patient's forehead, said, 'This man's idea is of course not scientific. He is one of the scheduled classes – an Untouchable, as we used to say. He has never eaten very much all during his life and so he will have only a little weak heart. It would never be a good heart in your father's body, to circulate all his blood properly.' With a proud gesture, he thumped Robert Pentecouth's chest. 'This is the body of the well-nourished man. In Calcutta, we shall find him a proper big heart that will do the work effectively.'

They arrived at the railway station. The sun was above the horizon and climbing rapidly. Rays of gold poured through the branches of the trees by the station on to the faces of people arriving to watch the great event, the stopping of the great Madras–Calcutta express, and the loading-aboard of a white man going for a heart-transplant.

Furtively, Jane looked about the crowd, searching to see if her man happened to be there. But, of course, he would be back in his village by now, with his wife and the children.

Intercepting the look, Amma said, 'Jane, you did not give that man baksheesh, did you?'

Jane dropped her gaze, not wishing to betray herself.

'He would have robbed you,' Amma insisted. 'His heart would be valueless. These people are never free from hookworms, you know – in the heart and the stomach. You should have bought the vase if you wanted a souvenir of Naipur Road – not a heart, for goodness' sake!'

The train was coming. The crowd stirred. Jane took Amma's hand. 'Say no more. I will always have memories of Naipur Road.'

She busied herself about her father's stretcher as the great sleek train growled into the station.

Keith Roberts

Manscarer

By dawn most of the spectators are in their places in the stands and already making a din that is causing Roley Stratford to rage and fume. This the plebs will never understand: that the true introduction to the coming spectacle is Silence. One cannot play Silence, the primordial entity; so there is nothing to which to listen, and the people are not quiet.

Roley has dressed for the occasion as a British admiral of the early nineteenth century; his white breeches are soiled with grass stains where he has helped one of the working parties make last-minute adjustments to the great shanks of *Manscarer* lying along the clifftop. Jed Burrows, ADC for the day, fusses behind his temporary chief, carrying the bottle of rum Roley has declared indispensable to the period flavour. He also started out with a brass telescope and an astrolabe, but the latter was left behind as too unwieldy. The telescope he still carries, tucked in the crook of his blue-uniformed arm.

The dawn wind is cool; Jed shivers a little, stepping from one foot to the other as the shade of Nelson harangues the leader of the orchestra. A minor difficulty has arisen; the contract clearly specifies a thirty-minute overture before the 'Pomp and Circumstance' extracts that will herald the Assembly, but only part of the band awnings has arrived in time. A harassed group of City engineers is still at work erecting the rest, manhandling the awkward lengths of billowing pre-formed plastic. Leader, Strings and Woodwind are prepared to play in the open air; the brass section, keen union men one and all, are not. The boys claim it will chap their lips. Somewhat obscurely, Percussion and Effects are backing the argument. Jed tires of the row and wanders off, leaving the rum placed on a conspicuous outcrop of rock. Part of the book calls for volleys of Very lights; he will have ample warning of the start.

Most of the Colony are scattered round the concrete pads on which *Manscarer* will take-shape, by the grace of God and in spite of the force of gravity. The working teams lounge on the grass, still keeping roughly in position; here and there a bottle is raised in greeting to Jed as he paces solemnly the dural beams of the Crow. As he walks he rehearses again in his mind the complex stages of Assembly. The first members, once socketed into their pads, will serve as derricks for the raising of the greater beams, the weighted and counterbalanced shafts that will set the head of the sculpture in huge and complicated motion. The beak itself, the *corvus*, lies along the clifftop like an old-time ploughshare monstrously over-large. There could be trouble with the placing of the assembly; it is heavy, very heavy, and the triplefold tackles that will bear its weight are none too hefty for the job. The answer would have been a flying crane, but Roley refuses to countenance the use of such an apparatus. The machine would spoil the form of *Manscarer* at a critical moment, and its din would drown the orchestra.

Jed checks the donkey engine that will make the great pulls. Steam is already raised – steam and steam only has been deemed fit by Roley for his masterpiece – and Bil-Bil and Tam are fretting over their gauges. On the roof of the engine shed Reggy Glassbrook, nimble and hairy, sits grinning like an ape. He is the Colony's steeplejack; he will be first into the rigging today, handling the split-second alignments as the beams sail to their positions, sure-footed and quick as one of Meg's pet geckos. As far as Jed is concerned, he will be welcome to the job; the ADC has no head for heights, and from the feet of the *Scarer* to his main goosenecks will be all of ninety feet.

A hundred yards beyond the donkey shack a gully running to the cliff edge makes a shallow windbreak. Crouched in its lee, Bunny, Whore Nonpareil and the Witch of Endor eat alternate sandwiches of crab and caviare, and serve passers-by with hock from a Georgian coffeepot. At their feet a coffee machine heated by a small spirit-lamp glugs and burbles to itself. 'What are we, girls?' shouts Jed. 'Artists or engineers?' The gag, in the new 'flat humour' favoured by the Colony, raises a chorus of unanswers, nods and headshakes and somewhat glazed morning-after grinnings. Jed looks up, visualizing the great blue negative the sky will make round the whirling bars of *Manscarer*. Pushes his telescope more firmly under his arm, touches his hat and moves on.

Artists or engineers? As an artist Roley called for underpinnings to reach down unseen into the cliff, a hundred and fifty feet to sea-level. Through them *Manscarer* would have grown from earth's roots, sweeping up, continuing the lines of stress inherent in the bulging stone, shackling the ground firmly to the sky; but the City engineers refused him more than twenty feet, just enough to hold the ponderous swirling of the tophamper. It will serve, though; *Manscarer* will peck and thunder, nibbling perhaps at his own sinews and feet to fall one day in glorious dissolution into the water. Perhaps before that the Colony will hold a ritual destruction; there will be more stands and more admission charges and more selling of high-priced ice-cream. And the South Sector Symphonic again, if it can be arranged.

Symphonic . . . Jed, a quarter of a mile from the podium, can still hear in the breaks of the wind the evidence of Roley's apoplexy. The Overture was timed to start as the sun's disc broke clear of the sea; but the daystar has lifted now his own diameter from the horizon, and not a brass bleat has been heard from the pack of them. The occasion is ruined before it begins. Jed mounts a hillock of grass to gain a view of the distant stands. The State Police are having a mite of trouble keeping order over there; he marks a dozen separate and complicated scuffles taking place on the grass in front of the awnings. Programmes are being fluttered, and some sort of organized chanting has started. He sees a man running, another being belaboured by a mounted Cossack. He swears at the risk to the Colony's precious horses. An enthusiastic mob.

He looks along the coast. Symphonies are playing already, the mute works the plebs refuse to hear. The notes are of lilac and seething pale blue, touched with the thin glittering of sunlight. Far below at the feet of the cliffs are the crawling lace curtains of the tide. Jed turns away slightly giddy. The Assembly teams are standing now, chafing their hands and flapping their arms across and back against their shoulders. The jeans and reefer jackets of the men amount almost to a uniform, but no two girls are dressed alike. Jed sees a fine Firebird swirling in a mist of fluorescent nylon; nearer are a Pompadour, a Puck, a shivery paint job all black and white zebra-stripes. Meg Tranter is dolled up in ancient half-burned newsprint, the textured leaves flapping round arms and knees. She carries a placard with the legend 'Zeitgeist 1960'. That, too, is 'flat' humour; she is explaining to the plebs that they lack the mental equipment ever to understand.

Between the Assembly site and the nearest of the terracings a collection of Colony possessions has been set up on display. Armoured and well-guarded cases hold stacks of old books; dogs and beribboned goats are being paraded and Piggy and the Rat are doing a brisk trade in genuine hand-executed Seascapes. There is a constant coming and going from the ranks of sightseers. In the City, Colony artefacts fetch quaint prices; through them Jed's folk are self-supporting in theory at least. Jed wipes his face and looks farther along the cliffs. Way off and blue with distance he can see the City's impossible side, like the edge of a hundred-yard-thick carpet pulled across the land. The structure covers all England with its grinding weight and sameness. In its catacombs, trapped in the miles on honeycombed miles of chambers and passages, men can live and die, if they are born poor enough, without seeing the sun. The tiny open spaces round the coasts, full of the mad artefacts of the Colonies, provide a relief from Sameness that the people come trooping year after year to see. Without them, populations might run shrieking mad themselves. Artists are a therapeutic force now, recognized and protected by Government; the lunacy of the few safeguards the sanity of the many.

A bang-crock; the report and its echo lift a paperchase of gulls from beneath Jed's feet. He watches them soaring out under the glowing ball of the signal. Shreds of music reach him; at long last, the Overture has begun. He paces back methodically, lips pursed, keeping in character as he walks the quarterdeck of the cliff. From the tail of his eye he sees Reggy, stripped now to shorts and sleeveless leather jerkin, springing and posturing on the roof of his little shed. Someone runs to Jed and presents him with chipolatas on sticks and a stuffed olive. He munches as he walks, savouring the Surreal delicacy of the gesture, climbs the rostrum where Roley dances in a furor of creativity and apprehension. A speaking-trumpet is gripped in his hand; the fingers that hold it are white-knuckled with strain.

The music climbs towards its first climax. 'Lifting teams,' bellows Roley. 'Teams, *ha-ul* . . .' A jet of steam rises from the donkey hut; oddly assorted groups of Colonists, drilled to perfection, scurry across the grass, taking up the slack in the controlling tackles. The spars of the lowest Configuration rise with surprising speed, waver and . . . *bang-bang* . . . thump down, dead on beat, into their sockets. The thing is done, like a conjuring trick out of the grass. *Fortissimo* from the huge gaggle of musicians, a half-heard firework-gasp from the crowd and then cheering while Roley waves his arms again leaping up and down and damnblasting the plebs, lilac in the face with rage. The gestures are eloquent, even effective; the little blue-dressed figure, capering mad as a clockwork monkey, quietens the crowd. The occasion, after all, is a solemn one; the plebs, who have fought for tickets, are duly impressed. They are witnessing a demonstration of an art form in which Roley alone excels; the erection, to music, of a supermobile. Uncomprehending, they still stand in stark awe of lunacy. That, after all, is what they have paid good money to see.

The Interval. After an hour's work the main spars stand supported by their guys like the disfigured kingpoles of a Big Top. Smaller secondary beams, feathered with bright lapping sheets of metal, already spin and dip, humming in the wind; the goosenecks that will take the great spars of the main assembly are in place, and the lifting tackles. The donkey hut becomes obscured by steam as Tam blows pressure from his waiting boiler; on the roof, Reggy, still sweating from his exertions and wrapped in a hand-woven poncho, holds court before an admiring half-circle of Colonists. Roley, squatting on the edge of his rostrum, waves brief encouragement before re-addressing himself to his bottle of Captain Cat (home brewed in the Colony). Below him, musicians lounge on the grass; mush-sellers circulate between them bearing aloft feathery *incubi* of green and pink candyfloss. The machines of aerial observers, newsmen and photographers, hang racketing round the struts of the mobile, some dangerously close to the guys; people from the ground teams are waving their arms, trying to shoo them back.

The sun is hotter now; Jed mops his face with a bright bandanna. Beyond the half-completed *Manscarer* other mobiles loom; Jed, watching, sees *Fandancer* bow herself, making for an instant with her wobbling slats the outline of a hip, the big thrust of trochanter and the muscled curve below, before collapsing into Motion. One of Roley's most ingenious creations that, though maybe lacking a little in over-all strength. Bil-Bil and Tam approve of her, and that isn't always a good sign. She was a bitch on the drawing-board, and a bitch to put together as well. Her Assembly was a near-fiasco; it took weeks of patient adjusting and rebalancing before she condescended to shimmy in the airs of Heaven. Behind her are other sculptures, more distant still; Jed sees the flash and swoop of *Halcyon*, *Manscarer*'s forerunner, before his beams, flattening freakishly, lose themselves beneath a swell of grass. He looks up again lovingly at the new Structure, shielding his eyes against the sun, watching the lazily turning plates of dark blue and deathly iridescent violet. The mobile has already a drama that the others lack.

Manscarer is a crow, or the bones of one; a vast ghost that once complete will thunder and peck along the clifftop, the bird at last turned hunter and revenger of dead fields. Or so runs the Manifesto. Jed doubts if one in a hundred of the gaping Cityfolk have taken the trouble to read it; it would mean little enough to them if they did.

Jed moves to the hour-glass strapped on the side of the rostrum. The last few grains of sand are funnelling down. He raises his arm, palm flat, and there is a scramble as the orchestra runs for its instruments. Reggy erupts from the poncho; Roley raises his baton, and construction begins again with a quiet passage in which Reggy, balanced and slowly revolving in the blue, delicately attaches the featherings of the upper rings. While he works, the hundred-foot linked shafts of the main assembly are cleared for lifting.

The secondary Configurations are nearly complete now; hawsers run from them to anchor-points in the grass. Others are ready for the main beams. *Manscarer*, unshackled, would rampage across a 300-yard circle, tearing and clucking at the grass; before the last of the ropes are slipped, bandstand and engine house will be evacuated. Jed leaves the podium, where Roley still conducts in a berserk frenzy, runs to his pre-arranged position on the tackles. Every pair of hands the Colony can muster will be needed for the coming operation.

Hawsers snake upwards to humming tightness as Tam, the winch control-levers in his hands, leans from the window of his shack. The music drives towards its great central theme; a shout, a heavier thundering from the engine shed, and the *corvus* lifts clear of the grass, twenty feet long, glinting with a vicious rose-and-black shimmer. Reggy balances on the skullplates, sticky-footed. A medley of orders bellowed through the music, wiry strumming as the beams snub at their restraining tackles, and on the beat the whole assembly soars, weaving impatiently as the feathered tailplates feel the breeze. Jed loops his downhaul round a bollard, leans back as the creaking rope takes the strain. The beams swing higher, clang against the central masts to drop with a crash, sockets trued over the projecting goosenecks; the *corvus* falls and rises, dipping as it tastes the wind.

Triumph, and disaster. Somewhere in the rigging a shackle parts with a hard snap. Tackles come down flailing. The beams swing, driven by the wind, shearing the remaining cables. *Manscarer* rotates, unpredictable now and weighing tons, the focus of a widening circle of unhappiness. Jed sees a block swinging in decapitating arcs, falls flat and rolls on his back to watch the huge overhead clicking of violet bones. A dozen people skid past, drawn by their rope, chirping out a birdcage panic; a Cavalier's hat bowls across the ground, on edge like a little feathered wheel. The wind gusts; the *corvus* casts out far across the sea, swings back to rake screeching flinders from the awnings of the bandstand, tangles massively with the roof of the engine shed. Steam explodes outwards, gusting across to where the orchestra, on hands and knees, scuttles for its collective life. The beak, checked by the obstruction of the donkey shed, wavers and dips again to strike at the main struts, down which Reggy is still scurrying from danger. Another peck, a fleshy concussion, a shrill falling scream; a surprised gob of blood splashes across Jed's wrist from where Reggy, suitably scared, sails overhead, filling the close sky with legs and arms. He bounces against the cliff edge to fall again to the blue and white impatience of the water, his plunging splash lost far below in the morning noise of the sea. After him a French Horn, disembodied from its master, bounds disconsolately like a Surreal yellow snail.

Jed crawls to the cliff edge in the sunlight, and thoughtfully adds his quota of moisture to the ocean.

The flooring of the house is of polished yellow wood, broken by platforms and steps into various levels. Sunlight lies across it in calm rectangles. Round the dark blue walls white alcoves, circular-topped, house ancient ship models and tropical shells; hand-rails of copper and mahogany echo the nautical flavour. The end wall of the building is of glass; through it, distantly, can be seen the ocean. To one side of the living-space stands a bright-red twentieth-century MG, her nose butted into a recess in the floor; in the centre of the room is a table covered with a spotless linen cloth. A silver breakfast service adds a last note of elegance.

Above the carport in the wall the curtains of a sleeping-alcove are drawn back to reveal a plain divan covered by a heap of bright coloured scatter cushions. From the alcove, close under the oddly pitched roof, a thick white-painted beam spans the room. Jed stands beneath it, feet with their buckled shoes in a patch of sunlight, hand on the hilt of his sword. 'That's my beam,' he says crossly. 'Just you get off it, this minute.'

The girl above him makes no movement, staring down with eyes wide with fright as those of a tarsier. 'That's my beam,' says Jed again more carefully. 'Nobody can sit up there, except me.'

Silence.

'I'll run you through without mercy,' declares the Admiral, exposing six glittering inches of the swordblade.

There is no reaction.

'I'll do terrible things. I'll keelhaul you and flog you through the fleet. I'll throw you to the fishes . . .'

The girl grips the beam a little harder with her jean-clad legs, twining her bare ankles beneath it.

Jed looks thoughtful, pushes the sword back into its scabbard, walks to the table and wields a silver pot. Steam rises fragrantly. He adds sugar and milk, stirs carefully and picks up the cup in its saucer, turning as he does so to look back at the roof. 'If they make coffee in Heaven,' he calls, 'and tea in Hell, I'd take my turn at the stoking.' The hot drink soothes, steadying the shaking of his hands. He sits down, studies the table and selects a round of toast. He butters it and spoons a blob of marmalade on to his plate. 'After breakfast,' he says to the silence, 'I'll stop being an admiral. Is that what you want?'

A headshaking from the girl on the beam.

'Polly,' says the retiring Captain Hardy, 'if you won't come down I really shall knock you off. I shall do it with a broom.'

There is no response except a tensing of the legs. Polly indicates her determination to stay on the beam until killed. Jed fixes her again with a contemplative eye. 'I was sick this morning,' he says. 'I did it in the sea. Were you there when Reggy was pecked?'

A nodding. A violent reaction for Polly.

Jed pauses, the toast halfway to his mouth. 'He was killed,' he says, unnecessarily. 'Is that why you got up there?'

The nodding again.

'Were you frightened?'

Headshaking. No, no . . .

'I've decided,' says Jed. 'I won't knock you down after all. Instead I shall just wait till you get tired and fall off.' He lifts the pot again. 'Polly, you do make lovely tea.' He finishes the cup, lays down his toast and walks forward to grip the girl's dangling feet. On the ankles are faint brown watermarks. He pushes the toes under his chin, leans his forehead against the cool frontal curving of the shins. 'Poll,' he says, 'you've got mucky feet.' Then looking up, 'You are a funny girl . . .'

The Colony, cowed by death, keep to their separate homes; Roley to his bleak little sixteenth-century pub, Piggy and the Rat to their queer thatched tower-room, darkly glowing with light from fishtanks and crystal globes, Meg and the Witch of Endor to to their clifftop bunker full of juju dolls and scuttling lizards and the apparatus of magic. Visitors poke and pry, disappointed at the lack of activity and at missing the morning's disaster. They traipse through Polly's fragile house, empty now, leaving its doors ajar to gusts of sunlight; but nobody comes near Jed's home. He would almost welcome interference. He lounges against the rear wheel of the MG, a cushion at his back, his legs stretched out along the planking of the floor. He is reading from an ancient copy of the *Ingoldsby Legends*; from time to time he glances up half-aggravatedly from the verse to the *succubus* still straddling the beam. A mile away *Manscarer* spins angrily, clashing and banging in the circle he has cleared. His noise fills the peninsula on which the Colony lies, penetrates bumblingly through the glazed wall of the room.

At lunchtime Jed leaves, to be away from Polly's eyes. He hunts out sketchbook and pastels on the way, and lets the outer door slam. It is only then the girl becomes active. She slides off the beam in frenzied haste, scurrying with the nervous violence of an ant as she clears the table, washes, cooks. When Jed returns she is back on her perch. He looks a little disappointed; he had hoped to find his house no longer haunted. But the dinner simmering in the oven is very good.

Jed eats the meal in silence, carries the dishes and plates to the kitchen alcove and washes them, stacking them carefully in their racks. He clears the rest of the table, shakes the cloth outside the back door and folds it. By the time he has finished Polly has at least changed her attitude, she is riding the beam sidesaddle. It is a hopeful sign; perhaps at last the strain is telling. Jed stands underneath her again, looking up. 'I could pull you off quite easily now,' he says. 'You wouldn't be able to hang on at all.' She bites her lip, knowing he will do no such thing.

He scratches his head, badly worried. 'You're Making a Protest, aren't you?'

The girl nods.

'What's it about?'

No answer.

'Something's upset you terribly,' says the erstwhile admiral. 'It was to do with Reggy, but it wasn't him being killed. I don't know what it is. Couldn't you write it down?'

Negative. A large tear escapes from the corner of Polly's eye and runs down her cheek. She ignores it till it reaches her lip; then she fields it with the pointed tip of her tongue.

Jed fetches the sketchbook from where he flung it down carelessly, and holds it up. He says a little helplessly 'These are for you.' Polly grabs with surprising speed, like a monkey stealing a banana. The drawings of the *Manscarer*, his posturings and violent movements under the yellow searchlight-stabbings of sunlight. Polly clutches the book to her chest, rocking and crooning, burying her nose in the pages to catch the sweet scent of new fixative. She is still holding it when Jed leaves to drink five evening pints of beer at the Lobster Pot and tell Roley his beam has been invaded by a woman. A runner is instantly despatched to take Polly a little hat, a copy of the Rieu *Odyssey* and a picture book of sailing ships to look at if she's bored. Meg wants to send a gecko as well, but Jed says no. Polly is a little afraid of them, and it wouldn't be fair.

When he returns, the peninsula is blue with summer dusk and the last grasshoppers in the Universe are making the night shrill with their churring. He decides he can't face supper; he undresses in the dark, lies down and feels the bed swaying slightly from side to side. As long as he doesn't roll over violently he will be all right. An hour later a sudden thump wakes him from a doze. Muffled sounds follow at intervals as Polly pads about doing God only knows what. Jed draws himself up against the wall, waiting. He feels his heart, accelerating, bump faintly against the insides of his ribs; quick prickling sensations move across his skin. It seems an age before Poll swings up the ladder to the alcove. She moves a little stiffly, still suffering from her day of abstinence.

She wriggles her jeans off before sliding on to the divan. To Jed she feels soft and cool, a life-size doll.

* * *

The two figures swim in a morning dazzle of sunlight, seeing the cliffs rise giddily in the troughs between the waves. Above them the head of *Manscarer* appears once, violet and sullen, withdraws itself instantly with the ease and quick grace of a snake. The creaking of the slats carries down to the water.

Jed hangs on to a rock, seeing the long fringes of weed wash and swirl on the tide, watching the tiny close sunburnings reflect from water and bursting foam. The situation is baffling. Polly has him completely in her grasp now; he owes her a breakfast, a dinner and a night in bed, and he wants them all again. The whole affair is difficult in the extreme.

Reggy, swilling palely while the sea gurgles in his ruined side can do nothing but nod his head up and down in agreement.

Among the bushes scattered in the little gully lights play and flash, now here, now gone; wayward gleams follow the voices of Oberon and Puck. Farther up the cliff Bil-Bil and Tam, the engineers, sit at a console alive with whirling tape-spools, setting the words of the Dream spinning and fluting through the sky. The Colony listens sleepy with poetry, clustered in the summer night. *Manscarer* swirls and clacks, gaunt and small on the skyline; but he is forgotten.

Polly, sitting cross-legged just behind Jed, pulls grass-blades miserably, chewing them and spitting them away. By Act Three she can no longer control the tensions inside her. She puts her head back and shrieks, rendingly. Then again, and again. The *son et lumière* is disrupted, for ever.

The Colony panics. Dumb things that scream are bad; like the stuffed fox in the poem barking, the oak walking for love. Polly isn't a deaf-mute; it's just that two years ago she decided she had nothing else interesting to say and vowed never to speak again. But it's difficult to remember that now she's been quiet so long. A confused battle starts in the gully, figures tumbling over each other and hitting out in alarm while Polly eels about between them still making sounds like a steam carousel. The play shuts down; Bil-Bil and Tam squeak miserably, enveloped by tape. Piggy finally catches the culprit by the heel and pins her while the Rat, never far away from trouble, kisses her to make her stop. Polly is unco-operative. Meg yelps, kicked firmly in the crotch; the Rat claps his hands to an eye jabbed by a hard little elbow. The Witch of Endor joins battle decisively; she administers three sound thumps before Jed, raging, starts to hit her back. The skirmishing subsides; there is a silence, broken by the sea noise far below and the unhappy grunting of the Rat.

Roley Stratford mounts a rock and windmills his long arms against the sky. 'It's hopeless,' he booms, furiously. 'We can't hear plays if people have to scream. Polly, will you be quiet? And not start any more fights?'

Polly, still struggling, shakes her head violently and gulps. Jed claps his hand across her mouth, terrified in case she starts being ghastly again. She instantly bites his thumb. He swears, and calls up to the rock. 'She says no . . .'

The Witch of Endor mutters something about 'nasty little free-martin'. The words come out slightly thick; she is trying to cope with a split lip. Jed, one arm round Polly, raises his free fist. The Witch ducks prudently, wriggling back out of reach. Roley jumps up and down on his rock. 'Then it's a trial . . .' He raises his arms dramatically, fists clenched. '*A tri-al* . . .'

The shout, taken up by the Colony, becomes a chant. Figures surge round Polly and Jed, hoisting them to their feet; the Witch is propelled after them up the incline of the gully. Bil-Bil and Tam desert their tangled console, infected by the general enthusiasm.

'A *trial* . . . it's a *trial* . . .'

Heavy Dutch oil-lamps hanging from the rafters light the bars of the Lobster Pot with a soft brilliance. Beneath them the Colony is present in full strength, banging its tankards on the white-scrub-bed tables and yelling for proceedings to begin. Roley, the Chief Justice, hammers louder on the counter-top in front of him with the scarred and knotted shillelagh that is his staff of office. The Court Peculiar is convened; mine host calls for witnesses.

The Witch of Endor is shoved forward, willowy in an ankle-length dress of scrubbed hessian. Finding herself the centre of at-tention, she sticks out her chest importantly. 'I got smacked in the teeth . . .' She waves a bright-splotched hankie. 'I'm a witness . . .'

'Polly didn't do that!'

'Shame!'

'She did!'

'She didn't. It was Jed . . .'

'Well, it was all her fault . . .'

'It wasn't!'

'Was!'

'You always want to bully her!'

'I *don't*! She started it!'

'*Shame!*'

The shillelagh beats half-moons into the counter-top. 'Polly,' says the Judge. '*Did* you start it? Whatever it was?'

Polly, sitting on Jed's knee, jiggles happily and nods.

'What did you do?'

'*Nothing . . .*'

'She *did* . . .'

'It was the Rat kissing her. She didn't like it . . .'

'That wasn't the start . . .'

'Well, that was when she hit him in the eye . . .'

Roley hammers again for order. 'Did you mind him kissing you, Polly?'

Polly shakes her head.

'It wasn't that, then,' says the Judge decisively. 'Now, is there an Indictment?'

'Tam's got it . . .' Tam is driven into the open, protesting. He stammers badly; his olive-skinned woman's face is suffused with embarrassment.

'That P-Polly did wilfully d-d-disrupt a performance of Sh-Shakespeare. And upset J-Jed getting his b-breakfast for him, and his d-d-dinner . . .'

'And she went to bed with him . . .'

'That doesn't matter . . .'

'It does. It ought to be included anyway . . .'

The Rat has hauled a chair into a window recess; enthroned on its temporary eminence he feels secure. His one serviceable eye leers horribly. '*She was a virgin too . . .*'

'She wasn't . . .'

'She *was* . . .'

'She couldn't have been . . .'

Roley whirls the shillelagh. 'This might be *very important* . . . Were you a virgin, Polly?'

Polly blushes, and hides her face against Jed's shoulder. The Colony, impressed, makes a concerted 'aaahhhh' noise, like a crowd of plebs when a rocket explodes. The Rat hiccups inconsequentially. 'C-c'n I have s'more beer, somebody . . . ?'

A jug is handed up to him. It gets well swigged from on the way. He pours what is left into his pot, mumbling to himself. Roley clears his throat. 'The Indictment is very confused,' he says, 'but evidently the whole affair's to do with Jed. That's the first point . . .'

'She just wants him to do something back . . .'

'Well, he won't . . .'

'He will. He'll do anything now; look at his face . . .'

The counter-top suffers again. 'It's to do with Jed,' says Roley loudly. 'And it's also to do with Reggy, because it started when he was killed. It started with the beam in Jed's house; that should have been in the Indictment. Right?'

Polly, nodding, seems to be trying to shake her head off her shoulders.

'Then, we're getting somewhere,' says the Judge, very satisfied. He swigs violently from a quart pewter mug. His neck muscles writhe in the lamplight as he swallows.

'We'd get on quicker if she'd *talk*,' says the Witch of Endor, glaring. 'I think it's just *stupid* . . .'

'*It isn't!*'

'*IT IS!*'

Proceedings instantly threaten to degenerate into another brawl. Splinters fly from the counter-top as the Judge calls the court to order. '*I* think', says the Witch primly as soon as she can make herself heard, 'she should be *made* to talk.' She tosses her wild yellow hair. 'We should push spills under her fingernails and light them. It would be quite proper.'

Polly clenches her hands protectively and starts to shiver.

'It seems to me', says Roley reprovingly, 'that all in all you've rather got it in for the defendant.'

'*I haven't.*' Then, sullenly, 'All right, I suppose I have. I think she's an ungrateful little beast.'

'Why?'

''Cos I sent her a picture book,' howls the Witch, dancing with sudden temper. 'An' all I got back was a slosh in the chops . . .'

'And I rule that *irrelevant* . . .'

The Rat, very drunk, starts to interrupt, sees the shillelagh poised to hurl at his head and subsides.

'Irrelevant,' says Roley again, to clinch the matter. He glares round him. 'All right. We've got the Indictment, or most of it; we need a Defence. Polly can't tell us why she started to be difficult. That's annoying, but it just can't be helped. So does anybody else know?'

'Yes,' says Jed quietly. 'I do.'

A hush, in which the shrilling of the grasshoppers sounds very loud. Polly turns startled to peer into Jed's face. He puts her aside, carefully, and stands up. He's wishing belatedly he'd worn his uniform and turned the proceedings into a Court Martial. Lacking lapels, he hooks his thumbs in his belt. 'Mr Chief Justice,' he says. 'Ladies and gentleman. This, I believe, is what she means. No more mobiles should be built. Furthermore; the figures already erected should be knocked down as soon as possible. Further—'

A gale of disagreement. Jed, shouted down, starts to jump about and wave his arms, mouth popping shut and open uselessly. Polly, looking desperate, sees above her a heavy beam. She is on the table instantly, and jumping for it. Roley howls his alarm; the Witch, quicker off the mark than the rest, dives at her, wrapping her arms round Polly's knees. A swaying confusion; Jed, leaping to the rescue, skids and vanishes under a scuffling pile of bodies; beer is spilled noisily; the Rat, whirling his pot in his excitement, falls headlong from his perch. Order is finally restored, and Polly restrained; but not before Piggy has been knocked half-silly by a brickbat, and Meg and the Witch have had their heads banged together for punching. Roley returns to his position of authority, breathing a little heavily.

'Now, then,' he says, surveying the court. 'I built these mobiles.' As he speaks he bangs with the handle of the shillelagh, emphasizing each word. 'I gave 'em the best years of me wanin' youth. *I* want to know why Jed says to scrap 'em; so the rest of you, *SHAR-RAP*!' The head of the club, whirling, inflicts a final wound on the counter; Roley bows with great gravity to Jed. 'Mr Burrows, if you would proceed . . .'

'It isn't only the mobiles,' says Jed quickly. He feels oddly certain of his words. 'It's everything we do. The horseriding and the archery and reading Shakespeare in the dark and holding séances, and building all those castles about the place and knocking 'em down again like the last time we had a Medieval War. Piggy and the Rat must stop painting their pictures and put all their fish back in the sea, and Meg must burn her jujus, and you must stop pretending to be a sort of man who doesn't exist anymore, Roley, and so must I. We must destroy the Colony, we must burn it. That's what we must do.'

In the awed silence, the Judge turns to Polly. He asks gently, '*Is* that what you meant?'

She nods again slowly, tears glistening in her eyes.

Nobody else seems able to speak. Roley says carefully, 'Why, Poll? Just because Reggy was killed?'

'No.' Jed is still quite sure of himself. 'Reggy's to do with it, but he isn't the reason. He just brought things to a head. You see, they'd never murdered any of us before.'

'Who?'

'The plebs. Oh, Christ, it's so obvious . . .' He stares round at faces changing from anger to puzzlement. 'We've failed; can't anybody else see that except Polly? All of us, in all the Colonies. When they let us come out here and gave us land and money to spend, and people to help us do every crazy thing that came into our heads, when we took their terms, that was when we failed. We let ourselves down; we sold our birthright. *And theirs* . . .

'We were too dangerous to them scattered about anywhere and everywhere all over the City. We couldn't be pushed about and led by the nose and hammered into the same shape as everybody else. When the trivvyscreens yelled at us we threw things at them, and when the plebs put us in jail for it we sat and laughed because we knew what they didn't, that we were the makers of dreams. The movers and shapers of the world, or something like that. There's a poem about it somewhere. But we took their terms; and now we aren't artists anymore. We don't deserve the name.'

He waves a hand angrily at his surroundings; the stone, the warm wood, the pools of light from the old lamps. 'Polly is telling us, all this is acting and pointless make-believe. That our lives are more sterile than the lives of the people we're supposed to despise.' He raises a declamatory finger. 'We let them short-circuit us. We let them put us where they could see us and count us, where they could come every day to laugh and know they were safe from us and all the nasty things that happen when people start to think. They made us into state-licensed buffoons; and we fell off the thin edge, the tight-rope between creativity and dilettantism, between free thought and aimless posturing for applause. That's why we lost, and how; and that's why we've got to stop now, before we burn ourselves up any further. If we . . . etiolate right out of existence there's no hope left. Not for anybody.' He swings slightly, and returns Roley's bow. 'Sir,' he says, 'I believe I have done . . .'

The Witch of Endor, sitting rather dazedly on the floor, dabs at her lip with the hankie and frowns at the fresh mark it leaves. 'Well, all right,' she says. 'All right. But you haven't said anything new, have you? I mean, we all felt like that. Sort of empty inside, pointless. Only we didn't talk about it. We knew we'd been had all right, all of us.' She looks at the faces behind her, then back to Jed. 'It didn't need saying. But what I want to know is this. Suppose we do what you want, set fire to everything and smash it all up. They'll only build it for us again tomorrow. It won't prove anything. It'll just give them some fresh kicks, won't it? And what else *can* we do?'

Everybody looks at Polly, including Jed. She brushes one eyelid with the back of a finger, and gulps. Jed frowns, pulls at his lip with his teeth. 'There's a lot more in this,' he says. 'But I don't rightly know how to get to it.' Polly's eyes lock on to his and the frown becomes deeper. 'I think,' he says, '*I think* . . . we must leave the Colony. Go back into the City, where we came from.'

Silence intensifies. Only Meg can find a voice. It sounds scratchy and thin.

'*Why* . . .?'

'Because . . . I don't know. Because I think' – again watching Polly – 'because they *need* us. The plebs. They don't know it; but in a funny sort of way the . . . uncertainty . . . matters to them. Not knowing where we are, where we shall pop up next, the crazy things we shall do. They need people who've made lunacy a profession; and that's us. Without us, they'll forget they're living in Hell; they'll just sludge down into a sort of great doughy mass, and forget how to think, and how to eat, and one day they'll forget how to breathe. I think we've got to help them . . . keep things stirred. Like worms tunnelling through earth, letting the air in. Us. The subversives. The Unsavoury Elements, the won't-do-gooders and won't-stay-putters. And I think we've got to do this even if it hurts because it's important to them as well. Because we might not like it, and we might refuse to face it, but in the long term the plebs are what matter to us more than anything else. Once we all opted for the Humanities. Well, there they are. The proper study of mankind. The plebs. *Man* . . .'

Polly's lips move, echoing the words; he catches her eye again and she nods, positively and sorrowfully.

The Witch says very quietly 'What about the sea?'

'We shan't see it anymore.'

'Birds?'

'Not for us. Soon there won't be any anyway. The City will spread over the Colony holdings as soon as we go and that'll be the end.'

'No houses of our own?' That from Meg, in a squeak.

Jed shakes his head. 'No houses. Just miniflats in the levels, the same as everybody else.'

'Sculpting?'

'Mobiles?'

'None. There won't be any room.'

'The sky?'

'We shall see it when we get a Liftpass. Like all the others.'

'We shall go mad . . .'

Jed nods. 'Yes, I think some of us will. But properly mad. Effectively mad. Not like this. This is just . . . keeping up appearances.'

Slowly at first, the idea catches on. 'I've had a monkey on my back for years,' says the Witch. 'Here's where I shuck him right the Hell off . . .'

'Jujus,' says Meg, brightening. 'New ones of all the Controllers. We shall be outlawed. Sent to jail again.'

'Shot at on sight!'

'Brainwashing!'

'Trepanning!'

'Leucotomy! Loads of fun!'

'But we shan't give up . . .'

'Menacing letters in the news-sheets!'

'Secret societies!'

'Things ticking in ventshafts!'

'Reign of terror!'

'Popping out all over!'

'Everything breaking up!'

'Arson!'

'Murder!'

'Incest!'

'Rape!'

'Secret printing presses!'

'Forbidden plays!'

'Subversive novels!'

'Art galleries in all the sewer flats!'

'Passwords!'

'Cloaks and daggers!'

'*Orgies!*'

Roley jumps on to his mangled counter, brandishing a bottle.

'Illicit stills!'

'Moonshining!'

'The plebs can't do this to us!'

'We demand our rights!'

'Summary execution!'

'Imprisonment without trial!'

'Curtailment of free speech!'

'We'll start tonight . . .'

The Colony, transformed on the instant to a mob, surges for the doors. Shouts rise outside; voices call for torches, levers, fire. There are smashings and bangings in the night.

Jed doesn't run with the others. He stands in the doorway of the little phoney pub, slightly staggered at the revolution he has started. Flames are already springing up from a dozen points in the blackness as homes and artefacts begin to burn. Meg runs past screaming, hair blowing in the wind, a blazing brand shedding a bright trail of sparks. Jed turns back, rubbing his face, and sees he isn't alone. He walks across to where Polly is waiting, puts an arm round her shoulders and gives her a little shake. She watches up at him steadily. He says, 'I didn't finish, did I? I still didn't go down all the way, to what you're really trying to do.'

She gives him no help.

'I'm still trying to think,' he says. He looks over her brown hair at the beams of the pub, the high nicotine-glazed ceiling. An extra-loud crash comes from outside; smoke begins to drift thin and acrid across the bar. 'They're all drunk now,' he says. 'They'll be sorry for this in the morning. When they see the houses burned down, and all the things destroyed.'

He swallows, and purses his lips. 'I think,' he says, 'I think . . . there was a painter once called Van Rijn. He was famous, and rich, and he had a wife and I suppose he loved her. Then everything went wrong. His wife died and he lost his house and his money and his patrons forgot about him. Everything he had was taken away. And so . . . he started painting again. He made a portrait, 'The Man in the Golden Helmet'. And then more. And more And more . . .'

Polly watches mistily, lips slightly parted.

'I think,' says Jed, 'if there's a Thing you can call by the name of Art, if it isn't all just a delusion . . . then the roots of the Thing have to reach right down, into bitterness and darkness. Somehow it needs them, it's like a . . . swelling, a wanting to live where there's nothing but death, a needing the sky when there's no sky left to see. It's a . . . longing, an anger. That's what you've let loose; because after tonight, when there's nothing left but the City, there'll be Art again. Something locked away and suffocated, growing, not seeing the sun. Like a . . . great flower in a box, thrusting and pushing and pushing till one day it bursts the seams . . . is that what you really wanted. Polly? Just for there to be Art again? Am I right now?'

Polly hugs him suddenly, kissing and nibbling at his neck.

He lifts her head, tugging gently at her hair. 'In the City,' he says. 'Will you talk?'

She shakes her head, slowly.

'Funnyface,' he says. 'Funnyface . . .' He holds her against him, tightly.

In the night are pink blossomings of fire. The explosions carve out the cliff edges, altering land that is soon to vanish. In their light the mobiles flail, fall with thunderings and scrapings and long-drawn bell-notes into the sea. Ploughshares and vanes, wings and sinews and metal feathers clanking and toppling; *Goliath, Civil War, Cutty Sark, Juliet, The Ant, Titania, Excalibur, Fandancer, Halycon* . . . and *Manscarer*, hugest and last. The procession of Colonists winds between the ruins, tired now, ragged and smoke-blackened and feverish-eyed. Leading them as they turn toward the distant loom of the City is a tiny red car. Its driver sports the sword and froggings, the buckles and epaulettes, the full panoply of a British admiral; beside him a slighter shadow, topped by a bonnet of gull feathers clutches a picture book of sailing ships. Behind, Meg carries boxes of scuttling animals, the Witch of Endor leads prancing dogs and a goat. The cavalcade, improvised banners swirling, fades in distance; and in time the last tarara-rattan of a drum is gone.

The dawn wind drones up from the sea. But the wind is alone.

Keith Laumer
Hybrid

Deep in the soil of the planet, rootlets tougher than steel wire
probed among glassy sand-grains, through packed veins of clay
and layers of flimsy slate, sensing and discarding inert elements,
seeking out calcium, iron, nitrogen.

Deeper still, a secondary system of roots clutched the massive
face of the bedrock; sensitive tendrils monitored the minute
trembling in the planetary crust, the rhythmic tidal pressures, the
seasonal weight of ice, the footfalls of the wild creatures that
hunted in the mile-wide shadow of the giant yanda tree.

On the surface far above, the immense trunk, massive as a cliff,
its vast girth anchored by mighty buttresses, reared up 900 yards
above the prominence, spreading huge limbs in the white sunlight.

The tree was only remotely aware of the movement of air over
the polished surfaces of innumerable leaves, the tingling exchange
of molecules of water, carbon dioxide, oxygen. Automatically it
reacted to the faint pressures of the wind, tensing slender twigs to
hold each leaf at a constant angle to the radiation that struck
down through the foliage complex.

The long day wore on. Air flowed in intricate patterns; radiation waxed and waned and the drift of vapour massed in the
substratosphere; nutrient molecules moved along capillaries; the
rocks groaned gently in the dark under the shaded slopes. In the
invulnerability of its titanic mass, the tree dozed in a state of
generalized low-level consciousness.

The sun moved westward. Its light, filtered through an increasing depth of atmosphere, was an ominous yellow now. Sinewy
twigs rotated, following the source of energy. Somnolently, the
tree retracted tender buds against the increasing cold, adjusted its
rate of heat and moisture loss, its receptivity to radiation. As it

slept, it dreamed of the long past, the years of free wandering in the faunal stage, before the instinct to root and grow had driven it here. It remembered the grove of its youth, the patriarchal tree, the spore-brothers . . .

It was dark now. The wind was rising. A powerful gust pressed against the ponderous obstacle of the tree; great thews of major branches creaked, resisting; chilled leaves curled tight against the smooth bark.

Deep underground, fibres hugged rock, transmitting data which were correlated with impressions from distant leaf surfaces. There were ominous vibrations from the north-east; relative humidity was rising, air pressure falling – a pattern formed, signalling danger. The tree stirred; a tremor ran through the mighty branch system, shattering fragile frost crystals that had begun to form on shaded surfaces. Alertness stirred in the heart-brain, dissipating the euphoric dream-pattern. Reluctantly, long-dormant faculties came into play. The tree awoke.

Instantly, it assessed the situation. A storm was moving in off the sea – a major typhoon. It was too late for effective measures. Ignoring the pain of unaccustomed activity, the tree sent out new shock roots – cables three inches in diameter, strong as stranded steel – to grip the upreared rock slabs a hundred yards north of the tap root.

There was nothing more the tree could do. Impassively, it waited the onslaught of the storm.

'That's a storm down there,' Malpry said.

'Don't worry; we'll miss it.' Gault fingered controls, eyes on dial faces.

'Pull up and make a new approach,' Malpry said, craning his neck from his acceleration cradle.

'Shut up. I'm running this tub.'

'Locked in with two nuts,' Malpry said. 'You and the creep.'

'Me and the creep are getting tired of listening to you bitch, Mal.'

'When we land, Malpry, I'll meet you outside,' Pantelle said. 'I told you I don't like the name "Creep".'

'What, again?' Gault said. 'You all healed up from the last time?'

'Not quite; I don't seem to heal very well in space.'

'Permission denied, Pantelle,' Gault said. 'He's too big for you. Mal, leave him alone.'

'I'll leave him alone,' Malpry muttered. 'I ought to dig a hole and leave him in it . . .'

'Save your energy for down there,' Gault said. 'If we don't make a strike on this one, we've had it.'

'Captain, may I go along on the field reconnaissance? My training in biology—'

'You better stay with the ship, Pantelle. And don't tinker. Just wait for us. We haven't got the strength to carry you back.'

'That was an accident, Captain—'

'And the time before. Skip it, Pantelle. You mean well, but you've got two left feet and ten thumbs.'

'I've been working on improving my co-ordination, Captain. I've been reading—'

The ship buffeted sharply as guidance vanes bit into atmosphere; Pantelle yelped.

'Oh-oh,' he called. 'I'm afraid I've opened up that left elbow again.'

'Don't bleed on me, you clumsy slob,' Malpry said.

'Quiet!' Gault said between his teeth. 'I'm busy.'

Pantelle fumbled a handkerchief in place over the cut. He would have to practise those relaxing exercises he had read about. And he would definitely start in weight-lifting soon – and watching his diet. And he would be very careful this time and land at least one good one on Malpry, just as soon as they landed.

Even before the first outward signs of damage appeared, the tree knew that it had lost the battle against the typhoon. In the lull as the eye of the storm passed over, it assessed the damage. There was no response from the north-east quadrant of the sensory network where rootlets had been torn from the rock face; the tap root itself seated now against pulverized stone. While the almost indestructible fibre of the yanda tree had held firm, the granite had failed. The tree was doomed by its own mass.

Now, mercilessly, the storm struck again, thundering out of the south-west to assault the tree with blind ferocity. Shock cables snapped like gossamer; great slabs of rock groaned and parted, with detonations lost in the howl of the wind. In the trunk, pressures built, agonizingly.

Four hundred yards south of the tap root, a crack opened in the sodden slope, gaping wider. Wind-driven water poured in, softening the soil, loosening the grip of a million tiny rootlets. Now the major roots shifted, slipping...

Far above, the majestic crown of the yanda tree yielded imperceptibly to the irresistible torrent of air. The giant north buttress, forced against the underlying stone, shrieked as tortured cells collapsed, then burst with a shattering roar audible even above the storm. A great arc of earth to the south, uplifted by exposed roots, opened a gaping cavern.

Now the storm moved on, thundered down the slope trailing its retinue of tattered debris and driving rain. A last vengeful gust whipped branches in a final frenzy; then the victor was gone.

And on the devastated promontory, the stupendous mass of the ancient tree leaned with the resistless inertia of colliding moons to the accompaniment of a cannonade of parting sinews, falling with dream-like grace.

And in the heart-brain of the tree consciousness faded in the unendurable pain of destruction.

Pantelle climbed down from the open port, leaned against the ship to catch his breath. He was feeling weaker than he expected. Tough luck, being on short rations; this would set him back on getting started on his weight-lifting programme. And he didn't feel ready to take on Malpry yet. But just as soon as he had some fresh food and fresh air—

'These are safe to eat,' Gault called, wiping the analyser needle on his pants leg and thrusting it back into his hip pocket. He tossed two large red fruits to Pantelle.

'When you get through eating, Pantelle, you better get some water and swab down the inside. Malpry and I'll take a look around.'

The two moved off. Pantelle sat on the springy grass, and bit into the apple-sized sphere. The texture, he thought, was reminiscent of avocado. The skin was tough and aromatic; possibly a natural cellulose acetate. There seemed to be no seeds. That being the case, the thing was not properly a fruit at all. It would be interesting to study the flora of this planet. As soon as he reached home, he would have to enroll in a course in ET botany. Possibly he would go to Heidelberg or Uppsala, attend live lectures by eminent scholars. He would have a cosy little apartment – two rooms would do – in the old part of town, and in the evening he would have friends in for discussions over a bottle of wine—

However, this wasn't getting the job done. There was a glint of water across the slope. Pantelle finished his meal, gathered his buckets, and set out.

'Why do we want to wear ourselves out?' Malpry said.

'We need the exercise. It'll be four months before we get another chance.'

'What are we, tourists, we got to see the sights?' Malpry stopped, leaned against a boulder, panting. He stared upward at the crater and the pattern of uptilted roots and beyond at the forest-like spread of the branches of the fallen tree.

'Makes our sequoias look like dandelions,' Gault said. 'It must have been the storm, the one we dodged coming in.'

'So what?'

'A thing that big – it kind of does something to you.'

'Any money in it?' Malpry sneered.

Gault looked at him sourly. 'Yeah, you got a point there. Let's go.'

'I don't like leaving the Creep back there with the ship.'

Gault looked at Malpry. 'Why don't you lay off the kid?'

'I don't like loonies.'

'Don't kid me, Malpry. Pantelle is highly intelligent – in his own way. Maybe that's what you can't forgive.'

'He gives me the creeps.'

'He's a nice-looking kid; he means well—'

'Yeah,' Malpry said. 'Maybe he means well – but it's not enough...'

From the delirium of concussion, consciousness returned slowly to the tree. Random signals penetrated the background clatter of shadowy impulses from maimed senses—

'Air pressure zero; falling . . . air pressure 112, rising . . . air pressure negative . . .

'Major tremor radiating from— Major tremor radiating from—

'Temperature 171 degrees, temperature −40 degrees, temperature 26 degrees . . .

'Intense radiation in the blue only . . . red only . . . ultraviolet . . .

'Relative humidity infinite . . . wind from north-north-east, velocity infinite . . . wind rising vertically, velocity infinite . . . wind from east, west . . .'

Decisively, the tree blanked off the yammering nerve-trunks, narrowing its attention to the immediate status-concept. A brief assessment sufficed to reveal the extent of its ruin.

There was no reason, it saw, to seek extended personal survival. However, certain immediate measures were necessary to gain time for emergency spore-propagation. At once, the tree-mind triggered the survival syndrome. Capillaries spasmed, forcing vital juices to the brain. Synaptic helices dilated, heightening neural conductivity. Cautiously, awareness was extended to the system of major fibres, then to individual filaments and interweaving capillaries.

Here was the turbulence of air molecules colliding with ruptured tissues, the wave pattern of light impinging on exposed surfaces. Microscopic filaments contracted, cutting off fluid loss through the wounds.

Now the tree-mind fine-tuned its concentration, scanning the infinitely patterned cell matrix. Here, amid confusion, there was order in the incessant restless movement of particles, the flow of fluids, the convoluted intricacy of the alphaspiral. Delicately, the tree-mind readjusted the function-mosaic, in preparation for spore-generation.

* * *

Malpry stopped, shaded his eyes. A tall thin figure stood in the shade of the uptilted root mass on the ridge.

'Looks like we headed back at the right time,' Malpry said.

'Damn,' Gault said. He hurried forward. Pantelle came to meet him.

'I told you to stay with the ship, Pantelle!'

'I finished my job, Captain. You didn't say—'

'OK, OK. Is anything wrong?'

'No, sir. But I've just remembered something—'

'Later, Pantelle. Let's get back to the ship. We've got work to do.'

'Captain, do you know what this is?' Pantelle gestured toward the gigantic fallen tree.

'Sure; it's a tree.' He turned to Malpry. 'Let's—'

'Yes, but what kind?'

'Beats me. I'm no botanist.'

'Captain, this is a rare species. In fact, it's supposed to be extinct. Have you ever heard of the yanda?'

'No. Yes.' Gault looked at Pantelle. 'Is that what this is?'

'I'm sure of it. Captain, this is a very valuable find—'

'You mean it's worth money?' Malpry was looking at Gault.

'I don't know. What's the story, Pantelle?'

'An intelligent race, with an early animal phase; later, they root, become fixed, functioning as a plant. Nature's way of achieving the active competition necessary for natural selection, then the advantage of conscious selection of a rooting-site.'

'How do we make money on it?'

Pantelle looked up at the looming wall of the fallen trunk, curving away among the jumble of shattered branches, a hundred feet, two hundred, more, in diameter. The bark was smooth, almost black. The foot-wide leaves were glossy, varicoloured.

'This great tree—'

Malpry stooped, picked up a fragment from a burst root.

'This great club,' he said, 'to knock your lousy brains out with—'

'Shut up, Mal.'

'It lived, roamed the planet perhaps 10,000 years ago, in the young faunal stage. Then instinct drove it here, to fulfil the cycle of nature. Picture this ancient champion, looking for the first time out across the valley, saying his farewells as metamorphosis begins.'

'Nuts,' Malpry said.

'His was the fate of all males of his kind who lived too long, to stand for ever on some height of land, to remember through unending ages the brief glory of youth, himself his own heroic monument.'

'Where do you get all that crud?' Malpry said.

'Here was the place,' Pantelle said. 'Here all his journeys ended.'

'OK, Pantelle. Very moving. You said something about this thing being valuable.'

'Captain, this tree is still alive, for a while at least. Even after the heart is dead, the appearance of life will persevere. A mantle of new shoots will leaf out to shroud the cadaver, tiny atavistic plantlets without connection to the brain, parasitic to the corpse, identical to the ancestral stock from which the giants sprang, symbolizing the extinction of a hundred million years of evolution.'

'Get to the point.'

'We can take cuttings from the heart of the tree. I have a book – it gives the details on the anatomy – we can keep the tissues alive. Back in civilization, we can regenerate the tree – brain and all. It will take time—'

'Suppose we sell the cuttings.'

'Yes, any university would pay well—'

'How long will it take?'

'Not long. We can cut in with narrow-aperture blasters—'

'OK. Get your books, Pantelle. We'll give it a try.'

Apparently, the yanda mind observed, a very long time had elapsed since spore-propagation had last been stimulated by the proximity of a female. Withdrawn into introverted dreams, the tree had taken no conscious notice as the whispering contact with the spore-brothers faded and the host-creatures dwindled away. Now, eidetically, the stored impressions sprang into clarity.

It was apparent that no female would pass this way again. The yanda kind was gone. The fever of instinct that had motivated the elaboration of the mechanisms of emergency propagation had burned itself out futilely. The new pattern of stalked oculi gazed unfocused at an empty vista of gnarled jungle growth, the myriad filaments of the transfer nexus coiled quiescent, the ranked grasping members that would have brought a host-creature near drooped unused, the dran-sacs brimmed needlessly; no further action was indicated. Now death would come in due course.

Somewhere a drumming began, a gross tremor sensed through the dead hush. It ceased, began again, went on and on. It was of no importance, but a faint curiosity led the tree to extend a sensory filament, tap the abandoned nerve-trunk—

Convulsively, the tree-mind recoiled, severing the contact. An impression of smouldering destruction, impossible thermal activity . . .

Disoriented, the tree-mind considered the implications of the searing pain. A freak of damaged sense organs? A phantom impulse from destroyed nerves?

No. The impact had been traumatic, but the data were there. The tree-mind re-examined each synaptic vibration, reconstructing the experience. In a moment, the meaning was clear: A fire was cutting deep into the body of the tree.

Working hastily, the tree assembled a barrier of incombustible molecules in the path of the fire, waited. The heat reached the barrier, hesitated – and the barrier flashed into incandescence.

A thicker wall was necessary.

The tree applied all of its waning vitality to the task. The shield grew, matched the pace of the fire, curved out to intercept—

And wavered, halted. The energy demand was too great. Starved muscular conduits cramped. Blackness closed over the disintegrating consciousness.

Sluggishly, clarity returned. Now the fire would advance unchecked. Soon it would by-pass the aborted defences, advance to consume the heart-brain itself. There was no other countermeasure remaining. It was unfortunate, since propagation had not been consummated, but unavoidable. Calmly the tree awaited its destruction by fire.

Pantelle put the blaster down, sat on the grass and wiped tarry soot from his face.

'What killed 'em off?' Malpry asked suddenly.

Pantelle looked at him.

'Spoilers,' he said.

'What's that?'

'They killed them to get the *dran*. They covered up by pretending the yanda were a menace, but it was the *dran* they were after.'

'Don't you ever talk plain?'

'Malpry, did I ever tell you I didn't like you?'

Malpry spat. 'What's with this *dran*?'

'The yanda have a very strange reproductive cycle. In an emergency, the spores released by the male tree can be implanted in almost any warm-blooded creature and carried in the body for an indefinite length of time. When the host animal mates, the dormant spores come into play. The offspring appears perfectly normal; in fact, the spore steps in and corrects any defects in the individual, repairs injuries, fights disease, and so on; and the lifespan is extended; but eventually the creature goes through the metamorphosis, roots, and becomes a regular male yanda tree – instead of dying of old age.'

'You talk too much. What's this *dran*?'

'The tree releases a hypnotic gas to attract host animals. In concentrated form, it's a potent narcotic. That's *dran*. They killed the trees to get it. The excuse was that the yanda could make humans give birth to monsters. That was nonsense. But it sold in the black market for fabulous amounts.'

'How do you get the *dran*?'

Pantelle looked at Malpry. 'Why do you want to know?'

Malpry looked at the book which lay on the grass. 'It's in that, ain't it?'

'Never mind that. Gault's orders were to help me get the heart-cuttings.'

'He didn't know about the *dran*.'

'Taking the *dran* will kill the specimen. You can't—'

Malpry stepped toward the book. Pantelle jumped toward him, swung a haymaker, missed. Malpry knocked him spinning.

'Don't touch me, Creep.' He wiped his fist on his pants leg.

Pantelle lay stunned. Malpry thumbed the book, found what he wanted. After ten minutes, he dropped the book, picked up the blaster and moved off.

Malpry cursed the heat, wiping at his face. A many-legged insect scuttled away before him. Underfoot, something furtive rustled. One good thing, no animals in this damned woods bigger than a mouse. A hell of a place. He'd have to watch his step; it wouldn't do to get lost in here . . .

The velvety wall of the half-buried trunk loomed, as dense growth gave way suddenly to a clear stretch. Malpry stopped, breathing hard. He got out his sodden handkerchief, staring up at the black wall. A ring of dead-white stalks sprouted from the dead tree. Nearby were other growths, like snarls of wiry black seaweed, and ropy looking things, dangling—

Malpry backed away, snarling. Some crawling disease, some kind of filthy fungus— But—

Malpry stopped. Maybe this was what he was looking for. Sure, this was what those pictures in the book showed. This was where the *dran* was. But he didn't know it would look like some creeping—

'Stop, Malpry!'

Malpry whirled.

'Don't be so . . . stupid . . .' Pantelle was gasping for breath. There was a bruise on his jaw. 'Let me rest . . . Talk to you . . .'

'Die, you gutter-scraping. Have a nice long rest. But don't muck with me.' Malpry turned his back on Pantelle, unlimbered the blaster.

Pantelle grabbed up a broken limb, slammed it across Malpry's head. The rotten wood snapped. Malpry staggered, recovered. He turned, his face livid; a trickle of blood ran down.

'All right, Creep,' he grated. Pantelle came to him, swung a whistling right arm, bent awkwardly. Malpry lunged, and Pantelle's elbow caught him across the jaw. His eyes went glassy, he sagged, fell to his hands and knees. Pantelle laughed aloud.

Malpry shook his head, breathing hoarsely, got to his feet. Pantelle took aim and hit him solidly on the jaw. The blow seemed to clear Malpry's head. He slapped a second punch aside, knocked Pantelle full-length with a backhanded blow. He dragged Pantelle to his feet, swung a hard left and right. Pantelle bounced, lay still. Malpry stood over him, rubbing his jaw.

He stirred Pantelle with his foot. Maybe the Creep was dead. Laying his creeping hands on Malpry. Gault wouldn't like it, but the Creep had started it. Sneaked up and hit him from behind. He had the mark to prove it. Anyway, the news about the *dran* would cheer Gault up. Better go get Gault up here. Then they could cut the *dran* out and get away from this creeping planet. Let the Creep bleed.

Malpry turned back toward the ship, leaving Pantelle huddled beside the fallen tree.

The yanda craned external oculi to study the fallen creature, which had now apparently entered a dormant phase. A red exudation oozed from orifices at the upper end, and from what appeared to be breaks in the epidermis. It was a strange creature, bearing some superficial resemblance to the familiar host creatures. Its antics, and those of the other, were curious indeed. Perhaps they were male and female, and the encounter had been a mating. Possibly this hibernation was normal process, preparatory to rooting. If only it were not so alien, it might serve as a carrier . . .

The surface of the organism heaved, a limb twitched. Apparently it was on the verge of reviving. Soon it would scurry away and be seen no more. It could be wise to make a quick examination; if the creature should prove suitable as a host . . .

Quickly the tree elaborated a complex of tiny filaments, touched the still figure tentatively, then penetrated the surprisingly soft surface layer, seeking out nerve fibres. A trickle of impressions flowed in, indecipherable. The tree put forth a major sensory tendril, divided and subdivided it into fibres only a few atoms in diameter, fanned them out through the unconscious man, tracing the spinal column, entering the brain—

Here was a wonder of complexity, an unbelievable profusion of connections. This was a centre capable of the highest intellectual functions – unheard of in a host creature. Curiously, the tree-mind probed deeper, attuning itself, scanning through a kaleidoscope of impressions, buried memories, gaudy symbolisms.

Never had the yanda-mind encountered the hyper-intellectual processes of emotion. It pressed on, deeper into the phantasmagoria of dreams—

Colour, laughter and clash of arms. Banners rippling in the sun, chords of a remote music and night-blooming flowers. Abstractions of incredible beauty mingled with vivid conceptualizations of glory. Fascinated, the tree-mind explored Pantelle's secret romantic dreams of fulfilment—

And abruptly encountered the alien mind.

There was a moment of utter stillness as the two minds assessed each other.

You are dying, the alien mind spoke.

Yes. And you are trapped in a sickly host creature. Why did you not select a stronger host?

I . . . originated here. I . . . we . . . are one.

Why do you not strengthen this host?

How?

The yanda-mind paused. *You occupy only a corner of the brain. You do not use your powers?*

I am a segment . . . The alien mind paused, confused. *I am conceptualized by the monitor-mind as the subconscious.*

What is the monitor-mind?

It is the totality of the personality. It is above the conscious, directing . . .

This is a brain of great power, yet great masses of cells are unused. Why are major trunks aborted as they are?

I do not know.

There was no more information from the alien brain which, indeed, housed multiple minds.

The yanda-mind broke contact, tuned.

There was a blast of mind-force, overwhelming. The yanda-mind reeled, groped for orientation.

YOU ARE NOT ONE OF MY MINDS.

You are the monitor-mind? gasped the yanda.

YES. WHAT ARE YOU?

The yanda-mind projected its self-concept.

STRANGE, VERY STRANGE. YOU HAVE USEFUL SKILLS, I PERCEIVE. TEACH THEM TO ME.

The yanda-mind squirmed under the torrent of thought impulses.

Reduce your volume. You will destroy me.

I WILL TRY. TEACH ME THAT TRICK OF MANIPULATING MOLECULES.

The yanda cringed under the booming of the alien mind. What an instrument! A fantastic anomaly, a mind such as this linked to this fragile host creature – and unable even to use its powers. But it would be a matter of the greatest simplicity to make the necessary corrections, rebuild and toughen the host, eliminate the defects—

TEACH ME, YANDA-MIND!

Alien, I die soon. But I will teach you. There is, however, a condition . . .

The two minds conferred, and reached agreement. At once, the yanda-mind initiated sweeping rearrangements at the submolecular level.

First, cell-regeneration, stitching up the open lesions on arm and head. Antibodies were modified in vast numbers, flushed through the system. Parasites died.

Maintain this process, the tree-mind directed.

Now, the muscular layers; surely they were inadequate. The very structure of the cells was flimsy. The yanda devised the necessary improvements, tapped the hulk of its cast-off body for materials, reinforced the musculature. Now for the skeletal members . . .

The tree visualized the articulation of the ambulatory mechanism, considered for a moment the substitution of a more practical tentacular concept—

There was little time. Better to retain the stony bodies, merely strengthen them, using metallo-vegetable fibres. The air sacs, too. And the heart. They would have lasted no time at all as they were.

Observe, alien, thus and thus . . .

I SEE. IT IS A CLEVER TRICK.

The yanda worked over the body of Pantelle, adjusting, correcting, reinforcing, discarding a useless appendix or tonsil here, adding a reserve air-storage unit there. A vestigial eye deep in the brain was refurbished for sensitivity at the radio frequencies, linked with controls. The spine was deftly fused at the base; additional mesenteries were added for intestinal support. Following the basic pattern laid down in the genes, the tree-mind rebuilt the body.

When the process was finished, and the alien mind had absorbed the techniques demonstrated, the yanda-mind paused.

It is finished.

I AM READY TO RE-ESTABLISH THE CONSCIOUS MIND IN OVERT CONTROL.

Remember your promise.

I WILL REMEMBER.

The yanda-mind began its withdrawal. Troublesome instinct was served. Now it could rest until the end.

WAIT. I'VE GOT A BETTER IDEA, YANDA . . .

'Two weeks down and fourteen to go,' Gault said. 'Why don't you break down and tell me what happened back there?'

'How's Malpry?' Pantelle asked.

'He's all right. Broken bones knit, and you only broke a few.'

'The book was wrong about the yanda spores,' Pantelle said. 'They don't have the power in themselves to reconstruct the host creature—'

'The what?'

'The infected animal; the health and life-span of the host is improved. But the improvement is made by the tree, at the time of propagation, to insure a good chance for the spores.'

'You mean you—'

'We made a deal. The yanda gave me this—' Pantelle pressed a thumb against the steel bulkhead. The metal yielded.

'– and a few other tricks. In return, I'm host to the yanda spores.'

Gault moved away.

'Doesn't that bother you? Parasites—'

'It's an equitable deal. The spores are microscopic, and completely dormant until the proper conditions develop.'

'Yeah, but you said yourself this vegetable brain has worked on your mind.'

'It merely erased all the scars of traumatic experience, corrected deficiencies, taught me how to use what I have.'

'How about teaching me?'

'Sorry, Gault.' Pantelle shook his head. 'Impossible.'

Gault considered Pantelle's remarks.

'What about these "proper conditions" for the spores?' he asked suddenly. 'You wake up and find yourself sprouting some morning?'

'Well,' Pantelle coughed. 'That's where my part of the deal comes in. A host creature transmits the spores through the normal mating process. The offspring gets good health and a long life before the metamorphosis. That's not so bad – to live a hundred years, and then pick a nice spot to root and grow and watch the seasons turn . . .'

Gault considered. 'A man does get tired,' he said. 'I know a spot, where you can look for miles out across the Pacific . . .'

'So I've promised to be very active,' Pantelle said. 'It will take a lot of my time, but I intend to discharge my obligation to the fullest.'

Did you hear that, yanda? Pantelle asked silently.

I did, came the reply from the unused corner he had assigned to the yanda ego-pattern. *Our next thousand years should be very interesting.*

Pamela Zoline
The heat death of the Universe

1. ONTOLOGY: That branch of metaphysics which concerns itself with the problems of the nature of existence or being.

2. Imagine a pale-blue morning sky, almost green, with clouds only at the rims. The earth rolls and the sun appears to mount, mountains erode, fruits decay, the Foraminifera adds another chamber to its shell, babies' fingernails grow as does the hair of the dead in their graves, and in egg-timers the sands fall and the eggs cook on.

3. Sarah Boyle thinks of her nose as too large, though several men have cherished it. The nose is generous and performs a well-calculated geometric curve, at the arch of which the skin is drawn very tight and a faint whiteness of bone can be seen showing through; it has much the same architectural tension and sense of mathematical calculation as the day-after-Thanksgiving breastbone on the carcase of turkeys. Her maiden name was Sloss, mixed German, English and Irish descent. In grade school she was very bad at playing softball and, besides being chosen last for the team, was always made to play centre field; no one could ever hit to centre field. She loves music best of all the arts, and of music Bach, J. S. She lives in California, though she grew up in Boston and Toledo.

4. BREAKFAST-TIME AT THE BOYLES' HOUSE ON LA FLORIDA STREET, ALAMEDA, CALIFORNIA. THE CHILDREN DEMAND SUGAR FROSTED FLAKES.
With some reluctance Sarah Boyle dishes out Sugar Frosted Flakes to her children, already hearing the decay set in upon the little milk-white teeth, the bony whine of the dentist's drill. The dentist is a short, gentle man with a moustache who sometimes

reminds Sarah of an uncle who lives in Ohio. One bowl per child.

5. If one can imagine it considered as an abstract object by members of a totally separate culture, one can see that the cereal box might seem a beautiful thing. The solid rectangle is neatly joined and classical in proportions; on it are squandered wealths of richest colours, virgin blues, crimsons, dense ochres, precious pigments once reserved for sacred paintings and as cosmetics for the blind faces of marble gods. Giant size. Net Weight 16 ounces, 250 grammes. 'They're tigeriffic!' says Tony the Tiger. The box blats promises: Energy, Nature's Own Goodness, an endless pubescence. On its back is a mask of William Shakespeare to be cut out, folded, worn by thousands of tiny Shakespeares in Kansas City, Detroit, Tucson, San Diego, Tampa. He appears at once more kindly and somewhat more vacant than we are used to seeing him. Two or more of the children lay claim to the mask, but Sarah puts off that Solomon's decision until such time as the box is empty.

6. A notice in orange flourishes states that a Surprise Gift is to be found somewhere in the package, nestled amongst the golden flakes. So far it has not been unearthed, and the children request more cereal than they wish to eat, great yellow heaps of it, to hurry the discovery. Even so, at the end of the meal, some layers of flakes remain in the box and the Gift must still be among them.

7. There is even a Special Offer of a secret membership, code and magic ring; these to be obtained by sending in the box top with 50 cents.

8. Three offers on one cereal box. To Sarah Boyle this seems to be oversell. Perhaps something is terribly wrong with the cereal and it must be sold quickly, got off the shelves before the news breaks. Perhaps it causes a special cruel Cancer in little children. As Sarah Boyle collects the bowls printed with bunnies and baseball statistics, still slopping half-full of milk and wilted flakes, she imagines *in her mind's eye* the headlines. 'Nation's Small Fry Stricken, Fate's Finger Sugar-Coated, Lethal Sweetness Socks Tots.'

9. Sarah Boyle is a vivacious and intelligent young wife and mother, educated at a fine Eastern college, proud of her growing family which keeps her busy and happy around the house.

10. BIRTHDAY.
Today is the birthday of one of the children. There will be a party in the late afternoon.

11. CLEANING UP THE HOUSE, ONE.
Cleaning up the kitchen. Sarah Boyle puts the bowls, plates, glasses and silverware into the sink. She scrubs at the stickiness on the yellow-marbled formica table with a blue synthetic sponge, a special blue which we shall see again. There are marks of children's hands in various sizes printed with sugar and grime on all the table's surfaces. The marks catch the light; they appear and disappear according to the position of the observing eye. The floor sweepings include a triangular half of toast spread with grape jelly, bobby pins, a green Band-Aid, flakes, a doll's eye, dust, dog's hair and a button.

12. Until we reach the statistically likely planet and begin to converse with whatever green-faced, teleporting denizens thereof – considering only this shrunk and communication-ravaged world – can we any more postulate a separate culture? Viewing the metastasis of Western Culture it seems progressively less likely. Sarah Boyle imagines a whole world which has become like California, all topographical imperfections sanded away with the sweet-smelling burr of the plastic surgeon's cosmetic polisher; a world populace dieting, leisured similar in pink and mauve hair and rhinestone shades. A land Cunt Pink and Avocado Green, brassièred and girdled by monstrous complexities of Super Highways, a California endless and unceasing, embracing and transforming the entire globe, California, California!

13. INSERT ONE. ON ENTROPY.
ENTROPY: A quantity introduced in the first place to facilitate the calculations, and to give clear expressions to the results of thermodynamics. Changes of entropy can be calculated only for a reversible process, and may then be defined as the ratio of the amount

of heat taken up to the absolute temperature at which the heat is absorbed. Entropy changes for actual irreversible processes are calculated by postulating equivalent theoretical reversible changes. The entropy of a system is a measure of its degree of disorder. The total entropy of any isolated system can never decrease in any change; it must either increase (irreversible process) or remain constant (reversible process). The total entropy of the Universe therefore is increasing, tending towards a maximum, corresponding to complete disorder of the particles in it (assuming that it may be regarded as an isolated system). See *Heat death of the Universe*.

14. CLEANING UP THE HOUSE, TWO.
Washing the baby's diapers, Sarah Boyle writes notes to herself all over the house; a mazed wild script larded with arrows, diagrams, pictures; graffiti on every available surface in a desperate/heroic attempt to index, record, bluff, invoke, order and placate. On the fluted and flowered white plastic lid of the diaper-bin she has written in Blushing Pink Nitetime lipstick a phrase to ward off fumy ammoniac despair. 'The nitrogen cycle is the vital round of organic and inorganic exchange on earth. The sweet breath of the Universe.' On the wall by the washing machine are Yin and Yang signs, mandalas, and the words 'Many young wives feel trapped. It is a contemporary sociological phenomenon which may be explained in part by a gap between changing living patterns and the accommodation of social services to these patterns.' Over the stove she had written, 'Help, Help, Help, Help, Help.'

15. Sometimes she numbers or letters the things in a room, writing the assigned character on each object. There are 819 separate movable objects in the living-room, counting books. Sometimes she labels objects with their names, or with false names; thus on her bureau the hair brush is labelled HAIR BRUSH, the cologne COLOGNE, the hand cream CAT. She is passionately fond of children's dictionaries, encyclopaedias, ABCs and all reference books, transfixed and comforted at their simulacra of a complete listing and ordering.

16. On the door of a bedroom are written two definitions from reference books, 'GOD: An object of worship'; 'HOMEOSTASIS:

Maintenance of constancy of internal environment.'

17. Sarah Boyle washes the diapers, washes the linen. Oh, Saint Veronica, changes the sheets on the baby's crib. She begins to put away some of the toys, stepping over and around the organizations of playthings which still seem inhabited. There are various vehicles, and articles of medicine, domesticity and war; whole zoos of stuffed animals, bruised and odorous with years of love; hundreds of small figures, plastic animals, cowboys, cars, spacemen, with which the children make sub and supra worlds in their play. One of Sarah's favourite toys is the Baba, the wooden Russian doll which, opened, reveals a smaller but otherwise identical doll which opens to reveal, etc., a lesson in infinity at least to the number of seven dolls.

18. Sarah Boyle's mother has been dead for two years. Sarah Boyle thinks of music as the formal articulation of the passage of time, and of Bach as the most poignant rendering of this. Her eyes are sometimes the colour of the aforementioned kitchen sponge. Her hair is natural spaniel brown; months ago on a hysterical day she dyed it red, so now it is two-toned with a stripe in the middle, like the painted walls of slum buildings or old schools.

19. INSERT TWO. THE HEAT DEATH OF THE UNIVERSE.
The second law of thermodynamics can be interpreted to mean that the ENTROPY of a closed system tends towards a maximum and that its available ENERGY tends towards a minimum. It has been held that the Universe constitutes a thermodynamically closed system, and if this were true it would mean that a time must finally come when the Universe 'unwinds' itself, no energy being available for use. This state is referred to as the 'heat death of the Universe'. It is by no means certain, however, that the Universe can be considered as a closed system in this sense.

20. Sarah Boyle pours out a Coke from the refrigerator and lights a cigarette. The coldness and sweetness of the thick brown liquid

make her throat ache and her teeth sting briefly, sweet juice of my youth, her eyes glass with the carbonation, she thinks of the Heat Death of the Universe. A logarithmic of those late summer days, endless as the Irish serpent twisting through jewelled manuscripts for ever, tail in mouth, the heat pressing, bloating, doing violence. The Los Angeles sky becomes so filled and bleached with detritus that it loses all colour and silvers like a mirror, reflecting back the fricasséeing earth. Everything becoming warmer and warmer, each particle of matter becoming more agitated, more excited until the bonds shatter, the glues fail, the deodorants lose their seals. She imagines the whole of New York City melting like a Dali into a great chocolate mass, a great soup, the Great Soup of New York.

21. CLEANING UP THE HOUSE, THREE.
Beds made. Vacuuming the hall, a carpet of faded flowers, vines and leaves which endlessly wind and twist into each other in a fevered and permanent ecstasy. Suddenly the vacuum blows instead of sucks, spewing marbles, dolls' eyes, dust, crackers. An old trick. 'Oh, my god,' says Sarah. The baby yells on cue for attention/changing/food. Sarah kicks the vacuum cleaner and it retches and begins working again.

22. AT LUNCH ONLY ONE GLASS OF MILK IS SPILLED.
At lunch only one glass of milk is spilled.

23. The plants need watering, Geranium, Hyacinth, Lavender, Avocado, Cyclamen. Feed the fish, happy fish with china castles and mermaids in the bowl. The turtle looks more and more unwell and is probably dying.

24. Sarah Boyle's blue eyes, how blue? Bluer far and of a different quality than the Nature metaphors which were both engine and fuel to so much of precedent literature. A fine, modern, acid, synthetic blue; the shiny cerulean of the skies on postcards sent from lush subtropics, the natives grinning ivory ambivalent grins in their dark faces; the promising, fat, unnatural blue of the heavy-tranquillizer capsule; the cool, mean blue of that fake kitchen

sponge; the deepest, most unbelievable azure of the tiled and mossless interiors of California swimming-pools. The chemists in their kitchens cooked, cooled and distilled this blue from thousands of colourless and wonderfully constructed crystals, each one unique and nonpareil; and now that colour hisses, bubbles, burns in Sarah's eyes.

25. INSERT THREE. ON LIGHT.
LIGHT: Name given to the agency by means of which a viewed object influences the observer's eyes. Consists of electro-magnetic radiation within the wave-length range 4×10^{-5} cm to 7×10^{-5} cm approximately; variations in the wave-length produce different sensations in the eye, corresponding to different colours. See *Colour vision*.

26. LIGHT AND CLEANING THE LIVING-ROOM.
All the objects (819) and surfaces in the living-room are dusty, grey common dust as though this were the den of a giant, moulting mouse. Suddenly quantities of waves or particles of very strong sunlight speed in through the window, and everything incandesces, multiple rainbows. Poised in what has become a solid cube of light, like an ancient insect trapped in amber, Sarah Boyle realizes that the dust is indeed the most beautiful stuff in the room, a manna for the eyes. Duchamp, that father of thought, has set with fixative some dust which fell on one of his sculptures, counting it as part of the work. 'That way madness lies, says Sarah,' says Sarah. The thought of ordering a household on Dada principles balloons again. All the rooms would fill up with objects, newspapers and magazines would compost, the potatoes in the rack, the canned green beans in the garbage can would take new heart and come to life again, reaching out green shoots towards the sun. The plants would grow wild and wind into a jungle around the house, splitting plaster, tearing shingles, the garden would enter in at the door. The goldfish would die, the birds would die, we'd have them stuffed; the dog would die from lack of care, and probably the children – all stuffed and sitting around the house, covered with dust.

27. INSERT FOUR. DADA.

DADA (Fr., 'hobby-horse') was a nihilistic precursor of Surrealism, invented in Zürich during the First World War, a product of hysteria and shock lasting from about 1915 to 1922. It was deliberately anti-art and anti-sense, intended to outrage and scandalize, and its most characteristic production was the reproduction of the 'Mona Lisa' decorated with a moustache and the obscene caption LHOOQ (read: 'Elle a chaud au cul') 'by' Duchamp. Other manifestations included Arp's collages of coloured paper cut out at random and shuffled, ready-made objects such as the bottle drier and the bicycle wheel 'signed' by Duchamp, Picabia's drawings of bits of machinery with incongruous titles, incoherent poetry, a lecture given by 38 lecturers in unison, and an exhibition in Cologne in 1920, held in an annex to a café lavatory, at which a chopper was provided for spectators to smash the exhibits with – which they did.

28. TIME-PIECES AND OTHER MEASURING DEVICES.

In the Boyle house there are four clocks; three watches (one a Mickey Mouse watch which does not work); two calendars and two engagement-books; three rulers, a yardstick; a measuring-cup; a set of red plastic measuring-spoons which includes a tablespoon, a teaspoon, a one-half teaspoon, one-fourth teaspoon and one-eighth teaspoon; an egg-timer; an oral thermometer and a rectal thermometer; a Boy Scout compass; a barometer in the shape of a house, in and out of which an old woman and an old man chase each other for ever without fulfilment; a bathroom scale; an infant scale; a tape measure which can be pulled out of a stuffed felt strawberry; a wall on which the children's heights are marked; a metronome.

29. Sarah Boyle finds a new line in her face after lunch while cleaning the bathroom. It is as yet barely visible, running from the midpoint of her forehead to the bridge of her nose. By inward curling of her eyebrows she can etch it clearly as it will come to appear in the future. She marks another mark on the wall where she has drawn out a scoring-area. Face Lines and Other Intima-

tions of Mortality, the heading says. There are thirty-two marks, counting this latest one.

30. Sarah Boyle is a vivacious and witty young wife and mother, educated at a fine Eastern college, proud of her growing family which keeps her happy and busy around the house, involved in many hobbies and community activities, and only occasionally given to obsessions concerning Time/Entropy/Chaos and Death.

31. Sarah Boyle is never quite sure how many children she has.

32. Sarah thinks from time to time; Sarah is occasionally visited with this thought; at times this thought comes upon Sarah, that there are things to be hoped for, accomplishments to be desired beyond the mere reproductions, mirror reproduction of one's kind. The babies. Lying in bed at night sometimes the memory of the act of birth, always the hue and texture of red-plush theatre-seats, washes up; the rending which always, at a certain intensity of pain, slipped into landscapes, the sweet breath of the sweating nurse. The wooden Russian doll has bright, perfectly round red spots on her cheeks; she splits in the centre to reveal a doll smaller but in all other respects identical with round bright red spots on her cheeks, etc.

33. How fortunate for the species, Sarah muses or is mused, that children are as ingratiating as we know them. Otherwise they would soon be salted off for the leeches they are, and the race would extinguish itself in a fair sweet flowering, the last generations' massive achievement in the arts and pursuits of high civilization. The finest women would have their tubes tied off at the age of twelve, or perhaps refrain altogether from the Act of Love? All interests would be bent to a refining and perfecting of each febrile sense, each fluid hour, with no more cowardly investment in immortality via the patchy and too often disappointing vegetables of one's own womb.

34. INSERT FIVE. LOVE.
LOVE: A typical sentiment involving fondness for, or attachment to, an object, the idea of which is emotionally coloured whenever

it arises in the mind, and capable, as Shand has pointed out, of evoking any one of a whole gamut of primary emotions, according to the situation in which the object is placed, or represented; often, and by psychoanalysts always, used in the sense of *sex-love* or even *lust* (q.v.).

35. Sarah Boyle has at times felt a unity with her body, at other times a complete separation. The mind/body duality considered. The time/space duality considered. The male/female duality considered. The matter/energy duality considered. Sometimes, at extremes, her Body seems to her an animal on a leash, taken for walks in the park by her Mind. The lamp-posts of experience. Her arms are lightly freckled, and when she gets very tired the places under her eyes become violet.

36. Housework is never completed, the chaos always lurks ready to encroach on any area left unweeded, a jungle filled with dirty pans and the roaring of giant stuffed toy animals suddenly turned savage. Terrible glass eyes.

37. SHOPPING FOR THE BIRTHDAY CAKE.
Shopping in the supermarket with the baby in front of the cart and a larger child holding on. The light from the ice-cube-tray-shaped fluorescent lights is mixed blue and pink and brighter, colder, and cheaper than daylight. The doors swing open just as you reach out your hand for them. Tantalus, moving with a ghastly quiet swing. Hot dogs for the party. Potato chips, gum drops, a paper tablecloth with birthday designs, hot-dog buns, catsup, mustard, piccalilli, balloons, instant coffee Continental style, dog food, frozen peas, ice cream, frozen lima beans, frozen broccoli in butter sauce, paper birthday-hats, paper napkins in three colours, a box of Sugar Frosted Flakes with a Wolfgang Amadeus Mozart mask on the back, bread, pizza mix. The notes of a just graspable music filter through the giant store, for the most part by-passing the brain and acting directly on the liver, blood and lymph. The air is delicately scented with aluminium. Half-and-half cream, tea bags, bacon, sandwich meat, strawberry jam. Sarah is in front of the shelves of cleaning products now, and the baby is beginning

to whine. Around her are whole libraries of objects, offering themselves. Some of that same old hysteria that had incarnadined her hair rises up again, and she does not refuse it. There is one moment when she can choose direction, like standing on a chalk-drawn X, a hot-cross bun, and she does not choose calm and measure. Sarah Boyle begins to pick out, methodically, deliberately and with a careful ecstasy, one of every cleaning product which the store sells. Window Cleaner, Glass Cleaner, Brass Polish, Silver Polish, Steel Wool, eighteen different brands of Detergent, Disinfectant, Toilet Cleanser, Water Softener, Fabric Softener, Drain Cleanser, Spot Remover, Floor Wax, Furniture Wax, Car Wax, Carpet Shampoo, Dog Shampoo. Shampoo for people with dry, oily and normal hair, for people with dandruff, for people with grey hair, Tooth Paste, Tooth Powder, Denture Cleaner, Deodorants, Antiperspirants, Antiseptics, Soaps, Cleansers, Abrasives, Oven Cleaners, Make-up Removers. When the same products appear in different sizes Sarah takes one of each size. For some products she accumulates whole little families of containers: a giant Father bottle of shampoo, a Mother bottle, an Older Sister bottle just smaller than the Mother bottle, and a very tiny Baby Brother bottle. Sarah fills three shopping-carts and has to have help wheeling them all down the aisles. At the check-out counter her laughter and hysteria keep threatening to overflow as the pale-blonde clerk with no eyebrows like the 'Mona Lisa' pretends normality and disinterest. The bill comes to $57.53 and Sarah has to write a cheque. Driving home, the baby strapped in the drive-a-cot and the paper bags bulging in the back seat, she cries.

38. BEFORE THE PARTY.

Mrs David Boyle, mother-in-law of Sarah Boyle, is coming to the party of her grandchild. She brings a toy, a yellow wooden duck on a string, made in Austria; the duck quacks as it is pulled along the floor. Sarah is filling paper cups with gum drops and chocolates, and Mrs David Boyle sits at the kitchen table and talks to her. She is talking about several things. She is talking about her garden which is flourishing except for a plague of rare black beetles, thought to have come from Hong Kong, which are undermining some of the most delicate growths at the roots, and feasting on the leaves of other plants. She is talking about a sale of household linens which she plans to attend on the following Tuesday. She is talking about her neighbour who has Cancer and is wasting away. The neighbour is a Catholic woman who had never had a day's illness in her life until the Cancer struck, and now she is, apparently, failing with dizzying speed. The doctor says her body's chaos, chaos, cells running wild all over, says Mrs David Boyle. When I visited her she hardly *knew* me, can hardly *speak*, can't keep herself *clean*, says Mrs David Boyle.

39. Sometimes Sarah can hardly remember how many cute, chubby little children she has.

40. When she used to stand out in centre field far away from the other players, she used to make up songs and sing them to herself.

41. She thinks of the end of the world by ice.

42. She thinks of the end of the world by water.

43. She thinks of the end of the world by nuclear war.

44. There must be more than this, Sarah Boyle thinks, from time to time. What could one do to justify one's passage? Or, less ambitiously, to change, even in the motion of the smallest mote, the course and circulation of the world? Sometimes Sarah's dreams are of heroic girth, a new symphony using laboratories of machinery and all invented instruments, at once giant in scope and intelligible to all, to heal the bloody breach; a series of paintings which would transfigure and astonish and calm the frenzied art world in its panting race; a new novel that would refurbish language. Sometimes she considers the mystical, the streaky and random, and it seems that one change, no matter how small, would be enough. Turtles are supposed to live for many years. To carve a name, date and perhaps a word of hope upon a turtle's shell, then set him free to wend the world, surely this one act might cancel out absurdity?

45. Mrs David Boyle has a faint moustache, like Duchamp's 'Mona Lisa'.

46. THE BIRTHDAY PARTY.

Many children, dressed in pastels, sit around the long table. They are exhausted and overexcited from games fiercely played, some are flushed and wet, others unnaturally pale. This general agitation and the paper party-hats they wear combine to make them appear a dinner party of debauched midgets. It is time for the cake. A huge chocolate cake in the shape of a rocket and launching-pad and covered with blue and pink icing is carried in. In the hush the birthday child begins to cry. He stops crying, makes a wish and blows out the candles.

47. One child will not eat hot dogs, ice cream or cake, and asks for cereal. Sarah pours him out a bowl of Sugar Frosted Flakes, and a moment later he chokes. Sarah pounds him on the back and out spits a tiny green plastic snake with red glass eyes, the Surprise Gift. All the children want it.

48. AFTER THE PARTY THE CHILDREN ARE PUT TO BED.

Bath-time. Observing the nakedness of children, pink and slippery as seals, squealing as seals, now the splashing, grunting and smacking of cherry flesh on raspberry flesh reverberate in the pearl-tiled steamy cubicle. The nakedness of children is so much more absolute than that of the mature. No musky curling hair to indicate the target points, no knobbly clutch of plane and fat and curvature to ennoble this prince of beasts. All well-fed naked children appear edible. Sarah's teeth hum in her head with memory of bloody feastings, prehistory. Young humans appear too like the young of other species for smugness, and the comparison is not even in their favour, they are much the most peeled and unsupple of those young. Such pinkness, such utter nuded pinkness; the orifices neatly incised, rimmed with a slightly deeper rose, the incessant demands for breast, time, milks of many sorts.

49. INSERT SIX. WEINER ON ENTROPY.

In Gibbs' Universe order is least probable, chaos most probable. But while the Universe as a whole, if indeed there is a whole Universe, tends to run down, there are local enclaves whose direction seems opposed to that of the Universe at large and in which there is a limited and temporary tendency for organization to increase. Life finds its home in some of these enclaves.

50. Sarah Boyle imagines, in her mind's eye, cleaning and ordering the whole world, even the Universe. Filling the great spaces of Space with a marvellous sweet-smelling, deep-cleansing foam. Deodorizing rank caves and volcanoes. Scrubbing rocks.

51. INSERT SEVEN. TURTLES.
Many different species of carnivorous Turtles live in the fresh waters of the tropical and temperate zones of various continents. Most northerly of the European Turtles (extending as far as Holland and Lithuania) is the European Pond Turtle (*Emys orbicularis*). It is from 8 to 10 inches long and may live a hundred years.

52. CLEANING UP AFTER THE PARTY.
Sarah is cleaning up after the party. Gum drops and melted ice cream surge off paper plates, making holes in the paper tablecloth through the printed roses. A fly has died a splendid death in a pool of strawberry ice cream. Wet jelly beans stain all they touch, finally becoming themselves colourless, opaque white like flocks of tamed or sleeping maggots. Plastic favours mount half-eaten pieces of blue cake. Strewn about are thin strips of fortune papers from the Japanese poppers. Upon them are printed strangely assorted phrases selected by apparently unilingual Japanese. Crowds of delicate yellow people spending great chunks of their lives in producing these most ephemeral of objects, and inscribing thousands of fine papers with absurd and incomprehensible messages. 'The very hairs of your head are all numbered,' reads one. Most of the balloons have popped. Someone has planted a hot dog in the daffodil pot. A few of the helium balloons have escaped their owners and now ride the ceiling. Another fortune-paper reads, 'Emperor's horses meet death worse, numbers, numbers.'

53. She is very tired, violet under the eyes, mauve beneath the eyes. Her uncle in Ohio used to get the same marks under his eyes. She goes to the kitchen to lay the table for tomorrow's breakfast, then she sees that in the turtle's bowl the turtle is floating, still, on the surface of the water. Sarah Boyle pokes at it with a pencil but

it does not move. She stands for several minutes looking at the dead turtle on the surface of the water. She is crying again.

54. She begins to cry. She goes to the refrigerator and takes out a carton of eggs, white eggs, extra large. She throws them one by one on to the kitchen floor which is patterned with strawberries in squares. They break beautifully. There is a Secret Society of Dentists, all moustached, with Special Code and Magic Rings. She begins to cry. She takes up three bunny dishes and throws them against the refrigerator; they shatter, and then the floor is covered with shards, chunks of partial bunnies, an ear, an eye here, a paw; Stockton, California, Acton, California, Chico, California, Redding, California, Glen Ellen, California, Cadiz, California, Angels Camp, California, Half Moon Bay. The total ENTROPY of the Universe therefore is increasing, tending towards a maximum, corresponding to complete disorder of the particles in it. She is crying, her mouth is open. She throws a jar of grape jelly and it smashes the window over the sink. Her eyes are blue. She begins to open her mouth. It has been held that the Universe constitutes a thermodynamically closed system, and if this were true it would mean that a time must finally come when the Universe 'unwinds' itself, no energy being available for use. This state is referred to as the 'heat death of the Universe'. Sarah Boyle begins to cry. She throws a jar of strawberry jam against the stove; enamel chips off and the stove begins to bleed. Bach had twenty children. How many children has Sarah Boyle? Her mouth is open. Her mouth is opening. She turns on the water and fills the sinks with detergent. She writes on the kitchen wall, 'William Shakespeare has Cancer and lives in California.' She writes, 'Sugar Frosted Flakes are the Food of the Gods.' The water foams up in the sink, overflowing, bubbling on to the strawberry floor. She is about to begin to cry. Her mouth is opening. She is crying. She cries. How can one ever tell whether there are one or many fish? She begins to break glasses and dishes, she throws cups and cooking-pots and jars of food which shatter and break and spread over the kitchen. The sand keeps falling, very quietly, in the egg-timer. The old man and woman in the barometer never catch each other. She picks up

eggs and throws them into the air. She begins to cry. She opens her mouth. The eggs arch slowly through the kitchen, like a base-ball, hit high against the spring sky, seen from far away. They go higher and higher in the stillness, hesitate at the zenith, then begin to fall away slowly, slowly, through the fine, clear air.

Roger Zelazny
Devil car

Murdock sped across the Great Western Road Plain.

High above him the sun was a fiery yo-yo as he took the in-numerable hillocks and rises of the Plain at better than 160 miles an hour. He did not slow for anything, and Jenny's hidden eyes spotted all the rocks and potholes before they came to them, and she carefully adjusted their course, sometimes without his even detecting the subtle movements of the steering-column beneath his hands.

Even through the dark-tinted windshield and the thick goggles he wore, the glare from the fused Plain burnt into his eyes, so that at times it seemed as if he were steering a very fast boat through night, beneath a brilliant alien moon, and that he was cutting his way across a lake of silver fire. Tall dust-waves rose in his wake, hung in the air, and after a time settled once more.

'You are wearing yourself out,' said the radio, 'sitting there clutching the wheel that way, squinting ahead. Why don't you try to get some rest? Let me fog the shields. Go to sleep and leave the driving to me.'

'No,' he said. 'I want it this way.'

'All right,' said Jenny. 'I just thought I would ask.'

'Thanks.'

About a minute later the radio began playing – it was a soft, stringy sort of music.

'Cut that out!'

'Sorry, boss. Thought it might relax you.'

'When I need relaxing, *I'll* tell *you*.'

'Check, Sam. Sorry.'

The silence seemed oppressive after its brief interruption. She was a good car, though Murdock knew that. She was always concerned with his welfare, and she was anxious to get on with his quest.

She was made to look like a carefree Swinger sedan: bright red, gaudy, fast. But there were rockets under the bulges of her hood, and two fifty-calibre muzzles lurked just out of sight in the recesses beneath her headlamps; she wore a belt of five- and ten-second timed grenades across her belly; and in her trunk was a spray-tank containing a highly volatile naphthalic.

For his Jenny was a specially designed deathcar, built for him by the Archengineer of the Geeyem Dynasty, far to the east, and all the cunning of that great artificer had gone into her construction.

'We'll find it this time, Jenny,' he said, 'and I didn't mean to snap at you like I did.'

'That's all right, Sam,' said the delicate voice. 'I am programmed to understand you.'

They roared on across the Great Plain and the sun fell away to the west. All night and all day they had searched, and Murdock was tired. The last fuel-stop/rest-stop fortress seemed so long ago, so far back . . .

Murdock leaned forward, and his eyes closed.

The windows slowly darkened into complete opacity. The seat belt crept higher and drew him back away from the wheel. Then the seat gradually leaned backward until he was reclining on a level plane. The heater came on as the night approached, later.

The seat shook him awake a little before five in the morning.

'Wake up, Sam! Wake up!'

'What is it?' he mumbled.

'I picked up a broadcast twenty minutes ago. There was a recent car-raid out this way. I changed course immediately, and we are almost there.'

'Why didn't you get me up right away?'

'You needed the sleep, and there was nothing you could do but get tense and nervous.'

'OK, you're probably right. Tell me about the raid.'

'Six vehicles, proceeding westward, were apparently ambushed by an undetermined number of wild cars sometime last night. The Patrol Copter was reporting it from above the scene and I listened in. All the vehicles were stripped and drained and their brains were smashed, and their passengers were all apparently killed too. There were no signs of movement.'

'How far is it now?'

'Another two or three minutes.'

The windshields came clear once more, and Murdock stared as far ahead through the night as the powerful lamps could cut.

'I see something,' he said, after a few moments.

'This is the place,' said Jenny, and she began to slow down.

They drew up beside the ravaged cars. His seat belt unsnapped, and the door sprang open on his side.

'Circle around, Jenny,' he said, 'and look for heat tracks. I won't be long.'

The door slammed, and Jenny moved away from him. He snapped on his pocket torch and moved toward the wrecked vehicles.

The Plain was like a sandstrewn dance-floor – hard and gritty – beneath his feet. There were many skid-marks, and a spaghetti-work of tyre tracks lay all about the area.

A dead man sat behind the wheel of the first car. His neck was obviously broken. The smashed watch on his wrist said 2.24. There were three persons – two women and a young man – lying about forty feet away. They had been run down as they tried to flee from their assaulted vehicles.

Murdock moved on, inspected the others. All six cars were up-right. Most of the damage was to their bodies. The tyres and wheels had been removed from all of them, as well as essential portions of their engines; the gas tanks stood open, siphoned empty; the spare tyres were gone from the sprung trunks. There were no living passengers.

Jenny pulled up beside him, and her door opened.

'Sam,' she said, 'pull the brain leads on that blue car, the third one back. It's still drawing some energy from an auxiliary battery, and I can hear it broadcasting.'

'Okay.'

Murdock went back and tore the leads free. He returned to Jenny and climbed into the driver's seat.

'Did you find anything?'

'Some traces, heading north-west.'

'Follow them.'

The door slammed, and Jenny turned in that direction.

They drove for about five minutes in silence. Then Jenny said: 'There were eight cars in that convoy.'

'What?'

'I just heard it on the news. Apparently two of the cars communicated with the wild ones on an off-band. They threw in with them. They gave away their location and turned on the others at the time of the attack.'

'What about their passengers?'

'They probably mono'd them before they joined the pack.'

Murdock lit a cigarette, his hands shaking.

'Jenny, what makes a car run wild?' he asked. 'Never knowing where it will get its next fuelling – or being sure of finding spare parts for its auto-repair unit? Why do they do it?'

'I do not know, Sam. I have never thought about it.'

'Ten years ago the Devil Car, their leader, killed my brother in a raid on his gas fortress,' said Murdock, 'and I've hunted that black Caddy ever since. I've searched for it from the air and I've searched on foot. I've used other cars. I've carried heat trackers and missiles. I even laid mines. But always it's been too fast or too smart or too strong for me. Then I had you built.'

'I knew you hated it very much. I always wondered why,' Jenny said.

Murdock drew on his cigarette.

'I had you specially programmed and armoured and armed to be the toughest, fastest, smartest thing on wheels, Jenny. You're the Scarlet Lady. You're the one car can take the Caddy and his whole pack. You've got fangs and claws of the kind they've never met before. This time I'm going to get them.'

'You could have stayed home, Sam, and let me do the hunting.'

'No. I know I could have, but I want to be there. I want to give the orders, to press some of the buttons myself, to watch that

Devil Car burn away to a metal skeleton. How many people, how many cars has it smashed? We've lost count. I've got to get it, Jenny!'

'I'll find it for you, Sam.'

They sped on, at around 200 miles an hour.

'How's the fuel level, Jenny?'

'Plenty there, and I have not yet drawn upon the auxiliary tanks. Do not worry.'

'– The track is getting stronger,' she added.

'Good. How's the weapons system?'

'Red light, all around. Ready to go.'

Murdock snubbed out his cigarette and lit another.

'Some of them carry dead people strapped inside,' said Murdock, 'so they'll look like decent cars with passengers. The black Caddy does it all the time, and it changes them pretty regularly. It keeps its interior refrigerated – so they'll last.'

'You know a lot about it, Sam.'

'It fooled my brother with phoney passengers and phoney plates. Got him to open his gas fortress to it that way. Then the whole pack attacked. It's painted itself red and green and blue and white, on different occasions, but it always goes back to black, sooner or later. It doesn't like yellow or brown or two-tone. I've a list of almost every phoney plate it's ever used. It's even driven the big freeways right into towns and fuelled up at regular gas-stops. They often get its number as it tears away from them, just as the attendant goes up on the driver's side for his money. It can fake dozens of human voices. They can never catch it afterwards, though, because it's souped itself up too well. It always makes it back here to the Plain and loses them. It's even raided used-car lots—'

Jenny turned sharply in her course.

'Sam! The trail is quite strong now. *This* way! It goes off in the direction of those mountains.'

'Follow!' said Murdock.

For a long time then Murdock was silent. The first inklings of morning began in the east. The pale morning star was a white thumbtack on a blue board behind them. They began to climb a gentle slope.

'Get it, Jenny. Go get it,' urged Murdock.

'I think we will,' she said.

The angle of the slope increased. Jenny slowed her pace to match the terrain, which was becoming somewhat bumpy.

'What's the matter?' asked Murdock.

'It's harder going here,' she said. 'Also, the trail is getting more difficult to follow.'

'Why is that?'

'There is still a lot of background radiation in these parts,' she told him, 'and it is throwing off my tracking system.'

'Keep trying, Jenny.'

'The track seems to go straight towards the mountains.'

'Follow it, follow it!'

They slowed some more.

'I am all fouled up now, Sam,' she said. 'I have just lost the trail.'

'It must have a stronghold somewhere around here – a cave or something like that – where it can be sheltered overhead. It's the only way it could have escaped aerial detection all these years.'

'What should I do?'

'Go as far forward as you can and scan for low openings in the rock. Be wary. Be ready to attack in an instant.'

They climbed into the low foothills. Jenny's aerial rose high into the air, and the moths of steel cheesecloth unfolded their wings and danced and spun about it, bright there in the morning light.

'Nothing yet,' said Jenny, 'and we can't go much further.'

'Then we'll cruise along the length of it and keep scanning.'

'To the right or to the left?'

'I don't know. Which way would you go if you were a renegade car on the lam?'

'I do not know.'

'Pick one. It doesn't matter.'

'To the right, then,' she said, and they turned in that direction.

*   *   *

After half an hour the night was dropping away behind the mountains. To his right morning was exploding at the far end of the Plain, fracturing the sky into all the colours of autumn trees. Murdock drew a squeeze-bottle of hot coffee, of the kind spacers had once used, from beneath the dashboard.

'Sam, I think I have found something.'

'What? Where?'

'Ahead, to the left of that big boulder, a declivity with some kind of opening at its end.'

'OK, baby, make for it. Rockets ready.'

They pulled abreast of the boulder, circled around its far side, headed downhill.

'A cave, or a tunnel,' he said. 'Go slow—'

'Heat! Heat!' she said. 'I'm tracking again!'

'I can even see tyre marks, lots of them!' said Murdock. 'This is it!'

They moved toward the opening.

'Go in, but go slowly,' he ordered, 'Blast the first thing that moves.'

They entered the rocky portal, moving on sand now. Jenny turned off her visible lights and switched to infra-red. An i-r lens rose before the windshield, and Murdock studied the cave. It was about twenty feet high and wide enough to accommodate perhaps three cars going abreast. The floor changed from sand to rock, but it was smooth and fairly level. After a time it sloped upward.

'There's some light ahead,' he whispered.

'I know.'

'A piece of the sky, I think.'

They crept toward it. Jenny's engine but the barest sigh within the great chambers of rock.

They stopped at the threshold to the light. The i-r shield dropped again.

It was a sand-and-shale canyon that he looked upon. Huge slantings and overhangs of rock hid all but the far end from any eye in the sky. The light was pale at the far end, and there was nothing unusual beneath it.

But nearer...
Murdock blinked.

Nearer, in the dim light of morning and in the shadows, stood the greatest junkheap Murdock had ever seen in his life.

Pieces of cars, of every make and model, were heaped into a small mountain before him. There were batteries and tyres and cables and shock absorbers; there were fenders and bumpers and headlamps and headlamp housings; there were doors and windshields and cylinders and pistons, carburettors, generators, voltage regulators, and oil pumps.

Murdock stared.

'Jenny,' he whispered, 'we've found the graveyard of the autos!'

A very old car, which Murdock had not even distinguished from the junk during that first glance, jerked several feet in their direction and stopped as suddenly. The sound of rivet heads scoring ancient brake drums screeched in his ears. Its tyres were completely bald, and the left front one was badly in need of air. Its right front headlamp was broken, and there was a crack in its windshield. It stood there before the heap, its awakened engine making a terrible rattling noise.

'What's happening?' asked Murdock. 'What is it?'

'He is talking to me,' said Jenny. 'He is very old. His speedometer has been all the way around so many times that he forgets the number of miles he has seen. He hates people, whom he says have abused him whenever they could. He is the guardian of the graveyard. He is too old to go raiding anymore, so he has stood guard over the spare-parts heap for many years. He is not the sort who can repair himself, as the younger ones do, so he must rely on their charity and their auto-repair units. He wants to know what I want here.'

'Ask him where the others are.'

But, as he said it, Murdock heard the sound of many engines turning over, until the valley was filled with the thunder of their horsepower.

'They are parked on the other side of the heap,' she said. 'They are coming now.'

'Hold back until I tell you to fire,' said Murdock, as the first car – a sleek yellow Chrysler – nosed around the heap.

Murdock lowered his head to the steering-wheel, but kept his eyes open behind his goggles.

'Tell them that you came here to join the pack and that you've mono'd your driver. Try to get the black Caddy to come into range.'

'He will not do it,' she said. 'I am talking with him now. He can broadcast just as easily from the other side of the pile, and he says he is sending the six biggest members of his pack to guard me while he decides what to do. He has ordered me to leave the tunnel and pull ahead into the valley.'

'Go ahead then – slowly.'

They crept forward.

Two Lincolns, a powerful-looking Pontiac, and two Mercs joined the Chrysler – three on each side of them, in position to ram.

'Has he given you any idea how many there are on the other side?'

'No. I asked, but he will not tell me.'

'Well, we'll just have to wait, then.'

He stayed slumped, pretending to be dead. After a time, his already-tired shoulders began to ache. Finally, Jenny spoke:

'He wants me to pull around the far end of the pile,' she said, 'now that they have cleared the way, and to head into a gap in the rock which he will indicate. He wants to have his auto-mech go over me.'

'We can't have that,' said Murdock, 'but head around the pile. I'll tell you what to do when I've gotten a glimpse of the other side.'

The two Mercs and the Big Chief drew aside, and Jenny crept past them. Murdock stared upwards from the corner of his eye, up at the towering mound of junk they were passing. A couple of well-placed rockets on either end could topple it, but the auto-mech would probably clear it eventually.

They rounded the left-hand end of the pile.

Something like forty-five cars were facing them at about 120 yards' distance, to the right and ahead. They had fanned out. They were blocking the exit around the other end of the pile, and the six guards in back of him now blocked the way behind Murdock.

On the far side of the farthest rank of the most distant cars an ancient black Caddy was parked.

It had been beaten forth from assembly during a year when the apprentice engineers were indeed thinking big. Huge it was, and shiny, and a skeleton's face smiled from behind its wheel. Black it was, and gleaming chromium, and its headlamps were like dusky jewels or the eyes of insects. Every plane and curve shimmered with power, and its great fishtailed rear end seemed ready to slap at the sea of shadows behind it on an instant's notice, as it sprang forward for its kill.

'That's it!' whispered Murdock. 'The Devil Car!'

'He is big!' said Jenny. 'I have never seen a car that big!'

They continued to move forward.

'He wants me to head into that opening and park,' she said.

'Head toward it, slowly. But don't go into it,' said Murdock.

They turned and inched toward the opening. The other cars stood, the sounds of their engines rising and falling.

'Check all weapons systems.'

'Red, all around.'

The opening was twenty-five feet away.

'When I say "now", go into neutral steer and turn 180 degrees – fast. They can't be expecting that. They don't have it themselves. Then open up with the fifty-calibres and fire your rockets at the Caddy, turn at a right angle and start back the way we came, and spray the naphtha as we go, and fire on the six guards . . .

'Now!' he cried, leaping up in his seat.

He was slammed back as they spun, and he heard the chattering of her guns before his head cleared. By then, flames were leaping up in the distance.

Jenny's guns were extruded now and turning on their mounts, spraying the line of vehicles with hundreds of leaden hammers. She shook, twice, as she discharged two rockets from beneath her partly opened hood. Then they were moving forward, and eight or nine of the cars were rushing downhill toward them.

She turned again in neutral steer and sprang back in the direction from which they had come, around the south-east corner of the pile. Her guns were hammering at the now retreating guards, and in the wide rear-view mirror Murdock could see that a wall of flame was towering high behind them.

'You missed it!' he cried. 'You missed the black Caddy! Your rockets hit the cars in front of it and it backed off!'

'I know! I'm sorry!'

'You had a clear shot!'

'I know! I missed!'

They rounded the pile just as two of the guard cars vanished into the tunnel. Three more lay in smoking ruin. The sixth had evidently preceded the other two out through the passage.

'Here it comes now!' cried Murdock. 'Around the other end of the pile! Kill it! Kill it!'

The ancient guardian of the graveyard – it looked like a Ford, but he couldn't be sure – moved forward with a dreadful chattering sound and interposed itself in the line of fire.

'My range is blocked.'

'Smash that junkheap and cover the tunnel! Don't let the Caddy escape!'

'I can't!' she said.

'Why not?'

'I just can't!'

'That's an order! Smash it and cover the tunnel!'

Her guns swivelled and she shot out the tyres beneath the ancient car.

The Caddy shot past and into the passageway.

'You let it get by!' he screamed. 'Get after it!'

'All right, Sam! I'm doing it! Don't yell. *Please don't yell!*'

She headed for the tunnel. Inside, he could hear the sound of a giant engine racing away, growing softer in the distance.

'Don't fire here in the tunnel! If you hit it we may be bottled in!'

'I know. I won't.'

'Drop a couple of ten-second grenades and step on the gas.

Maybe we can seal in whatever's left moving back there.'

Suddenly they shot ahead and emerged into daylight. There was no sign of any other vehicle about.

'Find it's track,' he said, 'and start chasing it.'

There was an explosion up the hill behind him, within the mountain. The ground trembled, then it was still once more.

'There are so many tracks . . .,' she said.

'You know the one I want. The biggest, the widest, the hottest! Find it! Run it down!'

'I think I have it, Sam.'

'Okay. Proceed as rapidly as possible for this terrain.'

Murdock found a squeeze-bottle of bourbon and took three gulps. Then he lit a cigarette and glared into the distance.

'Why did you miss it?' he asked softly. 'Why did you miss it, Jenny?'

She did not answer immediately. He waited.

Finally, 'Because he is not an "it" to me,' she said. 'He has done much damage to cars and people, and that is terrible. But there is something about him, something – noble. The way he has fought the whole world for his freedom. Sam, keeping that pack of vicious machines in line, stopping at nothing to maintain himself that way – without a master – for as long as he can remain un-smashed, unbeaten – Sam, for a moment back there I wanted to join his pack, to run with him across the Great Road Plains, to use my rockets against the gates of the gas forts for him . . . But I could not mono you, Sam, I was built for you. I am too domesti-cated. I am too weak. I could not shoot him, though, and I mis-fired the rockets on purpose. But I could never mono you, Sam, really.'

'Thanks,' he said, 'you over-programmed ashcan. Thanks a lot!'

'I am sorry, Sam.'

'Shut up— No, don't, not yet. First tell me what you're going to do if we find "him".'

'I don't know.'

'Well, think it over fast. You see that dust cloud ahead as well as I do, and you'd better speed up.'

They shot forward.

'Wait till I call Detroit. They'll laugh themselves silly, till I claim the refund.'

'I am *not* of inferior construction or design. You know that. I am just more . . .'

'"Emotional",' supplied Murdock.

'. . . Than I thought I would be,' she finished. 'I had not really met many cars, except for young ones, before I was shipped to you. I did not know what a wild car was like, and I had never smashed *any* cars before – just targets and things like that. I was young and . . .'

'"Innocent",' said Murdock. 'Yeah. Very touching. Get ready to kill the next car we meet. If it happens to be your boyfriend and you hold your fire, then he'll kill us.'

'I will try, Sam.'

The car ahead had stopped. It was the yellow Chrysler. Two of its tyres had gone flat and it was parked, lopsided, waiting.

'Leave it!' snarled Murdock, as the hood clicked open. 'Save the ammo for something that might fight back.'

They sped past it.

'Did it say anything?'

'Machine profanity,' she said. 'I've only heard it once or twice, and it would be meaningless to you.'

He chuckled. 'Cars actually swear at each other?'

'Occasionally,' she said. 'I imagine the lower sort indulge in it more frequently, especially on freeways and turnpikes when they become congested.'

'Let me hear a machine swear-word.'

'I will not. What kind of car do you think I am, anyway?'

'I'm sorry,' said Murdock. 'You're a lady. I forgot.'

There was an audible click within the radio.

They raced forward on the level ground that lay before the foot of the mountains. Murdock took another drink, then switched to coffee.

'Ten years,' he muttered, 'ten years, . . .'

The trail swung in a wide curve as the mountains jogged back and the foothills sprang up high beside them.

It was over almost before he knew it.

As they passed a huge, orange-coloured stone massif, sculpted like an upside-down toadstool by the wind, there was a clearing to the right.

It shot forward at them – the Devil Car. It had lain in ambush, seeing that it could not outrun the Scarlet Lady, and it rushed toward a final collision with its hunter.

Jenny skidded sideways as her brakes caught with a scream and a smell of smoke, and her fifty-calibres were firing, and her hood sprang open and her front wheels rose up off the ground as the rockets leapt wailing ahead, and she spun around three times, her rear bumper scraping the saltsand plain, and the third and last time she fired her remaining rockets into the smouldering wreckage on the hillside, and she came to rest on all four wheels: and her fifty-calibres kept firing until they were emptied, and then a steady clicking sound came from them for a full minute afterwards, and then all lapsed into silence.

Murdock sat there shaking, watching the gutted, twisted wreck blaze against the morning sky.

'You did it, Jenny. You killed him. You killed me the Devil Car,' he said.

But she did not answer him. Her engine started once more and she turned toward the south-east and headed for the fuel-stop/rest-stop fortress that lay in that civilized direction.

For two hours they drove in silence, and Murdock drank all his bourbon and all his coffee and smoked all his cigarettes.

'Jenny, say something,' he said. 'What's the matter? Tell me.'

There was a click, and her voice was very soft:

'Sam – he talked to me as he came down the hill . . .,' she said.

Murdock waited, but she did not say anything else.

'Well, what did he say?' he asked.

'He said, "Say you will mono your passenger and I will swerve by you",' she told him. 'He said, "I want you, Scarlet Lady – to run with me, to raid with me. Together they will never catch us," and I killed him.'

Murdock was silent.

'He only said that to delay my firing, though, did he not? He said that to stop me, so that he could smash us both when he went to smash himself, did he not? He could not have meant it, could he, Sam?'

'Of course not,' said Murdock, 'of course not. It was too late for him to swerve.'

'Yes, I suppose it was. Do you think, though, that he really wanted me to run with him, to raid with him – before everything. I mean – back there?'

'Probably, baby. You're pretty well equipped.'

'Thanks,' she said, and turned off again.

Before she did, though, he heard a strange mechanical sound, falling into the rhythms of profanity or prayer.

Then he shook his head and lowered it, softly patting the seat beside him with his still unsteady hand.

Michael Moorcock

The nature of the catastrophe

Introduction

The one-part actress

Miss Brunner was firm about it. With her lips pursed she stood in the school's dark doorway. She knew she had him over a barrel.

Pretending to ignore her, Jerry Cornelius leafed through the tattered copy of *Business Week*. 'The future that rides on Apollo 12 . . . Hunt for cancer vaccine closes in . . . What delayed the jumbo jets? . . . New sales pitch for disposables . . .'

Miss Brunner moved fast. She snatched the magazine from his hands.

'Look at me,' she said. 'Look at me.'

He looked at her. 'I'll be too many people by 1980. By 1980 I'll be dead,' he said.

Her nostrils flared. 'You've got to go.'

His legs trembled. 'It'll be murder.'

She smiled. 'It'll be murder,' she said, 'if you don't. Won't it?'

Jerry frowned. 'It had to come. Sooner or later.'

'It'll clear the air.'

'What fucking air?' He gave her a hurt look. 'Then?'

'Get busy, eh. You've got fifty years to play about in, after all.'

'Fuck you!'

'And we'll have no more of that.'

In the gym a wind-up gramophone played 'Bye, bye, Blackbird'.

Le fratricide de la rue Clary

Genes began to pop.

Scenes fractured.

Jerry screamed.

They took his bicycle away. It was a black gent's roadster: 'The Royal Albert'. He had kept it up nicely.

'Hang on tight, Mr Cornelius.'
'I'll bloody go where I . . .'
'This is it!'
The seedy street in Marseille disappeared.
He didn't mind that.

In the net
There was a drum beating somewhere and he could bet he knew who was beating it. Of all the superstitious notions he had encountered, the notion of 'the future' was the most ludicrous. He was really lumbered now.

Development
The nerve gas plant at Portreath, Cornwall, is a pilot establishment for the Ministry of Defence, which has been manufacturing small quantities of gas for some time. Mrs Compton said the widow of one victim had not been allowed to see the pathologist's report or any other medical papers on her husband.
The Guardian, *21 November 1969*

Fantasy review
After the gas attack Jerry Cornelius finished the washing-up and went out into the street. A rainbow had formed over Ladbroke Grove. Everything was very still. He bent to put on his bicycle clips.
'Jerry!'
'Yes, Mum?'
'You come back and dry up properly, you little bugger!'

The impatient dreamers
5 June 1928: Fifty-two years since Owen Nares and Jeanne de Casalis opened in Karen Bramson's *The Man They Buried* at the Ambassadors Theatre, London. The *Daily News* had said: '. . . at the end of all the tumult of life is "Time and the unresolved hypothesis".'

People like you
Jerry groped his way from the car and turned his sightless eyes

upward. Sunlight would not register. He was completely blind.

So it hadn't paid off.

Tears began to cruise down his cheeks.

'Mum?'

Somewhere in the distance the chatter of the Graf Zeppelin's engines died away.

He was abandoned.

Am I blue? You'd be too. If each plan with your man done fell through. Watcha gonna do? Watcha gonna do?

World to conquer

We regret to say that Prince Jewan Bukhy, son of the late Shah Bahudur Sha, the last titular King of Delhi, is dangerously ill . . . He is the last of his race that was born in the purple. He leaves a son, also in bad health, who was born in Rangoon while his father was in confinement. With Prince Jewan Bukhy passes away the last direct descendant of the once famous house of Timour.
Rangoon Times, *28 July 1884*

He struggled out of that.

Number 7

Jerry stumbled and fell, gashing his knee. He felt about him with his stone-cold hands. He touched something as smooth as steel. He stroked the surfaces. A discarded suit of armour? And yet everywhere now were sounds. Engines. Screams.

Didn't he know there was a war on? Was he making it back?

He heard a bus draw up nearby, its motor turning over.

He shouted.

There was silence again. A V2 silence.

Coming in on a wing and a prayer . . .

The ill wind

The rush of water.

He was grasping at anything now.

He should never have tried it. A certain amount of diffusion could have been anticipated, but nothing as terrifying as this. He'd been conned.

Distantly: *One o'clock, two o'clock, three o'clock rock . . .*

The adapters

There were strong sexual overtones which only became apparent as he concentrated, speaking aloud into the thinning air:

'Miss Jeanne de Casalis, who is the subject this week for our "Is the Child Mother to the Woman?" series . . .'

'My father, who came from *le pays Basque*, had gone to Basutoland for the purpose of scientific investigations in connection with cancer and probable cures for this terrible disease, when a baby was announced . . .'

'Once the best and most popular fellow at Greyfriars – now the worst boy in the school! Such is the unhappy pass to which Harry Wharton's feud with his form master leads him! You cannot . . .'

'Issued 15 July 1931, to be used to prepay postage on mail carried aboard the Graf Zeppelin on its prospective flight to the North Pole. It was on this voyage that the *Nautilus*, a submarine commanded by Sir Hubert Wilkins, was to meet the Graf Zeppelin and transfer mail from one ship to the other at the North Pole. The *Nautilus* did not keep the rendezvous.'

'Long Service Certificate. Presented by the Board of Directors to Ernest Frederick Cornelius of the W. D. & H. O. Wills Branch of the Imperial Tobacco Company (of Great Britain and Ireland) Limited, in Recognition of Faithful Service Rendered During the Past 25 Years and as a Mark of Appreciation and Goodwill. Signed on Behalf of the Board, Date 28 March 1929. Gilbert A. H. Wills, Chairman.'

'Georges Duhamel, who has discovered a serum for cancer, is suddenly stricken with pain. He lives for the rest of the play in dread expectation of death. His whole nature changes . . . [He] will not face an operation, because that will proclaim to the world that his serum is a failure.'

Jerry closed the scrapbook and opened the stamp album. It contained hundreds of Zeppelin issues from Paraguay, Liechtenstein, Latvia, Italy, Iceland, Greece, Germany, Cyrenaica, Cuba, Canada, Brazil, the Argentine, the Aegean Islands, the United States of America, San Marino, Russia. There were also a couple of Spanish autogiro issues and an Italian issue showing Leonardo da Vinci's flying machine.

From the little linen envelope beside the album, Jerry took with his tweezers his latest discovery, a set of Salvador airmail stamps issued on 15 September 1930. The stamps had become so brittle that they would split unless handled with great care. They were deep red (15¢), emerald green (20¢), brown violet (25¢), ultramarine (40¢) and all showed a biplane flying over San Salvador. This issue had just preceded the Simon Bolivar airmail issue of 17 December 1930.

'Jerry! You get down outa there an' 'elp yer mum!'

Jerry was oscillating badly.

The merit award

Jerry wandered over the bombsite, kicking at bits of broken brick. The catharsis had come at last, then. But wasn't it a trifle disappointing?

Now he could go for miles and nothing would interrupt him.

Taking an apple from his pocket, he bit it, then spat, flinging the apple away. It had tasted of detergent.

He looked down at his hands. They were red and grey and they shook. He sat on a slab of broken concrete. Nothing moved. Nothing sang.

Shapers of men

Changes in jewellery design styles tend to take place over a period of many years. In the past one could think in terms of millennia, centuries or generations, at the very least. Not so today.
Brian Marshall, Illustrated London News, *22 November 1969*

Coming next issue

Jerry wondered why the scene had got so hazy. A few buildings stood out sharply, but everything else was drowned in mist. He put the Phantom X into reverse.

He wished they'd let him keep his bike.

How little time you were allowed for yourself. Twenty-five years at most. The rest belonged to and was manipulated by the ghosts of the past, the ghosts of the future. A generation was a hundred and fifty years. There was no escape.

A rocket roared by.

When the red, red robin comes bob, bob, bobbin' . . .

Prisoner in the ice

By 1979, industrial technology will make the sixties seem like the dark ages. Automatic highways – computerised kitchens – person-to-person television – food from under the sea. They are ideas today, but industrial technology will make them a part of your life tomorrow . . . Our measuring devices are so accurate they're used by the US Bureau of Standards to measure other measuring devices. Our fasteners were selected for the space suits on the men who walked the moon. Our plastic parts are in almost every automobile made in the USA.

In these ways, and more, we help make today's ideas tomorrow's realities.

US Industries Inc., ad., New York Times, *16 October 1969*

'The waterline length is 1004 ft, and when completed her tonnage will probably exceed 73,000. The *Queen Mary*'s maiden voyage (from Southampton to New York) begins on 27 May 1936 . . .'

'Britain's toy soldiers have been . . .'

'By 1980 there will be . . .'

His voice was hoarse now. Fifty years was too long. He had no one, and no one to blame but himself.

Little man you're crying; I know why you're blue . . .

Lucifer!

A hundred and fifty years itched in his skull and yet he could not get back to the only year in which he could survive.

From time to time his sight would return, allowing him horrifying visions – fragments of newspapers, buildings, roadways, cars, planes, skulls, ruins, ruins, ruins.

'MUM!'

'DAD!'

(CRASHED CONCORDE HAD RECEIVED FULL OVERHAUL)

'CATHY!'

'FRANK!'

(MARS MEN BACK IN DOCK)

'GRANDMA!'

'GRANDPA!'

(CHINESE MAKE FRESH GAINS)

'JERRY!'

(METS DO IT AGAIN – TEN IN A ROW!)

'Je . . .'

His voice whispered into near-vacuum.

If only he had been allowed to bring his 'Royal Albert' bike. It would have seen him through. It would have been an anchor.

But he was alone.

'M . . .'

Rootless, he was dying.

The cold was absolute. His body fell away from him.

The resurrection, if it came, would be painful.

Conclusion

A man of qualities

'That's a boy!'

'That's what you say.' Jerry had had enough of it all. He shivered.

They unstrapped him from the chair. 'Don't you feel better now?'

Jerry glanced around the Time Centre. All the chronographs were going like clockwork. 'I told you it didn't exist,' he said, 'because I don't exist. Not there.'

'It was worth a try, though, wasn't it?'

Jerry bunched himself up and tried to stop shaking.

A kind and thoughtful friend

'It boils down to a question of character, doesn't it?' Miss Brunner said. 'Character. Character.'

She always knew how to get to him. She always chose a moment when his energy was at a low ebb.

He looked miserably up from the desk, hoping to touch her heart.

She knew he was confused. 'And if,I told your mother . . .'

He lowered his head again. Maybe it would all blow over.

It's a beautiful, glamorous age

It had all gone now, of course. He'd used up the last of it. No more past to draw on. He felt at his skin.

'Smooth,' he said.

'You see.' She held her thin body in an attitude of triumph. 'It was all for the best.'

Other texts used:
The Sketch, 13 January 1926
The Bystander, 5 October 1927
T.P.'s Weekly, 26 November 1927
Daily Mail, 15 December 1927
Le Petit Marseillais, 22 October 1930
The Story of Navigation, Card No. 50, published by
The Imperial Tobacco Co., 1935
Standard Catalogue of Air Post Stamps, Sanabria, New York, 1937
Modern Boy, 9 July 1938
The Illustrated Weekly of India, 6 July 1969
Vision of Tomorrow, November 1939

Robert Silverberg
Hawksbill Station

1

Barrett was the uncrowned king of Hawksbill Station. He had
been there the longest; he had suffered the most; he had the
deepest inner resources.

Before his accident, he had been able to whip any man in the
place. Now he was a cripple, but he still had that aura of power.
When there were problems at the Station, they were brought to
Barrett. That was axiomatic. He was the king.

He ruled over quite a kingdom, too. In effect it was the whole
world, pole to pole, meridian to meridian. For what it was worth.
It wasn't worth very much.

Now it was raining again. Barrett shrugged himself to his feet
in the quick, easy gesture that cost him an infinite amount of
carefully concealed agony and shuffled to the door of his hut.
Rain made him impatient; the pounding of those great greasy
drops against the corrugated tin roof was enough even to drive a
Jim Barrett loony. He nudged the door open. Standing in the
doorway, Barrett looked out over his kingdom.

Barren rock, nearly to the horizon. A shield of raw dolomite
going on and on. Raindrops danced and bounced on that continental slab of rock. No trees. No grass. Behind Barrett's hut lay
the sea, grey and vast. The sky was grey too, even when it wasn't
raining.

He hobbled out into the rain. Manipulating his crutch was
getting to be simple for him now. He leaned comfortably, letting
his crushed left foot dangle. A rockslide had pinned him last year
during a trip to the edge of the Inland Sea. Back home, Barrett
would have been fitted with prosthetics: a new ankle, a new in-
step, refurbished ligaments and tendons. But home was a billion
years away; and home there's no returning.

The rain hit him hard. Barrett was a big man, six and a half feet tall, with hooded dark eyes, a jutting nose, a chin that was a monarch among chins. He had weighed 250 pounds in his prime, in the good old agitating days when he had carried banners and pounded out manifestoes. But now he was past sixty and beginning to shrink a little, the skin getting loose around the places where the mighty muscles used to be. It was hard to keep your weight in Hawksbill Station. The food was nutritious, but it lacked intensity. A man got to miss steak. Eating brachiopod stew and trilobite hash wasn't the same thing. Barrett was past all bitterness, though. That was another reason why the men regarded him as the leader. He didn't scowl. He didn't rant. He was resigned to his fate, tolerant of eternal exile, and so he could help the others get over that difficult heart-clawing period of transition.

A figure arrived, jogging through the rain. Norton. The doctrinaire Khrushchevist with the Trotskyite leanings. A small, excitable man who frequently appointed himself messenger whenever there was news at the Station. He sprinted toward Barrett's hut, slipping and sliding over the naked rocks.

Barrett held up a meaty hand. 'Whoa, Charley. Take it easy or you'll break your neck!'

Norton halted in front of the hut. The rain had pasted the widely spaced strands of his brown hair to his skull. His eyes had the fixed, glossy look of fanaticism – or perhaps just astigmatism. He gasped for breath and staggered into the hut, shaking himself like a wet puppy. He obviously had run all the way from the main building of the Station, 300 yards away.

'Why are you standing around in the rain?' Norton asked.

'To get wet,' said Barrett, following him. 'What's the news?'

'The Hammer's glowing. We're getting company.'

'How do you know it's a live shipment?'

'It's been glowing for half an hour. That means they're taking precautions. They're sending a new prisoner. Anyway, no supply shipment is due.'

Barrett nodded. 'OK. I'll come over. If it's a new man, we'll bunk him with Latimer.'

Norton managed a rasping laugh. 'Maybe he's a materialist. Latimer will drive him crazy with all that mystic nonsense. We could put him with Altman.'

'And he'll be raped in half an hour.'

'Altman's off that kick now,' said Norton. 'He's trying to create a real woman, not looking for second-rate substitutes.'

'Maybe our new man doesn't have any spare ribs.'

'Very funny, Jim.' Norton did not look amused. 'You know what I want the new man to be? A conservative, that's what. A black-souled reactionary straight out of Adam Smith. God, that's what I want.'

'Wouldn't you be happy with a fellow-Bolshevik?'

'This place is full of Bolsheviks,' said Norton. 'Of all shades from pale pink to flagrant scarlet. Don't you think I'm sick of them? Sitting around fishing for trilobites and discussing the relative merits of Kerensky and Malenkov? I need somebody to *talk* to, Jim. Somebody I can fight with.'

'All right,' Barrett said, slipping into his rain gear. 'I'll see what I can do about hocusing a debating partner out of the Hammer for you. A rip-roaring objectivist, OK?' He laughed. 'You know something, maybe there's been a revolution Up Front since we got our last man. Maybe the left is in and the right is out, and they'll start shipping us nothing *but* reactionaries. How would you like that? Fifty or a hundred storm troopers, Charley? Plenty of material to debate economics with. And the place will fill up with more and more of them, until we're outnumbered, and then maybe they'll have a *putsch* and get rid of all the stinking leftists sent here by the old régime, and—'

Barrett stopped. Norton was staring at him in amazement, his faded eyes wide, his hand compulsively smoothing his thinning hair to hide his embarrassment.

Barrett realized that he had just committed one of the most heinous crimes possible at Hawksbill Station: he had started to run off at the mouth. There hadn't been any call for his outburst. He was supposed to be the strong one of this place, the stabilizer, the man of absolute integrity and principles and sanity on whom the others could lean. And suddenly he had lost control. It was a bad sign. His dead foot was throbbing again; possibly that was the reason.

In a tight voice he said, 'Let's go. Maybe the new man is here already.'

They stepped outside. The rain was beginning to let up; the storm was moving out to sea. In the east over what would one day be the Atlantic, the sky was still clotted with grey mist, but to the west a different greyness was emerging the shade of normal grey that meant dry weather. Before he had come out here, Barrett had expected to find the sky practically black, because there'd be fewer dust particles to bounce the light around and turn things blue. But the sky seemed to be weary beige. So much for theories.

Through the thinning rain they walked toward the main building. Norton accommodated himself to Barrett's limping pace; and Barrett, wielding his crutch furiously, did his damnedest not to let his infirmity slow them up. He nearly lost his footing twice and fought hard not to let Norton see.

Hawksbill Station spread out before them.

It covered about 500 acres. In the centre of everything was the main building, an ample dome that contained most of their equipment and supplies. At widely spaced intervals, rising from the rock shield like grotesque giant green mushrooms, were the plastic blisters of the individual dwellings. Some, like Barrett's, were shielded by tin sheeting salvaged from shipments from Up Front. Others stood unprotected, just as they had come from the mouth of the extruder.

The huts numbered about eighty. At the moment, there were 140 inmates in Hawksbill Station, pretty close to the all-time high. Up Front hadn't sent back any hut-building materials for a long time, and so all the newer arrivals had to double up with bunkmates. Barrett and all those whose exile had begun before 2014 had the privilege of private dwellings, if they wanted them. (Some did not wish to live alone; Barrett, to preserve his own authority, felt that he was required to.) As new exiles arrived, they bunked in with those who currently lived alone, in reverse order of seniority. Most of the 2015 exiles had been forced to take room-mates now. Another dozen deportees and the 2014 group would be doubling up. Of course, there were deaths all up and down the line, and there were plenty who were eager to have company in their huts.

Barrett felt, though, that a man who has been sentenced to life imprisonment ought to have the privilege of privacy, if he desires it. One of his biggest problems here was keeping people from cracking up because there was too little privacy. Propinquity could be intolerable in a place like this.

Norton pointed toward the big, shiny-skinned, green dome of the main building. 'There's Altman going in now. And Rudiger. And Hutchett. Something's happening!'

Barrett stepped up his pace. Some of the men entering the building saw his bulky figure coming over the rise in the rock and waved to him. Barrett lifted a massive hand in reply. He felt mounting excitement. It was a big event at the Station whenever a new man arrived. Nobody had come for six months, now. That was the longest gap he could remember. It had started to seem as though no one would ever come again.

That would be a catastrophe.

New men were all that stood between the older inmates and insanity. New men brought news from the future, news from the world that was eternally left behind. They contributed new per-sonalities to a group that always was in danger of going stale.

And, Barrett knew, some men – he was not one – lived in the deluded hope that the next arrival might just turn out to be a woman.

That was why they flocked to the main building when the Hammer began to glow. Barrett hobbled down the path. The rain died away just as he reached the entrance.

Within, sixty or seventy Station residents crowded the chamber of the Hammer – just about every man in the place who was able in body and mind and still alert enough to show curiosity about a newcomer. They shouted greetings to Barrett. He nodded, smiled, deflected their questions with amiable gestures.

'Who's it going to be this time, Jim?'

'Maybe a girl, huh? Around nineteen years old, blonde, and built like—'

'I hope he can play stochastic chess, anyway.'

'Look at the glow! It's deepening!'

Barrett, like the others, stared at the Hammer. The complex, involuted collection of unfathomable instruments burned a bright cherry red, betokening the surge of who knew how many kilowatts being pumped in at the far end of the line.

The glow was beginning to spread to the Anvil now, that broad aluminium bedplate on which all shipments from the future were dropped. In another moment –

'Condition Crimson!' somebody suddenly yelled. 'Here he comes!'

2

A billion years up the time-line, power was flooding into the real Hammer of which this was only the partial replica. A man – or something else, perhaps a shipment of supplies – stood in the centre of the real Anvil, waiting for the Hawksbill Field to enfold him and kick him back to the early Palaeozoic. The effect of time-travel was very much like being hit with a gigantic hammer and driven clear through the walls of the continuum: hence the governing metaphors for the parts of the machine.

Setting up Hawksbill Station had been a long, slow job. The Hammer had knocked a pathway and had sent back the nucleus of the receiving station, first. Since there was no receiving station on hand to receive the receiving station, a certain amount of waste had occurred. It wasn't necessary to have a Hammer and Anvil on the receiving end, except as a fine control to prevent temporal spread; without the equipment, the field wandered a little, and it was possible to scatter consecutive shipments over a span of twenty or thirty years. There was plenty of such temporal garbage all around Hawksbill Station, stuff that had been intended for original installation, but which because of tuning imprecisions in the pre-Hammer days had landed a couple of decades (and a couple of hundred miles) away from the intended site.

Despite such difficulties, they had finally sent through enough components to the master temporal site to allow for the construction of a receiving station. Then the first prisoners had gone through; they were technicians who knew how to put the Hammer and Anvil together. They had done the job. After that, outfitting Hawksbill Station had been easy.

Now the Hammer glowed, meaning that they had activated the Hawksbill Field on the sending end, somewhere up around A.D. 2028 or 2030. All the sending was done there. All the receiving was done here. It didn't work the other way. Nobody really knew why, although there was a lot of superficially profound talk about the rules of entropy.

There was a whining, hissing sound as the edges of the Hawksbill Field began to ionize the atmosphere in the room. Then came the expected thunderclap of implosion, caused by an imperfect overlapping of the quantity of air that was subtracted from this era and the quantity that was being thrust into it. And then, abruptly, a man dropped out of the Hammer and lay, stunned and limp, on the gleaming Anvil.

He looked young, which surprised Barrett considerably. He seemed to be well under thirty. Generally, only middle-aged men were sent to Hawksbill Station. Incorrigibles, who had to be separated from humanity for the general good. The youngest man in the place now had been close to forty when he arrived. The sight of this lean, cleancut boy drew a hiss of anguish from a couple of men in the room, and Barrett understood the constellation of emotions that pained them.

The new man sat up. He stirred like a child coming out of a long, deep sleep. He looked around.

His face was very pale. His thin lips seemed bloodless. His blue eyes blinked rapidly. His jaws worked as though he wanted to say something, but could not find the words.

There were no harmful physiological effects to time-travel, but it could be a jolt to the consciousness. The last moments before the Hammer descended were very much like the final moments beneath the guillotine. The departing prisoner took his last look at the world of rocket transport and artificial organs, at the world in which he had lived and loved and agitated for a political cause, and then he was rammed into the inconceivably remote past on a one-way journey. It was a gloomy business, and it was not very surprising that the newcomers arrived in a state of emotional shock.

Barrett elbowed his way through the crowd. Automatically, the others made way for him. He reached the lip of the Anvil and leaned over it, extending a hand to the new man. His broad smile was met by a look of blank bewilderment.

'I'm Jim Barrett. Welcome to Hawksbill Station. Here – get off that thing before a load of groceries lands on top of you.' Wincing a little as he shifted his weight, Barrett pulled the new man down from the Anvil.

Barrett beckoned to Mel Rudiger, and the plump anarchist handed the new man an alcohol capsule. He took it and pressed it to his arm without a word. Charley Norton offered him a candy bar. The man shook it off. He looked groggy. A real case of temporal shock, Barrett thought, possibly the worst he had ever seen. The newcomer hadn't even spoken yet.

Barrett said, 'We'll go to the infirmary and check you out. Then I'll assign you your quarters. There's time for you to find your way around and meet everybody later on. What's your name?'

'Hahn. Lew Hahn.'

'I can't hear you.'

'Hahn,' the man repeated, still only barely audible.

'When are you from, Lew?'

'2029.'

'You feel pretty sick?'

'I feel awful. I don't even believe this is happening to me. There's no such place as Hawksbill Station, is there?'

'I'm afraid there is,' Barrett said. 'At least, for most of us. A few of the boys think it's all an illusion induced by drugs. But I have my doubts of that. If it's an illusion, it's a damned good one. Look.'

He put one arm around Hahn's shoulders and guided him through the press of prisoners, out of the Hammer chamber and toward the nearby infirmary. Although Hahn looked thin, even fragile, Barrett was surprised to feel the rippling muscles in those shoulders. He suspected that this man was a lot less helpless and ineffectual than he seemed to be right now. He *had* to be, in order to merit banishment to Hawksbill Station.

They passed the door of the building. 'Look out there,' Barrett commanded.

Hahn looked. He passed a hand across his eyes as though to clear away unseen cobwebs and looked again.

'A late-Cambrian landscape,' said Barrett quietly. 'This would be a geologist's dream, except that geologists don't tend to become political prisoners, it seems. Out in front is Appalachia. It's a strip of rock a few hundred miles wide and a few thousand miles long, from the Gulf of Mexico to Newfoundland. To the east we've got the Atlantic. A little way to the west we've got the Inland Sea. Somewhere 2000 miles to the west there's Cascadia, that's going to be California and Washington and Oregon someday. Don't hold your breath. I hope you like seafood.'

Hahn stared, and Barrett, standing beside him at the doorway, stared also. You never got used to the alienness of this place, not even after you lived here twenty years, as Barrett had. It was Earth, and yet it was not really Earth at all, because it was sombre and empty and unreal. The grey oceans swarmed with life, of course. But there was nothing on land except occasional patches of moss in the occasional patches of soil that had formed on the bare rock. Even a few cockroaches would be welcome; but insects, it seemed, were still a couple of geological periods in the future. To land-dwellers, this was a dead world, a world unborn.

Shaking his head, Hahn moved away from the door. Barrett led him down the corridor and into the small, brightly lit room that served as the infirmary. Doc Quesada was waiting. Quesada wasn't really a doctor, but he had been a medical technician once, and that was good enough. He was a compact, swarthy man with a look of complete self-assurance. He hadn't lost too many patients, all things considered. Barrett had watched him removing appendices with total aplomb. In his white smock, Quesada looked sufficiently medical to fit his role.

Barrett said, 'Doc, this is Lew Hahn. He's in temporal shock. Fix him up.'

Quesada nudged the newcomer on to a webfoam cradle and unzipped his blue jersey. Then he reached for his medical kit. Hawksbill Station was well equipped for most medical emergencies, now. The people Up Front had no wish to be inhumane, and they sent back all sorts of useful things, like anaesthetics and surgical clamps and medicines and dermal probes. Barrett could remember a time at the beginning when there had been nothing much here but the empty huts, and a man who hurt himself was in real trouble.

'He's had a drink already,' said Barrett.

'I see that,' Quesada murmured. He scratched at his short-cropped, bristly moustache. The little diagnostat in the cradle had gone rapidly to work, flashing information about Hahn's blood pressure, potassium count, dilation index, and much else. Quesada seemed to comprehend the barrage of facts. After a moment he said to Hahn, 'You aren't really sick, are you? Just shaken up a little. I don't blame you. Here – I'll give you a quick jolt to calm your nerves, and you'll be all right. As all right as any of us ever are.'

He put a tube to Hahn's carotid and thumbed the snout. The subsonic whirred, and a tranquillizing compound slid into the man's bloodstream. Hahn shivered.

Quesada said, 'Let him rest for five minutes. Then he'll be over the hump.'

They left Hahn in his cradle and went out of the infirmary. In the hall, Barrett looked down at the little medic and said, 'What's the report on Valdosto?'

Valdosto had gone into psychotic collapse several weeks before. Quesada was keeping him drugged and trying to bring him slowly back to the reality of Hawksbill Station. Shrugging, he replied, 'The status is quo. I let him out from under the dream-juice this morning, and he was the same as he's been.'

'You don't think he'll come out of it?'

'I doubt it. He's cracked for keeps. They could paste him together Up Front, but—'

'Yeah,' Barrett said. If he could get Up Front at all, Valdosto wouldn't have cracked. 'Keep him happy, then. If he can't be sane, he can at least be comfortable. What about Altman? Still got the shakes?'

'He's building a woman.'

'That's what Charley Norton told me. What's he using? A rag, a bone—'

'I gave him surplus chemicals. Chosen for their colour, mainly. He's got some foul green copper compounds and a little bit of ethyl alcohol and six or seven other things, and he collected some soil and threw in a lot of dead shellfish, and he's sculpting it all into what he claims is female shape and waiting for lightning to strike it.'

'In other words, he's gone crazy,' Barrett said.

'I think that's a safe assumption. But he's not molesting his friends anymore, anyway. You didn't think his homosexual phase would last much longer, as I recall.'

'No, but I didn't think he'd go off the deep end. If a man needs sex, and he can find some consenting playmates here, that's quite all right with me. But when he starts putting a woman together out of some dirt and rotten brachiopod meat it means we've lost him.'

Quesada's dark eyes flickered. 'We're all going to go that way sooner or later, Jim.'

'I haven't. You haven't.'

'Give us time. I've only been here eleven years.'

'Altman's been here only eight. Valdosto even less.'

'Some shells crack faster than others,' said Quesada. 'Here's our new friend.'

Hahn had come out of the infirmary to join them. He still looked pale, but the fright was gone from his eyes. He was beginning to adjust to the unthinkable.

He said, 'I couldn't help overhearing your conversation. Is there a lot of mental illness here?'

'Some of the men haven't been able to find anything meaningful to do here,' Barrett said. 'It eats them away. Quesada here has his medical work. I've got administrative duties. A couple of the fellows are studying the sea life. We've got a newspaper to keep some busy. But there are always those who just let themselves slide into despair, and they crack up. I'd say we have thirty or forty certifiable maniacs here at the moment, out of 140 residents.'

'That's not so bad,' Hahn said. 'Considering the inherent instability of the men who get sent here and the unusual conditions of life here.'

Barrett laughed. 'Hey, you're suddenly pretty articulate, aren't you? What was in the stuff Doc Quesada jolted you with?'

'I didn't mean to sound superior,' Hahn said quickly. 'Maybe that came out a little too smug. I mean—'

'Forget it. What did you do Up Front, anyway?'

'I was sort of an economist.'

'Just what we need,' said Quesada. 'He can help us solve our balance-of-payments problem.'

Barrett said, 'If you were an economist, you'll have plenty to discuss here. This place is full of economic theorists who'll want to bounce their ideas off you. Some of them are almost sane, too. Come with me and I'll show you where you're going to stay.'

3

The path from the main building to the hut of Donald Latimer was mainly downhill, for which Barrett was grateful even though he knew that he'd have to negotiate the uphill return in a little while. Latimer's hut was on the eastern side of the Station, looking out over the ocean. They walked slowly toward it. Hahn was solicitous of Barrett's game leg, and Barrett was irritated by the exaggerated care the younger man took to keep pace with him.

He was puzzled by this Hahn. The man was full of seeming contradictions – showing up here with the worst case of arrival shock Barrett had ever seen, then snapping out of it with remarkable quickness; looking frail and shy, but hiding solid muscles inside his jersey; giving an outer appearance of incompetence, but speaking with calm control. Barrett wondered what this young man had done to earn him the trip to Hawksbill Station, but there was time for such inquiries later. All the time in the world.

Hahn said, 'Is everything like this? Just rock and ocean?'

'That's all. Land life hasn't evolved yet. Everything's wonderfully simple, isn't it? No clutter. No urban sprawl. There's some moss moving on to land, but not much.'

'And in the sea? Swimming dinosaurs?'

Barrett shook his head. 'There won't be any vertebrates for half a billion years. We don't even have fish yet, let alone reptiles out there. All we can offer is that which creepeth. Some shellfish, some big fellows that look like squids, and trilobites. Seven hundred billion different species of trilobites. We've got a man named Rudiger – he's the one who gave you the drink – who's making a collection of them. He's writing the world's definitive text on trilobites.'

'But nobody will ever read it in – in the future.'

'Up Front, we say.'

'Up Front.'

'That's the pity of it,' said Barrett. 'We told Rudiger to inscribe his book on imperishable plates of gold and hope that it's found by palaeontologists. But he says the odds are against it. A billion years of geology will chew his plates to hell before they can be found.'

Hahn sniffed. 'Why does the air smell so strange?'

'It's a different mix,' Barrett said. 'We've analysed it. More nitrogen, a little less oxygen, hardly any CO_2 at all. But that isn't really why it smells odd to you. The thing is, it's pure air, unpolluted by the exhalations of life. Nobody's been respiring into it but us lads, and there aren't enough of us to matter.'

Smiling, Hahn said, 'I feel a little cheated that it's so empty. I expected lush jungles of weird plants and pterodactyls swooping through the air and maybe a tyrannosaur crashing into a fence around the Station.'

'No jungles. No pterodactyls. No tyrannosaurs. No fences. You didn't do your homework.'

'Sorry.'

'This is the late Cambrian. Sea life exclusively.'

'It was very kind of them to pick such a peaceful era as the dumping-ground for political prisoners,' Hahn said. 'I was afraid it would be all teeth and claws.'

'Kind, hell! They were looking for an era where we couldn't do any harm. That meant tossing us back before the evolution of mammals, just in case we accidentally got hold of the ancestor of all humanity and snuffed him out. And, while they were at it, they decided to stash us so far in the past that we'd be beyond all land life, on the theory that maybe even if we slaughtered a baby dinosaur it might affect the entire course of the future.'

'They don't mind if we catch a few trilobites?'

'Evidently they think it's safe,' Barrett said. 'It looks as though they were right. Hawksbill Station has been here for twenty-five years, and it doesn't seem as though we've tampered with future history in any measurable way. Of course, they're careful not to send us any women.'

'Why is that?'

'So we don't start reproducing and perpetuating ourselves. Wouldn't that mess up the time-lines? A successful human outpost in one billion B.C., that's had all that time to evolve and mutate and grow? By the time the twenty-first century came around, our descendants would be in charge, and the other kind of human being would probably be in penal servitude, and there'd be more paradoxes created than you could shake a trilobite at. So they don't send the women here. There's a prison camp for women, too, but it's a few hundred millions years up the time-line in the late Silurian, and never the twain shall meet. That's why Ned Altman's trying to build a woman out of dust and garbage.'

'God made Adam out of less.'

'Altman isn't God,' Barrett said. 'That's the root of his whole problem. Look, here's the hut where you're going to stay. I'm rooming you with Don Latimer. He's a very sensitive, interesting, pleasant person. He used to be a physicist before he got into politics, and he's been here about a dozen years, and I might as well warn you that he's developed a strong and somewhat cock-eyed mystic streak lately. The fellow he was rooming with killed himself last year, and since then he's been trying to find some way out of here through extra-sensory powers.'

'Is he serious?'

'I'm afraid he is. And we try to take him seriously. We all

humour each other at Hawksbill Station; it's the only way we avoid a mass psychosis. Latimer will probably try to get you to collaborate with him on his project. If you don't like living with him, I can arrange a transfer for you. But I want to see how he reacts to someone new at the Station. I'd like you to give him a chance.'

'Maybe I'll even help him find his psionic gateway.'

'If you do, take me along,' said Barrett. They both laughed. Then he rapped at Latimer's door. There was no answer, and after a moment Barrett pushed the door open. Hawksbill Station had no locks. '

Latimer sat in the middle of the bare rock floor, cross-legged, meditating. He was a slender, gentle-faced man just beginning to look old. Right now he seemed a million miles away. Hahn shrugged. Barrett put a finger to his lips. They waited in silence for a few minutes, and then Latimer showed signs of coming up from his trance.

He got to his feet in a single flowing motion, without using his hands. In a low, courteous voice he said to Hahn, 'Have you just arrived?'

'Within the last hour. I'm Lew Hahn.'

'Donald Latimer. I regret that I have to make your acquaintance in these surroundings. But maybe we won't have to tolerate this illegal imprisonment much longer.'

Barrett said, 'Don, Lew is going to bunk with you. I think you'll get along well. He was an economist in 2029 until they gave him the Hammer.'

'Where did you live?' Latimer asked, animation coming into his eyes.

'San Francisco.'

The glow faded. Latimer said, 'Were you ever in Toronto? I'm from there. I had a daughter – she'd be twenty-three now, Nella Latimer. I wondered if you knew her.'

'No. I'm sorry.'

'It wasn't very likely. But I'd love to know what kind of a woman she became. She was a little girl when I last saw her. Now I guess she's married. Or perhaps they've sent her to the other station. Nella Latimer – you're sure you didn't know her?'

Barrett left them together. It looked as though they'd get along. He told Latimer to bring Hahn up to the main building at dinner for introductions and went out. A chilly drizzle had begun again. Barrett made his way slowly, painfully up the hill. It had been sad to see the light flicker from Latimer's eyes when Hahn said he didn't know his daughter. Most of the time, men at Hawksbill Station tried not to speak about their families, preferring to keep those tormenting memories well repressed. But the arrival of newcomers generally stirred old ties. There was never any news of relatives and no way to obtain any, because it was impossible for the Station to communicate with anyone Up Front. No way to ask for the photo of a loved one, no way to request specific medicines, no way to obtain a certain book or a coveted tape. In a mindless, impersonal way, Up Front sent periodic shipments to the Station of things thought useful – reading matter, medical supplies, technical equipment, food. Occasionally they were startling in their generosity, as when they sent a case of Burgundy, or a box of sensory spools, or a recharger for the power pack. Such gifts usually meant a brief thaw in the world situation, which customarily produced a short-lived desire to be kind to the boys in Hawksbill Station. But they had a policy about sending information about relatives. Or about contemporary newspapers. Fine wine, yes; a tridim of a daughter who would never be seen again, no.

For all Up Front knew, there was no one alive in Hawksbill Station. A plague could have killed everyone off ten years ago, but there was no way of telling. That was why the shipments still came back. The government whirred and clicked with predictable continuity. The government, whatever else it might be, was not malicious. There were other kinds of totalitarianism besides bloody repressive tyranny.

Pausing at the top of the hill, Barrett caught his breath. Naturally, the alien air no longer smelled strange to him. He filled his lungs with it. Once again the rain ceased. Through the greyness came the sunshine, making the naked rocks sparkle. Barrett closed his eyes a moment and leaned on his crutch and saw, as though on an inner screen, the creatures with many legs climbing up out of the sea, and the mossy carpets spreading, and the flowerless plants uncoiling and spreading their scaly branches, and the dull hides of eerie amphibians glistening on the shores and the tropic heat of the coal-forming epoch descending like a glove over the world.

All that lay far in the future. Dinosaurs. Little chittering mammals. Pithecanthropus in the forests of Java. Sargon and Hannibal and Attila and Orville Wright and Thomas Edison and Edmond Hawksbill. And finally a benign government that would find the thoughts of some men so intolerable that the only safe place to which they could be banished was a rock at the beginning of time. The Government was too civilized to put men to death for subversive activities and too cowardly to let them remain alive. The compromise was the living death of Hawksbill Station. A two billion years of impassable time was suitable insulation even for the most nihilistic idea.

Barrett struggled the rest of the way back toward his hut. He had long since come to accept his exile, but accepting his ruined foot was another matter entirely. The idle wish to find a way to regain the freedom of his own time no longer possessed him; but he wished with all his soul that the blank-faced administrators Up Front would send back a kit that would allow him to rebuild his foot.

He entered his hut and flung his crutch aside, sinking down instantly on his cot. There had been no cots when he had come to Hawksbill Station. He had come here in the fourth year of the Station, when there were only a dozen buildings and little in the way of creature comforts. It had been a miserable place, then, but the steady accretion of shipments from Up Front had made it relatively tolerable. Of the fifty or so prisoners who had preceded Barrett to Hawksbill, none remained alive. He had held the highest seniority for almost ten years. Time moved here at one-to-one correlation with time Up Front; the Hammer was locked on this point of time, so that Hahn, arriving here today more than twenty years after Barrett, had departed from a year Up Front more than twenty years after the time of Barrett's expulsion. Barrett had not had the heart to begin pumping Hahn for news of 2029 so soon. He would learn all he needed to know, and small cheer it would be, anyway.

Barrett reached for a book. But the fatigue of hobbling around the station had taken more out of him than he realized. He looked at the page for a moment. Then he put it away and closed his eyes and dozed.

4

That evening, as every evening, the men of Hawksbill Station gathered in the main building for dinner and recreation. It was not mandatory, and some men chose to eat alone. But tonight nearly everyone who was in full possession of his faculties was there, because this was one of the infrequent occasions when a newcomer had arrived to be questioned about the world of men.

Hahn looked uneasy about his sudden notoriety. He seemed to be basically shy, unwilling to accept all the attention now being thrust upon him. There he sat in the middle of the group while men twenty and thirty years his senior crowded in on him with their questions, and it was obvious that he wasn't enjoying the session.

Sitting to one side, Barrett took little part in the discussion. His curiosity about Up Front's ideological shifts had ebbed a long time ago. It was hard for him to realize that he had once been so passionately concerned about concepts like syndicalism and the dictatorship of the proletariat and the guaranteed annual wage that he had been willing to risk imprisonment over them. His concern for humanity had not waned, merely the degree of his involvement in the twenty-first century's political problems. After twenty years at Hawksbill Station, Up Front had become unreal to Jim Barrett, and his energies centred around the crises and challenges of what he had come to think of as 'his own' time – the late Cambrian.

So he listened, but more with an ear for what the talk revealed about Lew Hahn than for what it revealed about current events Up Front. And what it revealed about Lew Hahn was mainly a matter of what was not revealed.

Hahn didn't say much. He seemed to be feinting and evading.

Charley Norton wanted to know, 'Is there any sign of a weakening of the phoney conservatism yet? I mean, they've been promising the end of big government for thirty years, and it gets bigger all the time.'

Hahn moved restlessly in his chair. 'They still promise. As soon as conditions become stabilized—'

'Which is when?'

'I don't know. I suppose they're making words.'

'What about the Martian Commune?' demanded Sid Hutchett. 'Have they been infiltrating agents on to Earth?'

'I couldn't really say.'

'How about the Gross Global Product?' Mel Rudiger wanted to know. 'What's its curve? Still holding level, or has it started to drop?'

Hahn tugged at his ear. 'I think it's slowly edging down.'

'Where does the index stand?' Rudiger asked. 'The last figures we had, for '25, it was at 909. But in four years—'

'It might be something like 875 now,' said Hahn.

It struck Barrett as a little odd that an economist would be so hazy about the basic economic statistic. Of course, he didn't know how long Hahn had been imprisoned before getting the Hammer. Maybe he simply wasn't up on the recent figures.

Charley Norton wanted to find out some things about the legal rights of citizens. Hahn couldn't tell him. Rudiger asked about the impact of weather control – whether the supposedly conservative government of liberators was still ramming programmed weather down the mouths of the citizens – and Hahn wasn't sure. Hahn couldn't rightly say much about the functions of the judiciary, whether it had recovered any of the power stripped from it by the Enabling Act of '18. He didn't have any comments to offer on the tricky subject of population control. In fact, his performance was striking for its lack of hard information.

'He isn't saying much at all,' Charley Norton grumbled to the silent Barrett. 'He's putting up a smokescreen. But either he's not telling what he knows, or he doesn't know.'

'Maybe he's not very bright,' Barrett suggested.

'What did he do to get here? He must have had some kind of deep commitment. But it doesn't show, Jim! He's an intelligent kid, but he doesn't seem plugged in to anything that ever mattered to any of us.'

Doc Quesada offered a thought. 'Suppose he isn't a political at all. Suppose they're sending a different kind of prisoner back now. Axe murderers, or something. A quiet kid who quietly chopped up sixteen people one Sunday morning. Naturally he isn't interested in politics.'

Barrett shook his head. 'I doubt that. I think he's just clamming up because he's shy or ill at ease. It's his first night here, remember. He's just been kicked out of his own world and there's no going back. He may have left a wife and baby behind, you know. He may simply not give a damn tonight about sitting up there and spouting the latest word on abstract philosophical theory, when all he wants to do is go off and cry his eyes out. I say we ought to leave him alone.'

Quesada and Norton looked convinced. They shook their heads in agreement; but Barrett didn't voice his opinion to the room in general. He let the quizzing of Hahn continue until it petered out of its own accord. The men began to drift away. A couple of them went in back to convert Hahn's vague generalities into the lead story for the next handwritten edition of the Hawksbill Station *Times*. Rudiger stood on a table and shouted out that he was going night fishing, and four men asked to join him. Charley Norton sought out his usual debating partner, the nihilist Ken Belardi, and reopened, like a festering wound, their discussion of planning versus chaos, which bored them both to the point of screaming. The nightly games of stochastic chess began. The loners who had made rare visits to the main building simply to see the new man went back to their huts to do whatever they did in them alone each night.

Hahn stood apart, fidgeting and uncertain.

Barrett went up to him. 'I guess you didn't really want to be quizzed tonight,' he said.

'I'm sorry I couldn't have been more informative. I've been out of circulation a while, you see.'

'But you were politically active, weren't you?'

'Oh, yes,' Hahn said. 'Of course.' He flicked his tongue over his lips. 'What's supposed to happen now?'

'Nothing in particular. We don't have organized activities here. Doc and I are going out on sick call. Care to join us?'

'What does it involve?' Hahn asked.

'Visiting some of the worst cases. It can be grim, but you'll get a panoramic view of Hawksbill Station.'

'I'd like to go.'

Barrett gestured to Quesada, and the three of them left the building. This was a nightly ritual for Barrett, difficult as it was since he had hurt his foot. Before turning in, he visited the goofy ones and the psycho ones and the catatonic ones, tucked them in, wished them a good night and a healed mind in the morning. Someone had to show them that he cared. Barrett did.

Outside, Hahn peered up at the moon. It was nearly full tonight, shining like a burnished coin, its face a pale salmon colour and hardly pockmarked at all.

'It looks so different here,' Hahn said. 'The craters – where are the craters?'

'Most of them haven't been formed yet,' said Barrett. 'A billion years is a long time even for the moon. Most of its upheavals are still ahead. We think it may still have an atmosphere, too. That's why it looks pink to us. Of course, Up Front hasn't bothered to send us much in the way of astronomical equipment. We can only guess.'

Hahn started to say something. He cut himself off after one blurted syllable.

Quesada said, 'Don't hold it back. What were you about to suggest?'

Hahn laughed in self-mockery. 'That you ought to fly up there and take a look. It struck me as odd that you'd spend all these years here theorizing about whether the moon's got an atmosphere and wouldn't ever once go up to look. But I forgot.'

'It would be useful to have a commute ship from Up Front,' Barrett said. 'But it hasn't occurred to them. All we can do is look. The moon's a popular place in '29, is it?'

'The biggest resort in the system,' Hahn said. 'I was there on my honeymoon. Leah and I—'

He stopped again.

Barrett said hurriedly, 'This is Bruce Valdosto's hut. He cracked up a few weeks ago. When we go in, stand behind us so he doesn't see you. He might be violent with a stranger. He's unpredictable.'

Valdosto was a husky man in his late forties, with swarthy skin, coarse curling black hair, and the broadest shoulders any man had ever had. Sitting down, he looked even burlier than Jim Barrett, which was saying a great deal. But Valdosto had short, stumpy legs, the legs of a man of ordinary stature tacked to the trunk of a giant, which spoiled the effect completely. In his years Up Front he had totally refused any prosthesis. He believed in living with deformities.

Right now he was strapped into a webfoam cradle. His domed forehead was flecked with beads of sweat, his eyes were glittering beadily in the darkness. He was a very sick man. Once he had been clear-minded enough to throw a sleet bomb into a meeting of the Council of Syndics, giving a dozen of them a bad case of gamma poisoning, but now he scarcely knew up from down, right from left.

Barrett leaned over him and said, 'How are you, Bruce?'

'Who's that?'

'Jim. It's a beautiful night, Bruce. How'd you like to come outside and get some fresh air? The moon's almost full.'

'I've got to rest. The committee meeting tomorrow—'

'It's been postponed.'

'But how can it? The Revolution—'

'That's been postponed too. Indefinitely.'

'Are they disbanding the cells?' Valdosto asked harshly.

'We don't know yet. We're waiting for orders. Come outside, Bruce. The air will do you good.'

Muttering, Valdosto let himself be unlaced. Quesada and Barrett pulled him to his feet and propelled him through the door of the hut. Barrett caught sight of Hahn in the shadows, his face sombre with shock.

They stood together outside the hut. Barrett pointed to the moon. 'It's got such a lovely colour here. Not like the dead thing Up Front. And look, look down there, Bruce. The sea breaking on the rocky shore. Rudiger's out fishing. I can see his boat by moonlight.'

'Striped bass,' said Valdosto. 'Sunnies. Maybe he'll catch some sunnies.'

'There aren't any sunnies here. They haven't evolved yet.' Barrett fished in his pocket and drew out something ridged and glossy, about two inches long. It was the exoskeleton of a small trilobite. He offered it to Valdosto, who shook his head.

'Don't give me that cockeyed crab.'

'It's a trilobite, Bruce. It's extinct, but so are we. We're a billion years in our own past.'

'You must be crazy,' Valdosto said in a calm, low voice that belied his wild-eyed appearance. He took the trilobite from Barrett and hurled it against the rocks. 'Cockeyed crab,' he muttered.

Quesada shook his head sadly. He and Barrett led the sick man into the hut again. Valdosto did not protest as the medic gave him the sedative. His weary mind, rebelling entirely against the monstrous concept that he had been exiled to the inconceivably remote past, welcomed sleep.

When they went out Barrett saw Hahn holding the trilobite on his palm and staring at it in wonder. Hahn offered it to him, but Barrett brushed it away. 'Keep it if you like,' he said. 'There are more.'

They went on. They found Ned Altman beside his hut, crouching on his knees and patting his hands over the crude lopsided form of what, from its exaggerated breasts and hips, appeared to be the image of a woman. He stood up when they appeared. Altman was a neat little man with yellow hair and nearly invisible white eyebrows. Unlike anyone else in the Station, he had actually been a government man once, fifteen years ago, before seeing through the myth of syndicalist capitalism and joining one of the underground factions. Eight years at Hawksbill Station had done things to him.

Altman pointed to his golem and said, 'I hoped there'd be lightning in the rain today. That'll do it, you know. But there isn't much lightning this time of year. She'll get up alive, and then I'll need you, Doc, to give her shots and trim away some of the rough places.'

Quesada forced a smile. 'I'll be glad to do it, Ned. But you know the terms.'

'Sure. When I'm through with her, you get her. You think I'm a goddam monopolist? I'll share her. There'll be a waiting-list. Just so you don't forget who made her, though. She'll remain mine, whenever I need her.' He noticed Hahn. 'Who are you?'

'He's new,' Barrett said. 'Lew Hahn. He came this afternoon.'

'Ned Altman,' said Altman with a courtly bow. 'Formerly in government service. You're pretty young, aren't you? How's your sex orientation? Hetero?'

Hahn winced. 'I'm afraid so.'

'It's OK. I wouldn't touch you. I've got a project going, here. But I just want you to know I'll put you on my list. You're young and you've probably got stronger needs than some of us. I won't forget about you, even though you're new here.'

Quesada coughed. 'You ought to get some rest now, Ned. Maybe there'll be lightning tomorrow.'

Altman did not resist. The doctor took him inside and put him to bed, while Hahn and Barrett surveyed the man's handiwork. Hahn pointed toward the figure's middle.

'He's left out something essential,' he said. 'If he's planning to make love to this girl after he's finished creating her, he'd better—'

'It was there yesterday,' said Barrett. 'He must be changing orientation again.' Quesada emerged from the hut. They went on, down the rocky path.

Barrett did not make the complete circuit that night. Ordinarily, he would have gone all the way down to Latimer's hut overlooking the sea, for Latimer was on his list of sick ones. But Barrett had visited Latimer once that day, and he didn't think his aching good leg was up to another hike that far. So, after he and Quesada and Hahn had been to all of the easily accessible huts and had visited the man who prayed for alien beings to rescue him and the man who was trying to break into a parallel universe where everything was as it ought to be in the world and the man who lay on his cot sobbing for all his wakeful hours, Barrett said goodnight to his companions and allowed Quesada to escort Hahn back to his hut without him.

After observing Hahn for half a day, Barrett realized he did not know much more about him than when he had first dropped on to the Anvil. But maybe Hahn would open up a little more, after he'd been here a while. Barrett stared up at the salmon moon and reached into his pocket to finger the little trilobite before he remembered that he had given it to Hahn. He shuffled into his hut. He wondered how long ago Hahn had taken that lunar honeymoon trip.

5

Rudiger's catch was spread out in front of the main building the next morning when Barrett came up for breakfast. He had had a good night's fishing, obviously. He usually did. Rudiger went out three or four nights a week, in a little dinghy that he had cobbled together a few years ago from salvaged materials, and he took with him a team of friends whom he had trained in the deft use of the trawling-nets.

It was an irony that Rudiger, the anarchist, the man who believed in individualism and the abolition of all political institutions, should be so good at leading a team of fishermen. Rudiger didn't care for teamwork in the abstract. But it was hard to manipulate the nets alone, he had discovered. Hawksbill Station had many little ironies of that sort. Political theorists tend to swallow their theories when forced back on pragmatic measures of survival.

The prize of the catch was a cephalopod about a dozen feet long – a rigid conical tube out of which some limp squid-like tentacles dangled. Plenty of meat on that one, Barrett thought. Dozens of trilobites were arrayed around it, ranging in size from the inch-long kind to the three-footers with their baroquely involuted exoskeletons. Rudiger fished both for food and for science;

evidently these trilobites were discards, species that he already had studied, or he wouldn't have left them here to go into the food hoppers. His hut was stacked ceiling-high with trilobites. It kept him sane to collect and analyse them.

Near the heap of trilobites were some clusters of hinged brachiopods, looking like scallops that had gone awry, and a pile of snails. The warm, shallow waters just off the coastal shelf teemed with life, in striking contrast to the barren land. Rudiger had also brought in a mound of shiny black seaweed. Barrett hoped someone would gather all this stuff up and get it into their heat-sink cooler before it spoiled. The bacteria of decay worked a lot slower here than they did Up Front, but a few hours in the mild air would do Rudiger's haul no good.

Today Barrett planned to recruit some men for the annual Inland Sea expedition. Traditionally, he led that trek himself, but his injury made it impossible for him even to consider going anymore. Each year, a dozen or so able-bodied men went out on a wide-ranging reconnaissance that took them in a big circle, looping north-westward until they reached the sea, then coming around to the south and back to the Station. One purpose of the trip was to gather any temporal garbage that might have materialized in the vicinity of the Station during the past year. There was no way of knowing how wide a margin of error had been allowed during the early attempts to set up the Station, and the scattershot technique of hurling material into the past had been pretty unreliable. New stuff was turning up all the time that had been aimed for A.D. Minus One Billion, Two Thousand Oh Five, but which didn't get there until a few decades later. Hawksbill Station needed all the spare equipment it could get, and Barrett didn't miss a chance to round up any of the debris.

There was another reason for the Inland Sea expeditions, though. They served as a focus for the year, an annual ritual, something to peg a custom to. It was a rite of spring here.

The dozen strongest men, going on foot to the distant rock-rimmed shores of the tepid sea that drowned the middle of North America, were performing the closest thing Hawksbill Station had to a religious function. The trip meant more to Barrett himself than he had ever suspected, also. He realized that now, when he was unable to go. He had led every such expedition for twenty years.

But last year he had gone scrabbling over boulders loosened by the waves, venturing into risky territory for no rational reason, and his ageing muscles had betrayed him. Often at night he woke sweating to escape from the dream in which he relived that ugly moment; slipping and sliding, clawing at the rocks, a mass of stone dislodged from somewhere and came crashing down with an agonizing impact on his foot, pinning him, crushing him. He could not forget the sound of grinding bones. Nor was he likely to lose the memory of the homeward march across hundreds of miles of bare rock, his bulky body slung between the bowed forms of his companions.

He had thought he would lose the foot, but Quesada had spared him from the amputation. He simply could not touch the foot to the ground and put weight on it now, or ever again. It might have been simpler to have the dead appendage sliced off. Quesada veto'd that, though. 'Who knows,' he had said, 'some day they might send us a transplant kit. I can't rebuild a leg that's been amputated.' So Barrett had kept his crushed foot. But he had never been quite the same since, and now someone else would have to lead the march.

Who would it be, he asked himself?

Quesada was the likeliest. Next to Barrett, he was the strongest man here, in all the ways that it was important to be strong. But Quesada couldn't be spared at the Station. It might be handy to have a medic along on the trip, but it was vital to have one here. After some reflection Barrett put down Charley Norton as the leader. He added Ken Belardi – someone for Norton to talk to. Rudiger? A tower of strength last year after Barrett had been injured; Barrett didn't particularly want to let Rudiger leave the Station so long, though. He needed able men for the expedition, true, but he didn't want to strip the home base down to invalids, crackpots, and psychotics. Rudiger stayed. Two of his fellow-fishermen went on the list. So did Sid Hutchett and Arny Jean-Claude.

Barrett thought about putting Don Latimer in the group. Latimer was coming to be something of a borderline mental case, but he was rational enough except when he lapsed into his psionic meditations, and he'd pull his own weight on the expedition. On the other hand, Latimer was Lew Hahn's room-mate, and Barrett wanted Latimer around to observe Hahn at close range. He toyed with the idea of sending both of them out, but nixed it. Hahn was still an unknown quantity. It was too risky to let him go with the Inland Sea party this year. Probably he'd be in next spring's group, though.

Finally Barrett had his dozen men chosen. He chalked their names on the slate in front of the mess hall and found Charley Norton at breakfast to tell him he was in charge.

It felt strange to know that he'd have to stay home while the others went. It was an admission that he was beginning to abdicate after running this place so long. A crippled old man was what he was, whether he liked to admit it to himself or not, and that was something he'd have to come to terms with soon.

In the afternoon, the men of the Inland Sea expedition gathered to select their gear and plan their route. Barrett kept away from the meeting. This was Charley Norton's show, now. He'd made eight or ten trips, and he knew what to do.

But some masochistic compulsion in Barrett drove him to take a trek on his own. If he couldn't see the western waters this year, the least he could do was pay a visit to the Atlantic, in his own backyard. Barrett stopped off in the infirmary and, finding Quesada elsewhere, helped himself to a tube of neural depressant. He scrambled along the eastern trail until he was a few hundred yards from the main building, dropped his trousers and quickly gave each thigh a jolt of the drug, first the good leg, then the gimpy one. That would numb the muscles just enough so that he'd be able to take an extended hike without feeling the fire of the fatigue in his protesting joints. He'd pay for it, he knew, eight hours from now, when the depressant wore off and the full impact of his exertion hit him like a million daggers. But he was willing to accept that price.

The road to the sea was a long, lonely one. Hawksbill Station was perched on the eastern rim of the land, more than 800 feet above sea level. During the first half-dozen years, the men of the Station had reached the ocean by a suicidal route across sheer rock faces, but Barrett had incited a ten-year project to carve a path. Now wide steps descended to the sea. Chopping them out of the rock had kept a lot of men busy for a long time, too busy to worry or to slip into insanity. Barrett regretted that he couldn't conceive some comparable works project to occupy them nowadays.

The steps formed a succession of shallow platforms that switchbacked to the edge of the water. Even for a healthy man it was still a strenuous walk. For Barrett in his present condition it was an ordeal. It took him two hours to descend a distance that normally could be traversed in a quarter of that time. When he reached the bottom, he sank down exhaustedly on a flat rock licked by the waves, and dropped his crutch. The fingers of his left hand were cramped and gnarled from gripping the crutch, and his entire body was bathed in sweat.

The water looked grey and somehow oily. Barrett could not explain the prevailing colourlessness of the late-Cambrian world, with its sombre sky and sombre land and sombre sea, but his heart quietly ached for a glimpse of green vegetation again. He missed chlorophyll. The dark wavelets lapped against his rock, pushing a mass of floating black seaweed back and forth. The sea stretched to infinity. He didn't have the faintest idea how much of Europe, if any, was above water in this epoch.

At the best of times most of the planet was submerged; here, only a few hundred million years after the white-hot rocks of the land had pushed into view, it was likely that all that was above water on Earth was a strip of territory here and there. Had the Himalayas been born yet? The Rockies? The Andes? He knew the approximate outlines of late-Cambrian North America, but the rest was a mystery.

As he watched, a big trilobite unexpectedly came scuttering up out of the water. It was the spike-tailed kind, about a yard long, with an eggplant-purple shell and a bristling arrangement of slender spines along the margins. There seemed to be a lot of legs underneath. The trilobite crawled up on the shore – no sand, no beach, just a shelf of rock – and advanced until it was eight or ten feet from the waves.

Good for you, Barrett thought. Maybe you're the first one who ever came out on land to see what it was like. The pioneer. The trailblazer.

It occurred to him that this adventurous trilobite might well be the ancestor of all the land-dwelling creatures of the eons to come. It was biological nonsense, but Barrett's weary mind conjured a picture of an evolutionary procession, with fish and amphibians and reptiles and mammals and Man all stemming in unbroken sequence from this grotesque armoured thing that moved in uncertain circles near his feet.

And if I were to step on you, he thought?

A quick motion – the sound of crunching chitin – the wild scrabbling of a host of little legs –

And the whole chain of life snapped in its first link. Evolution undone. With the descent of that heavy foot all the future would change, and there would never have been any Hawksbill Station, no human race, no James Edward Barrett. In an instant he would have both revenge on those who had condemned him to live out his days in this place and release from his sentence.

He did nothing. The trilobite completed its slow perambulation of the shoreline rocks and scuttered back into the sea unharmed.

The soft voice of Don Latimer said, 'I saw you sitting down here, Jim. Do you mind if I join you?'

Barrett swung around, momentarily surprised. Latimer had come down from his hilltop hut so quietly that Barrett hadn't heard a thing. He recovered and grinned and beckoned Latimer to an adjoining rock.

'You fishing?' Latimer asked.

'Just sitting. An old man sunning himself.'

'You took a hike like that just to sun yourself?' Latimer laughed. 'Come off it. You're trying to get away from it all, and you probably wish I hadn't disturbed you.'

'That's not so. Stay here. How's your new room-mate getting along?'

'It's been strange,' said Latimer. 'That's one reason I came down here to talk to you.' He leaned forward and peered searchingly into Barrett's eyes. 'Jim, tell me: do you think I'm a madman?'

'Why should I?'

'The esp-ing business. My attempt to break through to another realm of consciousness. I know you're tough-minded and sceptical. You probably think it's all a lot of nonsense.'

Barrett shrugged and said, 'If you want the blunt truth, I do. I don't have the remotest belief that you're going to get us anywhere, Don. I think it's a complete waste of time and energy for you to sit there for hours harnessing your psionic powers, or whatever it is you do. But, no, I don't think you're crazy. I think you're entitled to your obsession and that you're going about a basically futile thing in a reasonably level-headed way. Fair enough?'

'More than fair. I don't ask you to put any credence in my research, but I don't want you to think I'm a total lunatic for trying it. It's important that you regard me as sane, or else what I want to tell you about Hahn won't be valid to you.'

'I don't see the connection.'

'It's this,' said Latimer. 'On the basis of one evening's acquaintance, I've formed an opinion about Hahn. It's the kind of an opinion that might be formed by a garden-variety paranoid, and if you think I'm nuts you're likely to discount my idea.'

'I don't think you're nuts. What's your idea?'

'That he's been spying on us.'

Barrett had to work hard to keep from emitting the guffaw that would shatter Latimer's fragile self-esteem. 'Spying?' he said casually. 'You can't mean that. How can anyone spy here? I mean, how can he report his findings?'

'I don't know,' Latimer said. 'But he asked me a million questions last night. About you, about Quesada, about some of the sick men. He wanted to know everything.'

'The normal curiosity of a new man.'

'Jim, he was taking notes. I saw him after he thought I was asleep. He sat up for two hours writing it all down in a little book.'

'Maybe he's going to write a novel about us.'

'I'm serious,' Latimer said. 'Questions – notes. And he's shifty. Try to get him to talk about himself!'

'I did. I didn't learn much.'

'Do you know why he's been sent here?'

'No.'

'Neither do I,' said Latimer. 'Political crimes, he said, but he was vague as hell. He hardly seemed to know what the present government was up to, let alone what his own opinions were toward it. I don't detect any passionate philosophical convictions in Mr Hahn. And you know as well as I do that Hawksbill Station is the refuse heap for revolutionaries and agitators and subversives and all sorts of similar trash, but that we've never had any other kind of prisoner here.'

Barrett said coolly, 'I agree that Hahn's a puzzle. But who could he be spying for? He's got no way to file a report, if he's a government agent. He's stranded here for keeps, like us.'

'Maybe he was sent to keep an eye on us – to make sure we aren't cooking up some way to escape. Maybe he's a volunteer who willingly gave up his twenty-first-century life so he could come among us and thwart anything we might be hatching. Perhaps they're afraid we've invented forward time-travel. Or that we've become a threat to the sequence of the time-lines. Anything. So Hahn comes among us to snoop around and block any dangers before they arrive.'

Barrett felt a twinge of alarm. He saw how close to paranoia Latimer was hewing, now. In half a dozen sentences he had journeyed from the rational expression of some justifiable suspicions to the fretful fear that the men from Up Front were going to take steps to choke off the escape route that he was so close to perfecting.

He kept his voice level as he told Latimer, 'I don't think you need to worry, Don. Hahn's an odd one, but he's not here to make trouble for us. The fellows Up Front have already made all the trouble for us they ever will.'

'Would you keep an eye on him anyway?'

'You know I will. And don't hesitate to let me know if Hahn

does anything else out of the ordinary. You're in a better spot to notice than anyone else.'

'I'll be watching,' Latimer said. 'We can't tolerate any spies from Up Front among us.' He got to his feet and gave Barrett a pleasant smile. 'I'll let you get back to your sunning now, Jim.'

Latimer went up the path. After a long while Barrett seized his crutch and levered himself to his feet. He stood staring down at the surf, dipping the tip of his crutch into the water to send a couple of little crawling things scurrying away. At length he turned and began the long, slow climb back to the Station.

6

A couple of days passed before Barrett had the chance to draw Lew Hahn aside. The Inland Sea party had set out, and in a way that was too bad, for Barrett could have used Charley Norton's services in penetrating Hahn's armour. Norton was the most gifted theorist around, a man who could weave a tissue of dialectic from the least promising material. If anyone could find out the depth of Hahn's Marxist commitment, if any, it was Norton.

But Norton was leading the expedition, so Barrett had to do the interrogating himself. His Marxism was a trifle rusty, and he couldn't thread his path through the Leninist, Stalinist, Trotskyite, Khrushchevist, Maoist, Berenkovskyite and Mgumbweist schools with Charley Norton's skills. Yet he knew what questions to ask.

He picked a rainy evening when Hahn seemed to be in a fairly outgoing mood. There had been an hour's entertainment that night, an ingenious computer-composed film that Sid Hutchett had programmed last week. Up Front had been kind enough to ship back a modest computer, and Hutchett had rigged it to do animations by specifying line widths and lengths, shades of grey and progression of raster units. It was a simple but remarkably clever business, and it brightened a dull night.

Afterward, sensing that Hahn was relaxed enough to lower his guard a bit, Barrett said, 'Hutchett's a rare one. Did you meet him before he went on the trip?'

'Tall fellow with a sharp nose and no chin?'

'That's the one. A clever boy. He was the top computer-man

for the Continental Liberation Front until they caught him in '19. He programmed that fake broadcast in which Chancellor Dantell denounced his own régime. Remember?'

'I'm not sure I do,' Hahn frowned. 'How long ago was this?'

'The broadcast was in 2018. Would that be before your time? Only eleven years ago—'

'I was nineteen then,' said Hahn. 'I guess I wasn't very politically sophisticated.'

'Too busy studying economics, I guess.'

Hahn grinned. 'That's right. Deep in the dismal science.'

'And you never heard that broadcast? Or even heard *of* it?'

'I must have forgotten.'

'The biggest hoax of the century,' Barrett said, 'and you forgot it. You know the Continental Liberation Front, of course.'

'Of course.' Hahn looked uneasy.

'Which group did you say you were with?'

'The People's Crusade for Liberty.'

'I don't know it. One of the newer groups?'

'Less than five years old. It started in California.'

'What's its programme?'

'Oh, the usual,' Hahn said. 'Free elections, representative government, an opening of the security files, restoration of civil liberties.'

'And the economic orientation? Pure Marxist or one of the offshoots?'

'Not really any, I guess. We believed in a kind of – well, capitalism with some government restraints.'

'A little to the right of state socialism, and a little to the left of *laissez-faire*?' Barrett suggested.

'Something like that.'

'But that system was tried and failed, wasn't it? It had its day. It led inevitably to total socialism, which produced the compensating backlash of syndicalist capitalism, and then we got a government that pretended to be libertarian while actually stifling all individual liberties in the name of freedom. So if your group simply wanted to turn the clock back to 1955, say, there couldn't be much to its ideas.'

Hahn looked bored. 'You've got to understand I wasn't in the top ideological councils.'

'Just an economist?'

'That's it. I drew up plans for the conversion to our system.'

'Basing your work on the modified liberalism of Ricardo?'

'Well, in a sense.'

'And avoiding the tendency to fascism that was found in the thinking of Keynes?'

'You could say so,' Hahn said. He stood up, flashing a quick, vague smile. 'Look, Jim, I'd love to argue this further with you some other time, but I've really got to go now. Ned Altman talked me into coming around and helping him do a lightning-dance to bring that pile of dirt to life. So if you don't mind—'

Hahn beat a hasty retreat, without looking back.

Barrett was more perplexed than ever. Hahn hadn't been 'arguing' anything. He had been carrying on a lame and feeble conversation, letting himself be pushed hither and thither by Barrett's questions. And he had spouted a lot of nonsense. He didn't seem to know Keynes from Ricardo, nor to care about it, which was odd for a self-professed economist. He didn't have a shred of an idea what his own political party stood for. He had so little revolutionary background that he was unaware even of Hutchett's astonishing hoax of eleven years back.

He seemed phoney from top to bottom.

How was it possible that this kid had been deemed worthy of exile to Hawksbill Station, anyhow? Only the top firebrands went there. Sentencing a man to Hawksbill was like sentencing him to death, and it wasn't done lightly. Barrett couldn't imagine why Hahn was here. He seemed genuinely distressed at being exiled, and evidently he had left a beloved wife behind, but nothing else rang true about the man.

Was he – as Latimer suggested – some kind of spy?

Barrett rejected the idea out of hand. He didn't want Latimer's paranoia infecting him. The Government wasn't likely to send anyone on a one-way trip to the late Cambrian just to spy on a bunch of ageing revolutionaries who could never make trouble again. But what *was* Hahn doing here, then?

He would bear further watching, Barrett thought.

Barrett took care of some of the watching himself. But he had plenty of assistance. Latimer. Altman. Six or seven others. Latimer had recruited most of the ambulatory psycho cases, the ones who were superficially functional but full of all kinds of fears and credulities.

They were keeping an eye on the new man.

On the fifth day after his arrival, Hahn went out fishing in Rudiger's crew. Rudiger never went far from shore – eight hundred, a thousand yards out – but the water was rough even there. The waves came rolling in with X thousand miles of gathered impact behind them. A continental shelf sloped off at a wide angle, so that even at a substantial distance off shore the water wasn't very deep. Rudiger had taken soundings up to a mile out, and had reported depths no greater than 160 feet. Nobody had gone past a mile.

It wasn't that they were afraid of falling off the side of the world if they went too far east. It was simply that a mile was a long distance to row in an open boat, using stubby oars made from old packing-cases. Up Front hadn't thought to spare an outboard motor for them.

Looking toward the horizon, Barrett had an odd thought. He had been told that the women's equivalent of Hawksbill Station was safely segregated out of reach, a couple of hundred million years up the time-line. But how did he know that? There could be another station somewhere else in this very year, and they'd never know about it. A camp of women, say, living on the far side of the ocean, or even across the Inland Sea.

It wasn't very likely, he knew. With the entire past to pick from, the edgy men Up Front wouldn't take any chance that the two groups of exiles might get together and spawn a tribe of little subversives. They'd take every precaution to put an impenetrable barrier of epochs between them. Yet Barrett thought he could make it sound convincing to the other men. With a little effort he could get them to believe in the existence of several simultaneous Hawksbill Stations scattered on this level of time.

Which could be our salvation, he thought.

The instances of degenerative psychosis were beginning to snowball now. Too many men had been here too long, and one crack-up was starting to feed the next, in this blank lifeless world where humans were never meant to live. The men needed projects to keep them going. They were starting to slip off into harebrained projects, like Altman's Frankenstein girlfriend and Latimer's psi pursuit.

Suppose, Barrett thought, I could get them steamed up about reaching the other continents?

A round-the-world expedition. Maybe they could build some kind of big ship. That would keep a lot of men busy for a long time. And they'd need navigational equipment – compasses, sextants, chronometers, whatnot. Somebody would have to design an improvised radio, too. It was the kind of project that might take thirty or forty years. A focus for our energies, Barrett thought. Of course, I won't live to see the ship set sail. But, even so, it's a way of staving off collapse. We've built our staircase to the sea. Now we need something bigger to do. Idle hands make for idle minds ... sick minds ...

Turning, he saw Latimer and Altman standing behind him. 'How long have you been there?' he asked.

'Two minutes,' said Latimer. 'We brought you something to look at.'

Altman nodded vigorously. 'You ought to read it. We brought it for you to read.'

'What is it?'

Latimer handed over a folded sheaf of papers. 'I found this tucked away in Hahn's bunk after he went out with Rudiger. I know I'm not supposed to be invading his privacy, but I had to have a look at what he's been writing. There it is. He's a spy, all right.'

Barrett glanced at the papers in his hand. 'I'll read it a little later. What is it about?'

'It's a description of the Station, and a profile of most of the men in it,' said Latimer. He smiled frostily. 'Hahn's private opinion of me is that I've gone mad. His private opinion of you is a little more flattering, but not much.'

Altman said, 'He's also been hanging around the Hammer.'

'*What?*'

'I saw him going there late last night. He went into the building. I followed him. He was looking at the Hammer.'

'Why didn't you tell me that right away?' Barrett snapped.

'I wasn't sure it was important,' Altman said. 'I had to talk it over with Don first. And I couldn't do that until Hahn had gone out fishing.'

Sweat burst out on Barrett's face. 'Listen, Ned, if you ever catch Hahn going near the time-travel equipment again, you let me know in a hurry. Without consulting Don or anyone else. Clear?'

'Clear,' said Altman. He giggled. 'You know what I think? They've decided to exterminate us Up Front. Hahn's been sent here to check us out as a suicide volunteer. Then they're going to send a bomb through the Hammer and blow the Station up. We ought to wreck the Hammer and Anvil before they get a chance.'

'But why would they send a suicide volunteer?' Latimer asked. 'Unless they've got some way to rescue their spy—'

'In any case, we shouldn't take any chance,' Altman argued. 'Wreck the Hammer. Make it impossible for them to bomb us from Up Front.'

'That might be a good idea. But—'

'Shut up, both of you,' Barrett growled. 'Let me look at these papers.'

He walked a few steps away from them and sat down on a shelf of rock. He began to read.

7

Hahn had a cramped, crabbed handwriting that packed a maximum of information into a minimum of space, as though he regarded it as a mortal sin to waste paper. Fair enough. Paper was a scarce commodity here, and evidently Hahn had brought these sheets with him from Up Front. His script was clear, though. So were his opinions. Painfully so.

He had written an analysis of conditions at Hawksbill Station, setting forth in about 5000 words everything that Barrett knew was going sour here. He had neatly ticked off the men as ageing revolutionaries in whom the old fervour had turned rancid. He listed the ones who were certifiably psycho, and the ones who were on the edge, and the ones who were hanging on, like Quesada and Norton and Rudiger. Barrett was interested to see that Hahn rated even those three as suffering from severe strain and likely to fly apart at any moment. To him, Quesada and Norton and Rudiger seemed just about as stable as when they had first dropped on to the Anvil of Hawksbill Station, but that was possibly the distorting effect of his own blurred perceptions. To an outsider like Hahn, the view was different and perhaps more accurate.

Barrett forced himself not to skip ahead to Hahn's evaluation of him.

He wasn't pleased when he came to it. 'Barrett', Hahn had written, 'is like a mighty beam that's been gnawed from within by termites. He looks solid, but one good push would break him apart. A recent injury to his foot has evidently had a bad effect on him. The other men say he used to be physically vigorous and derived much of his authority from his size and strength. Now he can hardly walk. But I feel the trouble with him is inherent in the life of Hawksbill Station and doesn't have much to do with his lameness. He's been cut off from normal human drives for too long. The exercise of power here has provided the illusion of stability for him, but it's power in a vacuum, and things have happened within Barrett of which he's totally unaware. He's in bad need of therapy. He may be beyond help.'

Barrett read that several times. *Gnawed from within by termites . . . one good push . . . things have happened within him . . . bad need of therapy . . . beyond help . . .*

He was less angered than he thought he should have been. Hahn was entitled to his views. Barrett finally stopped re-reading his profile and pushed his way to the last page of Hahn's essay. It ended with the words, 'Therefore I recommend prompt termination of the Hawksbill Station penal colony and, where possible, the therapeutic rehabilitation of its inmates.'

What the hell was this?

It sounded like the report of a parole commissioner! But there was no parole from Hawksbill Station. That final sentence let all the viability of what had gone before bleed away. Hahn was pretending to be composing a report to the government Up Front, obviously. But a wall a billion years thick made filing of that report impossible. So Hahn was suffering from delusions, just like Altman and Valdosto and the others. In his fevered mind he believed he could send messages Up Front, pompous documents delineating the flaws and foibles of his fellow-prisoners.

That raised a chilling prospect. Hahn might be crazy, but he hadn't been in the Station long enough to have gone crazy here. He must have brought his insanity with him.

What if they had stopped using Hawksbill Station as a camp for political prisoners, Barrett asked himself, and were starting to use it as an insane asylum?

A cascade of psychos descending on them. Men who had gone honourably buggy under the stress of confinement would have to make room for ordinary Bedlamites. Barrett shivered. He folded up Hahn's papers and handed them to Latimer, who was sitting a few yards away, watching him intently.

'What did you think of that?' Latimer asked.

'I think it's hard to evaluate. But possibly friend Hahn is emotionally disturbed. Put his stuff back exactly where you got it, Don. And don't give Hahn the faintest inkling that you've read or removed it.'

'Right.'

'And come to me whenever you think there's something I ought to know about him,' Barrett said. 'He may be a very sick boy. He may need all the help we can give.'

The fishing expedition returned in early afternoon. Barrett saw that the dinghy was overflowing with the haul, and Hahn, coming into the camp with his arms full of gaffed trilobites, looked sunburned and pleased. Barrett came over to inspect the catch. Rudiger was in an effusive mood and held up a bright red crustacean that might have been the great-great-grandfather of all boiled lobsters, except that it had no front claws and a wicked-looking triple spike where a tail should have been. It was about two feet long, and ugly.

'A new species!' Rudiger crowed. 'There's nothing like this in any museum. I wish I could put it where it would be found. Some mountain-top, maybe.'

'If it could be found, it *would* have been found,' Barrett reminded him. 'Some palaeontologist of the twentieth century would have dug it out. So forget it, Mel.'

Hahn said, 'I've been wondering about that. How is it nobody Up Front ever dug up the fossil remains of Hawksbill Station? Aren't they worried that one of the early fossil-hunters will find it in the Cambrian strata and raise a fuss?'

Barrett shook his head. 'For one thing, no palaeontologist from the beginning of the science to the founding of the Station in 2005 ever *did* dig up Hawskbill. That's a matter of record, so there was nothing to worry about. If it came to light after 2005, why, everyone would know what it was. No paradox there.'

'Besides,' said Rudiger sadly, 'in another billion years this whole strip of rock will be on the floor of the Atlantic, with a couple of miles of sediment over it. There's not a chance we'll be found. Or that anyone Up Front will ever see this guy I caught today. Not that I give a damn. I've seen him. I'll dissect him. Their loss.'

'But you regret the fact that science will never know of this species,' Hahn said.

'Sure I do. But is it my fault? Science does know of this species. Me. I'm science. I'm the leading palaeontologist of this epoch. Can I help it if I can't publish my discoveries in the professional journals?' He scowled and walked away, carrying the big red crustacean.

Hahn and Barrett looked at each other. They smiled, in a natural mutual response to Rudiger's grumbled outburst. Then Barrett's smile faded.

. . . termites . . . one good push . . . therapy . . .

'Something wrong?' Hahn asked.

'Why?'

'You looked so bleak all of a sudden.'

'My foot gave me a twinge,' Barrett said. 'It does that, you know. Here. I'll give you a hand carrying those things. We'll have fresh-trilobite cocktail tonight.'

8

A little before midnight, Barrett was awakened by footsteps outside his hut. As he sat up, groping for the luminescence switch, Ned Altman came blundering through the door. Barrett blinked at him.

'What's the matter?'

'Hahn!' Altman rasped. 'He's fooling around with the Hammer again. We just saw him go into the building.'

Barrett shed his sleepiness like a seal bursting out of water. Ignoring the insistent throb of his leg, he pulled himself from his bed and grabbed some clothing. He was more apprehensive than he wanted Altman to see. If Hahn, fooling around with the temporal mechanism, accidentally smashed the Hammer, they might never get replacement equipment from Up Front. Which would mean that all future shipments of supplies – if there were any – would come as random shoots that might land in any old year. What business did Hahn have with the machine, anyway?

Altman said, 'Latimer's up there keeping an eye on him. He got suspicious when Hahn didn't come back to the hut, and he got me, and we went looking for him. And there he was, sniffing around the Hammer.'

'Doing what?'

'I don't know. As soon as we saw him go in, I came down here to get you. Don's watching.'

Barrett stumped his way out of the hut and did his best to run toward the main building. Pain shot like trails of hot acid up the lower half of his body. The crutch dug mercilessly into his left armpit as he leaned all his weight into it. His crippled foot, swinging freely, burned with a cold glow. His right leg, which was carrying most of the burden, creaked and popped. Altman ran breathlessly alongside him. The Station was silent at this hour.

As they passed Quesada's hut, Barrett considered waking the medic and taking him along. He decided against it. Whatever trouble Hahn might be up to, Barrett felt he could handle it himself. There was some strength left in the old gnawed beam.

Latimer stood at the entrance to the main dome. He was right on the edge of panic, or perhaps over the edge. He seemed to be gibbering with fear and shock. Barrett had never seen a man gibber before.

He clamped a big paw on Latimer's thin shoulder and said harshly, 'Where is he? Where's Hahn?'

'He – disappeared.'

'What do you mean? Where did he go?'

Latimer moaned. His face was fishbelly white. 'He got on to the Anvil,' Latimer blurted. 'The light came on – the glow. And then Hahn disappeared!'

'No,' Barrett said. 'It isn't possible. You must be mistaken.'

'I saw him go!'

'He's hiding somewhere in the building,' Barrett insisted. 'Close that door! Search for him!'

Altman said, 'He probably did disappear, Jim. If Don says he disappeared—'

'He climbed right on the Anvil. Then everything turned red, and he was gone.'

Barrett clenched his fists. There was a white-hot blaze just behind his forehead that almost made him forget about his foot. He saw his mistake now. He had depended for his espionage on two men who were patently and unmistakably insane, and that had been itself a not very sane thing to do. A man is known by his choice of lieutenants. Well, he had relied on Altman and Latimer, and now they were giving him the sort of information that such spies could be counted on to supply.

'You're hallucinating,' he told Latimer curtly. 'Ned, go wake Quesada and get him here right away. You, Don, you stand here by the entrance, and if Hahn shows up I want you to scream at the top of your lungs. I'm going to search the building for him.'

'Wait,' Latimer said. He seemed to be in control of himself again. 'Jim, do you remember when I asked you if you thought I was crazy? You said you didn't. You trusted me. Well, don't stop trusting me now. I tell you I'm not hallucinating. I saw Hahn disappear. I can't explain it, but I'm rational enough to know what I saw.'

In a milder tone Barrett said, 'All right. Maybe so. Stay by the door, anyway. I'll run a quick check.'

He started to make the circuit of the dome, beginning with the room where the Hammer was located. Everything seemed to be in order there. No Hawksbill Field glow was in evidence, and nothing had been disturbed. The room had no closets or cupboards in which Hahn could be hiding. When he had inspected it thoroughly, Barrett moved on, looking into the infirmary, the mess hall, the kitchen, the recreation room. He looked high and low. No Hahn. Of course, there were plenty of places in those rooms where Hahn might have secreted himself, but Barrett doubted that he was there. So it had all been some feverish fantasy of Latimer's, then. He completed the route and found himself back at the main entrance. Latimer still stood guard there. He had been joined by a sleepy Quesada. Altman, pale and shaky-looking, was just outside the door.

'What's happening?' Quesada asked.

'I'm not sure,' said Barrett. 'Don and Ned had the idea they saw Lew Hahn fooling around with the time equipment. I've checked the building, and he's not here, so maybe they made a little mistake. I suggest you take them both into the infirmary and give them a shot of something to settle their nerves, and we'll all try to get back to sleep.'

Latimer said, 'I tell you, I saw—'

'Shut up!' Altman broke in. 'Listen! What's that noise?'

Barrett listened. The sound was clear and loud: the hissing whine of ionization. It was the sound produced by a functioning Hawksbill Field. Suddenly there were goosepimples on his flesh. In a low voice he said, 'The field's on. We're probably getting some supplies.'

'At this hour?' said Latimer.

'We don't know what time it is Up Front. All of you stay here. I'll check the Hammer.'

'Perhaps I ought to go with you,' Quesada suggested mildly.

'*Stay here!*' Barrett thundered. He paused, embarrassed at his own explosive show of wrath. 'It only takes one of us. I'll be right back.'

Without waiting for further dissent, he pivoted and limped down the hall to the Hammer room. He shouldered the door open and looked in. There was no need for him to switch on the light. The red glow of the Hawksbill Field illuminated everything.

Barrett stationed himself just within the door. Hardly daring to breathe, he stared fixedly at the Hammer, watching as the glow deepened through various shades of pink toward crimson, and then spread until it enfolded the waiting Anvil beneath it.

Then came the implosive thunderclap, and Lew Hahn dropped out of nowhere and lay for a moment in temporal shock on the broad plate of the Anvil.

9

In the darkness, Hahn did not notice Barrett at first. He sat up slowly, shaking off the stunning effects of a trip through time. After a few seconds he pushed himself toward the lip of the Anvil and let his legs dangle over it. He swung them to get the circulation going. He took a series of deep breaths. Finally he slipped to the floor. The glow of the field had gone out in the moment of his arrival, and so he moved warily, as though not wanting to bump into anything.

Abruptly Barrett switched on the light and said, 'What have you been up to, Hahn?'

The younger man recoiled as though he had been jabbed in the gut. He gasped, hopped backward a few steps, and flung up both hands in a defensive gesture.

'Answer me,' Barrett said.

Hahn regained his equilibrium. He shot a quick glance past Barrett's bulky form toward the hallway and said, 'Let me go, will you? I can't explain now.'

'You'd better explain now.'

'It's easier for everyone if I don't,' said Hahn. 'Let me pass.'

Barrett continued to block the door. 'I want to know where you've been. What have you been doing with the Hammer?'

'Nothing. Just studying it.'

'You weren't in this room a minute ago. Then you appeared. Where'd you come from, Hahn?'

'You're mistaken. I was standing right behind the Hammer. I didn't—'

'I saw you drop down on the Anvil. You took a time trip, didn't you?'

'No.'

'Don't lie to me! You've got some way of going forward in time, isn't that so? You've been spying on us, and you just went somewhere to file your report – somewhere – and now you're back.'

Hahn's forehead was glistening. He said, 'I warn you, don't ask too many questions. You'll know everything in due time. This isn't the time. Please, now. Let me pass.'

'I want answers first,' Barrett said. He realized that he was trembling. He already knew the answers, and they were answers that shook him to the core of his soul. He knew where Hahn had been.

Hahn said nothing. He took a few hesitant steps toward Barrett, who did not move. He seemed to be gathering momentum for a rush at the doorway.

Barrett said, 'You aren't getting out of here until you tell me what I want to know.'

Hahn charged.

Barrett planted himself squarely, crutch braced against the doorframe, his good leg flat on the floor, and waited for the younger man to reach him. He figured he outweighed Hahn by eighty pounds. That might be enough to balance the fact that he was spotting Hahn thirty years and one leg. They came together, and Barrett drove his hands down on to Hahn's shoulders, trying to hold him, to force him back into the room.

Hahn gave an inch or two. He looked up at Barrett without speaking and pushed forward again.

'Don't – don't—' Barrett grunted. 'I won't let you—'

'I don't want to do this,' Hahn said.

He pushed again. Barrett felt himself buckling under the impact. He dug his hands as hard as he could into Hahn's shoulders and tried to shove the other man backward into the room, but Hahn held him firm, and all of Barrett's energy was converted into a thrust rebounding on himself. He lost control of his crutch, and it slithered out from under his arm. For one agonizing moment Barrett's full weight rested on the crushed uselessness of his left foot, and then, as though his limbs were melting away beneath

him, he began to sink toward the floor. He landed with a rever-
berating crash.

Quesada, Altman and Latimer came rushing in. Barrett writhed
in pain on the floor. Hahn stood over him, looking unhappy, his
hands locked together.

'I'm sorry,' he said. 'You shouldn't have tried to muscle me
like that.'

Barrett glowered at him. 'You were travelling in time, weren't
you? You can answer me now.'

'Yes,' Hahn said at last. 'I went Up Front.'

An hour later, after Quesada had pumped him with enough
neural depressants to keep him from jumping out of his skin,
Barrett got the full story. Hahn hadn't wanted to reveal it so soon,
but he had changed his mind after his little scuffle.

It was all very simple. Time travel now worked in both direc-
tions. The glib, impressive noises about the flow of entropy had
turned out to be just noises.

'How long has this been known?' Barrett asked.

'At least five years. We aren't sure yet exactly when the break-
through came. After we're finished going through all the sup-
pressed records of the former government—'

'The former government?'

Hahn nodded. 'The revolution came in January. Not really a
violent one, either. The syndicalists just mildewed from within,
and when they got their first push they fell over.'

'Was it mildew?' Barrett asked, colouring. 'Or termites? Keep
your metaphors straight.'

Hahn glanced away. 'Anyway, the Government fell. We've got
a provisional liberal régime in office now. Don't ask me much
about it. I'm not a political theorist. I'm not even an economist.
You guessed as much.'

'What are you, then?'

'A policeman,' Hahn said. 'Part of the commission that's in-
vestigating the prison system of the former government. Including
this prison.'

Barrett looked at Quesada, then at Hahn. Thoughts were
streaming turbulently through him, and he could not remember
when he had last been so overwhelmed by events. He had to

work hard to keep from breaking into the shakes again. His voice quavered a little as he said, 'You came back to observe Hawksbill Station, right? And you went Up Front tonight to tell them what you saw here. You think we're a pretty sad bunch, eh?'

'You've all been under heavy stress here,' Hahn said. 'Considering the circumstances of your imprisonment—'

Quesada broke in, 'If there's a liberal government in power now and it's possible to travel both ways in time, then am I right in assuming that the Hawksbill prisoners are going to be sent Up Front?'

'Of course,' said Hahn. 'It'll be done as soon as possible. That's been the whole purpose of my reconnaissance mission. To find out if you people were still alive, first, and then to see what shape you're in, how badly in need of treatment you are. You'll be given every available benefit of modern therapy, naturally. No expense spared—'

Barrett scarcely paid attention to Hahn's words. He had been fearing something like this all night, ever since Altman had told him Hahn was monkeying with the Hammer, but he had never fully allowed himself to believe that it could really be possible.

He saw his kingdom crumbling.

He saw himself returned to a world he could not begin to comprehend – a lame Rip Van Winkle, coming back after twenty years.

He saw himself leaving a place that had become his home.

Barrett said tiredly, 'You know, some of the men aren't going to be able to adapt to the shock of freedom. It might just kill them to be dumped into the real world again. I mean the advanced psychos – Valdosto, and such.'

'Yes,' Hahn said. 'I've mentioned them in my report.'

'It'll be necessary to get them ready for a return in gradual stages. It might take several years to condition them to the idea. It might even take longer than that.'

'I'm no therapist,' said Hahn. 'Whatever the doctors think is right for them is what'll be done. Maybe it will be necessary to keep them here. I can see where it would be pretty potent to send them back, after they've spent all these years believing there's no return.'

'More than that,' said Barrett. 'There's a lot of work that can be done here. Scientific work. Exploration. I don't think Hawksbill Station ought to be closed down.'

'No one said it would be. We have every intention of keeping it going, but not as a prison.'

'Good,' Barrett said. He fumbled for his crutch, found it and got heavily to his feet. Quesada moved toward him as though to steady him, but Barrett shook him off. 'Let's go outside,' he said.

They left the building. A grey mist had come in over the Station, and a fine drizzle had begun to fall. Barrett looked around at the scattering of huts. At the ocean, dimly visible to the east in the faint moonlight. He thought of Charley Norton and the party that had gone on the annual expedition to the Inland Sea. That bunch was going to be in for a real surprise, when they got back in a few weeks and discovered that everybody was free to go home.

Very strangely, Barrett felt a sudden pressure forming around his eyelids, as of tears trying to force their way out into the open.

He turned to Hahn and Quesada. In a low voice he said, 'Have you followed what I've been trying to tell you? Someone's got to stay here and ease the transition for the sick men who won't be able to stand the shock of return. Someone's got to keep the base running. Someone's got to explain to the new men who'll be coming back here, the scientists.'

'Naturally,' Han said.

'The one who does that – the one who stays behind – I think it ought to be someone who knows the Station well, someone who's fit to return Up Front, but who's willing to make the sacrifice and stay. Do you follow me? A volunteer.' They were smiling at him now. Barrett wondered if there might not be something patronizing about those smiles. He wondered if he might not be a little too transparent. To hell with both of them, he thought. He sucked the Cambrian air into his lungs until his chest swelled grandly.

'I'm offering to stay,' Barrett said loudly. He glared at them to keep them from objecting. But they wouldn't dare object, he knew. In Hawksbill Station, he was the king. And he meant to keep it that way. 'I'll be the volunteer,' he said. 'I'll be the one who stays.'

He looked out over his kingdom from the top of the hill.

Frederik Pohl
Day Million

On this day I want to tell you about, which will be about a thousand years from now, there was a boy, a girl and a love story.

Now, although I haven't said much so far, none of it is true. The boy was not what you and I would normally think of as a boy, because he was 187 years old. Nor was the girl a girl, for other reasons; and the love story did not entail that sublimation of the urge to rape and concurrent postponement of the instinct to submit which we at present understand in such matters. You won't care much for this story if you don't grasp these facts at once. If, however, you will make the effort, you'll likely enough find it jampacked, chockfull and tiptop-crammed with laughter, tears and poignant sentiment which may, or may not, be worth while. The reason the girl was not a girl was that she was a boy.

How angrily you recoil from the page! You say, who the hell wants to read about a pair of queers? Calm yourself. Here are no hot-breathing secrets of perversion for the coterie trade. In fact, if you were to see this girl, you would not guess that she was in any sense a boy. Breasts, two; vagina, one. Hips, Callipygean; face, hairless; supra-orbital lobes, non-existent. You would term her female at once, although it is true that you might wonder just what species she was a female of, being confused by the tail, the silky pelt or the gill slits behind each ear.

Now you recoil again. Cripes, man, take my word for it. This is a sweet kid, and if you, as a normal male, spent as much as an hour in a room with her, you would bend heaven and earth to get her in the sack. Dora (we will call her that; her 'name' was omicron-Dibase seven-group-totteroot S Doradus 5314, the last part of which is a colour specification corresponding to a shade of green) – Dora, I say, was feminine, charming and cute. I admit she doesn't sound that way. She was, as you might put it, a dancer. Her art involved qualities of intellection and expertise of a very high order, requiring both tremendous natural capacities and endless practice; it was performed in null-gravity and I can best describe it by saying that it was something like the performance of a contortionist and something like Classical ballet, maybe resembling Danilova's dying swan. It was also pretty damned sexy. In a symbolic way, to be sure; but face it, most of the things we call 'sexy' are symbolic, you know, except perhaps an exhibitionist's open fly. On Day Million when Dora danced, the people who saw her panted; and you would too.

About this business of her being a boy. It didn't matter to her audience that genetically she was male. It wouldn't matter to you, if you were among them, because you wouldn't know it – not unless you took a biopsy cutting of her flesh and put it under an electron-microscope to find the XY chromosome – and it didn't matter to them because they didn't care. Through techniques which are not only complex but haven't yet been discovered, these people were able to determine a great deal about the aptitudes and easements of babies quite a long time before they were born – at about the second horizon of cell-division, to be exact, when the segmenting egg is becoming a free blastocyst – and then they naturally helped those aptitudes along. Wouldn't we? If we find a child with an aptitude for music we give him a scholarship to Juilliard. If they found a child whose aptitudes were for being a woman, they made him one. As sex had long been dissociated from reproduction this was relatively easy to do and caused no trouble and no, or at least very little, comment.

How much is 'very little'? Oh, about as much as would be caused by our own tampering with Divine Will by filling a tooth. Less than would be caused by wearing a hearing aid. Does it still sound awful? Then look closely at the next busty babe you meet and reflect that she may be a Dora, for adults who are genetically male but somatically female are far from unknown even in our own time. An accident of environment in the womb overwhelms the blueprints of heredity. The difference is that with us it happens only by accident and we don't know about it except rarely, after close study; whereas the people of Day Million did it often, on purpose, because they wanted to.

Well, that's enough to tell you about Dora. It would only confuse you to add that she was seven feet tall and smelled of peanut butter. Let us begin our story.

On Day Million, Dora swam out of her house, entered a transportation tube, was sucked briskly to the surface in its flow of water and ejected in its plume of spray to an elastic platform in front of her – ah – call it her rehearsal hall. 'Oh, shit!' she cried in pretty confusion, reaching out to catch her balance and finding herself tumbled against a total stranger, whom we will call Don.

They met cute. Don was on his way to have his legs renewed. Love was the farthest thing from his mind; but when, absent-mindedly taking a short cut across the landing-platform for submarinites and finding himself drenched, he discovered his arms full of the loveliest girl he had ever seen he knew at once they were meant for each other. 'Will you marry me?' he asked. She said softly, 'Wednesday,' and the promise was like a caress.

Don was tall, muscular, bronze and exciting. His name was no more Don than Dora's was Dora, but the personal part of it was Adonis in tribute to his vibrant maleness, and so we will call him Don for short. His personality colour-code, in Angstrom units, was 5290, or only a few degrees bluer than Dora's 5314, a measure of what they had intuitively discovered at first sight, that they possessed many affinities of taste and interest.

I despair of telling you exactly what it was that Don did for a living – I don't mean for the sake of making money; I mean for the sake of giving purpose and meaning to his life, to keep him from going off his nut with boredom – except to say that it involved a lot of travelling. He travelled in interstellar spaceships. In order to make a spaceship go really fast about thirty-one male and seven genetically female human beings had to do certain things, and Don was one of the thirty-one. Actually he contemplated options. This involved a lot of exposure to radiation flux – not so much from his own station in the propulsion system as in the spillover from the next stage, where a genetic female preferred selections and the subnuclear particles making the selections she preferred demolished themselves in a shower of quanta. Well, you don't give a rat's arse for that, but it meant that Don had to be clad at all times in a skin of light, resilient, extremely strong copper-coloured metal. I have already mentioned this, but you probably thought I meant he was sunburned.

More than that, he was a cybernetic man. Most of his ruder parts had been long since replaced with mechanisms of vastly more permanence and use. A cadmium centrifuge, not a heart, pumped his blood. His lungs moved only when he wanted to speak out loud, for a cascade of osmotic filters rebreathed oxygen out of his own wastes. In a way, he probably would have looked peculiar to a man from the twentieth century, with his glowing eyes and seven-fingered hands; but to himself, and of course to Dora, he looked mighty manly and grand. In the course of his voyages Don had circled Proxima Centauri, Procyon and the puzzling worlds of Mira Ceti; he had carried agricultural templates to the planets of Canopus and brought back warm, witty pets from the pale companion of Aldebaran. Blue-hot or red-cool, he had seen a thousand stars and their ten thousand planets. He had, in fact, been travelling the starlanes with only brief leaves on Earth for pushing two centuries. But you don't care about that, either. It is people that make stories, not the circumstances they find themselves in, and you want to hear about these two people. Well, they made it. The great thing they had for each other grew and flowered and burst into fruition on Wednesday, just as Dora had promised. They met at the encoding-room, with a couple of well-wishing friends apiece to cheer them on, and while their identities were being taped and stored they smiled and whispered to each other and bore the jokes of their friends with blushing repartee. Then they exchanged their mathematical analogues and went away. Dora to her dwelling beneath the surface of the sea and Don to his ship.

It was an idyll, really. They lived happily ever after – or anyway until they decided not to bother anymore and died.

Of course, they never set eyes on each other again.

*　　*　　*

Oh, I can see you now, you eaters of charcoal-broiled steak, scratching an incipient bunion with one hand and holding this story with the other, while the stereo plays d'Indy or Monk. You don't believe a word of it, do you? Not for one minute. People wouldn't live like that, you say with an irritated and not amused grunt as you get up to put fresh ice in a stale drink.

And yet there's Dora, hurrying back through the flushing commuter-pipes towards her underwater home (she prefers it there; has had herself somatically altered to breathe the stuff). If I tell you with what sweet fulfilment she fits the recorded analogue of Don into the symbol-manipulator, hooks herself in and turns herself on . . . if I try to tell you any of that you will simply stare. Or glare; and grumble, what the hell kind of lovemaking is this? And yet I assure you, friend, I really do assure you that Dora's ecstasies are as creamy and passionate as any of James Bond's lady spies, and one hell of a lot more so than anything you are going to find in 'real life'. Go ahead, glare and grumble. Dora doesn't care. If she thinks of you at all, her thirty-times-great-great-grandfather, she thinks you're a pretty primordial sort of brute. You are. Why, Dora is farther removed from you than you are from the Australopithecines of five thousand centuries ago. You could not swim a second in the strong currents of her life. You don't think progress goes in a straight line, do you? Do you recognize that it is an ascending, accelerating, maybe even exponential curve? It takes Hell's own time to get started, but when it goes it goes like a bomb. And you, you Scotch-drinking steak-eater in your Relaxacizer chair, you've just barely lighted the primacord of the fuse. What is it now, the six or seven hundred thousandth day after Christ? Dora lives in Day Million. A thousand years from now. Her body fats are poly-unsaturated, like Crisco. Her wastes are hemodialysed out of her bloodstream while she sleeps – that means she doesn't have to go to the bathroom. On whim, to pass a slow half-hour, she can command more energy than the entire nation of Portugal can spend today, and use it to launch a weekend satellite or remould a crater on the Moon. She loves Don very much. She keeps his every gesture, mannerism, nuance, touch of hand, thrill of intercourse, passion of kiss stored in symbolic-mathematical form. And when she wants him, all she has to do is turn the machine on and she has him.

And Don, of course, has Dora. Adrift on a sponson city a few hundred yards over her head or orbiting Arcturus, fifty light-years away, Don has only to command his own symbol-manipulator to rescue Dora from the ferrite files and bring her to life for him, and there she is; and rapturously, tirelessly they ball all night. Not in the flesh, of course; but then his flesh has been extensively altered and it wouldn't really be much fun. He doesn't need the flesh for pleasure. Genital organs feel nothing. Neither do hands, nor breasts, nor lips; they are only receptors, accepting and transmitting impulses. It is the brain that feels, it is the interpretation of those impulses that makes agony or orgasm; and Don's symbol-manipulator gives him the analogue of cuddling, the analogue of kissing, the analogue of wildest, most ardent hours with the eternal, exquisite and incorruptible analogue of Dora. Or Diane. Or sweet Rose, or laughing Alicia; for, to be sure, they have each of them exchanged analogues before, and will again.

Balls, you say, it looks crazy to me. And you – with your after-shave lotion and your little red car, pushing papers across a desk all day and chasing tail all night – tell me, just how the hell do you think you would look to Tiglath-Pileser, say, or Attila the Hun?

Philip K. Dick
The electric ant

At four-fifteen in the afternoon, TST, Garson Poole woke up in his hospital bed, knew that he lay in a hospital bed in a three-bed ward, and realized in addition two things: that he no longer had a right hand and that he felt no pain.

They have given me a strong analgesic, he said to himself as he stared at the far wall with its window showing downtown New York. Webs in which vehicles and peds darted and wheeled glimmered in the late afternoon sun, and the brilliance of the ageing light pleased him. It's not yet out, he thought. And neither am I.

A fone lay on the table beside his bed; he hesitated, then picked it up and dialled for an outside line. A moment later he was faced by Louis Danceman, in charge of Tri-Plan's activities while he, Garson Poole, was elsewhere.

'Thank God you're alive,' Danceman said, seeing him; his big, fleshy face with its moon's surface of pock marks flattened with relief. 'I've been calling all—'

'I just don't have a right hand,' Poole said.

'But you'll be OK. I mean, they can graft another one on.'

'How long have I been here?' Poole said. He wondered where the nurses and doctors had gone to; why weren't they clucking and fussing about him making a call?

'Four days,' Danceman said. 'Everything here at the plant is going splunkishly. In fact we've splunked orders from three separate police systems, all here on Terra. Two in Ohio, one in Wyoming. Good solid orders, with one-third in advance and the usual three-year lease-option.'

'Come and get me out of here,' Poole said.

'I can't get you out until the new hand—'

'I'll have that done later.' He wanted desperately to get back to familiar surroundings; memory of the mercantile squib looming grotesquely on the pilot screen careened at the back of his mind; if he shut his eyes he felt himself back in his damaged craft as it plunged from one vehicle to another, piling up enormous damage as it went. The kinetic sensations . . . he winced, recalling them. I guess I'm lucky, he said to himself.

'Is Sarah Benton there with you?' Danceman asked.

'No.' Of course; his personal secretary – if only for job considerations – would be hovering close by, mothering him in her jejune, infantile way. All heavy-set women like to mother people, he thought. And they're dangerous; if they fall on you they can kill you. 'Maybe that's what happened to me,' he said aloud. 'Maybe Sarah fell on my squib.'

'No, no; a tie rod in the steering-fin of your squib split apart during the heavy rush-hour traffic and you—'

'I remember.' He turned in his bed as the door of the ward opened; a white-clad doctor and two blue-clad nurses appeared, making their way toward his bed. 'I'll talk to you later,' Poole said, and hung up the fone. He took a deep, expectant breath.

'You shouldn't be foning quite so soon,' the doctor said as he studied the chart. 'Mr Garson Poole, owner of Tri-Plan Electronics. Makers of random ident darts that track their prey for a circle-radius of a thousand miles, responding to unique enceph wave patterns. You're a successful man Mr Poole. But, Mr Poole, you're not a man. You're an electric ant.'

'Christ,' Poole said, stunned.

'So we can't really treat you here, now that we've found out. We knew, of course, as soon as we examined your injured right hand; we saw the electronic components and then we made torso X-rays and of course they bore out our hypothesis.'

'What', Poole said, 'is an "electric ant"?' But he knew; he could decipher the term.

A nurse said, 'An organic robot.'

'I see,' Poole said. Frigid perspiration rose to the surface of his skin, across all his body.

'You didn't know,' the doctor said.

'No.' Poole shook his head.

The doctor said, 'We get an electric ant every week or so. Either brought in here from a squib accident – like yourself – or one seeking voluntary admission . . . one who, like yourself, has never been told, who has functioned alongside humans, believing himself – itself – human. As to your hand—' He paused.

'Forget my hand,' Poole said savagely.

'Be calm.' The doctor leaned over him, peered acutely down into Poole's face. 'We'll have a hospital boat convey you over to a service facility where repairs, or replacement, on your hand can be made at a reasonable expense, either to yourself, if you're self-owned, or to your owners, if such there are. In any case you'll be back at your desk at Tri-Plan, functioning just as before.'

'Except,' Poole said, 'now I know.' He wondered if Danceman or Sarah or any of the others at the office knew. Had they – or one of them – purchased him? Designed him? A figurehead, he said to himself; that's all I've been. I must never really have run the company; it was a delusion implanted in me when I was made . . . along with the delusion that I am human and alive.

'Before you leave for the repair facility,' the doctor said, 'could you kindly settle your bill at the front desk?'

Poole said acidly, 'How can there be a bill if you don't treat ants here?'

'For our services,' the nurse said. 'Up until the point we knew.'

'Bill me,' Poole said, with furious, impotent anger. 'Bill my firm.' With massive effort he managed to sit up; his head swimming, he stepped haltingly from the bed and on to the floor. 'I'll be glad to leave here,' he said as he rose to a standing position. 'And thank you for your humane attention.'

'Thank you, too, Mr Poole,' the doctor said. 'Or rather I should say just Poole.'

At the repair facility he had his missing hand replaced.

It proved fascinating, the hand; he examined it for a long time before he let the technicians install it. On the surface it appeared organic – in fact, on the surface, it was. Natural skin covered natural flesh, and true blood filled the veins and capillaries. But, beneath that, wires and circuits, miniaturized components, gleamed . . . looking deep into the wrist he saw surge gates, motors, multistage valves, all very small. Intricate. And – the hand cost forty frogs. A week's salary, in so far as he drew it from the company payroll.

'Is this guaranteed?' he asked the technicians as they fused the 'bone' section of the hand to the balance of the body.

'Ninety days, parts and labour,' one of the technicians said. 'Unless subjected to unusual or intentional abuse.'

'That sounds vaguely suggestive,' Poole said.

The technician, a man – all of them were men – said, regarding him keenly, 'You've been posing?'

'Unintentionally,' Poole said.

'And now it's intentional?'

Poole said, 'Exactly.'

'Do you know why you never guessed? There must have been signs . . . clickings and whirrings from inside you, now and then. You never guessed because you were programmed not to notice. You'll now have the same difficulty finding out why you were built and for whom you've been operating.'

'A slave,' Poole said. 'A mechanical slave.'

'You've had fun.'

'I've lived a good life,' Poole said. 'I've worked hard.'

He paid the facility its forty frogs, flexed his new fingers, tested them out by picking up various objects, such as coins, then departed. Ten minutes later he was aboard a public carrier, on his way home. It had been quite a day.

At home, in his one-room apartment, he poured himself a shot of Jack Daniel Purple Label – sixty years old – and sat sipping it, meanwhile gazing through his sole window at the building on the opposite side of the street. Shall I go to the office? he asked himself. If so, why? If not, why? Choose one. Christ, he thought, it undermines you, knowing this. I'm a freak, he realized. An inanimate object mimicking an animate one. But – he felt alive. Yet . . . he felt differently, now. About himself. Hence about everyone, especially Danceman and Sarah, everyone at Tri-Plan.

I think I'll kill myself, he said to himself. But I'm probably programmed not to do that; it would be a costly waste which my owner would have to absorb. And he wouldn't want to.

Programmed. In me somewhere, he thought, there is a matrix fitted in place, a grid screen that cuts me off from certain thoughts. Certain actions. And forces me into others. I am not free. I never was, but now I know it; that makes it different.

Turning his window to opaque, he snapped on the overhead light, carefully set about removing his clothing, piece by piece. He had watched carefully as the technicians at the repair facility had attached his new hand: He had a rather clear idea, now, of how his body had been assembled. Two major panels, one in each thigh; the technicians had removed the panels to check the circuit complexes beneath. If I'm programmed, he decided, the matrix probably can be found there.

The maze of circuitry baffled him. I need help, he said to himself. Let's see . . . what's the fone code for the class BBB computer we hire at the office?

He picked up the fone, dialled the computer at its permanent location in Boise, Idaho.

'Use of this computer is prorated at a five frogs per minute basis,' a mechanical voice from the fone said. 'Please hold your mastercreditchargeplate before the screen.'

He did so.

'At the sound of the buzzer you will be connected with the computer,' the voice continued. 'Please query it as rapidly as possible, taking into account the fact that its answer will be given in terms of a microsecond, while your query will—' He turned the sound down then. But quickly turned it up as the blank audio input of the computer appeared on the screen. At this moment the computer had become a giant ear, listening to him – as well as fifty thousand other queriers throughout Terra.

'Scan me visually,' he instructed the computer. 'And tell me where I will find the programming mechanism which controls my thoughts and behaviour.' He waited. On the fone's screen a great active eye, multilensed, peered at him; he displayed himself for it, there in his one-room apartment.

The computer said, 'Remove your chest panel. Apply pressure at your breastbone and then ease outward.'

He did so. A section of his chest came off; dizzily, he set it down on the floor.

'I can distinguish control modules,' the computer said, 'but I can't tell which—' It paused as its eye roved about on the fone screen. 'I distinguish a roll of punched tape mounted above your heart mechanism. Do you see it?' Poole craned his neck, peered. He saw it, too. 'I will have to sign off,' the computer said. 'After I have examined the data available to me I will contact you and give you an answer. Good day.' The screen died out.

I'll yank the tape out of me, Poole said to himself. Tiny . . . no larger than two spools of thread, with a scanner mounted between the delivery drum and the take-up drum. He could not see any sign of motion; the spools seemed inert. They must cut in as override, he reflected, when specific situations occur. Override to my encephalic processes. And they've been doing it all my life.

He reached down, touched the delivery drum. All I have to do is tear this out, he thought, and—

The fone screen relit. 'Mastercreditchargeplate number 3-BNX-882-HQR446-T,' the computer's voice came. 'This is BBB-307DR recontacting you in response to your query of sixteen seconds' lapse, 4 November 1992. The punched-tape roll above your heart mechanism is not a programming turret but is in fact a reality-supply construct. All sense stimuli received by your central neurological system emanate from that unit and tampering with it would be risky if not terminal.' It added, 'You appear to have no programming circuit. Query answered. Good day.' It flicked off.

Poole, standing naked before the fone screen, touched the tape drum once again, with calculated, enormous caution. I see, he thought wildly. Or do I see? This unit—

If I cut the tape, he realized, my world will disappear. Reality will continue for others, but not for me. Because my reality, my universe, is coming to me from this minuscule unit. Fed into the scanner and then into my central nervous system as it snailishly unwinds.

It has been unwinding for years, he decided.

Getting his clothes, he re-dressed, seated himself in his big armchair – a luxury imported into his apartment from Tri-Plan's main offices – and lit a tobacco cigarette. His hands shook as he laid down his initialled lighter; leaning back, he blew smoke before himself, creating a nimbus of grey.

I have to go slowly he said to himself. What am I trying to do? Bypass my programming? But the computer found no programming circuit. Do I want to interfere with the reality tape? And, if so, *why*?

Because, he thought, if I control that, I control reality. At least so far as I'm concerned. My subjective reality . . . but that's all there is. Objective reality is a synthetic construct, dealing with a hypothetical universalization of a multitude of subjective realities.

My universe is lying within my fingers, he realized. If I can just figure out how the damn thing works. All I set out to do originally was to search for and locate my programming circuit so I could gain true homeostatic functioning: control of myself. But with this—

With this he did not merely gain control of himself; he gained control over everything.

And this sets me apart from every human who ever lived and died, he thought sombrely.

Going over to the fone he dialled his office. When he had Danceman on the screen he said briskly, 'I want you to send a complete set of microtools and enlarging screen over to my apartment. I have some microcircuitry to work on.' Then he broke the connection, not wanting to discuss it.

A half-hour later a knock sounded on his door. When he opened up he found himself facing one of the shop foremen, loaded down with microtools of every sort. 'You didn't say exactly what you wanted,' the foreman said, entering the apartment. 'So Mr Danceman had me bring everything.'

'And the enlarging-lens system?'

'In the truck, up on the roof.'

Maybe what I want to do, Poole thought, is die. He lit a cigarette, stood smoking and waiting as the shop foreman lugged the heavy enlarging-screen, with its power supply and control panel, into the apartment. This is suicide, what I'm doing here. He shuddered.

'Anything wrong, Mr Poole?' the shop foreman said as he rose to his feet, relieved of the burden of the enlarging-lens system. 'You must still be rickety on your pins from your accident.'

'Yes,' Poole said quietly. He stood tautly waiting until the foreman left.

Under the enlarging-lens system the plastic tape assumed a new shape: a wide track along which hundreds of thousands of punchholes worked their way. I thought so, Poole thought. Not recorded as charges on a ferrous oxide layer but actually punched-free slots.

Under the lens the strip of tape visibly oozed forward. Very slowly, but it did, at uniform velocity, move in the direction of the scanner.

The way I figure it, he thought, is that the punched holes are *on* gates. It functions like a player piano; solid is no, punch-hole is yes. How can I test this?

Obviously by filling in a number of the holes.

He measured the amount of tape left on the delivery spool, calculated – at great effort – the velocity of the tape's movement, and then came up with a figure. If he altered the tape visible at the ingoing edge of the scanner, five to seven hours would pass before that particular time period arrived. He would in effect be painting out stimuli due a few hours from now.

With a microbrush he swabbed a large – relatively large – section of tape with opaque varnish . . . obtained from the supply kit accompanying the microtools. I have smeared out stimuli for about half an hour, he pondered. Have covered at least a thousand punches.

It would be interesting to see what change, if any, overcame his environment, six hours from now.

Five and a half hours later he sat at Krackter's, a superb bar in Manhattan, having a drink with Danceman.

'You look bad,' Danceman said.

'I am bad,' Poole said. He finished his drink, a Scotch sour, and ordered another.

'From the accident?'

'In a sense, yes.'

Danceman said, 'Is it – something you found out about your-self?'

Raising his head, Poole eyed him in the murky light of the bar. 'Then, you know.'

'I know,' Danceman said, 'that I should call you "Poole" instead of "Mr Poole". But I prefer the latter and will continue to do so.'

'How long have you known?' Poole said.

'Since you took over the firm. I was told that the actual owners of Tri-Plan, who are located in the Prox System, wanted Tri-Plan run by an electric ant whom they could control. They wanted a brilliant and forceful—'

'The real owners?' This was the first he had heard about that. 'We have two thousand stockholders. Scattered everywhere.'

'Marvis Bey and her husband Ernan, on Prox 4, control fifty-one per cent of the voting-stock. This has been true from the start.'

'Why didn't I know?'

'I was told not to tell you. You were to think that you yourself made all company policy. With my help. But actually I was feeding you what the Beys fed to me.'

'I'm a figurehead,' Poole said.

'In a sense, yes,' Danceman nodded. 'But you'll always be "Mr Poole" to me.'

A section of the far wall vanished. And, with it, several people at tables nearby. And—

Through the big glass side of the bar, the skyline of New York City flickered out of existence.

Poole said hoarsely, 'Look around. Do you see any changes?'

After looking around the room, Danceman said, 'No. What like?'

'You still see the skyline?'

'Sure. Smoggy as it is. The lights wink—'

'Now I know,' Poole said. He had been right; every punch-hole covered up meant the disappearance of some object in his reality world. Standing, he said, 'I'll see you later, Danceman. I have to get back to my apartment; there's some work I'm doing. Good night.' He strode from the bar and out on to the streets, searching for a cab.

No cabs.

Those, too, he thought. I wonder what else I painted over. Prostitutes? Flowers? Prisons?

There, in the bar's parking-lot, Danceman's squib. I'll take that, he decided. There are still cabs in Danceman's world; he can get one later. Anyhow it's a company car, and I hold a copy of the key.

Presently he was in the air, turning toward his apartment.

New York City had not returned. To the left and right vehicles and buildings, streets, ped-runners, signs . . . and in the centre nothing. How can I fly into that? he asked himself. I'd disappear.

Or would I? He flew toward the nothingness.

Smoking one cigarette after another he flew in a circle for fifteen minutes . . . and then, soundlessly, New York reappeared. He could finish his trip. He stubbed out his cigarette (a waste of something so valuable) and shot off in the direction of his apartment.

If I insert a narrow opaque strip, he pondered as he unlocked his apartment door, I can—

His thoughts ceased. Someone sat in his living-room chair, watching a captain kirk on the TV. 'Sarah,' he said, nettled.

She rose, well padded but graceful. 'You weren't at the hospital, so I came here. I still have that key you gave me back in March after we had that awful argument. Oh . . . you look so depressed.' She came up to him, peeped into his face anxiously. 'Does your injury hurt that badly?'

'It's not that.' He removed his coat, tie, shirt, and then his chest panel; kneeling down he began inserting his hands into the micro-tool gloves. Pausing, he looked up at her and said, 'I found out I'm an electric ant. Which from one standpoint opens up certain possibilities, which I am exploring now.' He flexed his fingers and at the far end of the left Waldo a micro screwdriver moved, magnified into visibility by the enlarging-lens system. 'You can watch,' he informed her. 'If you so desire.'

She had begun to cry.

'What's the matter?' he demanded savagely, without looking up from his work.

'I – it's just so sad. You've been such a good employer to all of us at Tri-Plan. We respect you so. And now it's all changed.'

The plastic tape had an unpunched margin at top and bottom; he cut a horizontal strip, very narrow, then, after a moment of great concentration, cut the tape itself four hours away from the scanning-head. He then rotated the cut strip into a right-angle piece in relation to the scanner, fused it in place with a micro heat element, then re-attached the tape reel to its left and right sides. He had, in effect, inserted a dead twenty minutes into the unfolding flow of his reality. It would take effect – according to his calculations – a few minutes after midnight.

'Are you fixing yourself?' Sarah asked timidly.

Poole said, 'I'm freezing myself.' Beyond this he had several other alterations in mind. But first he had to test his theory; blank, unpunched tape meant no stimuli, in which case the *lack* of tape . . .

'That look on your face,' Sarah said. She began gathering up her purse, coat, rolled-up aud-vid magazine. 'I'll go; I can see how you feel about finding me here.'

'Stay,' he said. 'I'll watch the captain kirk with you.' He got into his shirt. 'Remember years ago when there were – what was it? – twenty or twenty-two TV channels? Before the Government shut down the independents?'

She nodded.

'What would it have looked like,' he said, 'if this TV set projected all channels on to the cathode-ray screen *at the same time*? Could we have distinguished anything in the mixture?'

'I don't think so.'

'Maybe we could learn to. Learn to be selective; do our own job of perceiving what we wanted to and what we didn't. Think of the possibilities, if our brain could handle twenty images at once; think of the amount of knowledge which could be stored during a given period. I wonder if the brain, the human brain—' He broke off. 'The human brain couldn't do it,' he said, presently, reflecting to himself. 'But in theory a quasi-organic brain might.'

'Is that what you have?' Sarah asked.

'Yes,' Poole said.

*　　*　　*

They watched the captain kirk to its end, and then they went to bed. But Poole sat up against his pillows, smoking and brooding. Beside him, Sarah stirred restlessly, wondering why he did not turn off the light.

Eleven-fifty. It would happen any time, now.

'Sarah,' he said, 'I want your help. In a very few minutes something strange will happen to me. It won't last long, but I want you to watch me carefully. See if I—' He gestured. 'Show any changes. If I seem to go to sleep, or if I talk nonsense, or—' He wanted to say, if I disappear. But he did not. 'I won't do you any harm, but I think it might be a good idea if you armed yourself. Do you have your anti-mugging gun with you?'

'In my purse.' She had become fully awake now; sitting up in bed, she gazed at him with wild fright, her ample shoulders tanned and freckled in the light of the room.

He got her gun for her.

The room stiffened into paralysed immobility. Then the colours began to drain away. Objects diminished until, smoke-like, they flitted away into shadows. Darkness filmed everything as the objects in the room became weaker and weaker.

The last stimuli are dying out, Poole realized. He squinted, trying to see. He made out Sarah Benton, sitting in the bed; a two-dimensional figure that doll-like had been propped up, there to fade and dwindle. Random gusts of dematerialized substance eddied about in unstable clouds; the elements collected, fell apart, then collected once again. And then the last heat, energy and light dissipated; the room closed over and fell into itself, as if sealed off from reality. And at that point absolute blackness replaced everything, space without depth, not nocturnal but rather stiff and unyielding. And in addition he heard nothing.

Reaching, he tried to touch something. But he had nothing to reach with. Awareness of his own body had departed along with everything else in the universe. He had no hands and, even if he had, there would be nothing for them to feel.

I am still right about the way the damn tape works, he said to himself, using a non-existent mouth to communicate an invisible message.

Will this pass in ten minutes? he asked himself. Am I right about that, too? He waited . . . but knew intuitively that his time sense had departed with everything else. I can only wait, he realized. And hope it won't be long.

To pace himself, he thought, I'll make up an encyclopedia; I'll try to list everything that begins with an *a*. Let's see. He pondered. Apple, automobile, acksetron, atmosphere, Atlantic, tomato aspic, advertising – he thought on and on, categories slithering through his fright-haunted mind.

All at once light flickered on.

He lay on the couch in the living-room, and mild sunlight spilled in through the single window. Two men bent over him, their hands full of tools. Maintenance-men, he realized. They've been working on me.

'He's conscious,' one of the technicians said. He rose, stood back; Sarah Benton, dithering with anxiety, replaced him.

'Thank God!' she said, breathing wetly in Poole's ear. 'I was so afraid; I called Mr Danceman finally about—'

'What happened?' Poole broke in harshly. 'Start from the beginning and for God's sake speak slowly. So I can assimilate it all.'

Sarah composed herself, paused to rub her nose, and then plunged on nervously, 'You passed out. You just lay there, as if you were dead. I waited until two-thirty and you did nothing. I called Mr Danceman, waking him up unfortunately, and he called the electric-ant maintenance – I mean, the organic-roby maintenance people, and these two men came about four-forty-five, and they've been working on you ever since. It's now six-fifteen in the morning. And I'm very cold and I want to go to bed; I can't make it in to the office today; I really can't.' She turned away, sniffling. The sound annoyed him.

One of the uniformed maintenance-men said, 'You've been playing around with your reality tape.'

'Yes,' Poole said. Why deny it? Obviously they had found the inserted solid strip. 'I shouldn't have been out that long,' he said. 'I inserted a ten-minute strip only.'

'It shut off the tape transport,' the technician explained. 'The tape stopped moving forward; your insertion jammed it, and it automatically shut down to avoid tearing the tape. Why would you want to fiddle around with that? Don't you know what you could do?'

'I'm not sure,' Poole said.

'But you have a good idea.'

Poole said acridly, 'That's why I'm doing it.'

'Your bill', the maintenance-man said, 'is going to be ninety-five frogs. Payable in instalments, if you so desire.'

'OK,' he said; he sat up groggily, rubbed his eyes and grimaced. His head ached and his stomach felt totally empty.

'Shave the tape next time,' the primary technician told him. 'That way it won't jam. Didn't it occur to you that it had a safety factor built into it? So it would stop rather than—'

'What happens,' Poole interrupted, his voice low and intently careful, 'if no tape passes under the scanner? No tape – nothing at all? The photocell shining upward without impedance?'

The technicians glanced at each other. One said, 'All the neuro circuits jump their gaps and short out.'

'Meaning what?' Poole said.

'Meaning it's the end of the mechanism.'

Poole said, 'I've examined the circuit. It doesn't carry enough voltage to do that. Metal won't fuse under such slight loads of current, even if the terminals are touching. We're talking about a millionth of a watt along a cesium channel perhaps a sixteenth of an inch in length. Let's assume there are a billion possible combinations at one instant arising from the punch-outs on the tape. The total output isn't cumulative; the amount of current depends on what the battery details for that module, and it's not much. With all gates open and going.'

'Would we lie?' one of the technicians asked wearily.

'Why not?' Poole said. 'Here I have an opportunity to experience everything. Simultaneously. To know the universe in its entirety, to be momentarily in contact with all reality. Something that no human can do. A symphonic score entering my brain outside of time, all notes, all instruments sounding at once. And all symphonies. Do you see?'

'It'll burn you out,' both technicians said, together.

'I don't think so,' Poole said.

Sarah said, 'Would you like a cup of coffee, Mr Poole?'

'Yes,' he said; he lowered his legs, pressed his cold feet against the floor, shuddered. He then stood up. His body ached. They had me lying all night on the couch, he realized. All things considered, they could have done better than that.

At the kitchen table in the far corner of the room, Garson Poole sat sipping coffee across from Sarah. The technicians had long since gone.

'You're not going to try any more experiments on yourself, are you?' Sarah asked wistfully.

Poole grated, 'I would like to control time. To reverse it.' I will cut a segment of tape out, he thought, and fuse it in upside down. The causal sequences will then flow the other way. Thereupon I will walk backwards down the steps from the roof field, back up to my door, push a locked door open, walk backward to the sink, where I will get out a stack of dirty dishes. I will seat myself at this table before the stack, fill each dish with food produced from my stomach . . . I will then transfer the food to the refrigerator. The next day I will take the food out of the refrigerator, pack it in bags, carry the bags to a supermarket, distribute the food here and there in the store. And at last, at the front counter, they will pay me money for this, from their cash register. The food will be packed with other food in big plastic boxes, shipped out of the city into the hydroponic plants on the Atlantic, there to be joined back to trees and bushes or the bodies of dead animals or pushed deep into the ground. But what would all that prove? A video tape running backward . . . I would know no more than I know now, which is not enough.

What I want, he realized, is ultimate and absolute reality, for one microsecond. After that it doesn't matter, because all will be known; nothing will be left to understand or see.

I might try one other change, he said to himself. Before I try cutting the tape. I will prick new punch-holes in the tape and see what presently emerges. It will be interesting because I will not know what the holes I make mean.

Using the tip of a microtool, he punched several holes, at random, on the tape. As close to the scanner as he could manage . . . he did not want to wait.

'I wonder if you'll see it,' he said to Sarah. Apparently not, in so far as he could extrapolate. 'Something may show up,' he said to her. 'I just want to warn you; I don't want you to be afraid.'

'Oh dear,' Sarah said tinnily.

He examined his wristwatch. One minute passed, then a second, a third. And then—

In the centre of the room appeared a flock of green and black ducks. They quacked excitedly, rose from the floor, fluttered against the ceiling in a dithering mass of feathers and wings and frantic in their vast urge, their instinct, to get away.

'Ducks,' Poole said marvelling. 'I punched a hole for a flight of wild ducks.'

Now something else appeared. A park bench with an elderly, tattered man seated on it, reading a torn, bent newspaper. He looked up, dimly made out Poole, smiled briefly at him with badly made dentures, and then returned to his folded-back newspaper. He read on.

'Do you see him?' Poole asked Sarah. 'And the ducks?' At that moment the ducks and the park bum disappeared. Nothing remained of them. The interval of their punch-holes had quickly passed.

'They weren't real,' Sarah said. 'Were they? So how?'

'You're not real,' he told Sarah. 'You're a stimulus-factor on my reality tape. A punch-hole that can be glazed over. Do you also have an existence in another reality tape or one in an objective reality?' He did not know; he couldn't tell. Perhaps Sarah did not know, either. Perhaps she existed in a thousand reality tapes; perhaps on every reality tape ever manufactured. 'If I cut the tape,' he said, 'you will be everywhere and nowhere. Like everything else in the universe. At least as far as I am aware of it.'

Sarah faltered, 'I am real.'

'I want to know you completely,' Poole said. 'To do that I must cut the tape. If I don't do it now, I'll do it some other time; it's inevitable that eventually I'll do it.' So why wait? he asked himself. And there is always the possibility that Danceman has reported back to my maker, that they will be making moves to head me off. Because, perhaps, I'm endangering their property – myself.

'You make me wish I had gone to the office after all,' Sarah said, her mouth turned down with dimpled gloom.

'Go,' Poole said.

'I don't want to leave you alone.'

'I'll be fine,' Poole said.

'No, you're not going to be fine. You're going to unplug yourself or something, kill yourself because you've found out you're just an electric ant and not a human being.'

He said, presently, 'Maybe so.' Maybe it boiled down to that.

'And I can't stop you,' she said.

'No,' he nodded in agreement.

'But I'm going to stay,' Sarah said. 'Even if I can't stop you. Because if I do leave, and you do kill yourself, I'll always ask myself for the rest of my life what would have happened if I had stayed. You see?'

Again he nodded.

'Go ahead,' Sarah said.

He rose to his feet. 'It's not pain I'm going to feel,' he told her. 'Although it may look like that to you. Keep in mind the fact that organic robots have minimal pain circuits in them. I will be experiencing the most intense—'

'Don't tell me any more,' she broke in. 'Just do it if you're going to, or don't do it if you're not.'

Clumsily – because he was frightened – he wriggled his hands into the microglove assembly, reached to pick up a tiny tool: a sharp cutting-blade. 'I am going to cut a tape mounted inside my chest panel,' he said, as he gazed through the enlarging-lens system. 'That's all.' His hand shook as it lifted the cutting-blade. In a second it can be done, he realized. All over. And – I will have time to fuse the cut ends of tape back together, he realized. A half-hour at least. If I change my mind.

He cut the tape.

Staring at him, cowering, Sarah whispered, 'Nothing happened.'

'I have thirty or forty minutes.' He reseated himself at the table, having drawn his hands from the gloves. His voice, he noticed, shook; undoubtedly Sarah was aware of it, and he felt anger at himself, knowing that he had alarmed her. 'I'm sorry,' he said, irrationally; he wanted to apologize to her. 'Maybe you ought to leave,' he said in panic; again he stood up. So did she, reflexively, as if imitating him; bloated and nervous, she stood there palpitating. 'Go away,' he said thickly. 'Back to the office where you ought to be. Where we both ought to be.' I'm going to fuse the tape-ends together, he told himself; the tension is too great for me to stand.

Reaching his hands toward the gloves, he groped to pull them over his straining fingers. Peering into the enlarging-screen he saw the beam from the photoelectric gleam upward, pointed directly into the scanner; at the same time he saw the end of the tape disappearing under the scanner . . . he saw this, understood it; I'm too late, he realized. It had passed through. God, he thought, help me. It has begun winding at a rate greater than I calculated. So it's *now* that—

He saw apples and cobblestones and zebras. He felt warmth, the silky texture of cloth; he felt the ocean lapping at him and a great wind, from the north, plucking at him as if to lead him somewhere. Sarah was all around him, so was Danceman. New York glowed in the night, and the squibs about him scuttled and bounced through night skies and daytime and flooding and drought. Butter relaxed into liquid on his tongue, and at the same time hideous odours and tastes assailed him: the bitter presence of poisons and lemons and blades of summer grass. He drowned; he fell; he lay in the arms of a woman in a vast white bed which at the same time dinned shrilly in his ear: the warning noise of a defective elevator in one of the ancient, ruined downtown hotels. I am living, I have lived, I will never live, he said to himself, and with his thoughts came every word, every sound; insects squeaked and raced, and he half-sank into a complex body of homeostatic machinery located somewhere in Tri-Plan's labs.

He wanted to say something to Sarah. Opening his mouth he tried to bring forth words – a specific string of them out of the enormous mass of them brilliantly lighting his mind, scorching him with their utter meaning.

His mouth burned. He wondered why.

Frozen against the wall, Sarah Benton opened her eyes and saw the curl of smoke ascending from Poole's half-opened mouth. Then the roby sank down, knelt on elbows and knees, then slowly spread out in a broken, crumpled heap. She knew without examining it that it had 'died'.

Poole did it to itself, she realized. And it couldn't feel pain; it said so itself. Or at least not very much pain; maybe a little. Anyhow, now it is over.

I had better call Mr Danceman and tell him what's happened, she decided. Still shaky, she made her way across the room to the fone; picking it up, she dialled from memory.

It thought I was a stimulus-factor on its reality tape, she said to herself. So it thought I would die when it 'died'. How strange, she thought. Why did it imagine that? It had never been plugged into the real world; it had 'lived' in an electronic world of its own. How bizarre.

'Mr Danceman,' she said, when the circuit to his office had been put through. 'Poole is gone. It destroyed itself right in front of my eyes. You'd better come over.'

'So we're finally free of it.'

'Yes, won't it be nice?'

Danceman said, 'I'll send a couple of men over from the shop.' He saw past her, made out the sight of Poole lying by the kitchen table. 'You go home and rest,' he instructed Sarah. 'You must be worn out by all this.'

'Yes,' she said. 'Thank you, Mr Danceman.' She hung up and stood, aimlessly.

And then she noticed something.

My hands, she thought. She held them up. Why is it I can see through them?

The walls of the room, too, had become ill-defined.

Trembling, she walked back to the inert roby, stood by it, not knowing what to do. Through her legs the carpet showed, and then the carpet became dim, and she saw, through it, further layers of disintegrating matter beyond.

Maybe if I can fuse the tape-ends back together, she thought. But she did not know how. And already Poole had become vague.

The wind of early morning blew about her. She did not feel it; she had begun, now, to cease to feel.

The winds blew on.

Norman Spinrad

The last hurrah of the Golden Horde

Eastward across the Gobi, three hundred old men ride upon three hundred shaggy, wizened Mongolian ponies. The ponies, like their riders, are the tag-end of a dying breed. The men are dressed in filthy, cracked, badly tanned leathers. Across their backs are strapped short Mongolian bows; swords dangle from their waists, and they carry lances in their horny hands as they ride toward the sunrise.

In the dingy store-front on Sullivan Street identified as the D'Mato Social Club by the peeling green letters on the fly-specked translucent area above the black-painted area of the plate-glass window that hid the cave-like interior from the view of casual assassins in the street, Jerry Cornelius, a not-so-casual (or in his own way a *more* casual) assassin, sat on a grey-enamelled metal folding chair facing a gnarled old man with a Jimmy Durante nose across the cracked surface of a rickety card-table. Jerry wore a carefully dated black suit, a black silk shirt, a white tie and white boots. His black vinyl raincoat was draped across a counter which paralleled one wall of the room and which held a display of candy bars and a cardboard showcase of De Nobili cigars. Behind the counter hung a faded photograph of Franklin D. Roosevelt framed in black. The man with the Jimmy Durante nose was smoking a De Nobili, and the semi-poisonous smoke that he blew across the table was clearly designed to blow Jerry's cool. Jerry, however, had expected this, and as a counter-measure kept his violin case close at hand. It seemed a draw.

'This is a big one, Cornelius,' the old man said.

'Flesh is flesh, Mr Siciliano,' Jerry replied. 'Metal is metal.'

'Have you ever hit a Cabinet-level official before?'

Jerry pondered. 'It's open to doubt,' he finally admitted. 'I got a head of state once, but it was a benevolent despotism.'

The old man chewed his cigar, much to Jerry's disgust. 'It'll have to do,' he added. 'You've got the contract. How soon can you be in Sinkiang?'

'Three days. I'll have to change passports again.'

'Make it two.'

'I'd have to pull strings. It'll cost you.'

The old man shrugged. 'Do it,' he said.

Jerry grinned. 'My motto, Mr Siciliano. Who's the contract on?'

'Mao Tse-tung's heir-apparent.'

'Who's that these days?' Jerry asked. The situation in China had gotten somewhat muddled.

'That's your problem,' Durante-nose said.

Jerry shrugged. 'And my cover?'

'Arrange it yourself.'

Jerry got up clutching his violin case, ran his hand through his great bush of blond natural, retrieved his raincoat, took a De Nobili from the counter and said with an evil smirk, 'Don't say I didn't warn you.'

The railroad train consisted of a locomotive, a sealed boxcar, three flatcars and a caboose. The boxcar contained one ton of (uncut?) heroin. The open flatcars held three hundred members of the People's Army of China armed with machine-guns, protected from the elements by the thought of Chairman Mao. The caboose held the negotiating team. The locomotive was a diesel job.

'You'll be working with the Russians on this, Inspector Cornelius,' Q said. 'Our interests happen to coincide.'

Jerry frowned. The last time he had worked with a Russian he had contracted the clap. 'I don't trust those buggers,' he told Q.

'Neither do we,' Q said crisply, 'but it's the only way we can get into Sinkiang. You leave for Moscow on Aeroflot in the morning.'

'Aeroflot?' whined Jerry. Christ, those Russian stewardesses! he thought. 'I get airsick on Aeroflot,' he complained.

Q glared at Jerry firmly. 'We're getting the family-plan discount,' he explained.

'But I'm flying alone—'

'Precisely.'

'Dramamine?'

'If you insist,' Q said primly. 'But the Bureau frowns on foreign substances.'

'My mission?' Jerry asked.

'Catch the Chinks and the Maf in the act. Bust them.'

'But we have no jurisdiction.'

'Hence the Russians,' said Q. 'Use your head, Cornelius.'

'They have no jurisdiction either.'

'You're not that naïve, Cornelius.'

'I suppose not,' Jerry said wistfully.

According to the thought of Chairman Mao, the village was an anachronism: one hundred and fifty-three flea-bitten nomads, along with their animals (mostly diseased horses and threadbare yaks), encamped in a cluster of leather yurts on the margin of the Gobi. From the correct point of view, the village might be said not to exist.

From this same point of view (as well as from several others) the three hundred old men who galloped in from the wastes of the Gobi might also be said to be nonexistent. Nevertheless, the nomad encampment had a certain reality for the old warriors; in fact an archetypal reality stretching back in a line of unbroken tradition from the days of the Great Khan and his Golden Horde still burning clearly in their ancestral memory to the misty and arthritic present.

Village. Burn. Pillage. Rape. Kill.

Outside the umbrella of the thoughts of Chairman Mao, the old barbarians existed in a happier reality of simple, straightforward traditional imperatives.

Therefore, unmindful of the fact that the village was an anachronism, the old warriors, in the time-honoured tradition of the Golden Horde, rode into the encampment, slew the men and children, made a pass at raping the women to death, slaughtered the animals, burned the yurts, and continued to ride eastward, secure in the knowledge that they had fulfilled another quantum of their timeless destiny.

A long concrete runway broke the monotony of the Sinkiang wastelands with the more absolute monotony of its geometric perfection. At right angles to the runway, a railroad spur wandered off toward the horizon. From the viewpoint of the pilot of the C-5A approaching this three-dimensional nexus, the runway and the railroad spur formed a T with a finite bar and an infinite upright. If anything, the pilot thought this sloppy. It is likely that he did not fully comprehend the thought of Chairman Mao; a more erudite man might have appreciated the symbolism.

'It is a clear demonstration of the cynical perfidy of the Chinese gangster element enshrined behind the façade of the Maoist clique, Comrade Cornelius,' Commissar Krapotkin observed genially, drawing a glass of tea from the silver samovar and handing it across the table to Jerry. Krapotkin was a short barrel of a man who wore his double-breasted Mod suit like a uniform. Perhaps it is a uniform, Jerry thought, as he took a spiked sugar-cube out of his mother-of-pearl pillbox and inserted it between his teeth. The Russians were doing their best to be hip these days, and it was hard to keep up.

As Jerry sipped tea through the sugar-cube between his teeth, Krapotkin lit up an Acapulco Gold and continued to make small-talk: 'While they gibber and squeak their anti-Soviet obscenities in Peking, they deal with the worst gangster element of the decadent capitalist society by their back door in Sinkiang, which, by the way, is of course rightfully Soviet territory.'

'I wouldn't call the Maf the *worst* gangster element of decadent capitalist society,' Jerry observed mildly.

Krapotkin produced a metallic sound which Jerry tentatively identified as a laugh. 'Ah, very good, Comrade Cornelius. Indeed, one might argue that the distribution of heroin, contributing as it does to the further corruption of the already decadent West, is an act which contributes to the long-range progress of the working class.'

'But providing the reactionary adventurist régime in Peking with hard American currency does not,' Jerry rejoined.

'Exactly, Comrade! Which is why my government has decided to co-operate with the American narcs. Once the Maoist clique had been exposed in the act of selling heroin to the Maf, we should have no trouble totally discrediting them with progressive elements throughout the world.'

'And of course the Mafia will be discredited as well.'

'?'

'The Maf is essentially a patriotic organization like the K.K.K. or the Loyal Order of Moose.'

Krapotkin roached his joint. 'Enough of the pleasantries, Comrade,' he said. 'Are you prepared for the drop?'

Jerry fingered his violin case. 'My cover?' he inquired.

'You will be a Mafia hit man assigned a contract on the heir-apparent to Mao Tse-tung,' Krapotkin said. 'Our agents in Palermo have uncovered just such a plot.'

'The real hit man?'

Krapotkin smiled. 'He has been disposed of, I assure you.'

From a certain viewpoint, Jerry reflected, Krapotkin was right.

Not ninety seconds after the C-5A had taxied to a halt with its tail facing the juncture of the rail-spur–runway T as if preparing to fart along the track, the great doors in the nose opened like the petals of an aluminium flower, a ramp was lowered, and a black Cadillac disgorged, pulling a house-trailer of grandiose proportions and Miami Beach-Gothic design. The C-5A continued to disgorge Cadillacs like a pregnant guppy, each one pulling a trailer larger and more rococo than the last.

Something less than three hundred old men galloped haltingly across the wastes of Sinkiang on faltering ponies. A dozen or more of the Mongol warriors had burst blood vessels in their tired old brains from the excitement of the last massacre. The blood was running thin. Where once the steppes had echoed to the pounding hooves of the Golden Horde as a whole world trembled before a tide of barbarians that filled the field of vision from horizon to horizon, now there was naught but an expiring handful of decrepit savages. *Sic transit gloria mundi.* The spirit was willing, but the flesh was practically moribund. The survivors envied those few of their comrades lucky enough to have died a warrior's death sacking the last village in an endless chain reaching back to the glory days when the villages had names like Peking and Samarkand and Damascus.

But something – call it pride or manly virtue – kept the pitiful remnant of the Horde going, riding ever eastward into the sunrise. Perhaps it was the hope that somewhere on the endless steppe there still remained a village large enough (but not *too* large) to bring them all the glory of death in one last gory, triumphant, final massacre. Flailing like tattered battle-flags in their befuddled old brains the simple imperatives which shaped their lives and hopes and destinies: Village. Burn. Pillage. Rape. Kill.

Jerry Cornelius, still clutching the violin case, stood alone in the grey wasteland, and watched the Russian helicopter disappear into the slate-coloured sky with a certain sense of foreboding. You just can't trust those Russians, he thought. Now, where was the car?

To the east was a large boulder. Behind it, and not without a certain sense of relief, Jerry found a late model black Cadillac sedan, well waxed and shiny. So far, so good.

Inside the car, Jerry found his new persona. Doffing his clothes, he assumed the persona: a black pin-striped suit with pegged pants and thin lapels, a white button-down shirt, a white tie, a diamond stickpin, pointed black Italian loafers, argyle socks, a box of De Nobilis, and jars of black shoe-polish and vaseline, with which he gave himself a Rudolph Valentino job, atop which he affixed a green pork-pie hat with a leopardskin band. Thus accoutred, and with a round toothpick in his mouth at a jaunty angle, he sealed the car, turned on the air-conditioning, and set out across the wasteland.

Only when he discovered that the radio would bring in nothing but Radio Moscow and that the tape library contained naught but Tchaikovsky did the full extent of Krapotkin's treachery become apparent.

As the train hove into sight of the rail-spur–runway junction, the soldiers of the People's Army were able to contain cries of awe, amazement and dismay only by diligent application of the thought of Chairman Mao.

For there in the depths of Sinkiang was, considering the circumstances, quite a decent facsimile of Las Vegas. A semicircle of trailers rimmed a large kidney-shaped swimming-pool. Done up in pastels, sporting picture-windows, and sprouting numerous extensions, wings and breezeways, the trailers resembled the lower or casino floors of Las Vegas hotels. Complex mazes of cabanas, beach-chairs, bocci-courts, pavilions, greenhouses, handball-courts and pigeon-coups which filled the interstices between the trailers completed the illusion. Behind the semicircular Las Vegas façade towered the tail of the C-5A, reminiscent, somehow, of Howard Hughes and all that his shadowy persona implied. Parked among the spectral casino-hotels was an indeterminate number of black Cadillacs.

Around the pool, waiters in red tuxedoes served tepid Collinses to fat men in sunglasses stretched out in beach-chairs, warming themselves with complex arrays of sunlamps. Starlets in bikinis paraded their pinchable arses by the poolside.

The officials in the caboose immediately called for the reserve train which had been parked fifty miles down the track in anticipation of such a necessity.

Approaching his destination from the south, Jerry Cornelius spotted a cluster of pagodas, huts and barracks, among which huge billboards had been erected bearing immense portraits of Mao, Lenin, Stalin, Enver Hoxha and other popular personalities of the People's Republic of China. Everything was festooned with calligraphy like a wedding-cake. Intermittent strings of firecrackers exploded. Hatchet men chased each other through the winding streets. Soldiers of the People's Army performed calisthenics. The sharp syllables of Chinese dialects filled the air like razorblades. Gongs sounded. Paper dragons danced in the streets. Perpetual twilight hovered over the scene, which, upon closer inspection, proved to be constructed of balsa wood, rice paper and papier-mâché.

Warily, Jerry swung the Cadillac wide of this Chinese version

of Disneyland and circled toward the tail of a C-5A which dominated the landscape. Soon reality (such as it was) changed, and he
found himself on the outskirts of what appeared to be a suburb of
Las Vegas: the lower storeys of casino-hotels mounted on wheels
and parked in a semicircle around a huge kidney-shaped pool,
facing the Chinese apparition across the chlorinated waters.

Having spied a heavily guarded boxcar behind the façade of the
Chinese reality, Jerry was not surprised to see a dozen thugs with
machine guns guarding the C-5A. The $50,000,000 must be on the
plane.

For a moment, Jerry parked the Cad along the Orient–Vegas
interface, playing at pondering his next move.

Shortly, he drove on into the Mafia camp, parked the Cadillac
next to a fire hydrant outside a barber-shop, and melted into the
scene with barely a ripple. Yes, indeed, this was his kind of town!

Eastward across the wastelands, here and there a rider dead on
his horse, a scungy pony faltering under its rider, the spirit burning brighter as the blood thinned as if their ancient flesh were
ectoplasmating into naught but the weathered, parchment-dry
quintessence of tradition-cum-desire, the desperate determination
not to die a peasant's death, the image of the Final Massacre
burning its forlorn hope into the backs of what was left of their
arteriosclerotic brains, the husks of the Golden Horde doddered
onward, ever onward.

'Ya get da Big Picture, Cornelius?' the Rock said, sipping at his
Collins as he and Jerry lay side by side in beach-chairs, sunning
themselves at poolside. Jerry, dressed in neon-blue bathing-suit,
contrasting yellow terrycloth robe, Japanese rubber sandals and
silvered Air Force shades, had resisted the dangerous urge to
order Pernod, and as a consequence was nursing a foul rum con-
coction. Only the presence of his violin case close at hand soothed
his jangled nerves. And the sunlamps threatened to melt the shoe-
polish in his hair.

'I'm not paid to get the Big Picture, Rock,' Jerry said, keeping
in character, though from a certain viewpoint what he was saying
was true.

The Rock scratched his hairy paunch with one hand, and with

the other, claw-like, pinched the arse of a passing starlet, who giggled appropriately.

'I like yer style, kid,' the Rock said. 'But doncha have any curiosity?'

'Curiosity killed a cat.'

'I'm a dog man myself, Cornelius, so who gives a shit? What I says is dese Chinks have been asking for it. Just because da punks got a few H-bombs and ICBMs is no reason for them to get the idea they can burn the Maf and live ta talk about it. Yeah, after ya hit their number two *padron* that smart-arse punk in Peking will have ta look over his shoulder a few times before he tries putting milk-sugar in our heroin again.'

'Just who is their number two?'

Rock pointed his De Nobili at the empty raft anchored out in the centre of the kidney-shaped pool. 'De Big Boy will make this year's deal out on da raft – neutral turf. Whatever Chink is out there with him – zap!'

'Won't the Reds . . . ?' Jerry inquired.

'Da Cads are full of heavies with choppers,' the Rock grinned. 'When you hit da number two, dey hit da People's Army.' The Rock chucked himself under the chin with his right forefinger as if flicking a bead of sweat at the giant posters of Mao, Stalin, Hoxha and Lenin glowering like spectral Internal Revenue agents across the moat-waters of the pool.

Jerry decided to develop a sudden hankering for Egg Foo Yung.

Major Sung passed the opium-pipe across the black-lacquered table to Jerry, who inhaled the sweet smoke and fingered his violin case voluptuously as Major Sung caressed his copy of the Little Red Book obscenely and said, 'Of course I am familiar with your work in England, Colonel Kor Ne Loos.'

'Your English is excellent, Major,' Jerry lied. 'Harvard?'

'Berlitz.'

'I should be reporting to the honourable Heir-Apparent to god-like Mao,' Jerry chided.

Major Sung frowned and kicked the brass gong which sat upon the table. Kung Fu, Jerry noted warily. He revised his estimate of

Major Sung laterally. 'As you of course know,' Sung said with an oriental leer, 'the peacock often hides his egg behind an embroidered fan.'

Jerry started – he certainly hadn't expected anything like this! 'The dragon has been known to preen his scales before he pounces,' he rejoined.

Outside the pagoda, a chorus of two hundred kindergarten students were chanting the latest No. 1 on the Chinese Top 40, 'Death to the Violators of the Spirit of Mao's Urine'. Jerry tapped his fingers on the table in time to the catchy rhythm, which he recognized as a variation on 'Rock Around the Clock'.

'May I take that to imply that the pasta contains an asp?' Major Sung said. It was clearly not a question.

Jerry smiled. 'As Confucius says, a fox with a dagger may behead a drunken lion.'

Major Sung laughed. 'As Chairman Mao has observed, the enemies of the Revolution will devour their own entrails if they can make a fast buck in the process.'

Bowing and scraping, a sergeant in a kimono entered the chamber with tea and fortune cookies.

Major Sung cracked open his pastry and read aloud: 'Death to the revisionist running dogs of the Wall Street imperialists and their would-be lackeys in Prague.'

Jerry's fortune cookie said: 'Tension, apprehension and dissension have begun.'

As Jerry, in his pin-stripe suit, pork-pie hat and Italian loafers, lounged against the right-front fender of the Cadillac, which he had parked inconspicuously at poolside, a fat man in a flowered Hawaiian shirt and black Bermuda shorts boarded a speedboat at the Vegas end of the pool. Stuffed between his thick lips was an El Ropo Supremo Perfecto Grande. Set jauntily on his bald head was a red sailor-cap, on the brim of which 'The Big Boy' had been embroidered in Atlantic City in bold blue thread.

As a Meyer Davis orchestra in one of the poolside cabanas struck up 'Amore' and a stripper began to peel on the diving-board, the white speedboat set out across the pool toward the raft.

Meanwhile, across the pool, fifty soldiers of the People's Army marched back and forth bearing placards serializing the menu of Hong Fat's restaurant in severe calligraphy and psychedelic posters of Mao, Stalin, Lenin and Jim Morrison, while the People's Army Brass Band played 'Chinatown, My Chinatown' to which a chorus of Red Guards waving the Little Red Book sang the 'Internationale' in Sinosized Albanian. To this heady send-off, an old, bearded Chinese in a military tunic (with a curious if superficial resemblance to Ho Chi Minh) rowed a punt toward the raft in neutral waters.

At poolside, Jerry's trained eye picked out heavies in blue serge suits moving unobtrusively toward their Cadillacs. They all carried violin cases. Jerry placed a bet with a convenient bookie that the cases did not contain violins. The best he could get was the wrong end of 9–4 odds.

Alone on the raft at last, the Big Boy and the Heir-Apparent swapped *bon mots* as the strains of 'High Hopes' mingled with the thin voices of schoolchildren chanting 'My Mao Can Lick Your Mao' in a corrupt Canton dialect.

'Ya dirty mother, last year's dope was cut with milk-sugar.'

'As Chairman Mao has observed, when dealing with corrupt mercenaries of the exploitative class, the doctrine of "No tickee, no washee" is fully justified.'

'Remember what happened to Bugsy Siegel!'

'Confucius once said that a toothless dragon does not fear the orthodontist.'

Behind the Chinese Disneyland, the People's Army had placed six machine-gun nests in a circle around the boxcar of heroin.

Twenty heavies with choppers ringed the C-5A. Inside, five more heavies guarded $50,000,000 in unmarked small bills.

'Fifty million! That's robbery. You Chinks are crooks.'

The Meyer Davis orchestra played 'It Takes Two to Tango'. The People's Army Brass Band countered with a Chinese version of 'Die Fahne Hoch'.

'As Chairman Mao has said,' the Heir-Apparent threatened, 'I may not be the best man in town, but I'll be the best till the best comes round.'

Hidden behind a façade of placards, posters, pagodas, dancing paper dragons, hatchet men, schoolchildren performing calisthenics, rioting Red Guards, captured American airmen in chains, opium-dens and filthy peasant-huts, three hundred soldiers of the People's Army of the People's Republic of China girded themselves for a human-wave attack.

'We only deal with you Commie pinko Chink bastards because you're the only mass suppliers of heroin aside from the Federal narcs that we can find.'

'As Chairman Mao has said, tough shit.'

Ominously, the Meyer Davis orchestra began playing 'Hawaiian War Chant'.

Jerry Cornelius stubbed out his roach and reached for his violin case. 'The time has come, the Walrus said, to speak of many things,' he observed as, out on the raft, the Big Boy gave the finger to the Heir-Apparent.

'Fifty million for the boxcar. Take it or leave it,' the Heir-Apparent said.

The People's Army Brass Band broke into 'Light My Fire' as seven hundred Red Guards doused themselves with gasoline and immolated themselves while singing 'Chairman Mao ist unser Fuehrer' contrapuntally, but since they were all off-key the ploy was a failure.

'As Al Capone once observed, play ball, or we lean on you.'

Jerry Cornelius opened his violin case and withdrew a violin. To the untrained observer, it appeared to be merely an ordinary electric violin with self-contained power-supply, built-in amp and speaker rated at a hundred watts. However, an Underground electronics expert on 150 mg of methedrine had made a significant modification: the high notes registered well into the ultra-sonic and the lows were deep down in the sub-sonic, while all audible frequencies were eliminated.

* * *

When Jerry tucked the violin under his chin and began to play 'Wipeout', the brains of everyone within a five-mile radius began to vibrate to the beat of a drummer who was ultra- and supersonic as well as different and non-existent. To the naked human ear, Jerry appeared to be playing 'The Sounds of Silence'.

Out on the raft, the Big Boy was growing quite cross as the subliminal strains of 'Wipeout' inflamed cells deep within his paretic brain. 'Mao Tse-tung eats shit!' he informed the Heir-Apparent.

'Al Capone was a faggot, according to the infallible thought of Mao Tse-tung.'

The Meyer Davis orchestra began to play 'The Battle Hymn of the Republic'.

The People's Army Brass Band immolated their tuba-player.

As Jerry segued into a subliminal rendition of 'Heartbreak Hotel', fifty slot-machines produced spontaneous jackpots, Cadillacs gunned their engines, whores' poodles howled, thirteen plate-glass windows shattered, and every starlet at poolside achieved climax. (Some of them had not come since their first screen tests.)

Hatchet men began chopping at papier-mâché pagodas. A paper dragon set itself on fire. Three hundred soldiers preparing themselves for a human-wave attack began to drool and got erections. Seven hundred chanting kindergarten children achieved satori and began to devour an American flag drenched with soya sauce. A giant poster of Stalin broke a grin and thumbed its nose at a poster of Mao.

'Mao Tse-tung eats the hairy canary!'

'The Maf sucks!'

'Faggot!'

'Creep!'

'Chink!'

'Wop!'

'ARGH!'

Salivating, the Big Boy leapt at the Heir-Apparent, chomping his El Ropo Supremo Perfecto Grande to bits, and buried teeth and cigar in the old Chinaman's beard, setting it aflame. The two men wrestled on the raft, biting, spitting and cursing for a few moments, then toppled each other into the pool, which proved to be filled with crocodiles.

Pleased with his work, Jerry Cornelius began to play 'Fire'.

A phalanx of Cadillacs screamed around the pool and barrelled into the People's Army Brass Band spewing machine-gun bullets which ripped into a poster of Mao Tse-tung, enraging a rioting mob of Red Guards who set themselves on fire and threw themselves under the wheels of the cars, causing them to skid into a balsa-wood pagoda which toppled into the pool in splinters which were devoured by the blood-crazed crocodiles who expired in agony from the splinters in their stomachs some time later.

Three hundred soldiers of the People's Army launched a human-wave attack, firing their machine-guns at random.

Jerry continued to play 'Fire', seeing no particular reason to change the tune.

Major Sung shrieked, 'Capitalistic running dogs of the demographic People's revisionist lackeys of Elvis Presley have overrun the ideological manifestations of decadent elements within the amplifier of the pagoda!' and committed hara-kiri.

The Rock began smashing slot-machines with a baseball bat.

Starlets tore off their bikinis and chased terrified hatchet men around the poolside.

The human wave reached the pool, dove in, and proceeded to beat moribund crocodiles to death with their gun-butts.

A suicide squad hurled itself through the plate-glass window of a trailer and devoured the rug.

Cadillacs circled the boxcar of heroin like hostile Indians, filling the air with hot lead.

The sopping remnants of the human wave reached the trailer camp and began beating thugs to death with dead crocodiles.

Red Guards showered the C-5A with ink bottles.

Tongues of flame were everywhere.

Explosions, contusions, fire, gore, curses, looting, rape.

Jerry Cornelius began playing 'All You Need Is Love', knowing that no one was listening.

Riding eastward across the wastelands on their diseased ponies, something under two hundred decrepit remnants of what once had been the glorious Golden Horde, most of them incoherent with exhaustion, spied a great conflagration on the horizon.

Flaccid adrenals urged near-moribund hearts to beat faster. They flayed their ponies with the shafts of their spears. Drool flecked the lips of doddards and ponies alike. Their backbrains smelled blood and fire in the air.

The smells of gunpowder, gasoline, burning balsa wood and papier-mâché, sizzling flesh, gave Jerry Cornelius a slight buzz as he began to play 'Deck the Halls with Boughs of Holly'. The swimming-pool was coloured a bright carnelian, which did little to mask the chlorine odour. Bits of anodized aluminium struggled to keep afloat amid scraps of charred balsa wood and shards of placards.

A dented Cadillac careened through a barricade of beach-chairs and into a squad of Chinese soldiers beating a starlet to death with copies of the Little Red Book before sliding over the rim of the pool to sink bubbling into the churning depths.

The pillar of fire consuming the Chinese Disneyland reminded Jerry of the Dresden firestorm. Sentimentally, he began to play 'Bongo, Bongo, Bongo, I Don't Want to Leave the Congo'.

In a strange display of gallantry, Red Guards, hit men, capa mafiosas and Chinese soldiers joined hands in a ring around the ruined trailer camp, screaming, '*Burn*, baby, burn!' in English, Mandarin, Cantonese, Italian, Pidgin and Yiddish. At each '*burn*' a canister of napalm dropped from somewhere on to the conflagration.

Reduced to sentimentality despite himself, Jerry played 'God Save the Queen'.

Two hundred or so pairs of rheumy eyes lit up with feral joy at the sight of a great city (by current Horde standards anyway) going up in flames, at the sight of smashed cars, broken bodies, naked starlets shrieking, and a great pool of what appeared to be blood.

Weeping great nostalgic tears, the last generation of the Golden Horde shouldered their spears, whipped their ponies into a stumbling gallop and charged in a body into the fray, the image of the Final Massacre burning like a city in the fevered brains of the aged savages:

Village! Burn! Pillage! Rape! Kill!

Mongolian ponies wheezing and gasping under them, the crazed doddards reached the conflagration and found to their chagrin that there was precious little unburnt, unpillaged, unraped, un-killed.

They found a boxcar guarded by machine-gunners and charged it *en masse*, sacrificing half their number to impale the befuddled Chinese troops on their spears and set the boxcar aflame. As a strangely intoxicating, aromatic smoke billowed from the burning boxcar, the remnant of the remnant scattered, looking for more things or people to burn, rape and kill.

A dozen of the doddards expired attempting to rape an aged whore to death, and another dozen were compelled to shame-facedly trample her to death under the hooves of their ponies, eight of which expired from the effort.

Fifteen of the Horde had heart attacks trying to beat Cadillacs to death.

A half-dozen doddards died of broken hearts when the slot-machines they were torturing failed to cry out in pain.

Several of the Horde fell to devouring the corpses of crocodiles and choked to death on the splinters.

As the last Khan of the Golden Horde watched in senile befuddle-ment, the great silver bird issued a terrible battlecry and began to move. The doddard's bleary eyes bugged as the C-5A picked up speed, shot by him, and actually left the ground!

A feeble nervous impulse travelled spastically from his optic nerve into his brain, and thence to his arm and throat.

'Kill!' he wheezed asthmatically, and hurled his spear at the unnatural thing.

The spear was sucked into the intake of the left inboard jet engine, lodged in the turbine and shattered it. The jet engine exploded, shearing off the wing. The C-5A nearly completed a loop before it crashed upside down to the runway and exploded into flames.

From an aerial viewpoint, the runway and the railroad spur formed a T with a finite bar and an infinite upright, but the only living being in the area did not notice the symbolism. Riding into the sunset on his pony, his back to what in the distance seemed naught but a smouldering refuse-heap, the last Khan of the Golden Horde, sole survivor of the Final Massacre, filled his dying brain with one thought, like a dwindling chord: fulfilment; Golden Horde died in glory; village; burned; pillaged; raped; killed; ancestors proud.

This thought flared brightly in his brain like a dying ember, and then he went to that Great Carnage Heap in the Sky. The wheezing pony tripped over a rock, dislodging the body, which fell to the ground in a twisted heap. A vulture descended, pecked at the body, sniffed and departed.

The pony staggered on for a few steps, then halted, its dim brain perhaps mesmerised by the glare of the setting sun.

The Mongolian pony was still standing there an hour later when Jerry Cornelius, in his pin-stripe suit, pork-pie hat and Italian loafers, wandered dazedly up to it out of the wasteland.

'Here's a bit of luck,' Jerry muttered, perking up a bit. (The short-circuiting of his electric violin had seriously vexed him.)

Jerry mounted the pony, kneed its flanks and shouted, 'Git 'em up, Scout!'

The pony waddled forward a few steps, puked, and died.

Jerry extricated himself from the corpse, brushed himself off, and consulted a fortune cookie he had secreted in a pocket.

'It's a long way to Tipperary,' the fortune cookie informed him.

Munching the soggy rice pastry, Jerry trudged off into the setting sun whistling 'Dem bones, dem bones, dem dry bones, now hear de word of de Lord . . .'

Kingsley Amis
Hemingway in space

The woman watched him and he made another sweep. There was nothing again but he knew one of them was around. It got so you always knew. After twenty years it got so you always knew when one of them was around.

'Anything?'

'Not yet.'

'I thought you could tell just where to find these things,' she said. 'I thought we hired you because you could take us straight to one of these things. I thought that was why we hired you.'

'Easy now, Martha,' the young fellow said. 'Nobody can find xeeb where there aren't any xeeb, not even Mr Hardacre. We'll come across one any minute now.'

She moved away from the three of them at the instrument panel and her thighs were arrogant under the tight space-jeans. You bitch, Philip Hardacre thought suddenly. You goddam, bored, boring, senseless bitch. He felt sorry for the young fellow. He was a pretty nice fellow, and here he was married to this goddam senseless bitch, and it looked like he was too afraid of her to tell her to get the hell out, although you knew he wanted to.

'I feel him near,' the old Martian said, turning the bigger and more grizzled of his two heads toward Philip Hardacre. 'We shall see him soon now.'

The woman leaned against the ship's side and stared out the port. 'I can't think why you have to go hunting these monstrosities. Two days it's been since we left, and we could have been in Venusport all that while instead of cooped up in this steel jalopy a couple of light years from civilization. What's so good about getting a xeeb even if you do get one? What does it prove, getting a xeeb?'

'The xeeb is the largest life-form in this part of the galaxy.' The young fellow was a school professor or something like that, and you could tell it from the way he spoke. 'More than that, it's the only sentient creature living out here in free space, and it's ferocious; it's been known to take on a scout ship. It's the toughest damn thing there is. That's it, isn't it?'

'That's part of it,' Philip Hardacre said. There was that, although there was much more, the freedom out there and the stars against the black and the men small in their suits and afraid and yet not afraid and even the xeeb small in the vastness and the cool joy if the xeeb was a good one.

'He comes,' the old Martian said in his whistling tones, his smaller head bent toward the screen. 'See, lady.'

'I don't want to see,' she said, turning her back. It was a deadly insult under the ancient Martian code of honour, and she knew it and Philip Hardacre knew she knew it, and there was hate in his throat, but there was no time now for hate.

He got up from the panel. There was no doubt about it. An amateur could have taken the blip for an asteroid or another ship but after twenty years you knew immediately. 'Shut up,' he said. 'Spaceside in three minutes.'

He helped the young fellow with the helmet and what he had been dreading happened, the Martian had taken out his own suit and was stiffly putting his rear pair of legs into it. He went over to him and put his hand between the two necks in the traditional gesture of appeal. 'This is not your hunt, Ghlmu,' he said in the archaic Martian courtly tongue.

'I am still strong and he is big and he comes fast.'

'I know it, but this is not your hunt. Old ones are hunted more than they hunt.'

'All my eyes are straight and all my hands are tight.'

'But they are slow and they must be quick. Once they were quick but now they are slow.'

'Har-dasha, it is thy comrade who asks thee.'

'My blood is yours as in all the years; it is only my thought that must seem cruel, old one. I will hunt without you.'

'Hunt well, Har-dasha, then. I await you always,' the old creature said, using the ritual formula of acquiescence.

'Are we going to shoot this goddam whale or not?' The woman's voice was shrill. 'Or are you and that thing going on whistling at each other all night?'

He turned on her savagely. 'You're out of this. You're staying right here where you belong. Put that blaster back on the rack and take off that space-suit and start making food. We'll be back in half an hour.'

'Don't you give me orders, you bum. I can shoot as well as any man and you won't stop me.'

'Around here I say what everybody does, and they do it.' Over her shoulder he could see the Martian hanging up his suit and his throat went dry. 'If you try to get in that airlock with us we head right back to Venus.'

'I'm sorry, Martha, you'll have to do as he says,' the young fellow said.

The two big Wyndham-Clarke blasters were ready primed and he set them both at maximum, while they stood in the airlock and waited for the air to go. Then the outer door slid into the wall and they were out there in the freedom and the vastness and the fear that was not fear. The stars were very cold and it was black between the stars. There were not many stars, and the black was vast where there were no stars. The stars and the black together were what gave the freedom. Without the stars or without the black there would not have been the freedom, only the vastness, but with the stars and the black you had the freedom as well as the vastness. The stars were few and the light from them was small and cold, and around them there was the black.

He spoke to the young fellow over the suit radio. 'Can you see him? Toward that big star with the small companion.'

'Where?'

'Look where I'm pointing. He hasn't spotted us yet.'

'How does he spot us?'

'Never mind that. Now, listen. Each swoop he makes, give him one shot. Just one. Then go forward on your suit jet fast as you can. That confuses him more than lateral movement.'

'You told me.'

'I'm telling you again. One shot. He homes on your shot. Get ready; he's seen us; he's turning.'

The great beautiful phosphorescent shape narrowed as it came head-on to them, then appeared to swell. The xeeb was closing fast, as fast as any he'd known. It was a big, fast xeeb and likely to be a good one. He'd be able to tell for sure after the first swoop. He wanted the xeeb to be a good one for the young fellow's sake. He wanted the young fellow to have a good hunt with a good, big, fast xeeb.

'Fire in about fifteen seconds, then jet,' Philip Hardacre said. 'And you won't have too long before his next swoop, so be ready.'

The xeeb closed, and the young fellow's shot arc'd in. It was too early to be a good shot and it barely flicked the tail end. Philip Hardacre waited as long as he dared and fired toward the hump where the main ganglia were and jetted without waiting to see where he had hit.

It was a good xeeb all right. From the way its phosphorescence had started to pulsate you could tell it had been hit somewhere in the nervous system or what passed for that, but within seconds it had turned and begun another great beautiful graceful swoop on the two men. This time the young fellow held his fire a little longer and got in a good shot near the hump and jetted as he had been told. But then the xeeb dropped in the way they did once in a hundred times and xeeb and man were almost on each other. There was nothing for Philip Hardacre to do but empty his Wyndham-Clarke all at once in the hope that the loosing of so much energy would get the xeeb to change its mind and home on him instead. Then he was jetting forward at top speed and calling over the suit radio to make for the ship at once.

'It puffed something at me and I lost my blaster,' came the young fellow's voice.

'Make for the ship.'

'We won't get there, will we?'

'We can try. You may have damaged him enough with that last shot to slow him down or spoil his sense of direction,' Philip Hardacre said. He already knew that it was all over for them. The xeeb was only a few miles above them and beginning to turn for a fresh swoop, moving slower but not slow enough. The ship was above them too in the other direction. This was what you faced every time you hunted xeeb and when it happened at last it was just the end of the hunt and the end of the freedom and the vastness, and they would have had to end some time.

There was a long arc of light from the ship and the xeeb was suddenly brighter than ever before for an instant, and then the brightness went out and there was nothing there.

The Martian had fallen into a crouching position in the airlock and the third Wyndham-Clarke was still in his pincers. The two men waited for the outer door to close and the air to flood in.

'Why didn't he put on his suit?' said the young fellow.

'There wasn't time. He had about a minute to save us. A Martian suit takes much longer than that to put on.'

'What would have got him first, the cold?'

'Airlessness. They respire quickly. Five seconds at most. Just enough to aim and fire.' He was quick after all, Philip Hardacre thought.

Inside, the woman was waiting for them. 'What happened?'

'He's dead, of course. He got the xeeb.'

'Did he have to get himself killed doing it?'

'There was one weapon on board and one place to use it from.' Philip Hardacre said. Then his voice went quiet. 'Why are you still wearing your space-suit?'

'I wanted to get the feel of it. And you said to take it off.'

'Why couldn't you have taken the gun into the airlock?'

Her eyes went dull. 'I didn't know how the lock worked.'

'But Ghlmu did. He could have operated it from in here. And you can shoot, or so you said.'

'I'm sorry.'

'Sorry I like,' the young fellow said. He didn't sound like a school professor now, or afraid of her. 'Sorry brings back that old guy as alive as ever he was, doesn't it? Sorry is about the best I ever heard. And sorry is something else too. Sorry as all hell is how I feel when I drop you off in Venusport and take the shuttle to Earth by myself. You like Venusport, don't you? Well, here's your chance to get lost in it.'

Philip Hardacre finished composing the old Martian's limbs and appendages and muttered as much as he knew of the prescribed incantation. 'Forgive me,' he said.

'Get supper,' the young fellow said to the woman. 'Right away.'

'This was your hunt,' Philip Hardacre said to his friend's body.

A. E. Van Vogt
The Anarchistic Colossus 85p

In a future Earthworld, anarchy has become a way of life. Yet the anarchy is a strange sort – controlled by the mysterious Kirilian computers. Enter a race of alien beings, who look on the conquest of Earth as the amusing end-product of some extraordinary wargame ...

'The contemporary SF writer I enjoy most' COLIN WILSON

Richard Cowper
The Road to Corlay 80p

'A thousand years hence, when persistent rain has divided much of Britain into separate islands, the followers of a saintly boy are persecuted by the thuggish bully-boys of Church ... the struggles of the godly and ungodly are witnessed by a team of present-day researchers working on a technique of scanning the future ...' DAILY TELEGRAPH

'Brilliant ... quasi-mediaeval barbarism with a seasoning of time travel' TRIBUNE

Sir Arthur Conan Doyle
When the World Screamed 80p

A great classic of early science fiction, as well as one of the most extraordinary adventures ever undertaken by the eccentric Professor Challenger, the man who discovered *The Lost World*.

Accompanied in this volume by six more fine examples of masterly storytelling by Conan Doyle.

You can buy these and other Pan Books from booksellers and newsagents ; or direct from the following address :
Pan Books, Sales Office, Cavaye Place, London SW10 9PG
Send purchase price plus 20p for the first book and 10p for each additonal book, to allow for postage and packing
Prices quoted are applicable in the UK

While every effort is made to keep prices low, it is sometimes necessary to increase prices at short notice. Pan Books reserve the right to show on covers and charge new retail prices which may differ from those advertised in the text or elsewhere